Praise For a Great Novel Of American Life!

Other Avon books by
Dallas Miller

GIRLFRIENDS 31591 $1.75

DALLAS MILLER

Fathers and Dreamers

AVON
PUBLISHERS OF BARD, CAMELOT AND DISCUS BOOKS

All the characters in this book
are fictitious, and any resemblance
to actual persons, living or dead,
is purely coincidental.

AVON BOOKS
A division of
The Hearst Corporation
959 Eighth Avenue
New York, New York 10019

Copyright © 1966 by Harry D. Miller.
Published by arrangement with Doubleday and Co., Inc.
Library of Congress Catalog Card Number 66-18616
ISBN: 0-380-00950-1

First Avon Printing, January, 1969
Fifth Printing

AVON TRADEMARK REG. U.S. PAT. OFF. AND
FOREIGN COUNTRIES, REGISTERED TRADEMARK—
MARCA REGISTRADA, HECHO EN CHICAGO, U.S.A.

Printed in the U.S.A.

For K. B. M. *and* A. W. M.

One

A bicycle on the square!

On it was a little fillet of a boy with blue eyes, one of them wilder than the other, and thirty copies of the Cleveland *Plain Dealer*. Pedaling the bike with legs far too short, Parnell Gavin broke into an easy, early morning sweat, and felt his crewcut hair get sticky. He rubbed the stubbly top of it with one of his bandaged hands—God have mercy; he had poison ivy again—sprinkling dried calamine lotion over his forehead.

In the two narrow windows over the post office, the green blinds blew past the sills in a dry, hot breeze like the breath of a dying animal in the Cleveland Zoo. Slowly a shade was raised, and the face of the third and fourth grade teacher leaned out and scanned the sky for signs of clouds, promised on last night's nine o'clock news. It was vacant. The woman reached to the sill and pulled in a plant she had forgotten to take in the evening before, tapping the clay pot with her knuckles as if it were a cross schoolboy.

Parnell dug into the pouch on his back and tossed a folded paper at the door to one side of the post office. He looked up at the woman in the window, her bosom, un-girdled for the summer, almost touching the ledge. "G'morning, Miss Stickney," he said, and without waiting for an answer—wintry and scholarly it would be—he moved on.

Past Morrow's Hardware with its six rusting lightning rods on the roof, placed there at the turn of the century and still untested, though the store had burned twice from an overheated furnace. Past the Casto, a movie house, open all day Saturday and from one to seven on Sunday. And past the lunch counter next to it, its only name a very rude EAT, owned by the Rogers sisters who had turned down a free Coca-Cola outfit with their names because they shunned notoriety. At each he pitched a newspaper.

9

Past the Coal & Feed store, occupying what was once the best Greek Revival house in town; a Drug and Notion store, called just that, and painted red to match the Woolworths in the cities; Payne's Butcher Shop, its windows empty now except for a sleeping cat, other carcasses ripped apart and cooling in the back room; Youmain's Grocery, kept by very lovely people or by a bunch of gypsies, depending on whom you listened to, a half wheel of cheese on the counter inside, covered by cloth to ward off flies but black with them anyway, while the flypaper hanging from the ceiling contained nothing but a single gray thread of gypsy hair, snatched from Mrs. Youmain; a soda parlor called the Sugar Bowl, a saloon before the town went dry; an antique shop operated by a woman who was happy only when she had her hands on old-timey things and who even once seized a Victorian lapel watch from the chest of Miss Stickney at a PTA meeting and offered her ten dollars for it; and the Congregational church, a handwritten sign before it now that said *The Real Jesus Christ, 9 a.m. Sunday.* The Reverend Hill, who lettered his signs when he wasn't pumping gas at the station next to the church, hadn't arranged for a guest lecturer at all, but would himself deliver pretty much the same sermon that last week was called *Christianity: Fact or Fiction? 9 a.m. Sunday.* Christianity, as everyone in town knew, was a fact because the Reverend Hill said so, and he was a graduate of Oberlin College.

On the fourth and last side of the square stood a Civil War statue, clouds of dust blowing over its boots. The boy on the bicycle let himself coast while he surveyed its familiar face. Its maker was the late Amos Bennett of the firm called Monuments & Headstones, and its model, the boy had been told, the late Margaret Bennett, wife of the above. Behind it, a thin guardrail prevented automobiles from slipping off the road and shebanging over the side of a cliff that fell two hundred feet to the Grand River below. The other, less direct way to reach the river was by Tannery Hill, a steep, bumpy road down which the Cleveland bus bounced three times a week. At the bottom of the hill and to one side of the river was no tannery at all but the largest per-capita cemetery in the state, holding one hundred and fifty unclaimed bodies of strangers who had died in a train wreck nearby in the 1870s. The tannery that should have been there was nowhere. Ask Parnell Gavin about it, and he'll say—if he says anything,

10

and he won't if you're a smart aleck or too New Yorky—
"I figure that was way back when."

The town, Ventry. Just now getting over the last faint-
ing years of the Depression. Pop., 1400 or so. The Ornamental Iron Capital of the World. The state, Ohio. The
year? Way back when.

Earlier in the morning at the Nickel Plate depot where
he picked up the bundle of *Plain Dealers* for August 12,
1943, Parnell had quickly glanced at the headlines.
*Hamburg Leveled on Eighth Straight Day of Flying For-
tress Raids. Allies Rush Toward Northern Tip of Sicily;
Mainland Invasion Called Imminent. Russians Hold Firm
as Germans Mount Counter-offensive. War Administration
Announces More Butter for Civilians. Six New Cases of
Polio Reported in Northeastern Ohio. Orson Welles on
Gracie Fields' Show Tonight.* Butter, polio, and Orson
Welles he understood, but nothing else.

Sending the last of his papers flying at a stoop, he now
turned his bicycle over the rutted, dirt road toward home.
He deliberately steered close to the hedge of elderberry
bushes at his side, feeling the thorns against his legs, the
prickly music against the spokes. From the trees, still cool
and dark and dewy, came the noises of bullfrogs and small,
hopping animals. Parnell made the same cooing noises in his
throat, answering the darker ones from the trees.

On one side of the street, before the church, a dandelion
was growing out of the oiled dust, a flower of the morning.
It would be generous if the deliverer of the Cleveland *Plain
Dealer* would pick it to save it from being run over by the
eight o'clock bus. It would be sheer poetry if he hitched it
to the watch fob of his corduroy pants, sawed off at the
knees for the summer. But he did neither. He crushed it
with his red Flyer bike.

There!

The sign before the Congregational church nodded in
the morning breeze and sounds of the new day began to
rise from the village.

Coming upon Priest Street, Parnell saw his own house
at the end, sitting in the middle of a grove of trees on the
edge of a ravine, a weedy field on one side and a Victory
garden on the other. Only one other house had been built
on the street, across the way from the Gavins'; the two of

11

them were collectively known as Saint's Rest. Both names were relics of the days when the Gavins were still Catholics, the only ones in town. "Half-mad Irishmen," they had been called. "A house filled with candles and saints." Rather than any other mortifying name—Shanty Irish Street or Pope Street, to mention only two—the early people had called it Priest, and for a reason known only to them because there had never been a priest in Ventry, and, in fact, the Gavins had chucked out their candles back in the nineties and become Congregationalists like everyone else. But before they did, they had already buried the first of the family in a small plot of their own overlooking the valley, and it was this general region that was called Saint's Rest, and finally the whole area encompassing the two houses and the fields at the end of the street. On two of the stones there, the oldest ones, could be seen these words: *Pray for the soul of Patrick Gavin, 1831–1893* and *Nora Shannon Gavin, 1836–1871. Wife of Patrick. She was beloved.* Of the saints buried there, and before the county commissioners got after the family, seven were Gavins, one was a horse owned by the first non-Catholic, and nine were dogs—cockers, one red setter, a fancy English bull that belonged to Parnell's Aunt Cortez when she was a girl, and the rest mongrels.

Parnell rode his bicycle no-handed over the front lawn and rested it against the latticework at the bottom of the front porch. The porch itself and the two large windows on the first floor had been added around 1910 in a fit of friendliness and self-exposure. In one of the windows the iceman's sign was turned backward so that he wouldn't have to call today, and in the other was a banner with a small dark star. Parnell crept across the porch, quietly opened and closed the patched screen door, and walked into the hall. The house was still silent. He made his way on his toes up the large red roses on the Turkey carpet stair runner, past the wall with the glassed photograph of Uncle Desmond, aged four, in his child's coffin, past the high, spindly Victrola in the upstairs hallway, and to his bedroom for another hour's sleep.

Two

Parnell woke for the second time and began to crawl from the almost bottomless hole that had held him since a little after dawn, fingers wiping at his eyes. He was naked, dressed only in the fabric that covers all men, bare and bold, yet wearing a single white sock on his left foot. It concealed a tiny birthmark, no larger than a gherkin pickle and shaped like a brown wing. Fleet-footed Pegasus, Wingèd Foot himself! His grandmother, a woman cruelly kind, had said that if an angel happened to see the wing, his foot would be stolen at night quicker'n you could say Jack Robinson, leaving him with only a bleeding stub, not much good for a fellow who aspired to run as fast as Jesse Owens and to cut a figure in the world.

Words, as they say, cannot describe a boy at morning. Yet there *were* words, and they came from the upstairs hallway, outside the bedroom door. "You blackguardy, miserable excuses of men. A disgrace to God and the nation. You'd sleep until noon like a decaying Vanderbilt if it weren't for me. Up and at 'em! Set to! Scramble!"

Otherwise, the morning was sweet-tongued, full of flowers and earth. Even the sun, striking Parnell's bare leg, had a yellowish smell to it. A late-sleeping fly on the ceiling that Parnell had watched bed down the night before began buzzing toward the screen at the window, as if it alone had heard the voice of Simon Gavin, as perhaps it had.

From the other side of the room came the slow, measured breathing of Boyd—Wolfe Tone Boyd Gavin, but mercifully shortened—still caught in sleep. And, as if in time with the breathing, piano music began to drift across the small ravine that separated this house from the Ventrys', the family who had founded the town one hundred and fifty years ago and, even they admitted, had done mighty little since. It began, worked itself into confi-

13

dence, stumbled, whimpered another beginning, again, then again. From his pillow Parnell could see through the window past the exploding shrubs on the lawn into the Ventry parlor, somewhere in the early morning shadows of which a girl was sitting at the piano stool, already practicing, though there were no other signs of activity in that house.

Then, "Tina!" a girl's voice yelled. "Make Christina stop it!" The music stopped, waited a second, then began again.

Out of the corner of his itchy eye, over a ridge of poison ivy, Parnell watched his brother stir in his bed, sliding with that terrible grace he employed even when leaning over to pick up a ball from the ground. The single sheet that had covered him was twisted crazily at the bottom of the bed, half on the floor, and against the whiteness of the sheet he looked almost Nigerian, fair only where his swim trunks had covered him. He was upside down, his face buried in the pillow.

"Simon's going to be howling mad," Parnell said to the sleeping figure. "Are you awake?"

Boyd grunted and screwed his face farther into the pillow. "The loony," he said.

"Gramp?"

"Sweet mother of Jesus, no. Tina."

Relieved, Parnell stretched out his winged foot until it touched a tin box at the bottom of his bed. It contained his collection of Russo-Japanese War atrocity pictures, small, scented cards which came with bubble gum, and which the evening before he had arranged by degrees of horror, the dying Japanese on top because their last breaths were accompanied by more terrible gestures. Looking at them, he had imagined himself in scenes of adversity: being beaten with rubber truncheons, forced to drink urine, and hung by his fingers from rafters, all because he wouldn't tell the Gestapo how many air miles it was between Berlin and Ventry. He closed the lid with his big toe, lifted himself from his bed, and walked naked to the window. He jumped up to the window sill, half hoping that someone in the street might see him without any clothes, and said to the figure still in bed, "Where were *you*?"

"Where was I when?" Boyd partly turned over, his eyes opening, and as they did he looked down at his body and effortlessly pulled out a small blond hair growing from his shoulder in an otherwise clean patch of skin.

14

"Didn't that hurt?"

"A little bitty hair?"

"Sweet-mother-Jesus," Parnell said, searching his own shoulder, then his chest, then his belly. Finding nothing new or out of the way, he scratched at a scab on his knee. "Last night," he continued. "How come you were out so late last night? Were you with the dumb blonde? Were you da-runk?"

It was beyond Parnell's understanding why anyone would want to see the blonde anyway, or any other girl for that matter. He had once read an adults-only book in which the fatheaded hero, whenever he saw a woman, said, "And as I watched her, my bowels began to turn over." To Parnell it seemed to be a lot of trouble to go through for nothing.

Without waiting for an answer to his question, he went to Boyd's section of the dresser and drew out a pair of his brother's shorts. He now pulled them on, grabbing a fistful of cloth to keep them from sliding down again, then turned to see if Boyd had watched. Stepping into his corduroy shorts, he then said, "People get sick when they get drunk. Mr. Ventry always does."

"Who the hell says I got drunk?"

"I thought that's what you said."

"You can't get drunk until you're twenty-one. This is Ohio."

"How many years is that away?"

"Figure yourself. I'm eighteen." Boyd now leaned over the side of the bed, apparently looking for something. "Anyway, I wasn't with the dumb blonde if you mean Dor-o-thy." Dorothy, who squeezed every syllable out of her name, had been a friend of his the year before because she was the only one in school who was obliging enough to let anyone feel her tits. He'd finally given her up, saying that art was longer than sex; art in his case was running the mile on the track team. "Anyway," he resumed, "she's not a dumb blonde. She's a blonde dumb. It's a matter of emphasis." Then, "I was with Francine last night." Finally, "Toss me a pair of shorts."

Parnell looked into his brother's drawer with mock interest. "They're all gone."

"For the love of God, are you taking my clothes again? Mom said lay off that, didn't she?" He then reached over for a pair of shorts draped from a cane-bottomed chair next to his bed.

15

"I never take anything."

"Hah!" Boyd exclaimed. "Listen to him. He never takes anything. *Hah!*" He stood up now to draw his shorts around him.

"Toss me my pants."

"Which ones?"

"The ones I had on last night. On the door knob. There, stoopid. The good ones. I have to see Dr. Herron today. Very big deal."

Warily looking at his brother, Parnell remembered the office and the cold table where the doctor had put him to sleep, then cut below his ear, a long, jagged cut that Parnell, remembering, felt smart again. "That's where I had mastoid," he said somberly. "Criminee! Did you know he gave me e-ther?" He now inhaled deeply, feeling the dizzy smell of ether strike at his head. Nothing else had ever tasted that way—as if it had been buried for a very long time, an ancient taste—except the turtle soup he once had at his Aunt Cortez's house.

"All I have to get is a physical, for God's sake. You make it sound like a goddamn cancer operation." He paused, seeing the confusion on Parnell's face, ready now to explain. "They make you take a physical before you go to Oberlin. See? They want to make certain you're not a freak. Or that you don't have *Weltschmerz* or something."

Parnell knew that Oberlin could grope and tap his brother's body as much as they wanted to without finding anything wrong with it, even though his mother and his grandmother said that he once had rheumatic fever—St. Vitus's dance, they called it—as a baby. Not so, Parnell knew, because Boyd's body could do almost everything better than Parnell's. Even when they went to the Casto together, to see a new Betty Grable picture or a Laurel and Hardy, Boyd would always be able to find his way down the blackened aisle as if all the lights in the place were on. And with that advantage, he generally guided Parnell, rubbery and blind, and sat him in the darkness on top of the first fat lady he saw, smack-bang on her lap. "Oh, 'scuse *us*," Boyd would then say, howling and whooping.

"I know," Parnell now grunted. "I'm not so dumb."

"Sometimes I wonder."

Without too much dumbness, Parnell began again, "Anyway, I thought you were going into the Army. How

16

can you go to—how-you-call-it?—Oberlin and the Army at the same time?"

At the closet, Boyd turned his head and looked at his brother impatiently. "I'm getting a deferment, or haven't you heard? Boy, these wise guys who always want you to do something you can't do."

"I thought you were just pretending. Like Dewey Ventry. He's not supposed to have asa-mah at all."

"Who the hell says?"

"I don't know. Someone, I think."

"Well, why don't you ask him if he has asthma? You shouldn't believe everything you hear, bub. Dewey and I both got deferments, and we're going down to Oberlin to live it up. Get ourselves polished. Learn what irony means. Read Klopstock. Discuss is-sues. Boy, these guys who always want you to do something you can't."

Boyd's classification, though welcome, was a tender spot because almost everyone else in his high school class had already gone into the Army or Navy or was about to. Boyd himself didn't know precisely why the draft board had reclassified him at the last minute, but it seemed likely that it had something to do with his father. And he also had the vague notion that letters had passed between his grandmother and Aunt Cortez in Shaker Heights, and that Aunt Cortez, in turn, had written letters—pleading ones Boyd would be ashamed of—to any number of influential people she knew or pretended to know in the state. Whenever Boyd thought that perhaps it wasn't especially democratic, he remembered that Simon had said the richer you are, the easier it is to be democratic. Aunt Cortez was rich almost beyond good taste.

"If you go into the Army," Parnell now said, "you might run into Pop."

"Maybe," Boyd answered shortly. He very much did not like to talk about his father or even think much about him any more, partly because he was afraid if he did he would then have to face up to the truth which everyone else in the family had been avoiding for over a year—that a man couldn't be missing since June of last summer, suspended forever in that region between life and death. His father, he knew, was being kept alive now mostly by hopes—Parnell's, Simon's, and Rose's. On the day, the summer before, when they first learned that Lucas Gavin was missing in North Africa, the day that Rose had read the wire to the family, the small banner with the blue star

17

had been hung in the parlor window. It had been there ever since, a part of their lives, defying the war and the world itself.

"Pop can look after himself," Boyd announced, hoping that this would be the last he would have to say on the subject.

"Simon says he could have amnesia." Then, with real enthusiasm, "I saw a movie like that once." He now tilted his head back and let the scenes flash before his eyes like slides. "There was this guy who got hit on the head and couldn't even remember his wife. So he fell in love with a beautiful girl who was Deanna Durbin, I think, and he was going to marry her. What-you-call bigamy. But at the last minute—poweee!—he got hit on the head again and remembered his wife. Was *she* a rat. Brother! You should have seen him. He introduced the rat to a friend and . . ."

"Well, that's a movie," Boyd interrupted. "Those people in Hollywood get some nitwit to read a book about amnesia in about five minutes and then write a movie about it. And *who's* the only one in the world who believes every word? You. You believe everything. You think everything is a movie."

"Who, me? Not me."

Which was at least partly true. Parnell didn't think that everything was a movie; he merely wished that it was. His own world offered expectation alone, but nothing ever came of expectations except in the movies. There, while Parnell stuffed himself with popcorn, he watched the miraculous. Sonja Henie would have a gimpy leg one minute, and the next she'd win a skating contest on ice so slick it would send anyone else on his fanny. Tyrone Power would always get the snooty girl to fall in love with him even when he didn't know which fork to use at the dinner table. Everyone looked good. Everyone looked happy. Everyone looked *rich*. And no one was more partial to rich people than Parnell; his grandmother thought that poverty was ennobling, but he already knew better.

As if Boyd were this moment thinking of it, he groaned, "And who writes letters to John D. Rockefeller about his expedition to . . . to the fabled cities of Peru?"

"As a matter of fact," Parnell replied in a vaguely superior way, "it's for Yucatan. That's how much you know. The dig is for Yucatan."

"Listen to him! His dig! And you think that John D.

18

Rockefeller is going to send a nine-year-old kid to the jungles of Yuca ... Yuca*tan?*"

"He's supposed to sponsor cultural things."

"Like you?"

"That's what they told me at Yale University."

When Parnell was eight and first discovered his vocation, he had written a letter to the president of Yale, asking him how one went about getting an expedition financed. He had taken great pains with his letter, making certain that all the commas were in the right place, and it must have been favorably received because the chairman of the archaeology department had sent him a long, chatty answer which also included application forms for that fall's freshman class.

"Well, you're not going anywhere, bub. Maybe Yale didn't know you were a kid, but you can't fool Mr. Rockefeller."

"Those people in Yucatan even had a calendar," he sighed rather wistfully. "They even figured out the stars. They figured them *out*. They even had toilets. I have read up on it."

"Sometimes you're so showoffy smart. I suppose you got all that out of one of Simon's books?"

"The library. Miss Kane lets me read any book I want now except the dirty ones, and they're all in the glass case."

"Oh, my God," Boyd hooted, closing his eyes. "You've even read *Tobacco Road*. I saw it under your bed."

"It wasn't so dirty," Parnell answered cheerfully. "I mean, the words weren't. Some people were kind of dirty though."

"Well, act your age, for the love of God. If you read everything now, you'll run out of things by the time you're fifteen. And, anyway, you're not going anywhere. To Yucatan or even to Cleveland. You're as bad as Simon. Always wanting to be somewhere you aren't."

Animated now, Parnell said smugly, "Simon's taking me with him on his next trip. He says so. I'm going to help carry his suitcases."

Simon Gavin, their grandfather, ran away from home at least once a year, never telling anyone in advance, not even saying at the last minute that he couldn't bear their grandmother Rose one more second, but instead rushing up the stairs as if he were on fire, packing his bags, then throwing them—never carrying them—down the long flight of steps into the first floor hallway, and catching the next bus or train to Cleveland. So far he'd been to the Stony Mountains, as he called them; to Yallerstone Park; Denver, Colorado; Salt Lake City, Utah; Miami Beach, Florida; New York City; and two or three times, when he was short of cash, just as far as Jefferson, the county seat ten miles away, where he took a room in a boardinghouse and pretended that he was from the Far West. As for Rose, she said she didn't care one way or the other, but she wished he wouldn't throw his bags down the steps. Simon, for his part, explained rather importantly, "I've been in a hurry all my life, I expect," and everyone was polite enough not to ask for what. As for the noise of the falling suitcases, they knew that he simply wanted to make a strong, masculine sound.

"Simon's too old to be going on any more trips," Boyd said. "He's almost seventy-five."

"He's just waiting for his pass."

The pass—Simon dreamed of it for half the year and then waited for it to arrive in the mail the other half— was from the Pennsylvania Railroad and compensation for the outrage of having worked for them for most of his life. Simon had been a telegraph operator at the tower outside of town before he retired. Was *force*fully retired, Rose said, before he caused a one-hundred-thousand-dollar accident, reading *Liberty* magazine or *A Guide to Budapest,* feeling the lust for adventure while two trains ran into each other outside his window.

"And why would he want to have you around? I'd like to know."

"He said I could keep him company. I could cook for him among other things."

"A lot you can cook. Eggs is what you can cook."

"I can make shirred eggs," Parnell said loftily.

"Sweet Mary, mother of God, Queen of the May, will you listen to him!" Boyd yelled at the ceiling. Heavy footsteps could now be heard climbing the hall stairs, and as he heard them Boyd said, "Simon's going to give us another patriotic speech, I bet you anything. Hurry up and toss me my shoes."

The door burst open and Simon Gavin walked in, a tall, pink-faced man with a foxy head of white hair. He was already dressed in his linen suit and carrying the Panama hat which he would perch on the wooden cannonball at the end of the banister as he went down the stairs to breakfast, and which Rose Gavin would as quickly remove as it offended her eye. At seventy-five, he was still gingery-looking, and famous-looking, too, as if he could have been president of the Bank of America or Governor of Ohio or any other lordly thing if he hadn't gone swelling around in his youth. As it was, and as he often enough repeated, he had himself a tune as a young man. And it was a tune he never tired of singing in a deep, husky, senatorial voice that shook the house. The voice he ascribed to no gift of his own but to the fact that a druidy Gavin in the fifth century had stolen a goat that belonged to St. Patrick, had slain it and eaten it, for which Patrick—"One of God's most gorgeous saints, and anyone who thinks otherwise is a heathen"—had made the goat stick in his throat and in the throats of all Gavins for all time. He regarded anyone, especially the DAR type who couldn't trace his family back to the fifth century, as a pup.

Sweeping into the room now, Simon looked at his grandsons, Boyd pulling on his shoes, Parnell pinning his father's sharpshooter medal on his T shirt. "Well, I'll be danged," he roared huskily. "You'd be louting around here all day if it weren't for me. You'd sleep till noon like an English lord. Don't you know there's a war on?"

"That's what Bernard Baruch here," Boyd said, "has just been telling me."

"And what will you do when they start dropping Germans from Zeppelins? You ever considered that? The rape, the plundering, the destruction that would en-*sue?* Stand up straight, boys. Push out your chests. Look reckless and manly." Saying it, Simon himself showed them how.

"Drop Germans in Ohio?"

"If they do, I'll hide in the attic where it's good and dark," Parnell said quietly.

"The shame!" Simon boomed. "Here you are, named after the greatest men in Ireland—I can't hear their names without tears coming to my eyes—and you want to hide. No, *sir*. No Gavin in the long and de-plorable history of man has hid for a minute. Look 'em all up! There were Gavins who freed the Holy Land from the hands of the infidels!—and a pretty sight we made. There were Gavins who taught the ignorant Charlemagne how to read and drive darkness out of the whole of Europe! There was a Gavin who stood up to the Corsican himself, the greatest rascal of all time, at the battle of Water-looooo, and came home half-legged but in merry spirits!

21

Gavins who were bosom, *hu*-zum friends of all the great men in America. Washington! Jefferson! Ulysses S. Grant! My own grandfather, bless him, was so battle-shocked at Bull Run he was queer in the head for the rest of his life! My own mother saw Oscar Wilde in velvet breeches in Cincinnati, the year 1882! And don't forget your Uncle Tootie who stole Queen Victoria's hat from the Garfield Museum outside of Cleveland and burned it to a crisp because he couldn't sleep another night until that abomination was removed from the land of liberty. An IRA man to the last!"

"Oh, my God," Boyd muttered, afraid to say that he had never run across any Gavin exploits in history books, "you said you'd lay off that gung-ho stuff once it's summer."

"There's no telling when we'll be called on, young man. No, sir, there's no telling." He seemed now to be inspired, even perhaps willing to tell. "Why, take the time in the Philippines when I was summoned from ranks, a mere corporal, still wet behind the ears, by Arthur Mac-Arthur himself."

"Not a-gin," Boyd managed to say painfully, but Simon pretended not to hear, turning his deaf ear toward him.

"Douglas MacArthur's father, Parnell, in case you've forgotten. And you've never seen a man with such swank. Now, are you listening? I'll tell you something or two. On the night before his expected visitation, for such is what you call 'em, only one man in the whole scruffy 10th Pennsylvania Volunteers stayed up all night to pre-pare. Only one man spit-polished his shoes, rubbed his brass till it'd put your eye out to look at it, pressed his uniform by hand! Who was it, you'll ask."

Parnell, though he had heard the story many times, looked up, waiting for the answer.

"Simon Gavin! The sorry and neglected figure you're looking at this very minute. But back in those days, you'll have to remember that I was still young and brutish. A sight to behold! How could Arthur MacArthur or anyone else help but be drawn to me? I'd like to know. He walked up and down our ranks—it was shocking hot! The temperature 110 under a tree if you could find one alive— looking at all the miserable faces before him, and then his eyes fell on your own grandfather. 'Who,' said he to his adjutant, 'hooooo is that GIANT over there?' I stepped

22

out as smartly as you could ask, and he shook this very hand you're looking at now." In order that they could get a better view of it, Simon held it up, a kind of portable, everlasting reliquary. "And the point *is*, boys, I was ready for him. Pre-pared. In body and outlook. You'll find it all in the official history of the regiment that cost me two dollars and a quarter. It's all downstairs in the book for any human eye to see."

Both Parnell and Boyd had seen it, though the account lacked the exaltation of Simon's telling. Below a brownish photograph, a caption read: "A view of the troops during inspection." All that could be seen of the giant was the top of his head, but you couldn't deny that he looked proud. As for MacArthur, the historian had failed to mention him.

"Yup," Simon continued, "a man must always be pre-pared to walk before the spotlight of history. Has to know how to dee-port himself. Take the time . . . while I'm on the subject," he cleared more of the goat from his throat in order to press on, "the time I re-*fused* to shake the hand of Robert A. Taft in Cleveland, Ohio, the year nineteen hundred and thirty-nine."

Boyd, who hadn't followed the MacArthur story because he'd been exposed to it so often, now showed guarded interest.

"It was a bad year for Republicans," Simon resumed. "You couldn't get a crust of bread in a bread line unless you were a registered Democrat. Well, sir!" He wiped his mouth with the back of his sleeve, then squinted his eyes, as if to recall it more lucidly. "This was before Mr. Taft had presidential aspirations, you call 'em, but everyone saw he was a going thing. It looked actually like he might do. And I considered it my bounden duty to go to Cleveland to see the man close up, so to speak. I wanted to take the man's measure. See if he was up to the task. And let me tell you—the devil takes many forms—I was almost sucked in. Behold me therefore! As soon as Mr. Taft began to talk about the war in Europe, he said it was none of our danged business. People being killed, and it was none of our business, the man says. The fellow was a prune. Why, I was outraged, as you might well imagine. I was all for going up to the podium and giving the gent a good clout he'd remember for a long time. But my steady reason prevailed. I waited until he finished his de-plorable speech and then went up to have a little talk with him. To

23

set him straight. And didn't I tell him a thing or two! Oh, I was in great tune!"

Boyd, though he loved Simon dearly, was sure that he had, but he wasn't convinced that what had been said was as listened to as Simon believed it to be.

"Well!" Simon went on. "After I'd spoken my piece—and a proper dressing down I gave him—Mr. Taft said to me, 'I've always admired a man who isn't afraid to express his opinion. I'd be privileged to shake your hand.' And I said—do you know what I said?—I said, 'No, sir, I WON'T.' "

Simon paused to study the effect he had produced. It was a stunning one. Parnell's mouth was agape.

"Of course," Simon now said, more mildly, catching his breath, "it was all sup-pressed by the Cleveland newspapers. But still it's a part of unwritten history, the most re-vealing kind. The hand that had shaken Arthur MacArthur's wasn't going to be touched by a peacemongering prune!"

From downstairs came a sound that could only mean that Rose, their grandmother, was beating the pancake turner against the banister, her way of telling them to stop the foolish talk and come down to breakfast.

"Yup," Simon finished, the wind taken out of him slightly by the reminder of who and where he was, "a man can learn from great examples. And a man must be pre-pared for any eventuality. Now, I hope and pray to God they never drop Japanese in the fields—they're sneaky fellows, don't I know? Haven't I seen them with my own eyes in the city of Yokohama? They're monstrous beyond belief. They think nothing of swallowing a raw fish; they eat vipers; they *abuse* missionaries—I hope and pray they never do, as I say, but if they should come, dropping from the skies in great multitudes the way I see pictures of these parachuters, why, by God, I want us three Gavins to be the first to meet the foe." Then, apparently satisfied with the morning's call to arms—it would be duplicated tomorrow, and the next day, and the next—Simon said, "I'll give you two minutes to fall in. And I want you to do it with style this time. Boyd, you're getting to slouch like a fop. I want you to straighten up and march with *ginger*."

As quickly as he had appeared, he was gone, revolving on his heels and rushing out of the room. In a minute the boys could hear him begin to wind the Victrola in the upstairs hall.

"Criminee," Parnell complained, "I bet we're the only ones in America outside the Marines who have to march to breakfast."

Boyd waited for a while, and then, with wisdom that had only recently come to him, said, "I guess it pleases Simon."

Parnell brought the long metal tooth of his belt buckle to the last notch, tightening it around his pants as far as it would go to help keep up his stolen shorts. "They wouldn't do that, would they? Drop Japs from Zeppelins?"

Exasperation filled Boyd's face. "You're getting to be as ga-ga as Tina next door. Now, why would Emperor Hirohito take the trouble to send parachuters into our grape arbor, for Christ's sake? I think poison ivy's spread to your brain."

"I just wondered is all," Parnell said politely, wondering also if poison ivy could. "Then how come Simon said it?"

"Sweet mother of Jesus, don't you know Simon?"

"Sure, I know," Parnell answered, not knowing at all. He finished pinning his sharpshooter's medal on his T shirt, making certain that it was straight and that the tiny clasp wouldn't prick against him later on and stab him in the heart.

Dressed, Boyd looked at his brother, waiting by the door, the music from the Victrola already bringing the color to his cheeks. "Do you have to wear that?" he finally said.

"What?"

"That." He pointed to the small medal, the one his father had given to Parnell during his last leave before he went overseas. He now watched Parnell put his fingers over it protectively. "Oh, my God," Boyd then said, going through the door. "I wonder what would happen around this house if people ever begin to wake up."

Without waiting for an answer—Parnell wouldn't have been able to give one anyway—the two boys walked into the hall, the one behind the other, "The Stars and Stripes Forever" blaring from the Victrola at the top of the stairs.

Once in the hall, Parnell changed his easy, sleepy walk to a march, and Boyd did the same. Past the jardiniere filled with roses and snapdragons, past dead Uncle Desmond preserved forever in the frame on the wall, past the Victrola, and Simon himself.

"Step lively there, young man," Simon shouted at Parnell. "That's the way, boys. Make it bold. Throw your feet out like they're in flames. Let them leap! Think of the storied knights of old! Caesar's centurions! Hannibal! Think of the noble Alexander. The valiant Normans! Lord Nelson! The Battle of the Boyne, the darkest day in history! King Billy, Wolfe Tone, The gorgeous Parnell! That's the way. A little more swagger. 'Hoo-ray for the red, white, and ba-*lue! Da-da-da!* Da-da-da . . . Da-da-*Dum*-da!' Dig your heels into the carpet, Wolfe Tone. Dig 'em in, Charles Parnell. Oh, it's a lovely sight to behold. That's very lovely, boys."

A sharp, tired, impatient voice now came from the bottom of the stairs. "You've got the carpet worn to threads, Mister Gavin. Stop that racket before I call the police. Why, they can hear you all over town."

"No harm done," Simon answered sheepishly from the top. "That was very handsome, boys. Now, twenty push-ups apiece, and then you can fall out for breakfast. And I don't want to see a belly touching the floor." He picked up the arm of the Victrola and as he did, scratched it against the record, already bumpy from past scratchings. The music sometimes sounded as if it were coming from a box at the bottom of a stormy sea.

"Come on, gorgeous," Boyd said to his brother.

At the bottom of the stairs, Rose shivered, then shook her head at the two boys doing push-ups in the hall. "You won't be happy until you drive me crazy," she shouted.

"No harm done," Simon repeated, even more benignly this time, coming down the stairs into the hallway.

"Well, you'll be pleased to learn that you've succeeded in bursting my head wide open. I have half a notion to take the bus to Massillon and commit myself—yes, com-*mit* myself—to the state asylum." Having made this terrible threat, she looked without pleasure at the two convulsed bodies on the floor, pursed her lips, and touched her burst head. "The way your grandfather acts—it's a shame to mankind."

She was a woman with an elegant face and with eyes that were prodigies of color: black, brown, gray, and green, all at war with each other. Like an Oriental rug which becomes richer with age and abuse, she was better-

26

looking now than when she was young. Her upper eyelids were hooded, half closing her eyes; because of this and a restless and twitchy nose, caused by nervousness, she generally left the impression that she was about to sneeze. Yet she never did, thinking it in very poor taste. Instead she would catch her sneezes somewhere in her nasal cavities and swallow them before they exploded, making little slapping noises—a thud really, a half dollar dropped into wet mud—that were far more distracting than a one-hundred-percent sneeze.

About marriage, Simon and Rose had two minds—hers and his. It was, despite this, less a marriage of heaven and hell than it was one of heaven and heaven. The trouble, of course, was that each had fixed ideas about the place, unwilling to think that the other was suitable to live there. For Rose, expulsion took the form of "Now what has the old fool been telling you this time?" said with friendly animosity, while Simon in his turn suggested about his wife, "A thorny Rose indeed. She has a tongue that'll cut you flaming red."

To know why they had married in the first place is to know why men can't live without war. They married, it sometimes seemed, to suffer together. Simon, by his own account, had returned from the Spanish-American War at the turn of the century as free and footloose as a wild hog. He had money enough—his own fatted calf, he called it—to live for three years without turning his finger to work, but instead he had proposed to Rose Ann Boyd, almost as an act of contrition, almost as if to say, "Well, it's shameful and un-Christian for me to be so happy." Afterward—God is sometimes mysteriously obliging—he wasn't happy at all, yet happy, yes, when recalling how happy he had *been* before he took the step, happier even perhaps than he might have been with another woman who could have provided him with the monotony and tedium of bliss. It was strange, even Simon would admit, but except for the children the only real joy of his life was the past. Not just yesterday, but his dark past, his own perilous and beautiful youth, and all the tales which tended to make it unfold before his eyes. Rose, to be sure, was perhaps too often on hand, ready to lunge at his dreams and draw not blood but air, yet Simon was, as he said, always prepared for her. A man must always keep on his toes lest he be cut to the quick itself, he would say, naming it as if the quick were a bruised part of his body

27

which any moment he would uncover and display for all the world to see.

Yet he was cowed by his wife. Ineffably, unreservedly, inexpressibly cowed. The sword Rose carried was Truth. Her crime was terrible and marvelous. She knew him too well.

And probably because of that, one had to pity Rose, something she herself often did, volubly and with a faint, harmonious keening. She had listened to Simon's exploits, most of which had at least some basis in fact, for over fifty years. She had stood with him and fought the savage Filipinos in Manila, had braced him to the deck of his ship in the teeth of a typhoon in the China Sea, and had eaten octopus—unusually luscious, he said—with him in Hong Kong without even understanding the lingo of the land. She had looked on in disbelief when the Governor of Ohio had sent him a personal letter, an answer to one of his own imploring the good man to erect a statue of Admiral Dewey in the landlocked city of Columbus. She had heard him reel off answer after answer while they sat at night in the parlor listening to the Quiz Kids, saying that the Kids had no minds to speak of and no manners at all. She had worked long and tireless hours preparing a report for her Reading Club on Faulkner's *The Sound and the Fury,* which she really didn't get the hang of, only then to hear Simon say, "Well, he may be a bit on the obtuse side, as you call it, but he's a very likable man and plain to talk to. I suppose you know I ran into Mr. Faulkner, the poet lor-yut, in the bus station in Memphis, Tennessee, the year nineteen hundred and thirty-seven? We struck up a lively conversation—he was going to lecture at some college; danged if I know *why* I was there—and I gave him a few pointers on improving his books. He don't let people talk enough. Who cares if someone's lips are the color of the rosy-fingered dawn if they never move?" And Rose, under the impression she was the only one in Ventry who had ever heard of the man, pitched out her report and did one on *Tobacco Road* instead, later read by Parnell and pooh-poohed.

It was, of course, unfair. Rose had never been farther away from Ventry than Cleveland, and even then Simon, who was thrifty, would want to turn around and head back home the minute he got there to avoid driving the Hudson Terraplane at night and using its headlights and its precious battery juice. Coming after the years of privation spent in the presence of her sister Cortez, it was too much. As she said, and often truthfully, it burst her head.

Now, still holding her wavy head of hair, she walked from the hall into the parlor, where she made certain that the ice sign was turned around so that the one-armed man who speared chunks of ice with the iron at the end of his elbow, shivering and sweating at the same time, wouldn't have to stop. Rose next straightened the small banner in the bay window. Standing there, she seemed lost in thought, as if there were something written on the mass-produced flag that would perhaps now be revealed to her.

It was hers alone. Until the day she placed it in the window, it had been her opinion that such displays of emotion were vulgar. Yet on the day that she read the wire to the family announcing that her son was missing in action, the banner went up. Not, however, as an announcement to Ventry that her son was in the Army, for such was the purpose of these small, blue-starred flags. And not as a shrine by any means. Rather as a beacon almost, one that—its star there, blue and hopeful—would guide him home. For someone as strong as Rose, even unsentimental, it was a surprising confession of weakness.

As she looked at it now, Rose's heart was perhaps what her popular novelists call heavy. As were the hearts of those who watched her. If it would seem that the Gavins, for all their burdens, are on this morning unbecomingly happy, joyful almost, it should be remembered that they are still very Irish. And that even in the hunger years of the 1840s when over a million people died of starvation in that land, there could still be heard the sound of the fiddle, and *was* heard as long as there were arms to move a bow.

Imagine, then, this fiddling.

As Rose left the parlor, her face, momentarily softened by her thoughts, tightened again. She walked quickly into the hall in short, agitated steps, and to the boys heaving their bodies up and down on the floor finishing their push-ups, she said, "If you want any breakfast, I seriously advise you to remember that you're not one of those children they find in the jungles of Africa who've been nursed by wild boars. You'll kindly get off the floor. And straighten that rug, Parnell, before someone trips."

Pleased that he could point out an error made by Rose, Simon said, "If you can find a boar who can nurse children, we've got our fortune made." Rose narrowed her

29

small eyes, apparently wondering if he had said something carnal—loose talk of any sort she couldn't abide—and then continued on her way to the kitchen.

Boyd and Parnell wiped their hands on their pants and followed her as far as the dining room, where Catherine, their mother, was already sitting at the large round table, a low turn-of-the-century chandelier hanging from the ceiling before her, almost meeting the cut-glass dish filled with waxed apples and bananas. Boyd sat down, caught his breath, stood again, kissed his mother, then sat for a second time. "Is Rose mad at something again?" he whispered.

Catherine was buttering toast with great care, as if she were decorating it, watching it melt as it met the hot brown bread. "Your grandmother didn't sleep again last night," she said, her voice full of repose. Then to the boy next to her at the table, "Good morning, Parnell. Aren't you going to kiss me?"

Parnell pushed his chair closer to the table. "I'm too old." He punched a quarter of cantaloupe before him with his spoon to add manly emphasis, then looked at his brother for approval. Boyd replied with his "Who are you trying to kid?" expression. "Sweet Jesus," he then muttered to himself, unheard.

"Aren't you getting to be the cat's pajamas?" It was Rose, and she was now bent over Parnell, lifting a plate of sausages and eggs to the table, resting it, as if completing some perfect design, directly in front of Simon. Simon, who thought all animal flesh was vile and abominable, looked at it as if he were about to be sick to his stomach, then slowly pushed it away.

"Who loves you?" she now asked, running her hand through the stubble of Parnell's hair, stroking the front where a shameful wave used to be. She smelled vaguely of the creams, lotions, and pale pink liquids that preserved her.

Parnell had been through the game too often to care to respond. He knew somehow—he didn't exactly know why —that Rose liked for him to tell her that she loved him. It seemed very strange and backward. He now rested his spoon on the corner of his plate and replied, "I don't know."

"You know who loves you!" she coaxed, while Parnell studied his chipped cantaloupe, hoping that someone would rescue him. Next to him, out of the corner of one

eye, he saw his mother incline her head in such a way to indicate that he should answer in order to keep the peace. It was a look that said "Manners!" But he waited for his grandmother to commit herself more.

"Who loves you more than anyone in the world?"

He still kept his tongue, biting it hard.

"Who's going to buy you a pony one of these days?"

Parnell's face now broke into a glad smile that half closed his eyes. He dreamed about the pony almost every night, sometimes even waking up in the mornings sore from having been riding it, delivering his papers from its back, swashbuckling through town, raising the dust on Main Street, with no time even for a how-do-you-do to anyone he knew in school, galloping over fences, fields, rivers, a sight to quicken the heart, the one and only Parnell Gavin, son of the Wild West, handy with the lasso and the branding iron. A cowboy!

His eyes expectant, he now looked up at his grandmother slowly. "Y-y-*you?*" he said in disbelief, waiting for her to lead a pony in from the kitchen.

"Darn tootin'!" Rose cried, the winner, "Now give your grandmother a great big hug."

Sorrowfully, seeing that he had been duped again, he did, but as soon as she turned away he wiped his lips with his napkin, trying to remove the smell of cold cream. It could drive a man loco, as his friends in the movies said.

"Enough to turn your stomach."

"Eh? *Eh? EH?* What did Mister Gavin say?" This from Rose.

"I said," Simon began again, "that sausage is enough to turn your stomach." He waited, then caught Parnell's eye and addressed him personally, intensely. "The food you get nowadays isn't fit for human consumption. Correct me if I'm wrong. Time was when I liked to eat meat. *Meat!* Why, I'd eat a roast beef at a sitting. If anyone was fool enough to set a leg of lamb before me at a table, by the time I finished with it a starving man couldn't find enough on it to raise his saliva."

"Disgusting," Rose interrupted, not admiring the image.

"Virginia ham!" he now called out fondly, as if it were the name of an old sweetheart. "I ate my way through *two* of them one night in the city of San Francisco, the year eighteen hundred and ninety-seven. I've eaten . . . why, I've even eaten monkey meat. A very tasty dish."

Rose leaned over toward Catherine. "Never," she said,

31

then circled her head with her finger to suggest that Simon was a madman.

"But you're risking your life any more to eat the swill the government provides for civilians," Simon continued. "That's why I gave up animal flesh. Why, didn't I read just the other days that we're sending our best beefsteaks to the Bolsheviks in Russia? And all that's left for us is the entrails." He paused, apparently deciding to approach the matter a different way. "Of course, I expect my stomach was ruined in the Philippines where I lived on a diet of hardtack and muddy water so thick it'd crack your teeth to drink it. It's also where I picked up my malaria. Nothing has tasted right since 1900."

"It's all in his mind," Rose volunteered. "He ate like a field horse until this war came along and he remembered his stomach." She now turned toward Simon, shaking her spoon at him. "If I swallowed as much of that quinine as you do, well, sir, I'd have a bad stomach too. Whoever heard of anyone in the State of Ohio having malaria? I'd like to know."

"Here we go again," Boyd said to his brother, hitting him sharply against the arm. Parnell twisted his head to study his stinging flesh, wondering if it would become blue and bruised, hoping that it would.

"All I like any more is a mess of Jell-O," Simon continued earnestly, oblivious of everyone. Also truthfully: it now constituted the greatest part of his diet. "It's easy to digest and you get all your important nutriments. Why, I wouldn't eat meat any more even if Mr. Roosevelt handed me a presidential citation for every pork chop I'd consume."

"You can't keep a spider alive on Jell-O," Rose said. Then, more aroused, "He said the same thing last year about tapioca pudding, do you remember, Catherine? Do you rek-clect how I'd spend an hour stirring tapioca pudding until I thought my arm'd fall off into the pan because Mister Gavin said he couldn't abide the store-bought kind and as how his stomach couldn't accommodate anything else? Before he discovered Jell-O? And didn't I myself catch him in the refrigerator in the dead of night licking a chicken carcass down to the bone? That's a living fact, Mister Gavin."

The living fact was that Simon had given up meat because he didn't want to deprive American troops of their vittles. But sometimes, when the rest of the house was sleeping, he would lose his resolve.

"If the truth be known," he said weakly, "I was getting a drink of ice water because I was running a slight malarial fever."

"Shoo! If you wouldn't sit in that chair all night reading, you wouldn't *have* gas."

"I didn't say I had gas. I said I had a slight temperature." He caught Boyd's eye and looked into it deeply, as if he were about to reveal something of great importance. "I understand the government now has pills they give to soldiers in the Far East to ward off malaria. Correct me if I'm wrong." He screwed up his face, perhaps reaching for something that would erase the impression left by Rose's words. "Of course," he began again, "I was in perfect health until I took that terrible tumble into the shark-infested waters of Manila Bay the day we steamed into port. It was a shocking fall. Shocking. A two-hundred-foot drop, and I counted every inch on the voyage down. They said they could hear me recite the Rosary each time I popped up to the surface. I was resigned to a watery grave." He paused. "The mar-velous thing is that my father was the last Catholic in the family, and I can't recall that I ever even learned the Rosary. The strangeness of God! But I tell you. It undermined my health. I came out unscathed—it just didn't, bless the Lord, happen to be the shark season—but it undermined my health."

"Well, it undermined your something," Rose said, afraid that Simon's story had given him an advantage that couldn't be countenanced. "Anyone who sits in that chair in the parlor half the night, reading, just because you *know* it's keeping me awake, is undermined somehow."

Simon spooned his Jell-O slowly into his mouth, saying nothing. It was true, to be sure, that he liked to read when the house was quiet, and nothing pleased him more than to sit in the silent parlor late at night and read a history book or look through an atlas. But ten minutes after Rose went up to her own bedroom, she would start pounding on the floor above him with the heel of a shoe. "Simon," she would yell, the pictures on the walls shaking in the parlor downstairs, "how do you expect me to sleep with you down there? Simon, what are you *doing?*" Thump-thump-*thump* with the shoe. "Get to bed this instant. Are you deliberately trying to drive me crazy?" Thump! *Thump! THUMP!* Simon would then put his book down sadly, turn off the light, and climb the stairs, passing Rose's closed door—a room he hadn't been in for the last twenty years—imagining her in bed, her arm over the side, the shoe still in her hand like a forgotten plaster saint. Even during the daytime she kept the door double-locked, taking the extra precaution of placing a slip of paper between the door and the jamb to tell her if anyone had tried to tamper with it, though God knows, Simon said, why anyone other than the Marquis de Sade himself would want to.

"If you knew how many ration coupons that sausage took," Rose now said, "you wouldn't be so snooty. *Eat, Parnell.* Don't be so bold."

Parnell, who was boldly not eating, now dug his fork into the yellow of his egg and watched it spread over his plate. He impaled a sausage.

Catherine chose this moment to reach over and rest her hand on his forehead. "You look sleepy, honey. I bet you didn't get to bed until almost ten last night, did you?" Then to Rose, "I don't know that you should have brought him to Miss Osborne's funeral after all. Doesn't he look sleepy?"

Rose, who thought that all funerals were uplifting, always carried Parnell off to them when one of her Rebekah Lodge sisters died—heart attacks, cancer, and one poor woman who, she said, truly died of languor—as Simon, too, generally took his grandson with him to last rites of Spanish-American or First World War friends—coronaries or gassed lungs. Remembering Miss Osborne, a small woman who walked through life doubled over, a tiny hump on her back, Parnell shivered. He had looked at her closely, as his grandmother had told him to ("Go ahead, she's not going to bite you," she said, which even he thought was unsuitable), trying to see what the undertaker had done to her curved back and how it could be that she was, in her coffin, lying down straight for the first time in her life. All he had been able to imagine was a bone-crushing snap.

"Well," Rose said reverentially, "I'm glad she's finally dead. She was so tiny toward the end."

"People don't die of tinyness," Simon announced.

"Hah! He should have been a per-fessor at Harvard University." She fed her mouth for a minute, then permitted her eyes to become thoughtful. "I'll never forget that time I went down to Miss Osborne's about two years ago.

She was always a great one for spiritualism, you know. Anyway, the minute she came to the door, she said, 'Rose Anne Gavin, I clearly see a light around your head. It's your mama.' *Well*, I was scared to death, let me tell you. Mama dead for fifteen years, and then Miss Osborne telling me there's a light around my head." She paused, showing her agitation. "I ran home quicker than anything and looked in the mirror. Sure enough, there *was* a light. I went down on my knees and prayed to Mama and asked her how she was getting along."

"The woman was an old fool."

"Eh? What's that you're saying, Mister Gavin?"

"I said Miss Osborne was an old fool. She was so nearsighted she couldn't see a light even if there was one. Didn't she once call me up to her front porch and say that a man had been crouching at the corner of her house for the last three days? And when I went over for a look-see, it was the danged rhododendron she'd planted herself the spring before. A frustrated old maid!"

"The Mister doesn't believe in anything," Rose answered. "But mark my words, there's something *to* that." She now sucked in part of her bottom lip to help her think. "Why, did you know that Mama herself once told me that I was to prepare for a trip? She came to me all of a sudden and said, 'Rose Anne, prepare yourself. You're going on a trip.' And the next day wasn't I carted off to Cleveland at fifty miles an hour to have *two* gallstones removed I never even knew about?"

"Some trip," Boyd said to his brother.

A shadow now seemed to move over Rose's face, and a gentleness touched it. "Just last night," she began, "I was lying in bed, wondering if I could ever get to sleep. If I ever die, it'll be because of my nerves, mark my words. I could feel myself jumping all over, and I thought, Well now, Rose Anne, you're not going to get any sleep tonight. You'll just have to bear up under it. It must have been after five o'clock, because the room was already getting to be light around the window shades, and I must have dozed off for a minute. No more than a minute. Five at most. And who do you think I saw?" She looked from face to face at the table. "I saw Luke as clear as day."

Except for Boyd, everyone now rested his knife and fork upon hearing the name. Boyd waited for a second, during which he stopped chewing the toast in his mouth; then he, too, put his fork down.

"He looked just the way he did the last time he was home," she resumed. "Well, maybe a little tired. Yes, that was it. His eyes looked a little tired. But he could see me, and I could see him, oh so plain. It wasn't a dream, because he wasn't doing anything, if you follow me. He just appeared before me. Sometimes those things happen. He came and then he was gone. Well, it was a sign, I know that for sure. He came to tell me that he'll be home quicker than you can say Jack Robinson."

For a long time no one was able to say anything. It seemed somehow that they had jumped too quickly, without a moment's breath, from small talk to grief. It was Catherine who finally broke the silence. "Well," she began, "I hope so. I sincerely hope so."

"Yes, sir, a sign," Rose said, finished, unwilling perhaps to say any more. She pushed her chair back, then stood at the table, scooping up the plates before her which were now empty. As she began to walk toward the brown swinging door that separated the dining room from the kitchen, she looked through the white crisscross curtains at the window. "Now whoever is that?" she asked. "Walking across the Ventrys' lawn in her bare feet at this time of day and the grass still so wet. Is that Christina or Francine?"

They all turned to look through the window, relieved, each of them, that they had something to distract their attention from what Rose had told them. It was Boyd who recognized the girl in yellow shorts, barefoot, walking over the wet grass, squeezing her toes into it at every springing touch.

"It's Francine," he said almost with yearning. "Tina is a couple inches taller, and anyway she almost never goes outside." Tina Ventry, the oldest child in that family, was almost twenty, but her mind was still frozen at four or five. She had gone to school for just a few years, and then her mother had taken her out and tried to teach her at home. She had learned to play the piano—perhaps merely by rote, someone had said—but so well that in the past few years she had even been invited to play before clubs when they met. But she would never leave the house. She was Parnell's friend because, except for her younger sister Francine and her brother Dewey, she had no friends near her own age.

"Well," Rose said half playfully, "you should be able to tell them apart if anyone can. You spend more time with

36

Francine than you do with your own family. I've never seen anyone so sweet on a girl before."

"Aw, cut it out, Rose," Boyd answered, smiling and not displeased. He and Francine had been going steady, more or less, since the fall before; when he wasn't with her, he was with Dewey, her brother, who was a year and two months older than Francine but had failed one year in school—which put them all in the same class.

"Well, I bet a dollar Helen Ventry is keeping her eye on that girl. Don't you think she isn't," Rose now said at the kitchen door. "I bet a dollar she has high hopes for Francine; she's aiming as high as she can."

Catherine seemed offended, and for once she didn't try to conceal it. "Whatever do you mean? She couldn't have higher hopes for Francine than we have for Boyd."

"She was always a bit on the grand side, Helen was. I suppose that's why she married Frank Ventry in the first place. The Ventrys *used* to have money, of course, back in the days when they still owned the iron factory. Why I can even remember when they had peacocks on their lawn. Yes, they did. They had that wrought-iron fence they took down last year because the government needs all the metal it can get, and two of the loveliest peacocks you ever saw, just strutting from one end of the lawn to the other, like they were princes of the land. My sister Cortez always said, when we passed the house, that when she grew up that's what she wanted: peacocks on the lawn."

"Aunt Cortez has enough money to buy all the peacocks in the world," Boyd volunteered.

"Yes, and isn't it funny?" She pursed her lips, then ran her fingers over her chin. "She doesn't even have a pet. Not a dog or a cat. Just all by herself in that big house in Shaker Heights. The last time I said to her, 'Cortez, dear, when are you going to get those peacocks you were always talking about?' do you know she couldn't even remember? Not a bit. Money's a terrible thing that way. It burns people out. I hope to God we'll always stay poor, the way we are now. My own mama used to say that the only thing poor people have a lot of is water—you can get almost all you want for free, I suppose you've noticed. And maybe that's all we need. At least it keeps us clean. And not selfish, the way Cortez is."

Cortez—even her name was promising, glittering— belonged to the town as much as she did to the family.

37

Although a small white prewar sign at the city limits announced in black letters, *Ventry, est. 1797, the Ornamental Iron Capital of the World,* it might easily have read, *Birthplace, Because of the Grace of God, of Cortez Boyd Forrest.* She was, even more than the New Orleans-style of porch furniture made before the war, Ventry's most famous export. Unlike the iron sofas and chairs, Cortez had a way of coming back from time to time to enlarge her legend, so much so, in fact, that people in town often even dated natural and unnatural events according to one of her stately appearances: "It was the summer of the terrible drought, the year the wells went dry, the year Cortez came home from Cornell University." Or, "I'm not much of a drinking man. Fact is, the only time I ever had a drink in my life was a beer once, just to be polite, when I went to Columbus to the Fair, and the time Cortez Boyd made those fancy things—rum she said it was, whatever that is—out at the Gavins'." Or, "All we did this time was neaten up the house a little, just the one coat of white paint. Did you see that picture of Cortez Boyd's place in the *Plain Dealer* a while back? The day it was open for the Garden Club. Why, lands! I didn't know people lived in castles any more."

There was no summer in the Gavin house until Cortez made her annual visit, and once she appeared, there was no peace. If everyone else saw her as a bearer of beauty, Rose saw her as one more cross she had to put up with, terrible and mutilating. Simon would become young and even rather daring and courtly again, and Parnell would lie awake at night dreaming of the bounty Aunt Cortez might drop his way. But it was Rose who said, "I can't, for the life of me, figure out why she keeps coming back here. She's never grown up, no older today than she was on her thirteenth birthday. My own mama thought the sun rose and set on Cortez, and she killed herself working for her, trying to give her the *nice* things—letting her go to college when no girl in this county went to college, making dresses for her like she was the Duchess of Kent. And what did Mama get for her troubles? Nothing. Cortez wouldn't even kiss her on the day she died. And what did I get for going without the nice things so that she could have them? Nothing. Not even a thank you. Still she keeps coming back looking for more. I call that a queer thing, I do."

Now, as they heard her name, each one at the table

sank into his own private thoughts and expectations. "She's not selfish," Simon said, adding in a burst of propriety. "You shouldn't talk that way in front of the children."

It was all Rose needed. Her face reddened with anger, not pique. "Don't I know she's always turned *your* head? Yes, that's one thing I know."

It was hard for the family to understand, but it seemed to Boyd at least that Rose could never forgive her sister for being prettier than she was, for having all the lovely things Rose had never had, and for sending the rare and touching cards from all over the world when she went on trips and cruises. Boyd, though he knew he was on dangerous ground and that there were some things in the family that no one dared joke about, couldn't suppress his smile. "Simon turns every woman's head," he said. "That's why he's taking Parnell with him the next time he leaves home. To fight off all the ladies."

"He won't have much to do," Simon answered, half belligerently, half flattered that anyone would think that he spent time with fancy women.

"Well, he's taken the last of his famous trips if you ask me," Rose said, then turned toward Simon. "You've got a home. You're seventy-four, going on seventy-five. You can't expect me to go traipsing all over the country looking for you like the last time."

"I've never been the slightest inconvenience to anyone," Simon replied stuffily, as if he were addressing a judge in court, "except on that one occas-i-on. Correct me if I'm wrong."

His last trip, just a little over a year ago, ended not far from where it began. He had got just as far as Cleveland, and as he waited for his train connection to Chicago and the West he had a dizzy spell and fell. Had it happened at home, he wouldn't have thought twice about it, but the stationmaster had packed him off to St. Luke's Hospital and called the family before Simon had his wits about him again. He had been driven back home in defeat and humiliation; for Rose, it had seemed almost a confirmation of everything she said about him. Now no one except Parnell, who believed everything he was told, thought that Simon would go on another journey.

During a minute's quiet Parnell took the opportunity to say, "If there were . . . pea-cocks, what happened to them?"

Rose looked startled, as if she, like Cortez herself, had forgotten. "The Ventrys' peacocks? Well, I expect they died, Parnell. The winters around here were probably too cold for them. They made a fierce noise when they were unhappy. Yes, I expect they died."

Catherine leaned over from her place at the table and looked through the window, over the African violets on the sill, at a man crossing the lawn. "That's Frank Ventry coming around to the back of the house now," she said softly. "You don't want him to hear us talking about . . ."

"Well, if I had my way," Rose interrupted, "I wouldn't give the man the time of day. No, sir. I used to love Frank Ventry as I love my own son. I won't deny that. But not the drunkard he's become. Not the . . ."

"Shhhh, Mother. You seem to forget that he's had a great deal of bad luck."

Someone had once said of Rose that she always spoke the truth—hers, but no one else's. To question what she said was to question the woman herself. She now bristled. "He's been coasting on his bad luck for the last ten years. Once upon a time I thought Frank could blame everything on the Depression, and I was the first one to feel sorry for him. Yes, the very first one! Didn't he come over here into this very house and cry on my lap the night he came home from art school for the last time, after the Ventrys lost everything—the factory, the cars, and almost the house? And didn't I feel sick—so sick I couldn't eat anything for two days, just feeling for him when he had to go to work on the boat? Yes, I did. But no more. Any man who comes up this street, every day of the year, winter or summer, smelling of liquor the way he does, never sober enough to be a husband or a father . . . that man doesn't have my sympathy."

What Rose said about the man was, of course, only half the story, and those at the table knew that part of the reason for her abridging it came from the resentment she felt toward Frank for having remained in town while Lucas, her own son, had gone off to war right after Pearl Harbor. Luke hadn't been compelled to go, to leave his family and the law practice he had started in Cleveland, unless it could be said that he had been fired by Simon's grand notions of duty and glory. Frank himself, an America Firster and an idolater of Lindbergh, had called him a fool for doing it.

And only someone as close to the Gavins as one of the

Ventrys had the freedom to use such language. Partly because of the geography of the street—the two houses were almost an enclave, a secret place separated from the rest of the town—the one family was an extension of the other. And it had always been that way. Simon had been the best friend of Frank's father, Hosea Ventry; Lucas Gavin, until they went off to separate colleges, had been Frank's best friend; and now Boyd and Parnell were re-creating the arrangement, Boyd with Francine and Dewey, Parnell with Tina. It was almost as if they somehow wanted to perpetuate the self-sufficiency of Saint's Rest, and that the world beyond it didn't matter. A kind of incestuousness that offended no one.

Except Rose, who was, after all, a Gavin only through marriage. The Boyds, her own family, had lived in the country, just outside of town, in a house now abandoned. And as an outsider, almost as if to protect herself from the Gavins and the Ventrys, she had even brought a Boyd with her when she moved into the house for the first time. On the very day that Simon and Rose returned from their wedding trip to Cincinnati, Simon had opened the front door of his house, picked up his new bride to carry her across the threshold, and found Cortez Boyd waiting for them in the hall. But if Rose had hoped for her sister to bolster her, she was mistaken. Cortez and Simon got along *too* well. It seemed to her that her sister was almost flirting with Simon. So that, one day several months after her son was born, when Rose went into the parlor and saw Simon and Cortez sitting there by themselves, laughing, Rose assumed that she was the object of their derision. She went up to her sister, slapped her neatly on the face, and told her to get out of her house. Cortez moved to Cleveland a few days later and before the year was out, almost in spite, had married there a fifty-two-year-old man, a friend of the Hannas, the Chisholms, and the Severances, who had been married twice before and who was, people said, dying from a surfeit of money.

Added to the reasons why Rose could not defend Frank Ventry, the world of Saint's Rest was primarily a man's world: Simon himself, Lucas, Boyd, and Parnell. Catherine could never be any great ally of Rose's because she was, for one thing, unable to be aggressive, and any ally of Rose's would have to be aggressive to get on with her; and, for another, she was too exclusively involved with the children to pit herself against Simon or Frank or whomev-

41

er, as Rose was forever asking one to do. Catherine had, in fact, such a hold over the children and their love that Rose had never dared contest for any of that share. Instead, she contested with Simon for his, hoping, it sometimes seemed, that if enough ridicule was piled on him some of Boyd's love and Parnell's love for their grandfather would fall her way, as spoils of war.

Still, on those occasions when the children actually did something warm and pretty for Rose, some small act of love, more often than not she didn't know how to respond. "Oh, go on with you," she would say, flustered and embarrassed, if Parnell would try to cuddle up to her at the kitchen table while she was working. Or if Boyd, a smile on his face like a half-wit, would try to sneak a kiss from her in the hall as he was leaving the house, she would yell, "Hah! You think I have nothing to do but run around like a giddy eighteen-year-old girl!" But—and the children knew it by now—if the kisses were given to her in front of Simon, it was devilishly hard to free oneself. It sometimes seemed not merely that she wanted *some* of the wild affection the children brought to Simon, but that—God above, why?—she wanted all of it, and that having all of it would please her only if she could see with certainty that Simon had none, needing her more than ever.

A complex woman, yet not complex at all. She was, though she fancied she was too deep for it, understood by everyone in the family, even, curiously enough, by Parnell. But not by herself. So that when Rose waded into Frank Ventry on this morning, the table knew she did it at least partly because Frank had been Luke's best friend. Best friend? she seemed to say. Why did he need a best friend when he had his mother? And, aside from that, Frank was a man, and all men were devious and suspect because they tried to be stronger, braver, and, yes, manlier than Rose herself.

At the table, perhaps the recollection of his own humiliations that were somehow tied to Frank Ventry's or some nostalgia for his own badgered sex moved Simon to push his chair back and rise from it. He stood tall at his place and waited until Rose turned and looked toward him. "I'll have you keep a civil tongue in this house," he said, his voice almost shaking. "You don't think anyone in the world is worthy enough to have bad luck except you."

With this, he walked toward the kitchen door. "I'm letting Frank in, and I expect you to be cordial."

Rose shrugged her shoulders to indicate that she didn't know what had got into Simon, then followed him into the kitchen, the door swinging shut behind them. In the silence that followed, Parnell leaned over and rested his head on his mother's shoulder. Boyd, who was watching Frank Ventry circle around the house to the back door, was relieved when he finally heard the knock.

"God" he said, "they're always fighting."

"Don't say 'God' that way. If you say it all the time, why should He listen to you when you really want Him?"

"You know what I mean. Poor Simon. Sometimes I don't know why he stays in the house at all."

Catherine shook her head slowly. "Oh, Boyd," she said, drawing out his name, "you have a lot to learn if you think Rose is being cruel. It's just . . . her way. You can't expect everyone to be the same. She's had to be different in order to survive."

Boyd supposed that this was a reference to all the jobs Simon had held at one time or another. He had been in the wholesale candy business, he had worked in stores, he had owned a gas station, he had been a traveling salesman, and even a travel agent. And he had failed at all of them, not taking the job on the railroad until he was almost forty. It tended to make Rose a bit wary of her husband.

Parnell leaned more closely against his mother; he liked to feel her heart beat. At last he said, "She says she saw Daddy."

"Yes, she said she did."

"Does that mean he's coming home?"

After a long while Catherine replied, "You ask too many questions, Parnell. Your brother asks too few, and you too many. But sometimes I can't answer yours. Here, help me clear the dishes from the table like a good boy."

Catherine began to run her hand over the white tablecloth, gathering the crumbs and rolling them into her cupped palm. As she did, Boyd sat still in his chair, finishing his breakfast, though he was now the only one eating. Meals in the house were invariably like this. Plates were picked up by Rose sometimes even before the last spoonful of food had been removed. For her, eating seemed little more than the provocation that made the washing of dishes necessary.

As Simon and Frank Ventry came through the kitchen door, Boyd stuffed a crust of bread into his mouth and said, "Hi, Mr. Ventry. Want some breakfast? Boy, it sure looks like you fell into a coal pile."

Frank Ventry walked in half apologetically, his face blackened by coal dust, restricting himself to the uncarpeted patch of floor by the door. He had not fallen into a coal pile; he worked in one. More particularly, he worked in the engine room—as second engineer, though he began as a fireman—of the car ferry that sailed from the harbor in Ashtabula, north of Ventry, to Canada loaded with railroad cars filled with coal from the Pennsylvania mines. Even beneath the grime on his face, however, there could be seen a heightened color—probably, the Gavins knew, because he had already been drinking that morning, as early as it was.

"Hello, Catherine," the man said, making a feeble attempt to stretch out his hand toward her at the table. "Boyd, you're getting to look more like your father every day. Howdy, Parnell, old fellow—still reading up a storm, are you?" Then, greetings finished: "Excuse me for looking this way, Catherine, but we just got in and I haven't cleaned up yet. A couple hours of sleep and I'll be a new man, you wait and see." Holding his dirty hands behind him, he added, "Since we've been sailing at night, it seems I never get much of a chance to see any of you. I just thought I'd drop in a minute for a quick hello."

"Settle yourself, Frank," Simon said. "That's what my father always said when people came to call. I guess he just meant to sit down in the first empty chair you can find."

Frank smiled, showing Simon that he appreciated the gesture. "No, I'll just get your chair all dirty. I've got enough coal on these pants here to keep an eight-room house warm all winter. Well, how's our All-State miler? All set for Oberlin?"

"I guess so, Mr. Ventry. Mom—Mom and Rose are doing most of the worrying for me."

"Same way over at our house. Helen tells me she's worn to a frazzle getting Dewey ready. I—I don't get a chance to talk to him much; we've been working twelve hours a day, seven days a week; everything's so hurry-up in this war. And well, it doesn't give me much time at home. I'm always asleep when Dewey's awake, and I'm awake when he's asleep. But Helen says he's pretty excited."

Boyd, who was being addressed, knew that Frank had neglected to mention two things. One was that Helen Ventry had been worn to a frazzle long before she began to get Dewey ready for college. Simon had once said that there was no more to her than met the eye. What met the eye was fatigue. As for Frank's not being able to talk to his son, that was no surprise. So far as Boyd knew, they hadn't said more than four or five words to each other during the last year, and Frank's work schedule had nothing to do with it.

"You two are still rooming together, aren't you, Boyd?" Frank now asked.

"Why, of course they are," Simon bellowed. "Dewey's just like one of the family. Why, didn't I name him myself? After a man I admired greatly—even once saw from a distance—the liberator of the Philippines. Admiral Dewey!"

"Yes, Simon, and I'm grateful." He allowed a smile to come to his lips. "Helen always wanted him to be named Roderick or Bradford or something. Some name she picked up in an English story, I guess." He paused, smiling widely. "I remember that day like it was yesterday. You coming over and saying, 'For the love of God you can't call that poor, helpless thing Roderick. Call him Dewey in honor of one of the greatest men of the century'." He looked at Parnell, who appeared to be perplexed. "People were still born in the beds you slept in, Parnell, right in your own house. Not like it is now when everyone goes flying off to the hospital in Cleveland."

"Was *I?*" Parnell said slowly to his mother. "Where?"

Indulgently, yet firmly, Catherine answered, "Shhhh, you're interrupting. It was in the room where your grandfather sleeps now."

"What did I look like? Were you glad?"

"Shhhhhh," Catherine replied.

"The way I figure it, Dew and I are going to be about the only men on campus," Boyd said brightly. "Dewey's already gone through last year's directory and put check marks next to the names of all the girls he thinks might be heiresses. The posh ones from places like Lake Forest and Scarsdale."

For a second—it was barely perceptible—Frank Ventry's face clouded, then quickly recovered. "Well, I hope you two make the most of your opportunity. You're lucky to be going at all. I talked to a fellow I work with the other day, and he said he would have done anything to get his son down to Bowling Green, but he was 1-A the day he graduated from high school. I was always sort of sore that Dewey had ... well, that asthma, but not any more. It might be a godsend after all."

Boyd laughed easily. "There should be more of it. For a guy with asthma, he was the best left guard Ventry High ever had."

What seemed almost like pride crossed his face. It was hard to tell with Frank Ventry. What was there more than anything was injury. "I'll say *that* for Dewey—when he gets mad, watch out. And he's fast on his feet too. *I* can't keep up with him, that's for certain." He turned once more to Catherine. "Well, I'm holding you people up. I have to ... well, I better get some sleep."

They each understood, even Parnell, that Frank would now go home and up to his bedroom and drink until eleven, then fall off into a restless sleep until about four. His wife, Helen, would then try to wake him up to get ready to go back to work.

"You're always welcome, Frank," Simon said. " 'A thousand welcomes,' as my father would say." In a lower voice, "Are you sure ... absolutely sure that that's going to be enough to tide you over?" indicating with a nod of his head something that Frank apparently had in his pocket.

For a moment Frank seemed upset that Simon had brought it to the attention of the family, but then appeared to make the best of it. "More than enough, Simon, and I appreciate it. I think maybe it was just that we managed none too well these last two weeks. I was telling Helen the other day: back at the start of hard times, sometimes we were living on a quarter a day, but we always had a few pennies left over. And now, with the war and all, and the better salaries, we never seem to have much after we pay the bills. Of course, there's the money I've got set aside for Dewey. But I told Helen if she tried to take any of it she'd have to do it over my dead body. Not," he added darkly, "that that wouldn't probably be best for everyone."

"Frank!" Catherine said.

"I suppose I'm just getting self-pitying in my old age. I better get out of the house before Mrs. Gavin gets after me with the mop. She's already in the kitchen mopping up

46

where I walked through. I don't think I ever saw a cleaner woman."

"Well, there's nothing wrong with a little good clean dirt," Simon volunteered. "Someday, when I think I can get away with it, I'm going down to the pond, haul a wheelbarrow of sand back here, and dump it in the middle of the kitchen floor, and tell her to *leave* it there for a week. Yup."

"You think you could, Simon?" Frank said.

"No, the woman would have me put in jail for extreme cruelty."

When Frank left through the door with Simon, and before Rose came into the dining room to mop up the floor where he had been standing, Boyd turned to his mother and said, "Now I call that funny, don't you? Mr. Ventry borrowing money from *us* to pay for their groceries. So he won't have to use Dewey's college money."

"But that's very admirable," Catherine answered. "No matter what people say—about how he drinks and carries on—he's still a good man at heart. There's still something there." She looked at the table. "Sometimes I almost think that no one can blame him for drinking."

She began to pile several cereal bowls on top of one another, first draining the milk and mashy remnants into a teacup. "You'd never think it to look at him today," she went on, "but once he was the most . . . well, the most dashing boy in Ventry, if you can believe that. You should have seen him when he came calling on Helen French. He had the swankiest clothes! And he had his own car when most of the people in this town still had horses in the back yard. And when he was still in high school, he got his name in *The New York Times* of all places. I've forgotten exactly why, but it had something to do with a competition he won, a prize he got from the Cleveland Museum of Art. He was the youngest winner in the history of the contest, I think it was. And when he went to college in Cleveland, we all had such high hopes for him. Why, one weekend he came home wearing an *ascot!* Would you believe it? We'd never seen one in town before that. And then the Depression came along and the bottom fell out of everything. Mr. Foster over at the bank *could* have taken their house, along with everything else, but he knew that it would kill old Mr. Ventry, and he didn't."

She waited, apparently struck by something that had never before occurred to her. "The one it killed, I expect, was Frank. He had to leave everything and come home to help out. He went into the engine room of that boat, and Boyd—this is as true as I'm sitting here—he never came out. He had to work like a black man one hundred years ago, like a man who never in his life had a dream. And it broke him. That's why I always want you to respect him—even, well, even if sometimes he gets to drinking and you want to turn your eyes. Simon is right that way. When someone has fallen down, you should try twice as hard to pity him."

For the two boys, Frank Ventry's face still before them, it was hard to understand. Not so much that he drank—Parnell himself had more than once fled from the Ventry parlor when Frank, unable to sleep, had come downstairs roaring drunk and proceeded to throw up in the hall—but that he had ever done anything *but* that. They accepted him pretty much as he was, as someone who could be tender and warm one minute and terrifying the next, but it was difficult to think that he was the same man who had been their father's best friend. Difficult to think that he had ever been young and unbeaten.

"I do, Mom," Boyd said at last. "But you're talking to the wrong guy. I like Mr. Ventry. Dewey is the one who hates him. Dewey won't even talk to his own father."

Catherine seemed stunned. "You should never say a thing like that unless you know. I don't think Dewey is that way."

"But he says so."

"Well, then *he* doesn't know. He just hasn't looked at his father. Or even himself. He should be proud of Frank, because he has . . . well, he has so little else. God has seen fit to take almost everything away, and hatred, well, that could put out the little spark that's still there."

As they talked, Parnell had been listening, loving the words because they were about people he knew, not about people in long dresses or opera cloaks, the ones he read about in books. Through the window he watched Mr. Ventry shuffle across the lawn, going home to his own house. A spark, his mother had said. Everyone had to have a spark. Without it, you were dead.

Watching the man move across the street now, his head bowed, not looking at anything, Parnell imagined the strange animals that had once been on the lawn and were now gone. Oh, to have seen them! To have watched them—what had Rose said?—strut from one corner of the lawn to the other, their heads high, their feathers shining, princes, the color of . . . the color of . . .

"What-wha-*what* exactly is a pea-cock?" he now asked his mother.

Catherine laughed, and in a minute so did Boyd, and then Parnell himself, not quite knowing why.

In the front hallway Catherine took hold of her two sons by their arms. "We have a lot to do today," she said to Boyd. "You'll have to go through all your socks and your underwear to see what's good and what isn't. I don't want any son of mine to go to Oberlin with holey underwear." She watched Boyd nod his head up and down in listless agreement. "And I think some of yours must be in Parnell's drawer." She reached down Parnell's back and pulled at the blue shorts that came halfway up his chest under his T shirt. "Parnell, that isn't nice. You took your brother's shorts again."

"I made a mistake."

"Well, I suppose you did." She studied her two sons. Alike, yet not at all. Boyd was almost a man, and a heavy, sweet, even sensual look had recently come to his face. In Parnell there was still a kind of dumbness, innocence perhaps, and wonder. "You'll probably have to make do with the one suit," she resumed. "I don't see how we can buy you a new one. I'll bring it over to Mr. Levinson today and have it cleaned."

"It's brand-new," Boyd said, hoping that she was almost finished with her program for the day. "All I did was wear it once to the Prom. They're not that snappy at Oberlin."

Rose, finished with her mopping, flew by them to reach the closet under the stairs. "Well, if people around here went to church from time to time, they'd sure wear suits more often." She stopped before the open door of the closet, looked in, and held her chin in her hand. "He never does wear anything except those white pants Jimmy Morris sent him from the Army." Then, "Now whatever possessed me to open this closet door? What do I want?"

"Cock-eyes," Simon said, passing through the hall on his way to the front porch where he would do his morning breathing exercises. "It's an Indian word. From India. Some people, of course, call them kha-khees, but they're mistaken. Correct me if I'm wrong."

"He should have been a per-fessor at Harvard University," Rose said as Simon opened the screen door and walked onto the porch, already sucking in a long breath.

"And I'll go through your pajamas," Catherine continued. "We may have to buy you a new suit or two. I'll talk to Alice Heath down at the store."

"Only poor people wear pajamas, Mom. People with money sleep in their underwear or in the raw. Ask Parnell. He read it somewhere and told me."

"That's *very* true," Parnell said bookishly.

Rose seemed outraged, confronted by bestiality. "Why, that's the most perverse thing I ever heard in my life." Convinced that her standing before the closet door wouldn't refresh her memory, she walked to the center of the hall.

"Dr. Herron expects you at eleven," his mother went on. "Don't be late this time. You know how busy he is. And pay attention to what he tells you."

Rose tapped him on his chest with her finger, as if she were calling at someone's front door. "Are you listening to your mother, young man?"

"Yessum," he said automatically, "I'm listening."

"Well, look like it," she said, tapping him harder on the chest, this time with her knuckles. "Open your eyes." She disappeared into the dining room, Boyd shrugging his shoulders after her.

"There's nothing wrong with me," he now said. "Do you think they would have let me play football or go out for track if I had a busted heart?" His heart condition existed only in his mother's imagination and in Rose's, beginning early in the war as an idea even before Boyd's father went away, a recollection that he had had something in childhood that might well have been St. Vitus's dance, and now—against all reason—it had become a reality in their minds, to use at the last minute in the event that the draft board tried to reclassify him.

As if to suggest some of the infirmities a *good* doctor would be able to find—he had already been examined by Army physicians in Cleveland—his grandmother said from the dining room, "He was always sickly when he was a boy, Catherine. You remember the bronchitis? Why, sometimes I thought he'd cough himself away in the middle of the night. He would have been dead years ago but for the generosity of God and the mustard plasters I made for his chest." She saw infinite possibilities in his body, each one less hopeful than the last. And her remedy for just about everything, excepting eyestrain, was either a mustard plaster or an enema. She was the town's self-appointed enema administrator, and it was a task she performed fastidiously and with no small amount of pride. Whenever she visited friends who were ill—even poor Miss Osborne, almost breathless from cancer—she carried her enema outfit along with her, wrapped in a paper bag. "I don't know how many times I've saved people from the knife," she would say about her talent. Boyd hadn't been able to put a stop to the indignity until he was well past thirteen.

To change the subject, Catherine asked, "Did anyone listen to the news this morning?"

Over the noise of clinking dishes and tinkling silverware in the dining room, Rose answered. "I can't bear to listen to the news any more since Elmer Davis took that job in Washington. All those New York announcers are so lah-de-dah, like they're talking to the Queen of Hungary. Now, one voice I like is Mary Marlin's. I don't know why they can't use her."

On the porch, as he breathed in the early morning air, Simon's interest was aroused. "We bombed Hamburg again last night. Hommm*bourgh,* they call it themselves. From which ground meat got its name. They say you can see the city in flames from ten miles off, which I've calculated, by referring to my map, to be a village visited by the poet Heine the middle of the last century."

"He can't say a single thing without giving a history lecture."

Taking it as an invitation, Simon went on, "I recall that I once *met* a man from Hommmbourgh. It was in Hong Kong, China, the year eighteen hundred and ninety-eight. I suppose you think Hong Kong was an out-of-the-way place for me to be, eh?" He now looked through the screen to see if anyone did. "Well, in the ee-vent that your memory is faulty, I was blown there during a typhoon on the way to Manila Bay. Well, sir! This Hommmbourghian, as you call 'em, came up to me in the street, seeing as I was a white man, I expect, and asked me in unbroken English if I could be a friend in distress and give him money enough to get back to his ship before it sailed. Well, it took me a scant minute to look into his eyes to see if he was an honest man. *Was* he? He *was!* I don't remember much else about the fellow except that his hands smelled of sardines, which I now always think of

51

when I hear the name Hommmbourgh. I suppose the gent had just had supper. He sent me the money in a Christmas card many years later, and I've followed him in my fancy since then. Oh, those were merry days."

"Oh, my God," Boyd groaned to his mother, "was all *that* on the news?"

Catherine rested her hands in the pockets of her apron, as if they had suddenly become a burden. "Did they say anything about the poor Jews?"

"No," Simon answered from the porch, "but there was some talk about the whole thing being a lot of propaganda just to make us fight harder. And then they went on to say that the Lutheran ministers in Germany have asked the people to pray for Hitler. So it can't be as bad as the Levinsons think."

"I don't know what the world's coming to," Catherine said in a low, concerned voice. "I was talking to Mrs. Levinson yesterday and she's worried sick. They haven't heard a word from their families in Poland since 1941. You hear all these terrible stories about people being put in camps, and you don't know what to believe."

"We've put the Japanese in camps on the West Coast," Rose said quickly, "so we're as bad as the Germans. We're all marked. I know that for a fact. All mankind. And just think of those twenty-six colored people killed in that riot in Detroit last summer. Here, we pretend to feel sorry for the Jews, and we show it by killing Negroes. I'll tell you. They say everyone has a little Jew in him—the way we're all disappointed, the way the world seems to work against us—but I'll tell you what. We all have a little bit of Hitler in us too, and that's a fact."

Quiet, sobered by what Rose had said, the family stood where they were, in the hall, the dining room, the front porch, waiting for someone to break the spell. It was, in a minute, Parnell who finally said, "How can you be a Jew *here?*"

"Well, Parnell," his grandfather answered from the porch, "you can be a Jew anywhere. If you're a Jew, you bring it with you. There aren't many in this part of the country, but there are some." He waited, perhaps hoping that he could say something more understandable. "The Levinsons get their meat from Cleveland, for one thing. That helps remind them they're Jewish. Haven't you ever seen the man with the truck who brings it all the way out here?"

"The one with the beard?"

When, in fact, Simon discovered that a Jewish family had moved to Ventry, he withdrew several books on the subject from the library in Kingsville, and even from time to time listened on the radio to Friday services from a Cleveland synagogue. If anyone asked him why, he merely said that he was interested and that a man should keep informed about new developments. If Rose happened to pass while he was following the aching sounds of a rabbi or a cantor, she would say, "Look at him. He doesn't understand a word." But, strangely, somehow Simon felt that he could.

"Can I go now?" Boyd said at last.

"Just don't forget your appointment at the doctor's." Then, "I put a little something in your pocket as a surprise. You can get a soda or something on the way home."

"Me too!" Parnell cried.

At that moment there came from the parlor a low, swishing noise, as if someone were running a duster over the walls, or as if crepe paper were blowing over the floor, rising, falling, then rising again. Yet—how could one tell?—it was alive. Something was moving back and forth, bumping now into the chandelier, then into the pictures on the mantel, meeting a chair, a deep thud as it did, and then hitting against the soft curtains at the windows. A frightened, panicked noise.

Parnell was first to run to the doorway into the parlor and clap his hands in pleasure and surprise. "There's a birdie in here!"

From Catherine's mouth came a wordless, tongueless sound. She drew back toward the banister, her face slowly draining of color, as if for every second the bird was there—its wings rubbing against the walls, the ceiling, the very furniture on which the family sat—it deprived her of breath. She backed into the dining room and stopped only when she was next to Rose.

Simon, who had heard the commotion, was at the parlor door, at Parnell's back, standing half transfixed, watching the tiny bird flutter over the room, looking at it as if he were waiting for it to tell him something, to cry out his name. Only when it made a desperate swoop toward the door where he stood did he come to life and say to Parnell, "Close the danged door before it gets into

53

the rest of the house. Or get out of my way and I'll do it myself."

"It's only a birdie," Parnell said, too busy watching it rise and fall in the room to see his mother's face or even Simon's next to him.

In the dining room Rose seemed humbled, a look of terrible disappointment on her face, unlike the fear on Catherine's. But slowly she began to get hold of herself. "There now," she said to Catherine, "that's no way to be. Mister Gavin will have it out as quick as lightning. Why, lands, it's just a tiny bird that must have come down the chimney."

"Let me catch it!" Parnell yelled, but his grandfather, directly behind him, pushed him out of the way abruptly. "You hush, for God's sake!" he exclaimed, so angrily that Parnell would have burst into tears had not Simon touched him on the shoulder and drawn him away from the door. "Your mother's upset, can't you see that? It's . . . well, it's an old, old belief. Help me get these windows open and we'll chase the poor critter out. Why, he's scared half to death. Look at the poor fella. Don't seem hurt, though, does he?"

Only Boyd had seen everything—the bird itself, the terror on his mother's face, the exaltation on Simon's as he watched it. An old belief, Simon had said. Could it be so old that Boyd could know it without ever having heard it? For Boyd, when he first heard the wings, and before he knew what they were or before he had seen what they brought to his mother's face, had felt his own heart begin to fall.

Yet it was lunacy. As Boyd watched Simon and Parnell flap their arms in the air, trying to press the bird toward one of the open windows, he had to restrain himself from whooping and howling. Oh, my God, look at them! Like people two hundred years ago and just out of the bogs. He wanted to double over and stomp his feet on the floor. For the love of God, *look* at them!

"I'll get a magazine," he heard himself saying. "I'll try to scare him over to the windows with a magazine."

As if Simon had been waiting for advice, he, too, now picked up a magazine, as did Parnell, and the three of them flailed the air, driving the tiny bird across the ceiling, then toward the front of the room where it hovered, frightened, at the curtains over the window. "Get out where you belong, you blackguardy, misguided creature,

54

you," Simon yelled. "Why, it's nothing but a little warbler. Now what was he doing sneaking down our chim-i-ney? I'd like to know. There you go, and the devil take you, you rascally upstart. Out! That's the way!"

Fluttering through the open window, a panic in its wings that could be felt even by the three men in the room, the bird flew onto the porch, hit back and forth against its wooden ceiling, as if it were blind and could no longer see its way, and then—a sudden, gigantic push—it was free, flying over the front lawn and into the trees.

They stood before the window watching it disappear, each one's breath quickened from the labor, each thinking his own thoughts. Boyd slowly said, "What did you mean, Simon, about a belief?"

Simon waited for what seemed a long time. "Did I say that?" he answered at last. "Well, I don't rightly know. There's nothing to it anyway."

Yet Simon knew. He could remember what his own father had said, as if it were yesterday: that death announced itself in small, surprising ways, and that a bird, innocent and unthinking, a mere vessel for a larger purpose, was worst of all. Somehow—and only God knew how—a bird would divine that it had been chosen to elevate the stricken soul, to carry it to the uppermost regions of the sky, and with that knowledge would visit the house of the soon-to-die one last time to look again at all the things the soul held dear and loved and wanted to remember for all eternity. And, Simon understood, to bring black and mortal terror to the hearts of the living.

Slowly recovering himself, regaining his composure, Simon turned to his two grandsons. "A job well done, boys!" he yelled. "Didn't I tell you a man never knows when he's going to be called on! Yes, sir, we got that little critter out of here before its poor heart stopped from fear. That happens. Don't you think it don't. The littler the creatures, the fainter the hearts. Well, there's *one* who isn't going to come poking his nose down our chim-i-ney for a long time. A hero's job, boys!"

Three

The morning ripened and grew, drawing the Gavins out of the house, following the bird itself, now hidden somewhere in the trees, ignorant of its importance. As ignorant as the first flowers of spring that Rose picked each May Day and heaped artfully before the front door to celebrate the new season and to flatter some old, half-remembered pagan god, and which the Reverend Hill, sensibly Congregational, looked upon with horror. But as Simon himself once said, "Isn't it a blessing we believe in so many things?"

A talent, yes. A blessing, no.

Simon was already seated on the green porch swing, unfolding the newspaper Parnell had saved for him. He made arrangements to walk to the square with Boyd a bit later on in the morning, where, on a park bench, it was his habit to hold his open-air levee, catching all his old friends as they passed. Boyd, as he hopped off the porch steps, said that he would be just a few minutes at the Ventrys'.

"I see," Simon said, raising his newspaper in the air, "I see where Mrs. Roosevelt is in New Zealand."

"She gets around a lot." Boyd withheld what he preferred to say, knowing that Simon would regard any frivolous appraisal of Eleanor Roosevelt's war duties as a blow against democracy.

"An incredible woman. Why, I bet if those savages in New Zealand gave a feast for her, she'd pick up her plate at the end of the meal and lick it clean. Just to make them feel at their ease. A grand woman!"

Boyd wasn't sure that such an act constituted grandness, but he let it pass. He was glad to get away from the badgering that was a part of every breakfast in the house, glad that he wouldn't have to listen to Rose's analysis of what had happened in the parlor, or his mother's. Rose, he knew from past experience, thought with her will, believing only what she wanted to believe, while Catherine—it was far worse—thought through her nervous system, reacting to ideas and events as she would react to the hotness of fire or the coldness of snow.

From where he stood on the brick sidewalk he could see Parnell, sitting in the crook of the oak tree. "You're not supposed to be up there," Boyd yelled to him, to which Parnell predictably replied, "I know."

It was from the oak tree that their Uncle Desmond, their father's brother, had fallen when he was a small boy. It had been old Mr. Ventry on his front porch across the street who had watched the boy fall, ambled across the street to help dry his tears, and then, finding the child's head twisted behind his body, began to scream hysterically. A grown man, too. It was the suddenness of it, the family said years later. Mr. Ventry had never even had time to let go of the evening paper in his hands.

But because everyone agreed that lightning never struck twice, no one particularly cared that Parnell liked to climb the tree and sit there, looking down Priest Street, past Summer, past Spring to Satin Street, all the way to the square. They were upset, however, because he sometimes had long, intricate conversations with his Uncle Desmond while he was up there, leaning back against a branch, as still as an ancient sage. And because his only other playmate was Tina, a twenty-year-old girl who seldom said anything either, Rose was sometimes heard to mention to Catherine, "Excuse me for saying it, but I wonder if that boy of yours isn't getting to be a little queer in the head." Not a bit, Boyd knew. All the Gavins were mountainy men, as Simon often said. They just liked to be alone.

Boyd saw Frank Ventry at his bedroom window, without a stitch of clothes on, looking at him with vacant eyes—eyes that Boyd knew well because they were also Dewey's, Francine's, and Tina's. Yet Frank's were empty, hard, like colored enamel over metal. Boyd turned away, then bounded up the Ventry front porch and into the house without knocking. Tina was sitting on the rosewood sofa in the parlor, a notebook in her hands, and, seeing Boyd, she slowly rose and without a word walked to the curtains at the front window and hid there, just as he knew she would. A hated blush spread across his face. He waited a few seconds for the color to subside, then opened the door into the kitchen, where Helen Ventry was washing breakfast dishes at the sink.

Unlike Catherine, who tried to make herself look nice

57

in the mornings, fixing her hair carefully and sometimes even putting on a little eau de cologne that mixed with the fresh soap-and-water smell of her, Helen looked the way she must have looked when she got out of bed. She was wearing a housedress that had been worn the day before and probably the day before that. "Morning," Boyd said cheerfully. "Where's everyone?"

Helen Ventry jumped at the voice, as if she had been in deep thought. "Goodness, you should make a little noise when you walk into someone's kitchen. You almost made me drop the dish."

It wouldn't have made much difference, Boyd knew. Had he made noise, as she asked, she would have been put out with him because Frank was trying to sleep. In the mornings, until she was sure that her husband was entirely out of the way and unable to torment her for the next few hours, she was cross and a bit of a harpy.

"I'm sorry, Mrs. Ventry," he said. "Francine up?"

What Rose had said at the breakfast table about the protectiveness Helen felt toward Francine was uncannily accurate. Though she was cordial, he generally had the feeling that she didn't want Francine and him to become too thick. It was her hope, and she made no secret of it, to get Francine off to Cleveland in the fall, where she could meet *interesting* people. By "interesting," everyone supposed she meant people who had enough money so that Francine wouldn't have to live the kind of life Helen herself had lived. It didn't seem all that unreasonable; just rather humiliating if you happened not to be interesting.

"She's upstairs washing her hair now, but I expect she'll be down in a few minutes. She likes to dry it in the sun. Dewey's out in the garage. As usual."

If Helen Ventry tended to pamper Francine, she barely tolerated Dewey. It was Frank, not Helen, who insisted that Dewey go to Oberlin, though it would mean a great many sacrifices for the family. Helen would as soon use the money to help establish Francine in Cleveland or to buy a few things for the house. Dewey himself didn't, as he often said, give a rat's ass either way. He was at best an indifferent scholar and, at worst, an inconstant son— constant only in his hatred of his father, who was mortgaging the house to get him off to college.

As Boyd went toward the door that led to the back porch, Helen dried her hands on the wet apron, then pushed her graying hair back from her forehead. She had apparently decided to spend a few minutes chatting. "I suppose," she began, "that your Aunt Cortez will be showing up any one of these days. She's about due, I'd think."

A kind of transformation seemed to come over the woman, and Boyd could see how she might very well have been beautiful at one time. Even the patches of deep shadow under her eyes seemed to lighten. When she said Cortez's name, her face colored softly, as if she were feeling some of the splendor of Cortez's life.

"I don't think there's a letter yet," Boyd answered truthfully. "And it's just as well. You know how Rose always gets."

"Well, your grandmother never understood her sister. Cortez just wasn't like other people."

"And *how.*"

Helen now seemed to be fumbling for words. "I'd hoped I'd be able to talk to her about Francine. Cortez knows all those nice people in Cleveland, and I was hoping she might help Francine find . . . a suitable job."

Boyd heard "rich" for "nice" and "husband" for "job." "I bet she would," he said at last, not betting it at all. Cortez had never, to his knowledge, helped even his own family. Two summers ago, before the war broke out, she had bought a new Lincoln, a Continental, and had given her two-year-old Packard to Girl Scout headquarters in Cleveland, apparently as a tax benefit, though she knew perfectly well that the Gavins were still driving a 1932 Terraplane that couldn't be persuaded to leave the garage half the time.

Helen said, "It's always such a pleasure to see her."

Always a pleasure, Boyd knew she was trying to say, to see someone who lived such a beautiful life, who never got old, and who never worried about money. "Yeah," he said, limiting himself to this rich observation. "I'm going out to see Dewey. I suppose he's pulling some motor apart?"

What relaxation, almost warmth, that had spread over the woman's face as she talked about Cortez now disappeared and the hardness returned. She shook her head sadly as if suddenly tired. "He'll have to take a bath in strong yellow soap to get all that grease off him before he goes to college."

Boyd watched her reach over the oilcloth on the kitchen table for dirty cups, her hands puckered and red from the water. She held them against her soiled apron as if they were heavy, carried them to the sink, and rested them there. She was leaning against the sink, not standing at it, as he left.

Well, Boyd thought, going past the lilac bushes behind the house, there were some people you never knew what to say to. He always felt uncomfortable with her because he knew that she saw him as a threat, someone who might spoil her plans for Francine. As for Francine, she would do nothing to bring any more disappointment to her mother. Even though she was Boyd's girl, she was first and foremost her mother's daughter. If it pleased Helen for Francine to leave Ventry and go to Cleveland, then leave she must. It was as simple as that.

The Ventrys' garage, like the Gavins', had once been a barn, but was now used for the family car and as a place to store things that couldn't be accommodated in the attic. Through the wide, open doors, he saw Dewey lying on the hard-mud floor. The motor he was working on was protected from the dirt by a few newspapers.

"Howdy, *paisan*," Dewey said. "Don't step on any of the guts." He tenderly reached out for a small part, apparently something he had removed from the motor before him, to preserve it from Boyd's feet.

Dewey's hands could do almost anything. The old Ford now parked in the garage with its hood up—Boyd could never remember having seen it in the garage with the hood down—Dewey had been working on for over a year. No, not working on. Making love to. Sometimes as Boyd came into the garage he'd see Dewey sitting quietly next to it, his head resting against one of its highly polished fenders, as if the fender were a beautiful, smooth thigh. Or he would be standing before it, feet spread wide, hands in his pockets, looking at it as if he were watching a naked lady sleeping.

On Saturdays Dewey liked nothing better than to go to the junk yard outside of town and hunt up derelict radios and washing machines, cart them home, repair them, and then try to give them away. Those that couldn't be given away (the Gavins had eight radios in the house) were kept in the garage. There were at least fifteen radios there, of all varieties and all working, three washing machines, an old Ironrite mangle, four or five fans, electric mixers, toasters, an electric popcorn popper, curling irons, hair dryers, waffle irons, vacuum cleaners, and God knows what else, from the junk yard, all made love to by Dewey Ventry until they warmed, popped, and curled.

When his teachers in school said about Dewey that all he had working for him, really, was his hands—and, of course, his phenomenal Ventry face—it was clear that they had omitted any reference to his brain. His teachers were the first to admit that his head wasn't much of an asset. Boyd, who had coached him through most of his classes, was the second. Because of a shoddy high school record Dewey had barely got into Oberlin. His brain made for unreliable scholarship. He would become interested in a subject, then drop it impetuously as soon as he came upon a better one. While doing a tedious paper on mental health for a hygiene class the fall before, he had somehow unearthed a reference that hinted that Swinburne was more or less a masochist. It was a kicky subject—Dewey's own playful description, lost on most of his friends—that appealed to him. He had three volumes of Swinburne's letters sent to him from the library in Cleveland, read them, copied many of them, and even quoted them. But didn't bother to finish his mental health paper, for which subject he got an F for the six weeks, and so offended a priggish English teacher, for whom he *did* write a candid paper on masochism, that he got a D in that subject.

As for his face, it was probably too incredible, and, as such, it was his burden. Even Boyd, who didn't consider it manly to be a judge of these things, had to admit that he had never seen anything like it outside the movies. Moreover, Dewey's face was all his own; no capped teeth, no rechiseled nose, no machine-clefted chin. It was square, dark year-round, gamy, and full of warmth, and he had a look to his mouth and his chin that made almost everyone want to cuddle him, from spinster teachers in school to girls he had just met. Not surprisingly, he had been playing around with Victory Girls for the last two years, and nothing pleased him more—excepting ripping apart a motor—than to describe his adventures, step by step, or hand by hand, which was more often the case, from the minute he felt inside what he called a friendly brassiere to what he called "the truth of the moment," revising Hemingway, whom he had read and thought was a phony.

"What's up, bub?" Dewey now asked from the floor, wiping his hands over the single section of pants not already blackened.

"The usual," Boyd answered, settling back against one of the fenders of the precious Ford. "Rose wants me to be a saint. Mom wants me to be a little boy. Simon wants me to be a hero. Parnell wants me to be a father. Let's see ... is that all? Oh, yes, and a bird flew into the parlor after breakfast. No one knows what it wants me to be."

Dewey leaned back on his elbow, resting his head in the palm of his hand, spreading grease in his hair. He stared at Boyd quizzically, the cuddly look now on his face. "A real honest-to-God bird?"

"A real, authentic, one-hundred-percent bird. It came down the chimney like St. Nick. Simon just about got his old beat-up rifle to go after it. It scared hell out of everyone. Rose is probably over there now spreading her holy water from Lourdes all around the place."

The holy water had been carried back by a cousin more than fifty years ago before the family's lust for miracles had been tempered by Congregationalism. The water had been used ten times over. Rose simply freshened its essence—"Why, it's still there!" she'd say positively—from the kitchen tap. Though she was for the sake of form a Congregationalist, she was also secretly and obstinately a Catholic, performing her rites in the privacy of her room. Not only did she have popish tendencies, she had the Pope himself. His picture, chosen after much hemming and hawing over which view showed him to best advantage, was kept hidden in a drawer of her dresser. No one in the family was supposed to know, but of course everyone did.

A more serious look came to Boyd's face. "What's more," he said, "I think they all think it's a sign from heaven. I think they believe that! Honest to God, it's like we just got off the boat. A little-assed bird! Don't people ever start wising up after a while?"

"Here you have a fully wised-up guy. I ever tell you my great-great-granddad graduated from Harvard? We've been flowering ever since. I'm the last of the Ventrys—the last, perfect flower. And look at me. I'm a slob. When I die, they'll say, 'His name was writ in axle grease.' But I'm a wised-up guy, I am."

Boyd smiled. "How did you remember that—that 'was writ' thing?"

"How else? You made me cram old Keats for the English final, don't you remember? You said he was bound to be on it because old Miss Humphrey always cries when she tells how the feller died and then shows that postcard of the English Cemetery or whatever you call it, the one with all the pigeon droppings." She did. It was one of the highlights of Senior English, equaled only by her description of Shelley's burning on the beach. Before she dug her hand into her chest for her heart, she generally grabbed the glass paperweight on the desk.

"Christ-a-mighty," Dewey said, "you ever tried pulling a '36 Maytag apart? They're crazy, man."

"Fixing it for someone?"

"Hell, no. I'm just practicing. It keeps the mind and the fingers agile." He narrowed his eyes and surveyed the good clothes Boyd was wearing. "Why the clean duds? You going to a funeral or something? I thought they already planted Miss Osborne."

"You turn a very neat phrase," Boyd said. "Anyway, it so happens I'm going down to see Dr. Herron. Everyone over at the house is worried that maybe I won't have a heart attack before the war's over. He's supposed to give them away or something."

"You should try asthma, by God. Take it from an asthmatic noncombatant. It's the best. Much better than. say, closing a foot locker on your hand. like that screwball we saw in the movies. It don't deform you, bub."

"Is that asthma on the level?"

"Sure." Dewey coughed, holding a greasy finger up in the air, indicating that the richness of the tone could be appreciated only if Boyd paid perfect attention. "Listen! Great, eh? Doesn't it get you in the gut just to *hear* me wheeze? Don't you want to bundle up the Tenente and send him back to old Catherine Barkley? 'How-de-do, Miss Barkley. Just call me Tenente. God, I hope you will be good to me. Kiss me. Can you row? I'm sorry to disappoint you, m'dear, but I've had my private parts blown off.' "

"That's the other book, for the love of God. The Tenente got his while he was eating macaroni."

" 'I'm sorry to disappoint you, Miss Barkley, but I got it in my macaroni.' "

"You're irreverent, you know that?"

"Yup."

But it wasn't entirely irreverence, of that Boyd was certain. It sometimes seemed that Dewey used joking around as a kind of refuge. He had trouble finding any at all at home, with a father he hated and a mother who ignored him, and, like most people who are pained in one

63

way or another, he very much disliked to talk about painful things. But he was good company, even when he was hiding behind his silly talk.

"We're sure as hell going to make a big hit at school," Boyd now said. "Two 4-Fs."

"At Oberlin? Look, buddy, we're going to be the only men around. There's a war on. We have to do our doo-ty. Don't you read the posters? Didn't you see that WAC poster down at the post office? It has this sewer—at least she didn't have pimples; don't know where they found *her*—wiggling down a gangplank in Hawaii. And the headline says, 'The Woman Who Wouldn't Wait.' Well, who the hell's asking 'em to wait? I'm ready for them right now. Let 'em all come to Oberlin. Let 'em all finish their high school educations—the old matchbook spiel—and come to Oberlin."

"You're such a big sex deal, Dewey."

"You're not just a-talking, my friend. You know what? I was born with a what-do-you-call-it erection, and I've had one every day of my life, twenty-four hours a day. I ever tell you that? It's the honest-to-God truth. Ask Dr. Herron. Ask him and see if he doesn't say I had one two minutes after I was born. He patted old Dew on his wet bottom, dumped the ash of his stogie on the floor, and says, 'Well, by gum, if this isn't a marvelous and inspiring sight.' You just ask him."

"Oh, my God," Boyd said, only half glad that his friend had a flair for the preposterous. Then, "Did you get Janet home all right last night or did she rape you?" Dewey's date of the night before, though an amiable sort, had no great gift for anything except twirling the baton in the high school band.

"Christ-a-mighty!" Dewey now exclaimed, exploding with a grin. "That girl has a regular baton fetish. The more I ran, the harder she chased."

Boyd looked at him doubtfully, wondering just how much of what he was about to hear could be believed. Because Dewey could bear life only when exaggerated, it was damned hard to know when he was telling the truth and when he was merely providing the necessary extra color. "You're bull-crapping again, Dew. I can tell."

"Word of honor. Do you want to hear? I'll tell you all. Maybe you can even learn some of father Dew's wily old tricks. You, too, can become a dirty old man."

"I don't want to hear." Boyd was still getting over the

tale—how tall it was only Dewey knew—that involved Dorothy, the dumb blonde. No one in town had ever suggested that she was particularly wholesome, but even Boyd knew that she must still have some vestiges of pride. Dewey, however, said that he was willing to swear on a stack of Gideon Bibles that he had had her, standing up, in the back room of the Drug and Notion store, and as proof he offered to recite verbatim an Upjohn pimple poster that had been behind her head and that he had read while he was doing it.

"I asked her how much it would cost," Dewey went on. "What the tariff would be, and she said five dollars for one without feels and ten dollars for one with feels. You think it's hard to do the one without the other? Well, you just ask around. There are ways. Anyhow, I says to her, 'Honey, just what you gettin' at? Don't you like old Dew? You know he can't afford feels.' So . . ."

"I don't believe you, buster."

"God's honest truth, old buddy. Then, whilst Janet was trying to figure out how she was going to reduce the merchandise—looked to me, she was figuring on a fire sale—old Dew Ventry seized the opportunity and said, 'How about I take a dime's worth to start with?' So old Janet, she . . ."

"Damn it, Dew! This is exactly what you said happened between you and that what's-her-name, Dolly Something, the one you met last summer. The exact same thing."

"Listen, for Christ's sake. Don't interrupt the master, because I'm coming up with a dictum, an honest-to-God dictum. Quoth Dew Ventry, betrayer of girls: A girl, once you tickle her ear with your tongue, she's lost. She's as good as scarlet-lettered. All you do is flick the dandruff off her shoulders, say something pretty, then quick as hell bite her ear. She's yours forever. It never fails to work."

"I know. You already told me. And afterwards Janet said you were such a great guy you could have it all for nothing. It always happens. You bite an ear and then you ravish a girl for nothing."

"You're a goddamn soothsayer," Dewey said happily. "A regular sayer of sooth. My God, man, you could make money in the carnival racket. Did old Dew ever tell you about the dwarf he met at the county fair last summer? The one who wanted to show me how she candied apples? Yessir, her very words."

"I *know*, Dewey. The only trouble is that it happened to Homer Lane, and I was there when he told you."

"Never!" Dewey yelled. "Never! You're just jealous, old sod. You just don't like to see me get all the breaks. It's bad for your self-esteem. But, by God, let me tell you it's great. It's fine. It brings the roses to your cheeks! What I'd like to see, I'd like to see school boards all across the land open whorehouses in their gymnasiums. Forget about volleyball. Clear up the complexions of America's greatest asset, its horny youth. Tomorrow, by God, we may be dead, my friend. Let us fritter away our youth as best we can. In the sack. In dark garages. In gymnasiums. In back rooms of drugstores. It is sweet, man, sweet." He stopped. "That is absolutely Churchillian."

"Look, you," Boyd said, "one of these days you're going to come clean. One of these days you're going to tell me what really happens when you're with a girl. I just don't believe you, bub. Glamor boy that you are, you just can't make out *all* the time."

It wasn't anger that Boyd watched come into Dewey's eyes. Why the name should hurt him so much Boyd didn't know. It was, after all, just a tag for the image Dewey himself tried to create, but when someone said it Dewey seemed to hear questions in it. He didn't hear Glamor Boy, but Boy with Glamor, and it was a hell of a different thing. His face lost all its gladness and his fists were shaking. *"Don't call me. that."*

"Okay, Glamor Boy," Boyd said, waiting. He ducked as Dewey's fist flew past his chin, then caught his arms, holding them in a tight grip.

"Just don't bull-crap me, *hear?*" Boyd locked Dewey's arms, gave them a twist for emphasis, and then let them fall loose. As he did, Dewey backed away, getting a fender of the car between himself and his friend.

"You didn't have to do that," Dewey said at last, disappointment in his voice.

"What the hell did I do? I just kept you from taking a swing at me."

"You know damn well. You know I don't like it when people do that."

When people did *that,* as Dewey said, they touched him. He hated like hell to be touched, and yet he had to put up with it all through high school. Friends coming up to him in the hallways in school and throwing their arms around him until, his face burning, he was able to slide

66

away. The guys on the football team, goosing him and each other, and carrying him into the showers on top of their shoulders after a game as though they were carrying the rarest trophy they could find. It was strange, all right. For a man who spent a great deal of time talking about bodies, he didn't like his own to be touched.

Boyd hadn't meant for it to be a gratuitous injury, though he knew when he caught Dewey's arms that Dew would start bawling any minute if they weren't freed right away. There was in Dewey then the same kind of panic, almost, that Boyd had felt in the bird as it blindly hit against the ceiling that morning. Yet all Boyd wanted was for Dewey to level with him. That was all.

His animation gone, Dewey leaned over to the floor and picked up a part of his motor, then began to play with it in his hands. Boyd said, "How about doing something tomorrow night? We could have ourselves a hooley." A hooley was an Irishism for any mad and adventuresome thing.

"Yeah," Dewey answered sourly. "Some hooley you can have around this dump." Then, "Anyway, I thought you and Francine were doing something."

"That's tonight."

"Oh, Christ! Out at Howard's. I almost forgot. I've got a date with the Horse."

Boyd shook his head profoundly. "Betty Jo? For the love of God, no wonder you got all hopped up on that Swine ... Swine ... whatever his name is. You're a masochist too. Why the hell the Horse?"

The girl, in all fairness, was not a horse. She just wasn't much of a girl. At seventeen she was—and you couldn't deny that it was an achievement—already an old maid.

"She takes baths. She uses an underarm deodorant. Occasionally even a mouth wash. Who could ask for more? From a horse anyway."

"I didn't think you liked her."

"I don't."

"Then why see her?"

Dewey looked up angrily. "Because she doesn't have a date, wise guy. That's why. I don't pay any attention to her; she doesn't pay any attention to me. I think she hates me. It's a perfect relationship."

"Break the date. Ask someone else. Ask Nancy Taylor. You *said* you like her, and she's been crazy about you for the last year."

Helplessness groped its way over Dewey's face. "You know how I am. I never know what—to say or anything when I'm around a *nice* girl. I always think I got grease on my neck or something. Or that I lost a button on my fly. That's why I go after the pigs. They don't mind it. And the horses. Christ-a-mighty, I'm God's gift to the animal world."

Boyd smiled, then watched Dewey do the same. "Well, hell, we can make up for it tomorrow night, bub. We can go out to the Lake. It's supposed to be wild out there now." For anyone living in Ventry, the Lake was Arcola, a resort town five and one half miles to the north, right on Lake Erie. It attracted a great many girls—the secretarial type and those who had other, less identifiable skills—from Cleveland and Youngstown and Pittsburgh. The best and fairest description Boyd had ever heard given it was that you could get all the booze you wanted until two o'clock in the morning and, afterward, anything else you might want including an accommodating drugstore open until dawn. Once when Boyd and Dewey were driving by one of the beaches, bodies spilled everywhere in the moonlit dark, Dew had said, pointing, "Look. America singing."

Dewey now seemed to brighten. "Good idea. Maybe we can have a hooley after all. Maybe ... maybe we can even make it a Mother-Kill. How about that? That old Oedipus magic has got me in its spell. A Mother-Kill we'll make it. I'll get you to lose your blessed old maidenhead. Great idea!"

"The maidenhead, as you call 'im, may already be lost, bub." The quick experience Boyd had with Dorothy left him uncertain. He was, as he put it, almost a virgin, but through no fault of Dorothy's. The bell had happened to ring while they were at it in the book room in school, and they had to go back to a Civics class.

"Can we use your old man's car?" Boyd now asked. "The Terraplane is *kaput* again."

"If you toss in some gas coupons."

"I'll ask Simon." Then, "How's your old man anyway? I don't hear him storming around upstairs the way he sometimes does, and that's good."

Dewey turned his face aside. "Good, hell. He doesn't have to work tonight—the boat's not going out—so that means trouble. Me, all I want to be is out of the house

68

when he starts cutting up. Christ, sometimes when he looks at me, I think he wants to kill me."

"You imagine all that, Dewey."

As if he were showing something precious he had earned, Dewey pointed to the back of his greasy T shirt. "I imagined that?"

Under the T shirt were welts, old ones, nasty ones, maybe as many as six or seven, scarred ridges, some large, some small, all of them ugly and mean. And on a body like Dewey's—a near-perfect one because God had given him His best, and Dewey worked hard to improve even that, running with Boyd in the spring, playing football in the fall, baseball in the summer—it was the worst kind of violation, a sin against flesh.

Boyd could remember the night, less than a year ago, when Dewey had walked up the stairs of the Gavins' house to Boyd's bedroom, bent over and bleeding all the way. When Boyd first saw him, all he could think was that someone had knocked all his teeth out, because Dewey's mouth was flowing blood from where he had bitten through his lip to keep himself from screaming while his father beat him with a leather belt. Then Boyd had seen the rest. They'd called the doctor, and Rose the police, but neither Helen nor Dewey would file charges. Why Dewey had been punished he had never told, saying merely that it was between him and his old man.

"He was drunk," Boyd said now. "You have to forgive people when they do something like that, Mom says. You have to try to understand why they do it."

"I'll forgive him when he's dead." Then, as he began to go back to work on his motor, he added, "But he's on the gargle so much, boozed up all the time, I doubt that he'll know when it happens."

Boyd tapped his buddy on the shoulder affectionately—lightly, because anything else would have brought up the fists again—told him that he'd see him later, and left the garage, full of wonder, and doubts too, for every time he saw people it seemed as if he were seeing them for the first time. Only he was never sure that he was seeing them at all. As he walked across the lawn to the sidewalk, he looked up again and found Frank Ventry still standing at the bedroom window. In the tree across the street, Parnell continued to sit in the branches, his face leaning against the bark, his eyes only half open.

It was Simon who had once tried to explain Mr. Ventry

69

and other people who led several lives, several outside and several inside, by resorting to an analogy. God knows, Boyd had to admit that most Irish talk was tiresome, but now and then Simon chanced on something that seemed to make sense. He had told him about the small Irish bird, its name long forgotten, that waited until night to sit on the grass and sing. He said that no one had ever seen it because it hid during the day, but at night its song could be heard loud and clear. Simon had then said that a lot of people, Frank Ventry among them, were that way— singing on the grass in the darkness, yet no one was able to see them. It seemed to Boyd that Simon might have something.

He collected his grandfather from the porch swing, and the two of them started off for a walk to the square. The only sounds behind them came from the Ventry parlor, where Tina was again sitting at the piano, practicing. "Isn't that a fine noise?" Simon said about the music, but Boyd didn't answer.

"I don't reckon God knew what He was doing when He made her, begging His pardon," Simon now observed. "She doesn't have a thought in her head, still see how pretty she is—and *how* she can play the piano!"

Though he may not have followed her music as carefully as Simon, Boyd was very much aware of the girl. Each time that he went into the Ventry parlor, Tina would quickly stop playing, slide off the piano stool, and walk to the front window, standing there, almost hiding among the curtains. And as she did, Boyd always felt the hot blush begin at his neck and creep over his face. It was a terrible sensation—he hated it—and in a minute his face was as red as if it were newly sunburned, as red as the faces of the Finnish fishermen who lived in Ventry and fished out of Conneaut, faces that looked by August as if their own blood were washing over their foreheads.

So Boyd, when he went into the Ventry house, tried as often as he could to avoid the girl. If he heard her in the parlor as he came up the front steps, he would open the screen door quietly, then slip into the hall, waiting for Francine or Dewey to find him. As he stood there, not making a sound, invariably the piano music would stop anyway, and in a second he would hear her slide off the piano stool and glide slowly across the carpet to the window. By himself in the hall, he could feel the blush begin at his neck and cover his face. Francine, when she came from the kitchen or from upstairs, would say, "Good God, do you have a temperature or something?" or Dewey, more matter-of-fact and wiser in the ways of the world, would say, "Ah! I caught you, bub. Hands out of the pockets!"

And, strangely, Boyd sometimes felt as if he had been doing just what Dewey had suggested, even though it wasn't the sort of thing that much appealed to him, unlike the kids in school who were doing it all the time, proudly and conspicuously, for everyone to watch, even old-maid schoolteachers who didn't know how to word their complaint. He felt sometimes as if Tina had caught him at something, or that her eyes—how to say it?—almost undressed him, saw through all his layers of covering. The eyes were peaceful and still, like those of a small furry animal, alone in the forest. It was, Boyd had to confess, an eerie look and one that gave him a strange feeling, because it was hard to tell if the girl was afraid of him or he of her. And if she was, was she afraid of something in him that even he couldn't see?

Not that there wasn't plenty he *could* see, and none of it was the sort of thing to inspire him to want to spend much time with her in an otherwise empty parlor. She was certainly getting to be a woman, and she was—it took very considerable doing—the best-looking one in the family. Francine was pretty enough to turn over anyone's bowels, as Parnell would put it, and Dewey was, by common consent, the only one the people in town had ever seen who might, if he managed things right and kept his mouth shut, get a movie contract someday. Yet Tina beat them both. Her face was incredibly, desperately beautiful, but that of a child, attached to a body she didn't know what to do with. As for Boyd, and partly accounting for the blushes, he knew he had suggestions all right, but they came to him, shamefully, while he was sleeping. Twice during the last month he awoke at night, feeling all the ache rush from his body, and he knew that Tina's arms, not Francine's, had been around him during the last few seconds of sleep. The blush reached over his face until the sweat popped out of his forehead. He then went to the bathroom, cleaned up the humiliating mess on his body, wiped up the sheet as best he could, and went back to bed. He told himself, almost singing himself to sleep with the words, that Francine was his girl, even if she

71

couldn't be touched, and that he should never, *never* get close to her sister.

"What I think," Simon said, walking under the arched trees along Priest, "I think the cat's got her tongue. And one of these days she'll snap out of that quiet of hers and surprise us all."

Because it was the last thing in the world he wanted to cope with and because he thought it was nonsense, Boyd replied, "That's Parnell's old song—that she's in some witch's spell he's read about, but it just isn't true, Simon. She's supposed to be retarded. That's all there is to it. She's not goofy, I mean. She's just sort of retarded."

"But who can tell why?"

"She was born that way. That's why."

Simon spoke quickly and with passion, ready again to reach into the past for an explanation. "I remember it like yesterday, the first time I saw her. She was the prettiest baby in the world. Why, you didn't dare go up to her, catch her under her chin, and say 'Cootchy-coo' like you would with any other baby. All you wanted to do was cross yourself and wonder how something so beautiful could live. But live she did. And what I'm saying, I'm saying there was nothing wrong with her. Not a thing. She was full of tricks and as alert as any baby I've ever seen. The trouble was," he paused, apparently troubled by the recollection, "that even little babies know when they're not wanted. And the first time Frank Ventry saw that child, he said, 'Oh, God, take the damned thing away.' She *heard*."

"Si-mon," Boyd groaned, disappointed when his grandfather tried to peddle a farfetched view.

"Yes, she did," Simon went on with conviction. "Helen didn't want that baby, and neither did Frank. They named her the prettiest name they could think of—Christina— but, by God, they didn't want her. And Tina felt it and suffered."

"Babies don't know those things."

Simon looked up sharply. "You ever ask one?"

Boyd smiled, then shook his head.

"Well, then don't be a smart aleck. Some things a baby knows even if it don't know the words for 'em." He strode ahead, then continued. "You remember that time when you were still living in Cleveland and you came down here for a visit? Luke's old dog was still alive then, and the fuss he made over Luke! Parnell was about three, I expect, and it was the first time he saw his father's old dog. Well, damned if Parnell didn't go upstairs and hide under the bed, he was so hurt. I've heard of dogs that were jealous of kids, but how many kids are jealous of dogs? It took us a half hour to coax him out. He thought his father loved the dog more than he loved him."

"Parnell is . . . Parnell's strange." Boyd smiled as he said it, knowing that Parnell would have his fists up if he'd heard it.

"He's not. He's just a little boy and he has feelings. I'm telling you that Tina has feelings too. Sometimes it don't look that way, but they're there. All she's done, well, she did what Parnell did. She crawled under something a long time ago, and no one was around to coax her out."

At the corner, as they turned onto Summer Street, Boyd looked back, and he saw that Frank Ventry was still at the upstairs window of his house, still without any clothes on. Boyd smiled now, remembering what Simon had said about the human body. The most revolting machine on earth, he had said, and one that should be covered at all times. Young people, he had added, who thought bodies were beautiful were deluded because they were forever trying to give theirs away, and the beauty existed not in their bodies but in the gift.

Though Simon and the rest of the family often told how Frank had been the hope of the town back in the twenties, Boyd could remember best what Rose still referred to as Frank's hard-times sandwiches. When he first took the job on the car ferry at the beginning of the Depression, he carried his lunch with him. Rose said that his sandwich consisted of two slices of bread, held together by nothing. Of all the talk of the Depression—Boyd himself could remember little except that more rice than was palatable had been consumed in his own house, and that though ground steak went for twenty-five cents for three pounds, no one had the money to buy it—this seemed to spell out its full horror. To eat two slices of bread was to eat nothing, was to eat air, was to eat shame. For Boyd it was the most degrading thing that could happen to a man.

But there were plenty more. Back when Lucas Gavin had left for college, the same week Frank Ventry did, if the town had been asked to put its money on one of the two boys, they would have chosen Frank. Lucas was . . . well, he was too gentle to go very far, to get ahead in the world; he lacked whatever it was that propelled a man to do the remarkable. But Frank had it—the vision and the push, without which vision got nowhere. He hadn't, back in the twenties, asked his mother and father where he would be allowed to go to college; he had told them. No one in high school had particularly encouraged him to submit artwork of his to the Museum competition in Cleveland. He did it by himself, and the rest of the world be damned. It was *push,* a quality absent in the Gavins, a quality that kept them congenitally poor. But Frank, by God, had been blazing.

Oh, yes, *fired* by it. He had the genius if any man did. Why, with the stroke of a pencil on paper he could draw something that could make a happy man sad or a sad one happy. And now what did he have? Very damned little indeed. Not even a stitch of clothes on him.

"Was he an architect?" Boyd asked at last.

Simon seemed startled. It took a moment for him to realize that Boyd must have been pondering the man in the window.

"I don't know that he ever was," he answered. "He took a four-year course at Western Reserve, but it was mostly art, I think, and he never graduated. I seem to recall that he had a job at an architect's office in Cleveland while he was still in school—he was already married by then—but in a few years people weren't building houses; they were losing them."

There were deliberate omissions in what he had said. It had come as a real surprise to the people in town when Frank had married Helen French. The townsfolk had expected that he might be the first boy from Ventry to get as far as New York, or even Paris, that ultimate Elysium. But he had married Helen French instead and had shortly thereafter taken the job with the architect. Tina had been born too early, and people didn't like to talk about it; Helen had been carrying her on her wedding day. Then, in rapid succession, came Dewey and Francine. No, the Depression hadn't ruined Frank. It merely brought to his attention the ruin that was already there. He was a family man whether he liked it or not—he didn't—and family men didn't run off to New York or Paris. When, at last, the Depression did come, Frank lost his job in Cleveland and took one on the boat just as a stopgap, just until things got better. When in time they did, Simon had asked him one day, "Well, I suppose you'll be going back to

74

painting pictures soon?" All Frank had said was, "You suppose wrong."

The two now turned onto Satin, where the houses were white, in varying degrees of freshness, and each one, like the Gavins', had a spindly front porch with a green swing at one end. Most had been built in the thirties and forties, by which people meant the 1830s and 40s, and they had begun life as grand and symmetrical Greek Revival places. Subsequently, however, doors had been relocated, windows had been cut out, porches and gingerbread added, and shutters—because they were a nuisance—pulled off. The Greeks would have been aghast. William Jennings Bryan would have been pleased. The flamboyant additions were a kind of Victorian oratory set to wood.

The people in the houses differed, yet they seemed to be able to live with their differences. They dreaded the long, sunless winter because it brought out suicidal tendencies in the Finns, and Mrs. Kujala's seventy-year-old father had already been cut down twice from a rope which he had suspended from a creaking attic beam. Mrs. Morrison, a frumpy woman who once said she had washed her face with Gold Dust when she had run out of other soap, was thought to be carrying on with a Jewel Tea Company salesman, whose truck was often parked in her driveway, though she was no great tea drinker. Mr. Witherell had more or less gone off his rocker for a spell and had one night chopped down a perfectly harmless maple in the Andersons' back yard because he said its roots were reaching into his sewer. The Heinemans, though Lutheran, were passing through a Holy Roller stage. The Easterdays, originally from West Virginia, were so thrifty and so recently introduced to modern plumbing that they allowed their toilet to be flushed only once a day. Mr. Velbinger had had a two-pound gallstone taken from his body on which he had etched a portrait of Herbert Hoover. The Morrison boy had enticed the Ferrara girl to play doctor with him. The Metz boy, who didn't have all his marbles, had accused the Warren boy of making him take down his pants. The Fentons were ignorant. The Oxleys were smart. The Austins were pigs. And the Levinsons—who knew that they were being tested—were *nice*, so nice in fact that when they moved to town around Halloween the year before they hadn't even put up much of a fuss, after the first few terrifying moments, when a six-year-old girl had thoughtfully soaped on their screen door the word N-E-W.

In the middle of the block lived Abigail Clark, a sixty-year-old woman who once took a sun bath, stark naked, on the widow's walk on top of her house. Across from her were the Bells, mother and daughter, the latter a sour, plain-looking thing who had been courted for ten years by the same man, sending her mother to her bedroom whenever he called, where her mother flung herself on the floor and listened through the register for any sound of hanky-panky. In the house next door lived Henry Loose, a usually mild man who in 1938 got drunk at an Elks picnic and later urinated from his bedroom window, now commemorated in village lore as the year Henry peed out the window. A friend of his, Roy Burd, two doors down, once threw a Wedgwood lamp at a mailman who was walking over his newly seeded lawn. The Fitches had a stuffed Pekingese in their parlor. Rachel Young, whose father had owned the house that was now the Coal & Feed store, had a suit of armor in hers, visited each year by Miss Stickney's history class. Her sister, a piano teacher with poetic airs, had before her death asked that she be laid out on her rosewood sofa, one foot on the floor, a book of Browning on her lap. And at the very end of the street, where it met the square, lived the Reverend Hill in appalling solemnity, having forced the town council to change the name of the street from Satan—for such the pioneers had called it—to Satin, unwilling to fight the devil in his own front yard.

Yet the devil still lived in Ventry, and no one knew it better than Boyd and Simon.

When, the summer before, the Gavins learned that Lucas Gavin was missing in action, a euphemistic and governmental way of saying that no one knew where he was, the Gavins at first knew that no harm would come to him because he was a brave man and a cunning one too. But in time, as happens, doubts began to rise. The war no longer seemed to be one fought between brave men, but between single, helpless ones and machines and devices that took no account of a man's bravery or smartness. When, at last, the Allies finally landed in Sicily, the family thought, Well, now the Army will have a chance to find Luke. He was, they knew by this time, wounded somewhere—it cost them a great deal of grief even to admit this—in North Africa, and it was only a matter of finding

76

him, dazed and hurt, in one of the many hospitals. When still no news came, the family ceased talking about him altogether, thinking perhaps that speech would shatter the thin thread that held him to life.

And then the rumors, the talk on Satin Street. How it happened—what torn imagination first uttered it—no one knew, but people in town gradually began to think that there was something fishy about what was going on over at the Gavin house. Whoever it was who first suggested that Lucas might have got into trouble, no one could say, though perhaps it came from Mrs. Shaylor on Satin, whose own son had been killed in the Pacific, and it may very well have been her way of hating and at the same time coveting the hopes the Gavins still had. As happens sometimes in life, one event is clarified by another. So it was that when the *Plain Dealer* printed an account of an American soldier who had been sentenced to life imprisonment for some act of cowardice, someone in town speculated that this, too, might have happened to the Gavin boy. How could one otherwise explain the long silence? No one else in town, even the county, had still been missing over a year after the event was first reported. The government simply didn't operate that way; didn't *they* know? As for the unlikelihood of Luke's doing anything like this, the town knew that no man was infallible. Any man could fall. Any man. Back in the thirties, in fact, a youngster had left Ventry, a pleasant, well-behaved one, and had gone West, and the next the town heard about him was that he had robbed a store in Nebraska and even, before he was caught, shot and almost killed a man. Anything could happen once a man left his home.

Six months after the wire came to the Gavins, an Army car drove up Priest Street, stopped there, and two officers walked up to the Gavins' door; it seemed almost to be proof that the government was looking for Lucas. Rose had been by herself in the house, and she alone received the two men. People said afterward—Helen Ventry had watched it from across the street—that she was stony-eyed when they left. Not a tear. Now could a woman whose son wasn't in some shameful trouble be that cold and hard, that tied up inside? Rose herself had told the family, and the town soon enough learned, that the two men were friends of Luke, rotated back to the States, who had stopped in Ventry on their way to San Francisco. They themselves, Rose said, had seen Lucas carried back

77

to a field hospital, more shaken than wounded, before the company had moved on. Then they had lost track. But the town, the devil, had its own explanation.

It would be wrong to think that anyone *meant* to bring grief to the Gavins, but it happened. Again, how it happened—how perhaps a few foolishly spoken words could be enlarged, misunderstood, distorted, until they at last had a meaning far beyond what the sayer intended—no one knew. But it was now said by some people along Satin Street that Lucas Gavin had deserted. It was the only thing that seemed to make any sense. A man missing for one year and two months, and the Army had sent two men to look for him because they themselves didn't know where he was. It was a grievous and terrible thing, but hadn't they actually read about such desertions—men who jumped ship the day before they sailed overseas, or men in Europe or the Pacific who would, the next month, turn up in the towns they had left, hunted by the Army? Wasn't all that true? Well, perhaps not. But in their haste to understand what had happened to Lucas Gávin it seemed true enough. And in time it *was*—the town truth, that is.

Even sometimes to Simon and Boyd, the only two in the family who were aware of the talk. And yet, though they both knew, they had never dared to mention it to each other. As long as Lucas remained missing, as long as the blue-starred flag hung in the parlor window, they could only hope that the town was wrong. For his part, Simon was beginning to think that perhaps he knew nothing at all about his son. He knew what year the tomato had been introduced to Europe, what Joan of Arc said before her execution, and how Boswell had dressed on the night he had met Rousseau. But about his son, he didn't know. No more than Boyd. The way Rose told it, the Army had merely misplaced him, as one would misplace a slip of paper with a telephone number on it.

No one could ever accuse the Gavins of having much truck with reality. There was in most of them, and even in the people they married, a kind of intrigue against truth if it didn't conform to their notion of things. Even Simon himself, sitting alone in the parlor late at night, doing nothing but looking at the picture of the Bay of Manila on the wall—the one he had bought there during the Philippine Insurrection and carried from that strange land all the way to Ohio—and wishing somehow that he could relive it all, to feel the wonder and peril of youth again,

78

would remember how unhappy he had been, how he had suffered, how he had been sick, and how he had disliked most of the men in the regiment and had been disliked by them in turn. Still, there was *some*thing that he wanted to remember. By himself in the parlor, until Rose began pounding on the floor above him with her shoe, he would sometimes begin to cry, wondering, ashamed of himself for doing it.

What had his own father said? A man who had spent most of his life sad and unfulfilled, taking one job, then leaving it, starting a business, then losing it, loving his children, then hating them. "In every heart a child is crying." That's what it had been. "Simon," he had once told him, "when you're as old as I am, you'll know that you can never get half the things you want in life. All the grand and lovely things you dreamed about when you were small ... you'll never find them. Well and good. But the terrible thing is that you never forget the recollection; to the day you die you'll remember what it was— sometimes it's no more than a feeling—you were going to look for. And the child inside you never leaves you. It just gets disappointed, more and more as you get older. And sometimes that's all you can hear—the terrible crying inside. No matter what you do, the child is going to stay right with you, watching you, and crying to beat all hell when you let it down. It's a fact, Simon. This is no Irishism. A fact."

There was a lot of crying, Simon knew that. Sometimes in the darkness of the parlor, Simon fancied that he could hear Lucas far away, no longer a soldier but a boy again and frightened. It was then that the Irish sadness would wash over Simon, for it was then he thought that Lucas had done what the people in town said he had done. That he had been too soft to fight and that he had cried instead and then run.

As Simon and Boyd turned toward the square now, they looked beyond the façades of the buildings on one side of it and saw part of the red-brick building which housed the school—closed each winter for a few days because of needle ice in the pipes, each spring for outbreaks of the flu or measles, and even once to drive the frogs out of the basement because Miss Stickney had said she could teach nothing with all that croaking under her feet. Except for a sign strung between two trees, announcing the Third War Bond drive, there were no traces of the war at all.

"I've walked you out of your way, young fella," said Simon as they approached his bench.

"I wanted to get out of the house anyway," Boyd answered truthfully.

"Well, I think maybe I'll go over and have myself a talk with Mr. Levinson before I read the paper." When, back at the house, Catherine had asked about "the poor Jews," Simon had remembered that Lucas had spoken of them in just that way before he went overseas. It was during an argument with Frank Ventry, when Frank said that all the concentration-camp stories were packs of lies put out by Morgenthau and his cronies in Washington. Perhaps Mr. Levinson could tell Simon. Or perhaps Simon could cheer him up. Tell him that the war would be over in a few months and that the letters from Warsaw would start pouring in again.

Yet Simon already knew Herman Levinson's answer. "What's to say?" he would reply, saying everything.

While Simon made his way to the Levinsons' dry-cleaning shop, Boyd walked to the doctor's office over the Drug and Notion store.

Earlier, as soon as the family had chased the bird out of the parlor, Parnell had hurried off, like Eleanor Roosevelt, to perform certain war duties. They consisted of going into the basement and removing the labels from the tin cans there, washing them, and then crushing them with his tennis shoes. The cans would be turned in to a collection center in town, to be made into tanks, bazookas, howitzers, angry shells, and even perhaps—who could tell?—into other cans. For his labors, Parnell's canvas shoes were stained scarlet, a testimony to tomato soup. He then checked his wealth of fats which, as soon as they reached the rim of the old potato-chip container, would have to be carried off to Payne's Butcher Shop to be redeemed for coupons. He had helped the agonizingly slow accumulation by first sinking two choice stones selected from the garden into the container, hoping that Mr. Payne wouldn't notice them.

Finished with these exacting tasks, he climbed the tree in the front yard. As soon as Simon and his brother turned the corner onto Summer Street, Parnell climbed down the slippery trunk and went around the house to the back porch. There he kept his pollywog jar, handy for any lonely creature who wanted to put up in it for a day or two—crayfish, butterflies, hornets, houseflies, Canadian soldiers, caterpillars, garden snakes, toads, and once even something that no one in school, not even Miss Stickney, had ever seen before, a thing that looked like a small black button that crawled.

He wanted to try to catch the bird.

But he had tenants. In the old Mason fruit jar from the cellar, from which Parnell had, without her knowledge, drained Rose's preserved pears, there were now three embryonic frogs flitting around in the cloudy water he had provided. Instead of pouring them out on the lawn—only a Nazi would do that—he now made his way over the grass to the ravine behind the house and down the steep hill to the pond at the bottom. Once there, he poured the creatures back into the water, fancying that he could almost hear small joyous barks as he did. Not until then did he look around the bank to make certain that there was no poison ivy near him. The only patch he could see was directly beneath him, where he was stooping. "Criminee!" he said to it rather pathetically, as if the plant had legs and were following him, then jumped to a new place. Rose had said that she'd give him a good clout if he got poison ivy in one more place, though Parnell knew that he had just about run out of them.

He now watched the dragonflies dive-bomb over the pond, then stood up again and began to make his way back up the hill, grabbing at saplings for support, making excruciating sounds of effort as he did. From the top he could see the ravine follow Priest Street for about five hundred yards, then turn sharply and enter the deeper gulf. There, Parnell wasn't allowed to go by himself because the cliffs were too perilous and the water in the river was sometimes deep—had even, he remembered, drowned a classmate of his two summers ago, a boy who sat in front of Parnell that year in school, a boy who would have been alive today, everyone said, except that he got excited in the water and swallowed his tongue. Remembering, Parnell brought his own tongue as far back into the chasm of his mouth as it would go, preparing to swallow it, hoping to feel the exquisite agony, the blue-faced pain Billy Thompson had felt. You could die easy that way, he knew. He had even read that someone had died when he swallowed a green pea the wrong way at a Rotary Club dinner in Cleveland. "CLAUGHHHH! GDRRRRRR!

AGHHHHHHH!" he said desperately, freeing his tongue at last.

"The young Parnell, named after the well-known hero," he now said to himself, reciting the obituary he had prepared for the Ventry County *Sentinel* when he had scarlet fever, "was an amateur archaeologist and conducted correspondence with several notable people, among them José Guiterrez, a pen pal from Guatemala City, and John D. Rockefeller. He will be sorely missed by all who loved him. His body will be cremated and dropped from the sky by the daredevil pilot Tommy Fox and his Piper Cub at the Jefferson Fair following the sulky races. His family will remain in permanent seclusion."

And draw the curtains and blinds at the front of the house, Parnell continued, remembering that Rose had done that on the day old Mr. Ventry across the street had been carried from his house to the cemetery, dressed in his best blue suit but wearing his high boots, hidden under the satin covering, because he wanted something comfortable on his feet. The blinds were drawn, Rose had told him, not as he thought because they didn't want the dead man to look in as he passed, but out of respect for him.

Hearing voices in the kitchen now, Parnell crept up the steps of the back porch and stood next to the open door, listening. He was a terrible listener. A shocking listener, as Simon put it. If he wasn't listening, he was looking, even once going so far as reading the labels in the coats of twenty or so of Rose's Rebekah Lodge sisters when they came over to play cards. Peeping around the corner of the door, he could see his grandmother and his mother standing before the kitchen counter, their backs to him. Everywhere he could smell the richness of peaches, coming from the steaming pots on the stove. As his mother reached for a new peach to pare, Parnell looked closely, trying to etch it in his memory, wondering if he could still identify it when it appeared in the middle of his oatmeal sometime next winter. "Speaking of marvelous things," he would then say, echoing Simon's important way of talking, "I distinctly remember this peach."

Parnell watched his mother drop the bald peach into an almost filled pot, then reach into a second one—it would have hot water in it, Parnell knew, to loosen the skins—for another. "I'm a little worried about Parnell," he heard her say.

They were talking about him! He crept closer to the

door, the better to listen, especially if they began to whisper. If they said *one* mean thing, they'd have to pay for it, and good! If his mother told Rose how he'd wet the bed by mistake the week before, he'd never talk to anyone again as long as he lived.

"He's a little too imaginative is all," Rose answered, stabbing at a new peach. "Why, didn't Miss Stickney at school say he's the most imaginative child she ever saw? He'll be a genius, I bet a dollar."

Parnell smiled happily, bursting with immense pride. If only they would say more. More! Say how good his table manners were getting to be. Say how nice it was, how match-ure it was that he could go upstairs at night by himself. Say how . . .

But Catherine instead said, "Sometimes when I look at him it seems, well, it seems that he hasn't accepted any-thing at all."

"Accepted what? I'd like to know."

"The war or anything," he listened to Catherine say, then watched her pat her apron with one hand. "You know, Boyd has never asked me anything about his father. Still, I can tell that he's thinking a lot. Well, Parnell keeps asking all the time, but I'm afraid he's not thinking at all. Half the time it looks like he thinks . . ."

Quickly, almost angrily, Rose said, "Thinks what?"

"Well, that the war is just some sort of fairy tale and that his father is coming right home."

"Why, he *is!*"

Parnell watched his mother lean against the counter. "I don't know," she said, her voice low, barely audible. "You can't keep hoping forever."

"No such thing!" Rose slapped her peach into the pan so that Parnell could hear it even on the porch. "Didn't the government *per*sonally tell me that those things hap-pen? In the confusion of war? Didn't his friends make a special trip all the way out here just to see me and tell me it happens plenty of times? Plenty! Why, Luke will be home before we know it. They'll *find* him, Catherine. You mark my words. As soon as the Army has a minute's breath, they'll find him quicker'n," she snapped her fingers together, "quicker'n that."

"It's been so long," Catherine answered. "The minute . . . the minute I heard the bird in the parlor, I knew what it was. Luke sent it, Rose. I *know* that."

The bird! It came from his father! All the more reason

to catch it! But as Parnell now reached for the pollywog jar he had placed on the porch floor, he heard the sounds of whistling come from the end of the street, and a quick shiver of excitement ran through his body. His eyes opened wide, and with one leap—no longer caring if anyone heard him—he was off the porch and running around to the front of the house, even lacking the courtesy to turn to look at Rose, who had come flying to the screen door.

"That boy has been snooping on us again, Catherine! Standing out here listening to every word." She made a horn of her hand around her mouth and yelled through the screen. "Parnell Gavin! If I catch you spying again, I'll ... you'll," she seemed to be weighing her threats, "... I'll keep you away from the movies for a month, *hear?*" With that, she turned back into the kitchen, struck her head with her hand, and rushed to the stove. "Goodness! Look what that boy made me do! I'm boiling the daylights out of the peaches even before they're pared."

After she yanked a pot from the stove, she returned to the counter and resumed her work, calmer, perhaps even grateful for Parnell's interruption. "Do you remember, Catherine," she said, "how you could buy a whole bushel of peaches back in 1933 for just fifty cents? And not a one of us had enough money for the sugar to can them. But, my, don't they look good this year?" She sliced a quarter from a peach and rested it on her tongue, savoring it. "Last year they seemed to have the taste of the wind in them. *That* was a bad summer."

The two women became silent, each working on the peaches, each seeing the bird again, and then the face of Lucas, missing now since last summer, a sorrow that had changed the whole season, even the fruit of the trees, even the wind.

High in the oak tree in the front lawn, Parnell watched the blind man make his way down Priest Street, whistling loud into the morning air, his white cane tapping before him on the sidewalk. Across the street, he could see that Tina had left her piano stool and come to the screen door to wait. Around the man's belly, strapped to it, was the counter on which all the candy bars were displayed, a garden of bright colors and shapes. All summer, from May to September, the man walked from door to door in Ventry, whistling shrill and loud to let people know he was approaching, followed by running and hopping children and by wiggling dogs, and by the music itself that lingered in the air behind him.

From where he sat in the tree, Parnell watched Tina disappear into the Ventry hall, knowing that she would be back in a minute with a nickel in her hand. He reached into his own pocket, the one without a hole, and fished out the small, hard circle there, wrapped in tissue paper. Catherine put one in his pocket every morning, and he wasn't allowed to get at it, even to fondle it, until he heard the whistling. Tina was back at the door, her white dress bold against the screen. As the blind man's cane missed the turn to her sidewalk—it seemed to Parnell that he was just teasing her—Parnell saw the disappointment move over her face. But as quickly as he had missed, the man backed up, smiled as if he were apologizing, then tapped his way up the walk, up the porch steps, to the front door. "That you, Tina?" he said once he was before her.

The girl's lips said nothing, but Parnell could see the shy smile come to her mouth. "What'll it be—Chicken Dinner, Powerhouse, Oh Hen-ery?" he heard the blind man ask. Tina's eyes searched the counter and she quickly snatched a candy bar. With her other hand she began to offer the man her nickel, but changed her mind and instead dropped it into the slotted metal container that rode high on his stomach over the counter. "Will you whistle?" she asked.

"*You're* the dear one, Tina," the man replied, a smile crossing his face, even for a minute lighting up his eyes. He began to whistle, going down the steps sideways so that she could watch his lips. It was the best, the most *advanced* whistling Parnell had ever heard, better even than anything he'd ever heard on Major Bowes'. Somehow, it sounded as if two or three people were whistling all at once, there were so many flourishes and fiddle-de-doos.

> "For Cock-ils and Mock-ils
> and
> Idley-I-oooh!"

Parnell sang the few garbled words he knew to the tune, not even taking the trouble to wonder why Molly Malone was trying to sell a mock-il. He had once asked Simon, he remembered, what one was, and Simon had answered, "Well, a mockil is a bit like a winkle, I expect. A legless creature. A fish. We don't have 'em over here. Correct me if I'm wrong." No one corrected him, just as no one bothered telling Parnell that they were merely alive-o.

> "On stur-eets why-ed
> and narr-elll
> She pushed her
> wheel bar-elll . . .
> Singing Cock-ils
> and Mock-ils
> and Idley-I-oooh!"

Parnell waited a minute more, drinking in the sounds, letting them drown in his head, and slowly began to slide down the trunk of the tree. As he did, he almost touched something that fluttered as his hand reached toward it. Fluttered, then rested again. He stopped dead, his hand still as it rested on the branch above him, and he let his body grow limp and quiet. He closed his eyes almost shut, leaving only a small band of light enter them, so that in the darkness he made the bird would not see him.

It was directly above, no more than two feet away, jerking its head up, then down, avoiding Parnell with its eyes. And then—Parnell almost let go of the trunk where he was jackknifed—it looked directly at him, so that Parnell could see his own face mirrored in its two eyes. Holding his breath for fear of frightening the bird, Parnell slowly inched his hand along the branch, his palm flat, his fingers loose, until he was almost touching it.

And in a sudden flurry it flew off, shaking the leaves around Parnell's head as it did. Into first one maple, then another, and still another, and finally disappearing into the ravine at the side of the house. Just as Catherine had said, it *was* from his father. It was a bird Lucas had sent, like the homing pigeons Parnell had seen in the movies.

Happy, he let himself fall quickly to the ground, no longer even hungry for a candy bar. He looked down the street to see if Boyd was still there so that he could be told, but he had moved on. Instead of running after his brother and Simon, Parnell dashed across the dirt road to the Ventrys' house, up the steps, into the house, and to the parlor where Tina was sitting on the edge of the sofa, opening her Chicken Dinner. He would tell her . . . he would tell her as soon as he calmed down.

Tina broke off a piece of her candy and handed it to Parnell, whose resolve to tell her was lost as soon as he saw it. "Do you want me to help you count?" he asked, watching her nod her head up and down. In a notebook that she carried everywhere with her except when she was playing the piano, she had been counting for the last year. She was already writing in the book sideways to accommodate the long numbers.

"Where," Parnell began, stuffing his share of the candy into his mouth, "where are you at?"

The girl ran her fingers through her blonde hair—almost white, it was so yellow—and read from the sheet of paper before her. "Eight billion, five hundred and twenty-two million, sixty-eight thousand, two hundred and twenty," she paused, catching her breath, *"seven!"*

"That's a lot," Parnell said gravely. "That *is* a lot." He swallowed the last of his candy, then watched her as she began to write the next number. She did it carefully and elegantly, making each figure more beautiful than the last—as if they were flowers, not numbers—creeping up on the next tentatively so as not to scare it away. "And *eight!*" she cried.

When Parnell turned—an excitement he felt in Tina's body made him—he saw Mr. Ventry standing at the parlor door, wearing white undershorts but nothing else, one hand leaning against the dark oak frame.

"Papa!" Tina smiled broadly and jumped off the sofa, running to the piano stool. "I learned something new!" She sat down, opened the lid of the square, old-fashioned piano, and let her fingers play over the keys. Her fingers were the palest white because they had never been sunburned, had lived most of their life in the parlor. What she played sounded to Parnell's ears as if it might be something European, but it wasn't so fancy that you couldn't understand it. Standing behind her on the carpet, he let his head sway back and forth to the rhythm, then slowly tapped his foot on the floor, the way Miss Budd, the music teacher in school, did. When, a minute later, she had finished, her face was flushed with excitement and pleasure. She turned on the stool to meet her father's eyes at the door.

But he was no longer there. As soon as she started playing, Parnell had seen him walk toward the kitchen, and he could now hear his voice, loud and demanding, talking to Mrs. Ventry. The girl sat quietly for a moment, then ran her fingers through her long hair, bringing a strand of it over to her cheek.

"Tina?" Parnell said, walking up and pushing her over on the stool so that he could sit next to her. "Do you want to know a secret?" He waited for the loneliness to leave her face—the loneliness that had swept over it as she watched the empty doorway.

"My father's coming home."

Tina smiled, pleased, as if she were listening to music.

An hour or so later when Boyd returned from the doctor's, he stood on the Ventrys' lawn and heard Parnell's voice, confiding, speaking to Tina within the house, then made his way to the back yard, hoping to find Francine there.

As he turned the corner of the house, he saw her, lying face up on an Indian blanket spread out on the grass. For a moment—a very short one—he allowed himself the luxury of looking at her. She was wearing the yellow shorts he had seen her in earlier that morning, and a white blouse, not tucked in, and with the top two buttons free to let the sun color parts of her Boyd had never seen. Her hair, the lightest of honey blondes, was spread out behind her on the blanket to dry, streaked even lighter where the sun had bleached it.

A long-legged, big-footed, beautiful girl. She was the product of good food, of growing up in the sun, and of natural endowments that were just plain fantastic. Her eyes were worryless, the color of the cattails growing in the ravine—warm, humid, and dusty—and her face never entirely relinquished its summer tan. It was clear because she avoided all the mucky and binding foods that deform most young people, and it was kittenish because she willed it to be that. She had somehow mastered the highest accomplishment, and kindness too, of looking helpless and witless for the benefit of boys who liked the look, though she had been valedictorian of her class and outthought them at almost every turn. She ran like a demon at Fourth of July races, she swam better than half the boys on the swimming team, and she knew at least three poems of Emily Dickinson by heart. She could bake pies, fry pork chops, make jam; she could change the fuses in the basement, rewire lamps, and run the coil through the stopped-up sewer. She could wear a ratty, holey pair of sun-faded shorts and look elegant; she could wear an expensive dress from Cleveland, secretly bought by her mother, and look simple and natural. She washed her hair in Ivory Soap, and the only perfume she ever used came from a bar of Woodbury which she used for her face and her body. Her fingernails were cut like a boy's, but her figure was not. It was positively alarming. Contained sometimes by a T shirt and sometimes by a bra, it eluded both, thank God. She was sweet, thoughtful, wise, and she drove Boyd half mad. She was wasted. Militantly and antagonistically a virgin.

As softly as he could, he walked up to her from behind and then, careful not to cast a shadow that would fall across her and awaken her, leaned over and kissed her on the forehead. "Anything from the Fuller Brush man today, lady?" he asked.

"I knew it was you," she answered, opening her eyes. "I was just playing possum." Then, "I hope Mom didn't see. She'll think I'm getting wayward."

"Small chance." Boyd sat down on the blanket next to her, then stretched out. As he did, Francine carefully, prudently placed a white towel over the top of her legs and her midsection. She buttoned the two buttons of her blouse.

"You're being very liberated today," he finally said.

"I'm not really a prude. I'm just saving myself."

"For anyone I know?" He waited for her foot to reach out and kick his ankle, and when she did he was ready for it. He tried to cover her bare leg with his trousered one, but she pulled back quickly as he knew she would.

Lying in the sun on the blanket, Boyd felt under the towel and placed his hand on top of hers, feeling the relaxation spread over her body and then his own. With all his horniness, he sometimes thought that he would burst when he touched her, but instead all he felt was immense peace. In school he used to sit all day at a desk that was too small for him, feeling the hunger rise in him as if any minute it would send him howling into the street, but as soon as he touched Francine, in the halls between classes or after school, the urgency was gone. As long as he was with her and could console himself with the little thievery of a touch now and then, everything was fine. But alone, the old anxiety would reach into him again, spilling out at night, and sometimes—because he couldn't help it—spilled by himself.

He now said, "You smell nice and lemony."

"*One* lemon," she replied, adding, "a single, well-behaved one. I cut it in half, squeezed it . . ."

"Bliss," he interrupted.

". . . and used it to rinse my hair. It makes me blonder."

"And the goo on your face? What does that make you?"

"Browner," she answered, touching the sun oil there, through which tiny beads of perspiration were trying to break. "It's said that a tanned face and blonde hair can get a girl anywhere she wants to go in the world."

"Like where?"

"I honestly don't know. The ones you read about all seem sort of fallen, if that's the polite word to use. Or felled. But then you don't have to have blonde hair to fall. So, actually, I'm letting my face get darker and my hair get lighter so that I'll look pretty in my white dress tonight. That's for you. I want people to say, 'Who is that ravishing girl with that swine?' Or did you forget the party?"

"Out at Howard's? No, I remembered." Howard he didn't like, but that wasn't reason enough not to take advantage of his hospitality. A dull and sneaky fellow whose family, as he frequently reminded everyone, had more money than most people in town. They owned the Ornamental Iron factory that was, and had been since the war began, in the bayonet end of the business. The oldest and least ornamental of products.

"I'm supposed to go out to the Lake tomorrow night with your wicked brother," he now said. "Is that allowed?"

"Oh, God!" Francine yelled, sitting up on the blanket, pulling her hand away. "Not with Dewey. You *know* how he is. He's a maniac. And you know why he's going out to the Lake. You just want me to think that I'm driving you to it."

Boyd waited for a minute, and then said, "Has it ever occurred to you that God made women different from men for a reason?"

"That's what I've read. But why do you always remind me when you know I can't do anything about it?"

It was, everything considered, unanswerable. She probably couldn't do anything about it even if she wanted to. What bothered Boyd most was that he didn't know if she wanted to. Although he was, as he described himself, almost a virgin, he had talked to enough buddies in school to know that if God made women different for a reason,

He also sometimes erred and made some women who never got the message. One of his friends in school had said that he knew a woman who had been married for almost twenty years and had also slept around a bit on the side, but who had not once felt anything, as she put it. A cold fish. It scared the living hell out of Boyd. For a man to marry a woman like that was for him to eat nothing but slices of bread all his life, never to know salami or liverwurst.

There were great chunks of Francine he didn't understand at all. He wondered if whatever had made her cover herself with the towel, when he sat down next to her a minute ago, might make her always want to reach for something to cover herself. He didn't know. All he knew was that on those few occasions that he had tried to go beyond petting—not only for the gratification of his own senses, but because he wanted to bring pleasure to her too—Francine had become angry and made him stop. And if it had been only that, Boyd probably could have accepted things, but he often had the feeling that she was depriving the two of them of joy only in order to increase her mother's. Francine had great will in resisting him, but none at all in resisting Helen Ventry.

In the meantime, of course, he was also expected to preserve himself for her. Yet he was sufficiently emancipated from Victorianism to have decided that chastity was a pretty slippery thing anyway. A man brought whatever good and bad things he had in him to a woman, and the number of adventures of the flesh he'd allowed himself before would make him neither worse nor better. (As far as proficiency was concerned, Boyd was country boy enough to know that no one had to teach a beaver how to build a dam.) The perfect chastity, as he saw it, was that of the heart, and not of any less exalted organ. Yet to Boyd it sometimes seemed that Francine, in desperately trying to preserve the chastity of the one, was somehow losing the chastity of the other.

The worst of it was that Boyd couldn't figure out how the notion of self-denial had originated in the first place, unless the early church fathers had wanted to keep most people out of heaven. The more Boyd thought of an afterlife, and that was apparently the reward for self-mortification, the more it seemed that one was promised without even a shadow of a guarantee—an arrangement, were it civil rather than celestial, that no levelheaded businessman in the world would accept. It appeared now and then to Boyd that an afterlife might be no more than one of those shady land developments in the South or Southwest composed of nothing but waterless desert, sometimes not even that, existing only in the minds of developers. To Boyd, it was a bit like putting all your money, all of your life, into a bank, and then to learn—oh, my God—that the bank could fail.

"Well," Boyd said, not wanting to distress Francine any more, "I suppose I'll just become a dwarf."

"It might have its advantages," she replied, smiling easily. "For one thing, if you were a dwarf you probably wouldn't go around importuning me so often."

"I'm sorry, Francine. It's just that . . . well, I'm a very emotional guy. Sometimes I don't know what I'm doing or saying."

She stretched out on the blanket again, then turned and looked at him, a look that was full of sweetness, and part of what it was that almost drove Boyd barmy. "So am I an emotional guy," she answered. "But I just can't forget myself. Sometimes I almost do. Like last week when we were parked in the gulf. I can't, Boyd."

"I know. I'm sorry a hundred times over."

At that moment from within the house they could hear Frank Ventry shouting at Helen in the kitchen. One, two, and then three obscenities, and upon hearing each one Francine sunk her head deeper into her arms.

"The family at play," Boyd said. "He sounds nasty."

"He's terrible. He's not even sleeping because he doesn't have to work tonight. He's been up in the bedroom all morning, just lying there, looking at the ceiling, drinking. By tonight . . . by tonight, he'll be a madman."

Boyd had known the family long enough not to be shocked any more when Frank Ventry misbehaved, but what seemed incredible to him was that Helen Ventry put up with it. Whenever he thought of them, he thought of two dogs caught together in the love act, bleeding, unable to pull apart, howling, suffering, ripping themselves each time they tried to separate, but unable to. "I don't know why your mother doesn't leave him."

Francine made a small noise in her throat as if to say that she too had wondered. "What could she do? Where could she go? You can't just start all over again when you're almost forty years old."

"She could get a divorce. And a settlement or something."

"And she could also kill Papa. It would amount to the same thing. If she left him, he'd just sit around here and drink up everything. He wouldn't go to work. He'd drink up everything, and when he ran out of money, he'd sell the house and drink up that too. And afterwards he'd die."

"She must still have some kind of feeling for him then."

"It doesn't look like it sometimes, but there *had* to be something once. I think she just feels sorry for him now because he's such a mess. And if she left him and took a job, who would look after Tina? That's what's so terrible. Sometimes you have to live with someone even if you hate it. If you have money, you can do anything. You can keep looking for something better. But if you're like us, you simply have to make do."

Displeased, Boyd dug his own face into his arms. "You always get back to that, don't you? Money. You think you can do everything if you're as rich as Aunt Cortez."

"I didn't say that. All I said was that Mom could still have a life of her own if we had a little money. That's all."

"Well, we don't have any money, and Simon and Rose manage somehow. Rose is always telling everyone how unhappy she is, and Simon is always threatening to run away, but at least they hold on."

"But they talk to each other sometimes, Boyd. Not much maybe, but at least now and then. They can *hear* each other. But all Papa does any more when he's mad is take a crack at Mom. It's the only way he can speak. Through his fists.

"Maybe everyone who's been married for more than ten years feels that way. I don't know. Half the time bored to death, and the other half they want to hit each other."

"No," Boyd said with conviction. "My mom and pop weren't like that."

At the mention of his father, they became quiet.

Francine said, "Well, Lucas was different. He was . . . an exception. And look where it got him. You just can't win. It's all so senseless."

It wasn't the first time that Boyd thought it was senseless. It sure as hell seemed that way. A man as empty and depraved as Frank Ventry, still tormenting his family, hated by half of them, and Lucas was . . . well, wherever he was. Francine had said, Look where it got him, and

Boyd was aware of the omission. Where had it got him? he wanted to ask. Did she mean he had failed anyway, as almost everyone in town thought?

"Pop went away because he had a great feeling for people," Boyd now said. "I guess it was childish—that's what your old man says about it. But still he had the feeling. And if you have that, maybe nothing else is important."

"But you can't have any feeling at all for people if you're ..." she faltered and Boyd noticed it, "if you're missing or dead. Isn't it better to stay where you are? Twenty or thirty years from now, no one's even going to care. The war's going to be something you study in school. You'll have to take tests, and some kids will pass them and some kids will flunk them. Well, I don't call that reason enough to go out and get yourself shot at. Just so you can enrich history courses that no one pays any attention to anyway." She carefully ran her hand over her forehead, drying it. "What Lucas did ... was stupid, Boyd."

Maybe it was. Maybe even Lucas had in time seen the stupidity of it and had then run. If Boyd's father had been an ordinary man and had gone to war for ordinary reasons, he might have been able to cope with the disillusionment. But he was, as Frank Ventry said, such a fool. He actually thought that he could save people. On the very last night Boyd had talked with him, Lucas had reminded him of the first Gavin who came from Ireland to America. It had cost him eleven dollars to travel from Cobh to Boston, and it had taken the family two years to scrape together the money to pay for the ticket. He had fourteen brothers and sisters and because he was the oldest he had been chosen to save them all, to come to America and to send for them one by one. By the end of his first year in Boston, when he had money enough to pay for a single passage, not one of his family was alive. They had all died of starvation or typhus during the Famine. They had saved him; he hadn't saved them. And Lucas had said that it was about time for a Gavin to repay the Old World for the favor. It was stupid, it was insane, it was foolish. Every time Boyd thought of it, he blushed, not knowing if it was from shame or from pity.

Boyd rested his hand on Francine's shoulder, then quickly withdrew it. "Well, I'm not going anywhere. All I'm doing is going to Oberlin with Dewey. I'm not like my pop." And he wasn't. He knew it.

"You have to promise."

Why not? It seemed to Boyd that he had already promised two or three different things to his own family. Would it be impossible to add another promise, even though it contradicted an earlier, unspoken promise to Simon? "Sure," he answered.

Relieved, Francine said, "I wish I could go with you instead of Dewey. He doesn't even care. He hates school and he always has. I love to read, and I love to talk to people who read. So what do I get as a reward? I get to take a dismal job in Cleveland and Dewey gets to go to college."

Frank Ventry's grand gesture was entirely mystifying. Boyd had once almost concluded that Frank wanted Dewey in Oberlin to get him out of his hair, but Boyd was no longer sure. He didn't know why Frank was doing it. "Well," he now said, "you'll have fun in Cleveland. And you won't be that far from Oberlin either, so I can visit you."

"Who will I talk to when you're not there? My mother has some silly idea that I'm going to meet all kinds of swanky people just because your Aunt Cortez did."

"I don't think she ever worked in an office."

"No, but she met her husband in Cleveland. At Severance Hall, of all places, and my mother has never got over it. 'Now, Francine,' she says, 'I want you to plan on subscribing to all the concerts. And remember that the Museum is good too.' Good for what? To meet swanky people? Why would they talk to *me?* God, sometimes I wonder what's going to happen. I honestly do."

No more than Boyd himself did. Each time that he listened to Helen Ventry's plans for Francine, he became angry again. The well-known Gavins of the international set—Ireland and Ventry, that is—just weren't tony enough for her. "Well, just don't get mad at Dewey because your old man is sending him to college and not you. He's still a buddy."

"In case you haven't noticed, you're about the only real buddy he has. You're something of a pig that way, Boyd. You want everyone to love you sort of indiscriminately, but I don't think you're really all that prepared to accept the consequences."

Boyd smiled. "I've been inviting you to share the consequences with me for the last year, but you get very standoffish at the crucial moment."

She ignored what he said. "I don't mean that. I mean that Dewey relies on you too much. Maybe even more than I do, I think. He doesn't have a father—or at least he thinks he doesn't—so he makes you one. Dandy. But have you ever thought what would happen if you said, 'Dew, old fella, here's your walking papers. I'm tired of looking after you'? He'd go to pieces."

"Who said I was going to?"

"But you have to. If you ever want to grow up. Or if you ever want Dewey to grow up. It's as simple as that."

"Oh, God," Boyd groaned, "all that complicated stuff. Why don't you lay off? You're not supposed to spend all your time wondering what makes people tick."

"If you don't, who will? I hope like hell you wonder about me. I honest to God hope that. Because no one else I know is. My mother isn't. All she wonders about is herself."

"Well, it so happens I wonder about you a lot. All the time. Someday I'll do *all* your wondering for you."

"There you go. You're getting piggish again. You mad Gavins try to eat up everyone with love. Love them to death. But you've got to remember that a little bit has to be saved for Francine."

"I'm game. I'll save you about five and a half percent. How about that? That enough?"

"Agreed. But I get to choose which five and a half percent."

"I've got a feeling you've already chosen." In a way, he supposed, she had. He might wonder about Francine, who she was, and what she was doing, but the mystery of her body was withheld at least for the time being. They both apparently thought of it at the same time, because they both laughed.

Boyd half raised himself from the blanket and kissed her on her damp cheek. But even as his lips touched her, he heard the voice from the house. He sank back on the blanket, frustrated and angry.

"Fran-cine?" the voice yelled from the kitchen window. "Francine, would you come in here for a minute?"

Francine shrugged her shoulders and rose from the blanket, the towel demurely wrapped around her, and walked toward Helen Ventry, who had been watching them from the window over the sink, smoking cigarette after cigarette as she did, putting the last one down quickly only when she saw Boyd kiss Francine's face.

As he walked around the Ventry house to the street, Boyd could feel eyes looking at him even before he turned and saw Tina at the bay window, the curtain held to one side by her hand. Her forehead was touching the glass. He waved once, then twice, watching the small hand answer him, then waited for the blush to spread through his body, but it was warmness now, not a blush. Even Tina, separated from him by the pane of glass, seemed no longer afraid. At the curb he turned quickly to see if she was still looking, and when he saw that she was he smiled at her. For a second it seemed that she might, after all, let the curtain fall and retreat into the parlor, but then—wonder of wonders!—she smiled back.

Later in the afternoon Parnell found Boyd lying on his bed, parts of one of Dewey Ventry's radios strewn over and around him, tubes on his chest, buttons and knobs and wires in his hands, the stripped carcass next to the pillow and his sleeping head. To Parnell, it looked as if he might be able to turn him on, to walk up, revolve a knob on his chest, and hear Benny Goodman from deep inside his body. "That's what's wrong with this house," Parnell muttered, apparently to himself. "One minute everyone's hollering at everyone else and then—wham!—you can hear a mosquito cough." He looked for signs of consciousness in Boyd and, finding none, added, "Sweet-mother-Jesus."

At the dresser, Parnell rested his elbows on the smooth walnut top, then peered in the mirror. "Clark Gable," he said to his silent reflection. With patches of inflamed, poison-ivied skin near his eyelids, he looked bloated and vaguely Oriental. He stuck his tongue out, partly at the horrid sight before him and partly to see if it, too, was infected. Even in that most secret of places, small red spots had formed. Criminee!

To Parnell it seemed that something was always going wrong with him. All winter long he had colds and coughs and fevers of astonishing violence, and all summer he had one third-degree sunburn after another, burns that barely succeeded in drawing his attention away from his poison ivy or impetigo, the latter Rose's own diagnosis of a rash he picked up at the pond in the ravine and which she said was an epidemic carried by frogs. If it wasn't his skin— Parnell's idea of growing up was to pass from sores to pimples—it was his limbs. His left arm had been broken twice, his right once at the wrist, and each of his ankles, first the one and then the other, had been sprained badly enough so that on two separate occasions he had had to wear a bunny slipper to school for more than a week. The first sprain had been earned through honest sportsman's activity, but the second was acquired when he walked all the way home on his ankles from the frozen river in the gulf because he couldn't untie the laces of his ice skates. And once, as if virus and shattered limbs weren't enough, he had even swallowed a dime.

A walking *memento mori*. Parnell opened his mouth a second time, ignoring the poison ivy, and studied the vacant, the barren hole where his last . . . no, not his last pulled tooth, but where his last toothache had been. Though it had hurt so much that he yelled even if someone talked too loud, what it had done more than anything was to explode his jaw into a hideous, lopsided balloon. It had been Simon, unable to bear the sight any longer, who had bundled him up, wrapped a scarf around his huge face, and carted him off to the dentist's, invoking the names of all the Gavin heroes as he did. While Simon glanced through a *Look* magazine in the waiting room, Parnell politely sat in Dr. Corbero's chair. Less than fifteen seconds later he flew through the room as if he were being chased by a swooping tornado, the napkin the dentist had placed around his neck still there, virginal white, then ran down the steps to the street in three giant leaps, racing home where he locked himself in the bathroom for the rest of the afternoon. Boyd finally put a ladder up to the window and coaxed him out, and Boyd, causing twice as much pain as any dentist, finally wrenched the tooth free. Dr. Corbero had had to close his office for the rest of the day because of the swelling where Parnell had bitten his hand the minute he tried to stick a Novo-cained needle into him.

Looking into the mirror at Boyd's reflected body to see if there were signs of life, Parnell now brought his fingers over the pictures Boyd had stuck in the corners of the frame. Tina had some of the same in her bedroom, photos that were supposed to belong to Francine, but Tina had told Parnell that they were her own. One showed Boyd at a track meet the minute he broke through the tape. His mouth was flung open, as if he couldn't breathe, and his eyes were bursting. What Parnell could see if he looked at the eyes long enough was the mile Boyd had just run—all that space was right there, popping out of his eyes.

Of all the pictures on the mirror—there was one of Boyd and Luke, arms around each other like schoolboys; one of Francine in a bathing suit; one of the whole family taken in Aunt Cortez's garden that showed her big house behind them; and even one of Parnell himself, taken at the county fair, but he had wet his lips too much and part of his jaw was a blur—his favorite was of the twelfth-grade class at Ventry High. Parnell went from figure to figure, naming names, marveling that he knew so many people. A girl in the front row, Carmel Johnson, was twisted around, looking down her aisle, apparently to see if everyone was sitting up straight; she was the only one who wasn't. Francine was in the row behind her, the prettiest girl in the class, so pretty that Miss Haller, the homeroom teacher, had her arm around her protectively. Dewey was behind her, and he appeared to be either making a face or chewing gum; there was a rip in his shirt that he had probably got playing baseball during lunch hour. Boyd was in the last row and taller than anyone else. His eyes were completely closed, and his head was pointing down, away from the camera. It pleased Parnell to see that his brother was brave enough to look the way he *wanted* to look: bold and contemptuous. "Very neat," he now said to it, approving.

"What are you doing, meathead?"

When Parnell heard his brother, he started, and then in confusion answered, "I'm just . . . looking," the same thing his mother said to clerks when she shopped in stores where everything was too dear.

"Yeah. You walk in here five minutes ago, and all you've been doing is watching me. You know what they do to Peeping Toms?"

"What?"

"Oh, my God!" Boyd howled, disarmed whenever Parnell replied to a rhetorical remark. "Just cut it out, hear?" Half the time Boyd didn't know if Parnell was slow-witted or quick-witted, whether he asked his whys and his whats because he was too thick to figure things out for himself or because he liked to listen to explanations. Whenever Boyd was on the verge of concluding that his brother might not, after all, be *that* dumb, Parnell would ask something like, "How come if people eat all the time they don't weigh three thousand pounds?" to which Boyd had replied, as simply as he could, "Bathroom." "Oh!" Parnell had said, his face full of revelation, "I never connected

99

them before." Yes, sometimes Parnell missed the connections.

Trying to think of something adult that would interest Boyd, Parnell said, "Do you know that about two people are murdered every single day in New York City, three hundred and sixty-five days a year?"

"What do you mean *about* two people are murdered, for the love of God? Either you're murdered or you're not."

"I read it in the *World Almanac*. It has a lot of good things like that. Do you know that savages in Africa who eat ants vomit when they see a white man eating a poached egg? Do you know that fourteen people were de-voured by wolves in the city of Paris one night in 1438? Do you know that the emperor penguin sits on stones and tries to hatch them when he forgets where he put his real eggs? Do you know that . . .?"

"Mother of God! Didn't Mom say you should stop reading that fine-print stuff? You'll have to get glasses, and then look where you'll be." The latter was full of innuendo, somehow suggesting that glasses over all of Parnell's other infirmities would be too much for a man to bear, that final stroke of bad luck, that ultimate humiliation.

"I'm not allowed." Which was, everything considered, pretty close to the truth. Parnell was not allowed to become nearsighted, because Rose would not have it. No Boyd and no Gavin had ever worn glasses, and there was no reason to introduce the fashion now, she'd said. When Miss Stickney, the spring before, sent a note home with Parnell complaining that he couldn't see half the things she wrote on the blackboard, Rose said, "Well, that's no loss." Then, "He just wants to look superior. But *I'm* not going to let him deform himself with glasses." As a result, he was not deformed; he was instead half sightless, his red-rimmed eyes squinting most of the time.

"Can you get into the Army," Parnell now asked, "if you wear glasses?"

"You can get into the Army with a bleeding kidney."

Parnell appeared to be letting his mind wander, more or less its natural state. "What," he began, "if there's a hand grenade and all the dirt gets shot up in your face and breaks your glasses? What do you do?" Obviously stirred by the picture he'd created, he went on: "You don't know where you are! You could walk right into the German lines! Bumping into barbed wire all the way!"

Bored and impatient, Boyd looked at his brother's

squinting eyes, wondering when he'd finally ask what he came in to ask. "Do you really want to know or are you just wasting my time?"

Parnell was vaguely offended. "These things are very important. Because if it ever happened to me, I'd like to know what to do."

Jackknifing up in bed, Boyd then pushed his body into a sitting position on the side, his feet on the floor. "Well," he said, "what you should do if you see a hand grenade coming at you, you should catch it and swallow it. That way you won't have to worry about your glasses."

After a long while Parnell said, "Are you kidding me?"

"For the love of God, if you're close enough to see it, it doesn't make any difference *what* you do. You just close your eyes. When things get bad like that, close your eyes. I suppose you've noticed that I have mine closed half the time."

Parnell turned to the mirror over the dresser and pointed to the senior class picture. "Like in this picture?"

"Like in that picture. The guy next to me—see him?— did something, well, did something to Dorothy Larson, and I saw him so I closed my eyes. She's not much of a girl, but, hell, it was the class picture, and ten years from now she'll look at it to see what she used to be like. And she'll see old Bud Carlson goosing her. She's goosed for all time."

Parnell had been waiting for an opportunity like this for a long time. "Is that what people do when they have what-you-call sex?"

Boyd brought up his arm as if he were going to throw a poke at his brother. "Get lost, will you? You're asking too many questions."

"I just thought I'd ask is all."

"Well, you're too young."

"Who says?"

"I say."

Parnell was convinced. He wondered for a moment if he had told Boyd that he had once seen a lady's tit—or at least he thought it was one. A kid next to him in school had made one out of clay during art class and passed it from desk to desk under the nose of their red-haired, irascible art teacher who had none of her own to speak of. "Do you know," Parnell began, remembering that he *had* told his brother, "do you know what I'm going to get when I grow up? A red car!"

"You've told me a thousand times." Boyd also knew that what Parnell hated most about the Gavins' penury was the 1932 Terraplane in the garage. Whenever he was forced to ride in it, he crouched low in the back seat so that no one would see him, thinking as he did that it was a very unbecoming place for a pen pal of John D. Rockefeller. As it probably was. Both front fenders were rusting away, and the rear bumper traveled with the rest of the car only because a piece of clothesline held it in position.

"Simon said he wouldn't be surprised if Aunt Cortez's new car is red. Criminee! I hope she keeps it here when she comes and doesn't send that darky away."

"Well, that's her car, Parnell, not yours. And how could she keep it here anyway? Where would her *man*," Boyd said it authoritatively, the way Cortez herself did, "sleep? We don't have any room."

"He could sleep in my bed. I'll sleep on the couch."

Boyd smiled, then shook his head. "You'd go to all that trouble just to have a Lincoln parked in the driveway? Son of a gun. You know what you are? You're a gross materialist. That's what you are. But I'll tell you what I'll do." He waited for Parnell's eyes to get properly big and expectant. "If I ever get rich, I'll buy you a red car. The reddest car they make. People'll look at it and say, Wow, there goes the Shah of Iran!"

"One with a three-tone *horn?*"

"I'll throw that in for free."

"One with a . . . with a *coon* tail?"

"A big-assed one that'll blow in your face when you're going seventy miles an hour."

"And a . . ."

Parnell would have gone on, grossly—a chrome-plated soda fountain in the back seat, leopard-skin upholstery with the stuffed head looking out the rear window, Venetian blinds like those he had seen in the movies—but there was a knock at the door, a gentle sound that could mean only Catherine. The knob turned, the door opened.

"Are you pestering your brother again?" she said, catching Parnell's ear and giving it a tug. "You shouldn't be in the house on a nice day like today anyway. Outside, Parnell."

"Criminee! Everyone always pushes me around. How come you don't pick on someone else for a change?"

"Oh, God," said Boyd.

"Do as I say."

Parnell waited at the door. "I was going to tell Boyd ... a secret!"

"Yeah, I know your secrets. How many people were devoured by emperor penguins last year in New York City. How many ... poached eggs there are in darkest Africa."

"A *real* secret."

"Now scat," Catherine said in a no-nonsense tone. "I want to talk to your brother."

"Boy, I always get pushed around. Someday you're going to be sorry."

They smiled, listening to him descend the stairs, then heard him bang his way through the screen door to the porch. A loud squeak, followed by a regular, creaky humming, and they knew he was established in the swing.

Catherine sat on the edge of the bed, smoothing the spread with her fingers. Boyd knew, of course, that she would want a detailed description of what Dr. Herron had found. On the day he had gone on the bus to Cleveland for his Army physical, two months before he graduated from high school, all work in the house had been suspended, as if both Catherine and Rose could do no more than pray all morning and afternoon that something terrible and disabling might be wrong with him. When he returned early in the evening, he had walked in for his own wake. Now, as he looked at his mother, the same mixture of hope and desperation was on her face.

"The form he filled out is over there," he said. He pointed to the top of the dresser, where the medical report for Oberlin was folded in an envelope.

"Didn't you ask him anything?"

Angry, Boyd replied, "Ask what? Good God, Mom, there's nothing wrong with me."

Catherine rose slowly from the bed, picked up the envelope, and withdrew the form. To Boyd it seemed that her eyes weren't even reading the words. "There's so much of this I don't understand."

"Well, you don't have to. Hell, Mom, didn't the draft board already classify me? They're not going to change their minds."

"I thought there might be something ... little that we didn't know about. Those Army doctors don't have time to look properly."

"But the draft board didn't classify me because of the physical. You know why they did. It was because of Pop."

"I know," she said quietly. "I'll rest easier when you get to college. Yes, I'll rest easier then."

Boyd was pretty sure that she was trying to say she feared the draft board less than she feared Boyd himself. Well, she needn't worry on that score. It would take something stupendous to make him change his mind and enlist in the Army instead of going to Oberlin.

Catherine took a letter from the pocket of her apron. "I have a secret too," she said, the faintest smile on her face. "I haven't told Parnell yet. Guess who's coming to visit us for a few days?"

"Aunt Cortez!"

"Rose is downstairs worrying her head off."

Boyd laughed outright. "She'll start to pull everything apart, you wait and see. It always happens."

"Well, she doesn't have to turn the house upside down for Cortez. She's not company."

Boyd knew better. She *was* company. She was company like no other in the world. "Why," Boyd began, "why does she come if she knows that Rose is going to be mean to her?"

"Mean? Your grandmother isn't mean to her."

"It sure looks that way sometimes."

"She just has . . . Rose has unusual ways. Like getting the house all polished up—washing the clean curtains and painting the woodwork that was painted last spring. That," Catherine said, a helpless look on her face, "that's the only way she can say she's glad to see her."

Boyd waited, then said at last, "But why does she come? Really?"

He leaned back against the top of the bed, imagining Cortez as she walked into the parlor—cleaner than it had ever been, curtains still smelling of sun and fresh air, all the old family pieces of furniture glistening under new wax, the woodwork heavy under another coat of paint: all the small offerings Rose would place before her sister. Yet he knew that when Cortez entered the room the only thing that would be seen was Cortez herself, the only thing the Gavins would see, and the only thing the woman herself would see, her hands flashing with rings too large for her tiny fingers, her hair too brightly dyed, and a fur thrown over her shoulders, the stunned eyes of the silver fox watching the scene like Cortez's own.

Four

In the soft August twilight Simon, Rose, and Catherine sat on the front porch fanning themselves, listening to thunder over the lake, and watching heat lightning and then storm lightning tear across the sky. From the ravine behind the house came the cries of a thousand crickets, and on the porch itself the wings of Canadian soldiers fluttered back and forth, hitting against the screen door, the windows, and even the lifeless bulb on the ceiling. Before morning and light, they would fall in sudden swoons onto the swing, the wicker chairs, and the floor itself and then be swept away by Parnell into the rhododendrons.

Down the block, they could hear the voices of children, giddy with summer. A swift kick of a shoe against metal clanged through the night air, and light footsteps scurried down sidewalks and across lawns. Long, tortuous counting began, followed by "Comin' ready or not." The children sat hidden, crouching behind trees and bushes, waiting.

"We *need* a rain," Catherine said to no one in particular, then sat back in the rocker, inflamed by her own body, then feeling the first cool waves of fresh air blow in from the lake. "My, but that breeze feels good."

Rose leaned forward in her chair and peered into the night, trying to make out the figures hidden behind the trees. "I wonder if that boy of yours has sense enough to run home before it pours."

They sat and rocked, moving their bodies from time to time to find more comfortable, cooler positions. From across the street a radio blared from the Ventrys' kitchen. A night raid on Berlin. A retaliatory one on London. Naval victory in the Pacific. A boy from Mesopotamia, in the southern party of the county, killed in the Mediterranean. Then the high-pitched, hysterical voice of a man far away, rebroadcast from a rally in Cologne. *"Sieg Heil! Sieg Heil! Sieg Heil!"* echoed through the trees and died in the ravine. A second's silence, followed by: Tomorrow's high temperature would be ninety-three.

"I think I'll scrape the paper off the dining room walls the first thing in the morning."

Simon groaned. He knew that even he would be recruited for the frantic activity involved in getting the house ready for Cortez. Everyone in the family would have to help Rose peel off the wallpaper, billowing clouds of steam from the rented machine filling the first floor, their lungs, their eyes, and all the while they would have to listen to Rose's invective against her sister for being such a nuisance.

"There's no need to upset everything," Catherine said softly. "The house looks perfectly nice."

"I thought you said you're not going to wait on her hand and foot this year?" Simon asked.

"Well, you don't want her to think we live in a slum, do you?" It would take some imagination to regard the Gavin house as a slum. Most of the furniture was fragile and handsome Victorian and Empire. If anything, the place was on the elegant side, and was about every two years "discovered" by a traveling antique man from the city who generally offered to give Rose a blank check for about anything, even the long, rain-pocked, brass-handled cherry table next to them now on the porch and which the man said belonged in a museum. "Museum, my foot," Rose had said about it. "Next he'll want my own mama's bones for scrimshaw. I don't know why anyone'd want that old table anyway. It's a coffin table. We always laid out the Boyds on it at wakes, and here the old fool wants to use it in someone's dining room."

"Well," Simon now said, "you can just leave everything the way it is. How long does she say she'll stay?"

"Not a word. She doesn't say when she's due or how long she'll be here. Just that she's arriving. It's vague and just like her. Making everything difficult for us."

"As long as she comes in her new car, Parnell will be pleased," Catherine observed.

"Anything to make a theatrical entrance. And she'll carry all those moth-eaten furs with her too, the way she always does. In the middle of August in ninety-degree heat."

"I don't think she'd like to hear you call them moth-eaten," Catherine said, biting her smile. "Aren't they mink or something?"

"Well, it's shameful. At Mama's funeral you couldn't even see Cortez. She was bundled up in the biggest, most awful-looking piece of fur you've ever seen. Like the kind tarts in the city wear. And don't you think she didn't do it on purpose. She was looked at more than poor Mama."

"She's still a very pretty woman," Simon volunteered.

"Listen to him! Why, don't you think I'd be pretty too if I spent as much money on myself as she does?" She waited, apparently for someone to concur, but no one did. "The first thing she'll do when she walks in here is to ask someone to take off her shoes for her. Yes, she will. She can't do anything by herself. Wouldn't Mama be appalled if she saw Cortez down here, too *grand* to take off her own shoes?"

Patiently, Simon said, "Well, you're not going to rip the house apart. It happens every time she comes. You pull the house to shreds, and an army of men couldn't put it back together. Then Cortez walks in in the middle of it."

Her face showing signs of astonishment, Rose looked at Simon and declared, "Well, I can't truthfully say that *that* has ever happened. Yes, I disremember that."

A sudden crash of loud thunder split over their heads now, and the three Gavins on the porch waited for their ears to clear. "We're going to have a *storm*," Rose announced, rising from her chair. "I better shut the upstairs windows." As she stood by the screen door fanning her face, she said, "I hope Boyd doesn't stay out too late. I don't want to wait up half the night."

Wait up half the night for what? Simon wondered, knowing that Rose would sit on the porch or in the stuffy parlor, her eyes filled with sleep, until Boyd at last came up the walk. "He's old enough to look after himself."

"Hah!" Rose exploded, then walked into the hallway, leaving them, as she intended, with the impression that if Boyd was old enough to look after himself, she was old enough to make sure he did.

"Shhhhh," Catherine said tenderly after she had left, silencing Simon's comment. "She means well."

Simon reached into his pocket for his white handkerchief and wiped it across his face.

"Allee-allee-in-free!"

The clouds had thickened, and Parnell, huddled behind a bush at the edge of the ravine, watched a scudding shadow cross the moon, covering it. He waited to hear

107

another "Allee-allee-in-free" before getting up, pleased with himself for having chosen a hiding place no one else dared go near after dark, and as he heard it ring through the air he stood up straight. Then, hearing other voices, closer, he stopped suddenly, hiding again.

Only four or five feet away, and directly above him, Mr. Ventry was standing at the kitchen window, black curly hair poking out at the top of his undershirt. He appeared at first to be alone, but in a minute Parnell saw Mrs. Ventry behind her husband. She had been leaning over to pick something up—a blouse it seemed to be, perhaps from the wicker basket he knew she used for just-washed clothes—and placed it on the ironing board before her, sprinkling it with water, and then slowly moved an iron over it.

As Parnell half rose again to run home, Frank Ventry looked out of the window at the lawn, and Parnell sank down again, afraid they would think he had been spying. As soon as the man turned away, Parnell would creep up close to the house, make his way along the shrubs, and out of sight. In another minute ... another minute.

Yet Parnell didn't move. He watched Mr. Ventry grab Mrs. Ventry's arm—so suddenly that it almost upset the ironing board. "You made me burn myself," he heard her say, then watched her stroke her hand where the iron had brushed against it.

"I'm sick of listening to you tell me what to do." Frank Ventry stood big and strong in front of the woman now, his face red and flushed, the back of his head where the hair was long now flattened, as if he had been lying down.

Helen Ventry continued to run the iron back and forth over the board, moving it as though her arm were tired or pained. "It's not your money. It's the money I got from my own father's house, and I can use it any way I want to use it."

He rested his fists on top of the chair on which the ironed clothes had been piled, and as he did the chair toppled over, spilling the clothes to the floor. As Mrs. Ventry rested her iron, then stooped to pick them up, he shouted, *"Leave* them there!"

A look of tired confusion seemed to pass over her face. She held herself for a few seconds over the scattered clothes, her hand almost touching them, then slowly stood and returned to the board, resuming her work, looking only now and then at the floor. "Won't you please go to bed? Don't you even know how to sleep any more?" Her words were slow and fatigued, as if it were an effort for her to say anything at all.

Parnell heard Frank Ventry's wild laughter. "By God, you talk about sleep! Once upon a time you wouldn't even let me sleep, do you know that? Who was always ready for a roll in the hay? You talk about *sleep*."

"Please. Tina's in the parlor."

"Now it's something that's dirty. Well, I know once when you didn't think it was dirty. I know that. You'd do anything to keep me awake. You want me to yell it? You want me to tell people what you like in bed? Back in the days before you wore out? Before you got sick of it? Oh, yes, you're like all the women I've ever known. You'll do anything for a while until you get all *your* pleasure, and then you wear out, and you tell a man to go to hell."

"*Frank*. Please go to bed."

"You make me sick."

Parnell watched him cross to the sink, turn both faucets on full force, splattering water up against the window, then as quickly shut them off. "The girl doesn't have to go to Cleveland to get any job. She can work right here in town," he said at last.

"It's all settled. It's not your money. It's mine.

"Well, this is still *my* house."

The woman's face curled up in a tight smile, then fell again. "You would have lost it years ago if it hadn't been for me. It's as much my house as it is yours."

Suddenly, taking her by surprise, he rammed his wet fist into the ironing board, almost upsetting it. Mrs. Ventry merely backed away until it stopped shaking, then quietly stepped up to it again, as if these interruptions were nothing new.

"I want Dewey to live at college so he won't be ashamed of us, do you hear?" he said. "You've made up a budget so he won't have a nickel left over for chewing gum. You've put all that money aside for Francine, and the girl doesn't have to go anywhere."

"Dewey will have enough." She folded the blouse she'd been ironing, looked around to see where it could be placed—the overturned chair, the floor—and finally rested it at the end of the board. "Anyway, it's too late to try to buy him, Frank. He doesn't expect anything from you any more, so you might as well not even try."

"I've been a good father to him."

"You've been a good nothing to him."

"He doesn't like me."

There was exasperation on her face now. "Why should he? Haven't you done everything to make it impossible? Showing up at graduation half drunk and then walking out in the middle of it? Going to *one* football game all season, when any other father would have been proud to see his son play? And *then* making a scene. And all those times Dewey needed someone to talk to, where were you? You were up in your room, talking to yourself and drinking. No wonder he doesn't like you."

"I've tried to talk to him."

"You've whipped him. I can vouch for that. You've whipped him so he could hardly stand up, and now you want him to like you."

"I whipped him once, and I had good reason."

She closed her eyes, as if she were praying, then opened them again. "It was reason to talk to him, not whip him. You find your son doing something you don't like—my God, you were so drunk, how could you know if it was right or wrong? And you whipped him until he bled. There isn't a boy in this town who hasn't done what he was doing."

"I don't want any son of mine to be some kind of masturbating worm."

Parnell suddenly looked up, as if the wind had changed and had become cold. Frank Ventry's words were said with loathing, and Parnell, hidden outside the window, could feel it. Unconsciously he knotted his hands for warmth.

"It was the only time you ever noticed Dewey. You catch him doing something you don't like, and then you remember for five minutes that you're supposed to be a father, so you almost kill him."

"I don't like that. I won't *have* that. No son of mine is ever going to be a masturbating worm of a boy."

"You set a wonderful example. There's more than one way to go about self-abuse."

Angrily, Mr. Ventry said, "You don't know anything about it. You didn't *see* him in the locker room. They carried him into the shower room on their shoulders—you didn't *see* them—like he was, like he was some . . ." He stopped, unable to find the words. "I wish to God I had a son like other men. Pimpled and ugly. You didn't *see* the look in their eyes."

Parnell knew now what it was they were talking about. Boyd had come home from a football game last fall and said that after they had won, Frank Ventry had come into the shower room with all the other fathers, and then gone half berserk. He pulled Dewey out of the showers, knocked him around until Dewey began to bawl, made him put his clothes on, and then walked him home and locked him in his bedroom. No one knew what had come over him, unless he was mad at something his son had done during the game, but Boyd said that it couldn't have been that because Dewey had set up two touchdowns. It was the same night that Dewey had later crawled up the stairs of the Gavin house, his back all bloodied where he'd been beaten.

Mrs. Ventry rested her iron on the board and turned to the man. "I won't say I know Dewey. A woman isn't expected to, I suppose. But he's full of love. I don't know where he got it from. Not from you. And he couldn't have got much from me. But he's full of love. And if the friends he has can't like Dewey the way they like other people—if you see them and you think you see love—then why don't you get down on your knees and thank God you have a son who can bring that out in people!"

"You don't understand."

"Oh, Frank," she said, her voice finally breaking. "Go to bed. How can I talk to you when you're like this?"

"I'm talking to you!"

"Oh, dear God." She looked once more at the floor and the freshly ironed clothes there, then leaned over to the wicker basket and picked up a slip, placing it on the board. "I have all these things to do, and I'm dead tired. Can't we talk tomorrow?"

"Francine isn't going away, and that's final. All you want is for her to marry well so you can sit back on your can in your old age and let her support you. I know you good."

She shook her head. "I want her to have a life. That's all."

"If I had my way, she'd marry the Gavin boy tomorrow."

Boyd! The Gavin boy! When he heard the name, Parnell looked up boldly, rising from behind the bush.

"They have enough trouble as it is."

Frank Ventry stepped close to her now, almost breathing down her neck. "And what do you mean by that?"

111

"You know perfectly well. They have enough troubles of their own without getting mixed up with one of us."

He placed his hand on top of the slip she was ironing, so that she had to pull the iron away quickly. "I told you never again to say anything about that. I don't know where you pick up all your foul-mouthed gossip, but don't peddle it around here. I'm not going to listen to it."

"If you're not, then you're the only one in town who isn't. Rose Gavin is covering all that up, but she hasn't fooled anyone but herself."

"*You* say a thing like that about Luke! Don't you have any sense, for Christ's sake!"

"And they sent that Army car all the way out here just to pass the time of day? Didn't I see them with my own eyes and hear them with my own ears? They came right up to my door and said, 'Is this where Lucas Gavin lives?' as if he were in my very own parlor, hiding. And then Rose telling everyone that he's missing for a year and two months. I *know* how's he's missing. Luke was just too ... soft. He should never have gone. He was too soft."

Parnell listened to them now, puzzled. Were they saying that they knew Luke wasn't missing any more? But that's what Parnell already knew. Weren't they saying that he was going to come home—that maybe he was on his way home right now?

Mr. Ventry's voice was different. Before it had been quarrelsome, but now even Parnell could feel the rage in it. "You don't leave a man anything! Doubting everything— taking away everything! I try to help Dewey and you tell me I'm wrong. And then you come along and cut the manhood out of Lucas Gavin with a knife. *Get out of this house!*"

"Please, Frank. Everyone can hear you. Go lie down."

His words were thick, drunken, and irrational. "Did I want to marry you? Didn't you follow me to Cleveland like the whore that you are and *make* me marry you? Did I want to be the father of some goddamn idiot? You wanted my name and you got it, but, by God, I'm still a man and I'm not going to let you take that. Or to take away the manhood from the only person in the world I'd give my life for. I would. I honest to God *would*. I'd give my life to save Luke Gavin, but you wouldn't understand that either. Well, you and that idiot child of yours can just *get!*"

"Please ... please, Tina will hear you."

112

"Let her. Maybe it'll wake her up."

Mrs. Ventry leaned on the ironing board, no longer trying to do her work. "I don't want to hear any more. I'm dead tired."

"You'll listen!" He grabbed her arm, and Parnell could almost feel the fingers dig into his own flesh. With his other hand Mr. Ventry then struck her face hard. "I'm tired of you sucking the blood out of people. You like to see me crawl. You like to see *all* of us crawl. It gives you pleasure, doesn't it? You like to see me this way. You suck the manhood out of me because you like to see me this way so you can suffer more. Well, by God, you're not going to ruin my life any more."

As she spoke now, she no longer seemed afraid. "You did it all by yourself."

One, two, three seconds, and Parnell waited for the rage to break over the man. *"Get out of my house!* And take your idiot daughter! And your masturbating son! And take the high-priced whore you want to make out of Francine. And take . . ."

"It's *my* house. Who do. you think's. been paying for it? Not *you!"* As she said the words, she slowly backed into the door leading into the hall.

And as she did, Frank Ventry ran to the ironing board, yanked the iron's cord from the socket, and lunged at her with it in his hand. Helen screamed once, throwing her arms in front of her face, then ran headlong into the hall, shouting his name. The front door slammed open and shut once, then twice, and Parnell could hear feet running on the grass.

It was then that he saw Tina. She came from behind the dining room door where she'd been standing and walked hesitatingly into the kitchen, her hand on her face as if it too had been struck. She stood under the harsh ceiling light, her face empty of expression, and came alive only when her mother screamed again from the yard. She placed her hand over her own mouth, as if to stop a sound there, then ran to the kitchen door, down the steps to one side of Parnell, and into the night, her dress billowing behind her.

Parnell felt the terror reach into his throat at the same time he felt rain strike his head. His heart thumping, he raced to the side of the house. "Tina!" he yelled at the white dress, down the street now, her yellow hair streaming behind her in the rain. "Tina! You're no idiot. *Tina!"*

113

But as Parnell turned to run after her, he saw something enormous and black in front of him, and he fell into Frank Ventry, almost spilling him on the wet lawn, and as he broke away, he heard the iron whiz past him, close to his head.

"I'll kill you all. I'll kill you all!"

In terrible panic, his pants dripping from where he had wet them in fear when he ran into the man in the dark, his face flooded by rain, Parnell ran in confusion back behind the house, into the Ventry kitchen, up the stairs, and hid there in a dark closet, his throat too dry even to call his brother's name.

Dancing with Francine on the flagstone floor of the Fosters' recreation room, their shoes off, moving so slowly that it was almost a face-to-face walk rather than a dance, Boyd heard the rain begin to beat against the terrace outside the French windows, then watched Howard Foster, a drink in his hand, stride across the room and shut the doors. The rain became muted, except for a wild gust now and then as the wind picked it up and tossed it against the lighted windows.

The party was small and manageable, not only because it was easier to entertain twelve people than twenty, but because twelve could do proportionately less damage to the house. Howard had said, as Boyd and Francine walked in, "Do anything you like as long as you don't leave any traces." Boyd had answered with a smile, knowing the inference. About two months before, Howard had got into a bad scrape with his mother because he couldn't explain the ring of condom which she had found staring at her one morning as she piled groceries into the back seat of the family car. The explanation, Boyd knew, involved a trip Howard had made by himself to Cleveland after the Senior Prom and, from what he said, the not altogether inspired work of a streetwalker in the back seat.

The Fosters were proud of their house, and Boyd could see why. Mr. Foster, a pinch-faced man with an ulcer that always left his mouth looking as if he had just bitten into a garlic bud in a salad, had bought the place for a song at the end of the Depression. Until 1939 he had been a small-town banker, like his father before him, but then, when there was talk of war in the air, he began to reach out. The old Ornamental Iron factory—which the Ventrys had lost to the bank in '32—floated enough loans to retool

114

and get down to the serious business of making money again. A great deal of it had already been made, and at least part put to use in the house where Boyd was now a guest. A recently built addition was strung along the back, two stories high, and a porch with four Scarlett O'Hara columns had been added to the front, making the place sufficiently pretentious to be named, in the unlikely event that they were otherwise unnoticed, "The Pillars." Simon, with truth and rancor, called it the house that bayonets built.

It was decorated rather than furnished, the only house in Ventry that was, and by a Cleveland firm which appeared to specialize in packing as many expensive objects into a room as space would allow. The chairs were uncomfortable, but pleasing to the eye; the tables were inlaid with rare woods, and impractical as all hell. To call on Howard—a chore anyway, because Boyd didn't especially like him—involved a kind of contest between his body and Mrs. Foster's furniture. "Do be careful of the lamp," she would say, hovering over Boyd, who was perhaps five feet away from it, a monstrous vase topped by an even more monstrous shade. Or "Are your shoes clean?" if Boyd, instantly feeling that he had just walked through a field of cow pies, made the mistake of entering one of the two parlors at the front, original part of the house. These were decorated like display windows and used, it was unkindly said, only when Mrs. Foster put on her bedroom slippers every night at dusk to walk across the deep carpet to flick on the lights.

The Fosters erred only in thinking that anyone in Ventry cared. If there was a reaction at all, it was a contemptuous one. Already Boyd had seen his friends at the party rest Coke bottles on the tops of mahogany tables, sweating there on the finish, and then watched Howard run up to them and pluck them away. Boyd hadn't been able to resist saying, "Come off it, Howard. The war's going to last a long time. Your old lady can buy some new tables," to which Howard replied, "Screw you, buddy." Howard was by this time aware of the special, not to say ambiguous, position the family occupied in town. The factory, to be sure, gave what was called a living to about two hundred people, men and women who had been out of work during the Depression, but it was just barely a living. The only one making *money* was Mr. Foster. And whenever any of his old cronies suggested that the plant paid less to its workers than any other in Ohio, he answered, with the same meek, self-righteous tone he used in church where he was a deacon, "That's business," though of course what he meant was, That's my business, or, as his son said, Screw you, buddy.

Well, Boyd would take his own house any day. He had the feeling in the room where he now was that no one had ever known the furniture except the nameless workmen who had made it, while in his home he could look at the none too steady Victorian gentleman's chair in the parlor in which his great-grandfather had his last stroke one afternoon while having tea and cookies, look at the pedestal base of the round Empire table in the dining room and find the marks made by the terrier when it was teething, or even see the rising pencil scratches on the side of the walnut secretary where Rose had savagely recorded, and still did, Boyd's height and Parnell's.

Howard Foster now walked across the room to Boyd and Francine, then tapped Boyd on the back. "The party's dying," he said. "No one's drinking but the host. Is that good manners?"

Both Francine and Boyd smiled, but not sympathetically. They had, like their friends, seen the prewar scotch and bourbon laid out on the sideboard when they came in, but after one drink the boys went to the refrigerator for cold beer and the girls settled for Cokes.

"Everything's fine," Boyd answered. "I'd just as soon have beer. And Francine doesn't drink."

Howard seemed to know enough not to press. If, as the fancy women's magazines now and then suggested, the best way to guarantee at least nominal temperance among young people was to serve drinks occasionally, an even better way—not necessarily easier—was to have an alcoholic father. Francine was put out even when Boyd drank beer.

"Well, at least Dewey's in fine fettle and not bringing disgrace to the family," Howard went on. "You know, the last time he was out here he said he had eight bottles of beer. Is that possible?"

Boyd replied that with Dewey it was hard to tell. "If he's ever been drunk, he does it so politely you really don't know."

"Well, he's not being polite now. Do you see what he's doing? He's dancing with my date. I can't even get near her."

Francine and Boyd turned. Dewey was, in fact, dancing with Barb Travers. "What happened to Betty Jo?" Francine at last asked, knowing that Dewey had arrived with her.

"The Horse is out to pasture," Howard responded. "The last time I saw her she was in the garden looking at the goddamn flowers, but I think the rain chased her in. What's wrong with her anyway? Is she under the impression someone's out after her cherry? Sweet mother, I wouldn't try for it if someone offered me a thousand bucks. I bet it's sunk in Portland Cement."

"Howard!" Francine cried. "Don't talk that way."

"Oops. Forgot you were here. 'Scuse my filthy tongue. I didn't mean cherry; I meant . . ."

"*Howard!*" Francine interrupted, vexed now. There weren't many words that hadn't, at one time or another, been yelled by her father when he'd been drinking, but a knowledge of them didn't make them any more acceptable. As for Boyd, he didn't like to hear Howard's loose tongue in front of a girl.

"I'll go see if I can round up Betty Jo," Francine said quickly, not bothering to conceal her irritation. She touched Boyd's arm, then walked across the room into a hallway.

"Go easy on the language, bub," Boyd said as soon as Francine had left. "What are you trying to prove?"

It would be hard to say what it was. Boyd had read somewhere—God knows where—that some girls actually became excited by listening to dirty talk, but he didn't think that could be Howard's angle. Howard simply—how to say it?—liked almost to expose himself, as if by saying "cherry" he was also saying, bringing it into view almost, his own equivalent to it. And not to arouse a girl, but to arouse himself. Boyd remembered, in fact, that in school Howard had sometimes come up to a gang of buddies between classes saying, "Hey, look. I was just giving old Dorothy the eye in algebra class and look what she did to me," and then stand in profile so that everyone, including Dorothy, could see. He was, by his own admission, hung like an elephant, and no elephant had less modesty. Once, hearing that a wedding and birthday photographer in a town west of Ventry was also a sly Sunday pornographer, Howard had said that he wouldn't mind at all posing for pictures with some broad. The broad, Boyd knew, would have been no more than window dressing, because

Howard's eyes were for himself alone. Eyes for what he considered his gift. As fastidious as his family was, Boyd always felt that Howard smelled of last week's underwear.

But for all that, Howard was now going steady with Barb Travers, who providentially had a sinus condition, and he would probably marry her. No one could envy the girl, Boyd thought; she probably even deserved pity. Unless of course she went in for self-exposure too.

"For the love of God," Howard now said, "will you kindly get Dew Ventry away from my date or do I have to bust him in the nose?"

"All you have to do is tell him to shove off, my friend."

"I just tried, as nice as hell. But you know how Barb is. She's gaga for Dew, and always has been. You tell Glamor Boy to lay off. Barb'll get mad at me if I push him around."

"We'll have to find the Horse first. As soon as we do, I'll saddle her up."

"Gawd, what a girl she is. And Dewey is supposed to be the guy who's always making out. You ever listen to him tell you what he does? You get every single, panting detail." He bent over conspiratorially and whispered, "Between you and me and the lamppost, there's something wrong with him."

"With *Dewey?*"

"You find a hot-shot guy as good-looking as Dew Ventry, something's wrong with him. You know what they say about all those matinee idols in Hollywood, the ones who give all the middle-aged ladies hot pants? They don't even go for tail at all. They don't like it. And I mean, someone as sharp-looking as Dewey, he . . ."

"He manages," Boyd interrupted. Tail? Was tail somehow the test of a man? Not his own vestigial one, but whatever was offered by an accommodating broad? Hail to the ape, that most tailed of things, rutting at high noon in the Cleveland Zoo!

"I'll believe it when I see it."

Boyd grunted. "Some things you don't do in front of an audience. Most people, that is. Dew is okay for my money."

"Just get him away from my date before I knock his teeth in. And then—hell, man, what about driving the children upstairs to the land of milk and honey? You want to go upstairs?"

Because Howard's parents were seldom around the house when he gave parties, at some time during the evening there was generally an exodus to the bedrooms. Nothing sinister, so far as Boyd knew, ever happened. They would lie there on top of beds, a boy and a girl to a room, kiss a little, and talk a little, always leaving the door to the hall open in the terrible event that the Fosters returned in the middle of it, at which time they were prepared to line up stupidly in front of the two bathrooms.

"Sounds okay to me," Boyd answered. "I'll get Francine."

"Forget Francine. I'm dying. Just get Glamor Boy away from my date before we go upstairs."

"Better not let him hear you call him that. He doesn't like it, Howard."

"Hell, if *I* looked the way he does, I sure as hell wouldn't mind the name. Some guys get all the breaks. Here, it looks as if God really cared when he was making Dew Ventry, but He forgot to give the poor guy any balls. So there you have it. I've got balls to spare, but no face."

"And you better not let him hear you say that either, Howard, or you won't have them for long. Dewey is just likely to beat the living hell out of you."

"A guy who bawled out loud when his old man pulled him out of the shower room after that game! He couldn't."

Boyd didn't smile. "Maybe he couldn't, but I could."

Howard backed up in mock, exaggerated horror, but then very slowly—something inside him apart from his intellect, which was no great shakes, must have made him feel it—a look came over his face which announced, without words: Okay, you don't like me. I don't like you. But this is a small town, so we better be nice to each other. Boyd felt it clearly, and he was glad that Howard acknowledged what he himself had been thinking. There were some privileges a host at any party could take, but Boyd wasn't sure that tearing into a friend was one of them. You could give the Fosters credit for some things—they had an "E" flag at the plant for a production record; Boyd privately felt an "M" for money would have been more suitable—but you didn't have to be servile to them because they had more dough than anyone else in town. On second thought, Boyd withdrew the pity he had earlier offered Howard's as yet unmarried wife. Anyone who would marry the ass deserved none.

"I'll see you upstairs in a little while," Howard said as he picked up an empty ice bucket and left the room. Boyd in turn made his way to Dewey, who had left Barb Travers and was standing with a beer in his hand, a goofy smile on his face. Walking up to him, Boyd put his hand on his neck—a grip, really—and gave it a friendly, affectionate twist. Predictably, Dewey slid away from it.

"You've got to give Howard a break," Boyd said to him. "I like him like poison, but hell, this is his show. He's chomping at the bit. Chomp-chomp: like that. How about letting him dance with Barb a couple times? She's his date anyway."

"Christ-a-mighty, let Howard have the Horse if he's lonely. She can show him her teeth. When she laughs, you can see her appendix."

"You brought her, for the love of God."

"I brought her because it's easy to ask her. All I say is, 'Hey, you want to go to a party, eh?' And she looks like she's going to vomit, but then she says, 'Yeah, I don't have anything else to do.' " Dewey's face brightened. "Just wait until I get to Oberlin. Then you're going to see sparks."

"Okay, but you're not at Oberlin now. So how about giving Barb a breather like a good boy?"

Dewey, shy in almost every way, was not shy with tears. Whenever he felt hurt his eyes got wet, as they did now, whether from the request Boyd had made or the childlike "good boy" with which he had ended it. Unlike some people, Dewey could hide few of his feelings. His eyes moistened in the same way, and almost with the same regularity, that he grinned. It happened if a teacher in school gave him hell for talking in class, it happened during football games if he was benched for a quarter, and it happened if someone tossed a snowball at him on the school lawn. Everything was a very personal injury, and it didn't matter that the same teacher had yelled at five other talkers on the same day, that some men never got off the bench during games, and that snowballs were a fact of winter. Now, as he felt the wetness come to his eyes, he looked down at the floor, ashamed, and said, "I always get the shaft. Hell of a lot I care about these ruttin' girls in this lousy town anyway."

"Take it easy. Don't get mad at *me*."

"You're a fuckhead too."

"You say that again, and I'll think I really am."

The big, goofy grin returned to his face, pulling up his

lips. "All you sensitive guys. All you ... all you sensitive guys can't even get called a fuckhead without getting all cut up. You feel too much, bub. You know where it got Byron? It got him a mean wife and it got him a twisted foot. So just watch your mother-lovin' step." Then, having cheered himself, "Is God's little gift to the knife industry letting us go upstairs? I saw you talking with him."

"Why not? Like you say, tomorrow we may be dead. So let us fritter away our youth in bed."

Dewey's pleasure was unbounded, discovering that Boyd could remember things he had told him. Pleased, he said, "You actually *listen* to me."

"Sure."

"Well, how you like that." He nodded his head in approval, indicating that he did, and quickly added, "So what did I just say about bushy-haired Byron?"

"You said he had a twisted wife and a mean foot."

"Why?"

"Because he was ... he was bushy-haired."

"Ker-rect! And he died when he was left out in the wet. A right good man the feller was, only he didn't bundle up."

"He was Irish. That's what Simon says, I think. Anyway, he says that 'Shelley' is a corruption of 'Kelly.'"

"Wrong. Byron was a Greek. He must have meant Blake. *His* old man changed his name from O'Brien or something to get away from the bill collectors."

"It could only happen to an Irishman."

"Pity the poor Irish. Pity the poor Greeks." He tilted his head up to the ceiling. "God in heaven, in all Your infinite wisdom and mercy, pray for us and pay our bills and shower us with grace."

"That," Boyd said slowly, wiping his hair where Dewey had soaked it, "is beer you're showering me with, *paisan.*"

"*Paisan!*" Dewey yelled.

Standing on the back porch under the light, a torrent of rain falling before him on the steps from the leaky eave spout, Simon rested his rifle on his hip and looked across the dark lawn. A minute ago he had seen Frank Ventry by the barn, quietly watching the house and the kitchen where Helen sat at the table with Catherine. Seeing him there, Simon had bounded up the stairs to the attic where he kept his old Spanish-American War rifle, loaded it, and returned to the porch. "Frank, you better go home now," he said into the blackness. "Leave these people alone. You've done enough for one night."

Simon looked into the rain again, wishing that he had replaced the burned-out bulb at the barn door when he first saw that it was out several days ago. He couldn't make out the man any more, but he had heard his running feet on the grass only a few seconds ago. Frank had probably gone around to the front of the house to see if that door was open, but Simon had already made certain that it wasn't. Rose, now making up the spare room, had locked it as soon as Helen Ventry had run in.

The damned rifle wasn't much good, Simon knew, unless a man was frightened by noise. As long as no one was particular about what part of the body it lodged in, Simon figured that a bullet could still pass through the bore that hadn't been oiled in more than a year and a half. Still, as he stood there, his feet apart, holding it in his arms, he liked the feel of it. It was a good feeling. A man couldn't ask for anything finer than a rifle in his arms. A woman's hands were made for holding a baby, but a man's always felt at home when they were touching a rifle, even if he had never touched one before.

And there were damned-sight worse ways to hurt people than with a bullet. When the Gavins, sitting on the front porch listening to the first drops of rain splatter on the tin roof, heard Helen Ventry's screams, each one more or less instinctively knew what had to be done, because it had happened before when Frank had been drinking. There could be no reasoning with him when he was this way. The best bet was simply to provide refuge for the family, to lock the man out, and to hope that he might change overnight, be visited by God or by the man he used to be. But it wouldn't happen. Early tomorrow morning Simon would have to walk over to the Ventry house, because Helen would still be too afraid to go by herself, and he would have to rouse the drunken man from the sofa or the floor, or wherever he had finally fallen, and then try to get him ready for work if the boat was making a day run. It had happened too many times. Frank's eyes would be every bit as full of wrath in the morning as they were right now. Later, tomorrow night, he would come home from work, unsteady from drink, his face darkened from the engine room of the boat, and the wrath would still be there in his eyes.

122

Simon turned slightly, stepped back out of the rain, and watched Helen and Catherine through the open kitchen window. It was funny, he thought, how hard a woman's face could become. Looking at Helen, she seemed almost as beaten as Frank himself, as if the disease of one had infected the other. Her hair, matted from the rain, lay lifeless on her head, her lips seemed to be parched and swollen, and the two deep, blue-black shadows under her eyes almost engulfed her face. On her lap Simon saw that she was holding what appeared to be a slip. She must have been ironing, he decided, when Frank went after her, and hadn't had even a second to drop it.

"I'm so ashamed," the woman said, kneading the edge of the slip with her fingers.

"Cry all you like. It's good to get it out of your system." Catherine rose from her chair, looked out the window to make certain that Simon was still between them and Frank Ventry, and reached into the cupboard for two cups and saucers. She carried the coffeepot from the stove, then poured the steaming coffee.

"We should be used to it," Helen said, regaining more of her voice, "but each time it happens, it's like it never happened before." She tried to pick up the cup which Catherine had placed before her, but her hand was still shaking too much. She rested it on her lap again. "I don't know what we'd do without you."

"That's what friends are for. To help each other."

"I'm so ashamed," she said. "Frank doesn't know what he's doing when he's this way."

"A person just has to make the best of it, Helen."

Simon watched the woman nod her head silently, then followed Catherine as she leaned over and rested her hand on top of Helen's. There was about Catherine a calmness, a peace, and he hoped that some of it might drain into Helen Ventry. Seeing her, Simon was again overwhelmed that Luke had chosen such a fine woman to be his wife and mother of his children. Perhaps that was the highest and proudest achievement of a father: to raise a boy who would know how to tell the difference between a good wife and one who wasn't. How wise Luke had been to choose a quiet and peaceful woman.

Hearing a noise on the lawn, Simon raised his gun before him. He could feel Frank, but he couldn't see him. "I'll shoot, Frank," he said, and as he heard his own words echo across the yard Frank stopped moving. In another minute all he could hear was the rain, the wet branches as they brushed against the roof of the porch, and the voices from the kitchen. He backed up again, closer to the screen door.

"I thought a terrible thing tonight," Helen said. "I thought—God forgive me—how Frank would be better off dead." She brought her hands to her face, as if she were going to break down again, but recovered. "I've thought how it would be if he went away and never came back. It's a sin, but I've thought it, Catherine."

Catherine left her chair and went over to the woman, resting a hand on her shoulder. "The more hopeless things look, the more you need to hope. You need it then more than ever."

The tears finally came. "We were so happy, Catherine. I never thought life could be that happy. And then, when things started going wrong, I actually thought I could help him forget his disappointments. To help him love his children. To live through them. That's what I've had to do, Catherine. I have no life of my own. I have their lives." She wiped her face with the tip of her fingers. "But he wouldn't. He sees the same disappointments in his children that he sees in himself."

"It's hard sometimes to know what a man thinks."

"He sees the same disappointments in Dewey that he sees in himself, and he won't forgive him for it. It's as if he's saying to his own son, 'Be a man,' and his son is saying, 'But how?' and Frank hates him for not knowing."

"You can't punish your children because they're not perfect." What crossed Catherine's face under the light was almost the beginning of a smile. "I remember Lucas and how he talked about Parnell. He knew that Parnell depended on him too much, and that Parnell shouldn't be weak because it might hurt him later on. But Luke said—do you know what he said? He said, 'I'm glad my son is so gentle.' He was. And so am I."

Helen's lips trembled before she spoke. "I don't think there's a God, Catherine. I honestly don't think there's a God. A man like Lucas gone. And Frank here tormenting us all."

"They say you can learn through suffering."

"I don't know what."

Catherine said, after a moment, "Kindness."

As she heard the word, Helen looked up and all the bitterness returned to her eyes. "You have to fight to get ahead in the world. I've learned that. There's no place for kind people."

"To get ahead in the world, but not to live in it. I don't care what my sons do—what kind of jobs they have or what kind of money they make—as long as they're kind. If they don't have that, they don't have anything."

Helen shook her head slowly from side to side as if she were trying to apologize to herself for what she had just said. "I try. I try to be as good a mother as I know how. All my children are different, so I have to be something different to each one of them. I have to be one way to Dewey so I won't hurt him. And another way to Francine. And still another to Tina. But I have to do it all by myself. I have no husband to help me. Frank left me. He left me so that I don't know who he is any more."

On the porch Simon turned away from the door and walked to the top of the steps. Oh, there was a deal of crying in the world—widows with husbands, and widowers with wives, fatherless children and motherless children with fathers and mothers. And suffering? There was as much of that as there was air, as there was earth and water. But kindness? Wasn't there a point when you had to stop being kind and fight back against the unreasonableness of it all? Against a world that would cripple one man and steal another, that would leave Frank here, on this night in Ventry, crazed and with hatred in his heart, while Luke hadn't the words in him any more to help the people who needed him? Oh, there was crying in the world. There was crying in every heart, and Simon could hear it plain.

Slowly, perhaps not even knowing what he was doing except that he felt something move his hands, he raised the rifle to his shoulder, the sight at his eye, and aimed into the darkness, his finger throbbing at the trigger, seeing all the disorder and cruelty and despair in the night before him, ready now to send a bullet breaking into heaven itself, ready to make a sound, to fire a shot that Lucas—eyeless and lost—could hear, ready . . .

And as Simon began to tighten his finger around the trigger, Frank Ventry stepped before him in the sights, his face coming straight at Simon, looking at him without turning his eyes, daringly, almost imploringly, his hands at his sides, the rain pouring down his face, no more than fifteen feet away, then ten, then five.

For a moment Simon didn't move—until, his arms

125

shaking, he slowly lowered the rifle. As he did, Frank stopped, spat once on the lawn, and began to walk around the house in the direction of his own.

Revulsion like nausea came to Simon's throat—not at what he saw on the lawn, but at himself. He placed the rifle by the kitchen door and sank on the top step, letting the rain fall over his head, his shoulders, and onto his knees.

From within the kitchen Catherine said to Helen Ventry, "Come to bed now. Rose is fixing the spare room for you. I'll be sleeping in the parlor, and Francine and Tina can have my room."

"Tina!"

Catherine rushed quickly through the door. "Par-nell!" she yelled into the night. "PAR-NELL?"

At last, still sitting on the floor of the closet, the door open only an inch or two for air, Parnell heard his name being called across the street. He opened the door another inch, listening to the sounds in the house—the leaves of a tree stroking against the wet siding, a shade at an opened window sailing in and out over the sill in the wind, and even a low sigh from the house itself, as if the heat collected there during the day were seeping out of the roof, cooled by the rain. At the bottom of every sound, Parnell thought he heard Mr. Ventry.

Pulling back again, Parnell waited, knowing that sooner or later someone would come for him. He heard his mother call his name, and soon Simon—his voice hollow and tired—took it up. And in a minute they both began to yell Tina's name too.

Tina would be far down Summer by now, the way she'd been running. In the few seconds after Parnell had bumped into Frank Ventry and even as he heard the iron fly past him, he had seen her fall on the sidewalk. Instead of getting up, she lay there, as close to the concrete as she could get, as though she were waiting for her father's hand to strike her. Then, as Parnell ran to the back of the house, he saw her bring her face up to the sky, her neck bent back, letting the rain fall on it. "Down Summer to Spring and Satin." That's probably what she'd been saying to herself so she wouldn't get lost. She and Parnell often hummed it together in the parlor, and it always seemed strange to them that you could go down summer and find spring.

126

When, in a minute, Parnell heard Frank Ventry's step on the stairs, he was almost relieved. At least now he knew where the man was. When Mr. Ventry snapped the hall light on, Parnell's first thought was to try to inch the door all the way shut, but he was afraid that it would make a noise and afraid, too, that he might not be able to breathe. If you couldn't breathe, Parnell knew, you could die. Once, when he was no more than a baby and visiting Rose and Simon for the summer, he had what they said was a convulsion and had begun to turn blue, unable to draw breath, and Frank Ventry, who had heard Rose's frantic screams, came running into the house, held him upside down by his feet, beat him on his back, and then breathed into his mouth. Catherine always said that if it hadn't been for Frank, Parnell might be dead today, yet here the man was, out in the hall with an iron in his hand. "I'll kill you *all*," he had shouted at Parnell in the yard.

Through the crack in the door Parnell could see him, his clothes soaking wet, his feet leaving small puddles where he was standing on the hall carpet. Motionless for a moment, he turned and walked into the bedroom which Parnell knew he shared with Mrs. Ventry, flicking on the light, moving across the room, and resting both of his hands on one side of the high, old-fashioned headboard of the bed. Then—Parnell couldn't at first make out what he was doing—he seemed to run his fingers over the scratches in the wood.

It was an old bed, Parnell figured, and people had probably died in it and been born in it. Was that why he was touching the scratches? Maybe old Mr. Ventry had dug into the wood when he was dying, or maybe Mrs. Ventry when she was having a baby. Or maybe—what had Frank said in the kitchen?—those times she wouldn't let him sleep, and then they had scratched the bed. You could tell a lot from little marks like that.

He watched Frank Ventry move toward the foot of the bed, rest his hands against his work pants, hung from one of the short posters there, and proceed to the wall over the dresser. There he removed a framed picture and, carefully studied it. There were two others in the house that Frank had painted. One was supposed to be of Mrs. Ventry, but to Parnell it looked more like a girl; and one was a picture of the gulf and the river in early fall when the leaves were changing, and which Boyd had once called corny. The picture the man was holding now was of

Euclid Avenue in Cleveland as it was when he had gone to art school. In the middle was a yellow streetcar filled with faces and hats, to one side of which people were passing, dressed in old-timey clothes. Tina and Parnell often took it down, saying, "Look at this woman with the pink face!" or, "Here's a man with a gold-knobbed cane!" or, "There are exactly twenty-one people on the streetcar."

Frank Ventry seemed to tire of it, for he placed it on the bed, walked to the door, leaving the room without switching out the light, then stood in the hall as, if he didn't know what to do next. Parnell held his breath, hoping that he would leave. In a second or two he did, opening the door of the next room, turning on the ceiling light, and picking up a cane-bottomed chair and carrying it next to the bed.

He was doing nothing. He sat on the chair in Dewey's room as if he were in a doctor's waiting room, letting his eyes play over the bed, the walls, the dresser, the Oberlin pennant, and the letters from Ventry High. So far as Parnell could see, he might be falling asleep. But, no, his hands were opening and closing, first in a tight fist, then flung out straight. Sometimes, Parnell knew, Tina would do the same thing before sitting down to play the piano, stretching her fingers until they became nimble, freeing them of nervousness.

The man leaned over in the chair, looking at the pillow on the bed for a second, then slowly rested his head on the sharp edge of his hand, catching it high at the forehead over his eyes. He sat that way, tapping one foot on the floor, for so long that Parnell heard his own breathing quicken, afraid that any minute Frank Ventry might spring up again, howl, and begin to rip the bed apart with his hands.

Yet if Mr. Ventry never talked to Dewey, why was he in the room now, talking to the things that belonged to him?

Whatever it was Frank Ventry was doing in the bedroom, he now appeared to be finished. Before he left the room, Parnell watched him fluff up the pillow on the bed where Dewey's head had made a hollow. He walked back into the hall and turned the knob of a little-used door to the top story of the house.

As the man began to climb the steps to the attic, Parnell began to breathe easier. Now he would be able to sneak home. He waited until he heard Frank's feet on the floor directly over his head, first shuffling around, then settling, apparently as he found another chair to sit on. Slowly Parnell opened the closet door and began to tiptoe down the hall to the stairs. At the open attic door he looked up and saw Mr. Ventry, his back toward him, sitting on a small stool.

Spread out on a table—Parnell had seen them many times before when Tina and he went to the attic to play on rainy days—were small, dried-up, hardened tubes of oil paint, and Frank now seemed to be arranging them, as if to make some pattern pleasing to the eye. To one side of him was his tilted drawing board, heavy with dust, bright splotches of color in the margins. In the center was the clean, yellowed wood that had been covered by countless pieces of paper and canvas board. And as Parnell watched him, listening to the rain beat against the roof, it seemed almost as if Frank Ventry were looking hard into that clean space for something he had never put there. In a minute the man closed his eyes.

Parnell crept down the stairs, avoiding the noisy one, out of the door and the silent house, and into the rain. He looked once more down the street for Tina, and then ran across the puddles to his own house.

Boyd and Francine had been quiet for a long time, lying on a bed, holding each other, the door to the hall opened only enough to let a band of light cut across the carpet at the foot of the bed, lighting their stocking feet.

"This is almost like being grown up, Francine," he said at last. "Isn't this a crazy bed? I bet you could get ten people in it."

"I have a feeling the Fosters have never tried."

"More's the pity." Boyd now removed his arms altogether and stretched out beside her. "But, you know, I don't think I want to come out here any more. Is that okay with you?"

"Did you and Howard have a fight?"

"No. You don't fight with people like Howard. You just bear them and keep your mouth shut. What I meant is that . . . well, hell, we don't have to come out here to have fun."

"Who else is so accommodating? Where else can you borrow a bed with *down* pillows? Do you know how much down pillows cost?"

"I'd like to stuff one of these pillows down Howard's throat."

"Then you did have a fight."

"No. I just sort of got tired of him all of a sudden. Hasn't that ever happened to you?"

"Get tired of something all of a sudden? The only thing I'm tired of is this town, and it didn't happen all of a sudden. It's been going on ever since I discovered the wheel. And that if you put something on top of three or four of them, you can *go*."

Boyd laughed, then pinched her hand. "It's not the town you don't like."

Boyd could feel her shoulders shrug. "You know what I used to dream when I was little? Every time your Aunt Cortez came here, I'd dream that she'd see me on the porch swing looking at her and she'd come over and say, 'What a lovely girl! What a treasure! You don't belong here at all. Come live with me.' Only she never did. She can't even remember my name half the time. She calls me Tina, and she calls Tina my name."

"Would you have gone away?"

She pondered it, and said, "It would have been nice to ... well, to get away from Papa's hollering for a while. I guess I would have liked that. And nice things. I wish I knew more about nice things."

"Like what?"

"Well, like ... have you ever seen that old chair we have next to the fireplace? Papa's chair? Every spring Mom says that this year she's finally going to Cleveland and buy a new one. She's got it all picked out. It's a wing chair and it's covered in gold damask. Do you know what damask is? She says that there should be one really nice chair for Papa. Isn't that funny? Can you imagine Papa in a silky wing chair? I don't know what she's thinking. Maybe if he had a chair to be proud of, he'd be proud too. I don't know. Anyway, every year she counts her money and she's always a little short. Or Tina has to have her teeth filled. Or I have to buy a new dress. Or Dewey says if we don't have the brakes on the car relined or re-somethinged, we'll all be dead." She began to laugh quietly, as if she saw the joke of it. "Well, I'd like to sit on that chair."

"Tell you what," Boyd answered. "Before I go to Oberlin I'll treat you to a trip to the city. I'll take you to all the department stores and we can sit in all the chairs we see."

"It wouldn't be the same. It has to be Papa's chair, and right where I can see it when I come down the stairs for breakfast."

"I sort of like that old chair you have anyway. Didn't you and your mom make a slipcover for it? And didn't Dew tie all the springs about a year ago? That makes it special. That makes it *your* chair."

"It makes it so when you sit on it your fanny hurts. That's what it makes it."

Half wistfully Francine added, "I don't think we've ever had anything in our house that's new. Except the refrigerator and the stove. And I think it would be nice if Mom could walk into a store, see something she likes, and say, 'I'll take that.' "

"She's had a lot of tough breaks. But if you go to Cleveland, it'll please her. Even if you don't stay long, I think you'll make her happy."

"It'd kill her if I didn't. All she has left from the money she got from Grandpa's house is about two hundred dollars, and that's supposed to set me up. Buy me a few new clothes so I won't look like a bumpkin, and find me a place to live. I tell her that she should use it on herself, but she won't hear of it."

But, Boyd wanted to say, wasn't Helen Ventry using it on herself? Wouldn't her own heart flutter to see Francine board the train to the city, and wouldn't she, from her own kitchen window, be able to walk down the crowded streets with Francine, look in the shop windows during lunch hours, go to concerts, to the museums? As much as Boyd saw the rightness of it—that Francine owed her mother at least that—he also saw the silliness. No matter where Francine went, her mother would get no farther away than her own kitchen window, no closer to whatever it was she wanted than she was right now.

"I wish you could come with me instead." Boyd leaned over and kissed her, his tongue reaching far into her mouth, a way of kissing they'd tried for the first time only a few months ago. Lying there in the half darkness, he could feel himself grow. Very quickly he pulled away from her and turned over on his stomach.

"What's wrong?"

"Nothing," he lied, waiting for his body to obey him again.

Francine touched his shoulder, half turning him over, then wiped the hair from his eyes and the sweat from his

131

forehead. "Poor Boyd," she said. "I wonder if we'll ever be alone."

"We are right now."

"No, we're not. I can feel my mother standing," she pointed across the room, "right there. And when I get home, she'll be waiting in that terrible old chair, asleep with the newspaper on her lap, and she'll wake up and ask me if I've had a good time. Then she'll look at me, Boyd. She just looks. To see if I've changed or anything, I suppose. Or done something I shouldn't have. I actually think she could tell."

"Is it important?"

"That she could tell? I don't know. I think so."

"Sometime or other, you have to start living your own life." Even as he said it, he saw the hypocrisy of it. Boyd himself wasn't living his own life any more than Francine was. He was living one prescribed for him. And in all the maze it was hard even to know what kind of life he would choose if the choice was his.

"It would be different if it weren't for Tina. Did I ever tell you I think Mom was carrying Tina before she got married? I think she was. I also think that's why she dosen't want me to get in the same kind of trouble."

"Who told you that?"

"No one. I figured it out. One day I saw their marriage certificate. It was in a drawer in her bedroom, and I was looking for something else. They were married around Christmas, and Tina was born in June. It doesn't work out right."

"She could have been premature."

"I don't think so. And if only Tina had been ... right, I don't think Mom would look at me the way she does. But with Tina the way she is, and Papa always drinking, it's almost like she's paying for a mistake, and that's why she won't take her eyes off me. As if she's afraid I'll do the same thing."

"What do you mean, the way Tina is? I think she's fine."

Francine touched her lip with the tip of her finger. "I meant that she's so ... well, you don't know what to do for her. If we were living in the city, I bet there'd be someone who could help her. But around here! Do you know why Mom finally took her out of school? Miss Stickney said that sometimes Tina was almost in a trance and wouldn't even answer when she was called on. She

132

was afraid Tina was going to have a fit! A seizure! And what it was, Tina was just too shy to talk in front of everyone. She's always been scared to death to be with people. If we were living in the city, she'd be all right now, I bet. Mom is the one who took her out of school. As if she thought Tina had to be hidden."

Boyd remembered Rose telling him about an October day when Tina had come running home from school in the middle of the day and said that she was never going back. There followed conferences with the teacher and with the school principal, Helen going by herself because the girl wouldn't leave the house. It was during one of them that the teacher finally admitted that she had yelled at Tina because she wasn't paying attention, then ever so gently, she said, tapped her across the knuckles with a ruler. What happened next had sent the class into roars of laughter. Tina, sitting at the desk, shaking, had wet her pants the moment she felt the teacher hit her hand, and the fluid had flowed from the hard wooden seat to the floor, the puddle seeping to the front of the room, while Tina herself had sunk lower and lower at her desk, unable to stop. Not until the entire class had been dismissed would she even leave her seat. When Helen heard what had happened, she said that she didn't want her daughter in school any more, and after a few desultory tests that Tina was forced to take, the superintendent had signed the forms that allowed her to withdraw. Afterward, Tina seldom went out of the house.

"They say that in the city they can figure out what's wrong with people like Tina. Simon says she's not even retarded. And Parnell says she's very smart. *He's* crazy about her. I bet he spent a week and a half making that valentine he gave her last year."

"Well," Francine replied, "as long as he's the only Gavin. But sometimes I have the feeling she thinks *you're* her boy friend."

"Me?" Boyd asked.

"She talks about you all the time. I'll be sitting on my bed painting my nails or something, and she'll come in and tell me you've just left the house. Then she'll tell me exactly, down to the color of your socks, what you're wearing."

Boyd could feel his blush, and in the half darkness he hoped that Francine couldn't see it. "I don't think she's ever said more than two or three words to me."

"Oh, she talks when she's with me. She asks me all about Oberlin and what people do there. She gets so excited. And then she'll go back to that silly notebook of hers and count to calm down or something. She knows as much about Oberlin as I do. Where you'll be living, where you'll be eating, what courses you'll be taking. But then as soon as she sees you, she pretends she doesn't even know who you are and won't say a word. She's the quiet one in the family. But I make up for it. I talk all the time. Do you think I'm a witchy woman?"

He leaned over and brought her into his arms again. "If you are, I'm all for it."

They lay in the darkness, thinking of the years that would have to be suffered before they could know each other. If it were just four years at college, it would be enough for two bodies to bear. But the war? Boyd felt the joy ebbing from him, the certainty he'd felt become another dismal uncertainty. He tried not to think of it, but, as if Francine were weighing the same things in her mind, she said, in a whisper, "Please God, I hope we'll always be as happy as we are now."

Later, somewhere in the darkened room, there was a sound—a kind of noisy, hard swallow—and Francine sat up in bed. "Boyd, there's someone *here*."

"The Green Hornet," Dewey answered from the floor where he was sitting. In the narrow sliver of light entering the room, they could see that he was leaning against the bed, his legs jackknifed before him.

"Dewey! You sneak. When did you come in?"

"A long time ago. The piebald mare downstairs is reading a magazine. Every now and then she says, 'Dew, listen to this. It's very droll,' and then she reads something from Life in These Yew-nited States. She's full of good times." He sighed. "There *can't* be pigs like that at Oberlin. It would break my heart."

"I heard somewhere that all Oberlin girls have thick ankles and crossed eyes. I'm counting on it," Francine replied.

"If there's one, you'll find her, Dew. Honest to God, you attract them. You could be in Atlantic City with forty-eight bosomy Miss America candidates, and the only pig in the room, the one who's handing out programs upside down, she'll go right up to you and say, 'Hullo, my name's Geraldine.' "

134

"I already met her," Dewey said. "In fact, I met her twice. You remember those two years we went up to Shore High in Euclid for the basketball tournament? Some cheerleader-dog named Geraldine got very palsy-walsy with me. Said she was from Garfield Heights and she'd love to get a letter from me. She had a nose that went from her forehead to her chin. Anyway, the second time I met her she said, 'Don't you remember me, baby?' And the thing was bobbed. Trimmed. By now it was a *cute* nose. An itty-bitty nose. She was breathing through her mouth. I told her I'd write her, but I never did. I think she was hot for me. I made seven baskets and two free throws at that game, running to get away from her."

"You don't know what you want," Francine said.

"You just wait until I get to Oberlin."

Francine seemed a little angry. "You're not going to Oberlin to bob your sex problems. You're going there to study."

"Listen to her, will you? What kind of books have you been reading? I'm a virile, clean-cut American boy. I don't *have* sex problems. You're just sore because Pop is making me go to college, and you'd rather go yourself. Hell, I can't help that, Francine."

"I know it," she admitted.

"What were you two guys talking about before I came in? The war effort? Is Stalin a good guy or a bad guy? What to do with Hitler after the war—make him a college president?"

"For one thing, we were talking about your old man's chair."

"Oh, for Christ's sake, that," Dewey answered. " 'Number 431, Thomasville Furniture Company, the gold damask, thank you.' I learned that about the time I learned the Lord's Prayer. It's legendary around the house. It'll appear neck and neck with the next Messiah."

"Mom will have it someday. You wait and see."

"By that time we'll have to tie Pop to it to keep him from falling out. Don't you get—what do you call 'em?—delirium tremens after a while?"

"He's not that bad," Boyd said. "When he came over this morning while we were having breakfast, he was real nice."

"He's real nice like Goering is real nice."

"That's not *true*, Dewey. You shouldn't say things like

135

that. Isn't Papa doing everything he can to get you to college?"

"So he won't have to look at me."

"Do you believe that?"

Dewey hesitated. "I don't know."

"He just wants you to make something of yourself."

"With what?" Dewey replied sullenly. "What I'd like to do, I'd like to go to General Motors Institute and maybe open a garage someday. So I get to go to Oberlin instead. Big favor." He shook his head. "He's got some idea I'm going to be a doctor or a lawyer, for Christ's sake. 'But, Pop, I like cars,' I say, and all he says is that it's a nice hobby."

"If you wanted to be an artist, I bet it'd be different. He'd be all for it."

"So I get my kicks from cars instead of drawing apples in a bowl. So what's wrong with that? And you wait until after this war is over, everyone and his whiskered old mother is going to be buying a new car. A mechanic, he'll be a big shot."

"Someday maybe even President."

"Someday even that. Five terms. And why should I want to be a lousy doctor anyway? You think doctors give a rat's ass about people? Some maybe, but most of them are in it for the loot. You go around any town in Ohio and see who's living in the biggest house, and nine times out of ten it's kindly old Dr. Christian. You know what we got from Doc Herron two days after Grandpa Ventry died? A bill for twenty-five dollars. And that was in the middle of hard times when Pop was making maybe six dollars a week breaking his back on the boat, on call, whenever they wanted him. Twenty-five lousy bucks. He sent the bill twice so it wouldn't slip our minds. That goddamn old . . ."

"Dewey!"

Dewey had never thought one way or another about doctors, Boyd knew, until right before he went to Cleveland with Boyd for his Army physical. Frank Ventry had made him see Dr. Herron first, and it was Herron who had said that Dewey's asthma would probably keep him out of the Army. Afterward, Dewey never had anything good to say about doctors.

"Get your degree from Oberlin and then open a garage," Boyd now suggested. "Be the first brainy mechanic.

It can all be a part of your Gladness Through Poverty campaign."

"What I'd like to do, I'd like to open a garage right on the square. A big neon sign: 'D. V. Ventry, poet and mechanic. Cheapest rates. He loveth the poor and cars.'"

"Sounds good to me," Boyd replied.

"You'll be greasy all your life."

"I loveth grease. I was born with a greasy spoon in my mouth." Dewey seemed to become sober. He brought his hand up before him, as if he were trying to judge something in the air. "The trouble is, every time I dream about the garage—I *dream* that way; I dream like the movies; no symbols at all; does that mean I'm dumb?—whenever I see it, I see it good and clear, but *I'm* never there. I see the garage all right, but where the hell is the poet-mechanic? He's not there. It bugs me. What I figure . . . I figure I'm dead."

Playfully Boyd reached over the side of the bed and tapped Dewey's shoulder. "Well, stick around. You're the world's buddy. You are, once and for all, the world's buddy. No sense dying. Long may you live, old pal."

"You get all moldy anyway, I hear. Not for me. You get like cheese left out in the sun—little feathers start growing out of you. I'll pass it up. Anyway, I'm going to live to be a dirty old man. And then I'm going to ascend to heaven, body and all. I'll say, 'Lookee here, if you don't want my hot-shot body, you guys aren't gettin' *nothin'*, hear?'"

"No, keep alive."

"Oh, by God, I will. I'm going to go rovin' through life like nothing you ever saw before."

"Lovin' it up in sacks with women who have lust in their eyes."

"Wandering hither and yon, one glad day after the other."

Francine punched Boyd on the arm. "Where do I come in? Don't I get to hither and yon too?"

"You hither and yon with me."

In the quiet that followed, Boyd felt that he could spend the rest of his life right where he was, never to go to Oberlin, never even leave Ventry. Was it, after all, wrong to stay where you were, to take a job that worried your hands, not your mind? What did you get by being smarter anyway? Wouldn't you just lose what you now had?

But there was the world, and it hated simplicity and yelled for change. For Francine to go to Cleveland, to meet new people, and in time perhaps to become like them; for Dewey to go to college, grease still under his fingernails, and to find that rovers come in last, and that for his bread every man had to do penance at a job he hated; and Boyd ... for Boyd, what? He didn't know. All he knew was that hithering and yonning would become harder and harder. That even now there was a war, far away and yet as close as the other side of the window, and that he and Dewey and Francine would all be changed by it, whether they wanted to or not. No, it wasn't any longer just Rose and Catherine who were pulling and pushing him. Or Simon and Parnell. It was the world itself.

Minutes later, when Francine said, "Shhhh," even though they weren't making a sound, each lost in his own thoughts, and, "Isn't that someone calling you, Boyd?" he almost started, as if it was a call he'd been waiting for. But then, listening to his name echoing up the stairs and down the hall, he knew who it was.

"It's the Horse," Dewey said. "Time to put the feed bag around her neck."

"No, it isn't. Listen."

Why had she called *his* name? Why not Francine's? Why not Dewey's? Why was she coming to *him?* "That's Tina," he said at last, hurrying off the bed. "Something must have happened."

When he reached the bottom of the stairs, the frightened girl ran into his arms, her face and her hair wild and wet, her knee cut from where she must have fallen. Boyd whipped his tan summer jacket around her because she was shivering and then dried her face with his handkerchief. She couldn't speak, not even to tell them what had happened, but as soon as Dewey saw her, he had said, "It's Pop again." Everything spoiled, Boyd quietly got them all together, said a hasty good-by to Howard, and walked out into the light rain that was falling. Tina held on to him all the way home, not willing to leave go until they reached the Gavin porch and Rose took over, pulling the frightened girl upstairs and into a hot tub.

Boyd and Dewey stood on the porch, their eyes on the house across the street, blazing with lighted windows, all their silliness and joy drained from them. "What does he *want?*" Dewey asked. "What the holy hell does he *want?*"

If only it had a name, Boyd thought. If you could figure

out what he wants, you could figure out what everyone wants, even yourself. And as he stood there, watching the house, he remembered Simon's remark. Everyone was sitting on the grass in the dark and singing, and you could hear it, but you couldn't see anyone. Oh, for the power of seeing! To know what it was. To know what the man in that house wanted, what Tina wanted, Dewey, Francine, Simon, Cortez, Parnell, anyone.

Instead he said, "To hell with him. Let's hit the sack."

Early in the morning, his head heavy from lack of sleep, Simon put on his clothes before anyone else was up, walked down the stairs, onto the lawn, and across the street to the Ventry house, hating to meet the eyes of the man inside. Standing on the back porch the night before with the rifle in his hands, Simon had been ready to shoot. Frank knew it. Even now as he opened the screen door to the house, his arm shook.

As he stepped into the hall, he snapped out a light that had been left burning all night, then looked into the parlor. How many times Simon had had to beat Frank awake on the sofa he didn't know, but he saw now that the sofa hadn't been slept on. Before making his way upstairs, he heard a noise from the kitchen and reluctantly, he walked toward it.

Frank Ventry was dressed for work—a clean dark blue shirt and clean gray cotton pants—and he had already eaten his breakfast, rinsed his dishes, and placed them on the counter top. The wicker basket of damp, rolled clothes was almost empty; neatly folded, ironed clothes were stacked on the dining room table. Frank must have stayed up most of the night. Over the ironing board, without looking up at Simon, he drew the iron back and forth, with all the grace and beauty that was still in his hands, over one of his son's faded plaid shirts.

Five

In the Gavin house a high-pitched disorder prevailed. Boyd was in the bathroom meanly spreading paint over the walls, Parnell was in the back yard flaying a rug hanging from a clothesline, and Catherine in the kitchen was scrubbing cupboards from which everything had been removed and placed on the counters, on the table, and on chairs. Earlier in the morning Simon had filled a pail with soapy water and washed the front porch, taking great pains, but even before it was dry, Rose had filled a pail of her own, repeating the task, not even bothering to say to Catherine, as she sometimes did, "He just *half* does things," but instead scraping her brush against the already clean wooden floor, driving her red knees into the boards, knocking over the wicker chairs, upsetting a pot of geraniums, and hosing everything in sight, including the Ventry dog and herself, all with a fine frenzy. Then she left both her pail and the coiled hose at the top of the steps so that Simon couldn't fail to see how thorough she had been.

Which, as he sat at the dining room table, pasting cards in a scrapbook before him, he now did, looking across the room through the parlor window at all the chaos she had created, smiling as he watched her wipe her hand over her wet forehead. He picked up a card, one Cortez had sent from Stockholm, read its short message, and studied the Stockholm town hall on the other side, rising from the water. Next to it Cortez had childishly written, "Was here." He pasted four black tips on the page of the scrapbook and gently fitted the card into the created space. Other cards before him on the table—some from North Africa, some from Europe, some from the Orient, the most recent ones from the Caribbean and South America—had been growing in number since 1939, the year her husband had died, and Cortez had, the last time she visited Ventry, carried the album down with her in order that Parnell and Simon could arrange them by country: "England, Land of Shakespeare." "Spain, Land of Cervantes." And, apparently because it had no literature to speak of, but possessed geography, "Norway, Land of the Fiords."

As Simon looked up, he saw Rose silhouetted against the front window, pulling curtains from their rods. Across the street, he could clearly see the Ventry house, where, two days after the quarrel, everything was tranquil. When Frank had come home from work the day before, in fact, Simon had watched him walk up the street, and he had a strong, lively step to him. "Well, I hope it lasts," Simon had said at the time. "God give him strength."

"My hip is killing me," Rose cried as she made her way through the dining room. The curtains were at her bosom, and her lips moving; she was making an inventory of things that still had to be done. Simon knew, of course, that she had already begun too many projects and that there would be too little time to finish all of them, but to bring this to her attention would only invite wrath. Cortez, frivolous woman, would walk into the house and not notice that anything had been readied for her. Or, worse, she would go to the high, old-fashioned floor lamp with the beaded shade in the parlor, and say, "This dear old thing. I used to count the beads on it such a long time ago. I bet there isn't another one in the country that hasn't been pitched out of the house." Mollifying her remarks, she would add, "I hope you always keep it, Rose, even if it looks shabby," and Rose, her hands still scented with ammonia, her face pink from exhaustion, would be unable to say anything at all for a minute. By that time her hip would truly be aching, and she'd look at her sister with an expression of pure pain and say that she better not expect any special attention because it was hard enough to look after Simon—she would point an ammoniaed finger at him—let alone wait hand and foot on Cortez. "This isn't Rio de Janeiro," she would add in confusion.

Walking into the kitchen en route to the basement, Rose spoke to Catherine from behind her mountain of curtains. "I don't think I'll repaper the dining room after all. I'll just get Boyd to help me touch up the walls a bit here and there."

"*What* walls?"

"The paper's dirty over the radiators, Catherine. I'll

141

have Boyd pick up some wallpaper cleaner at the hardware and we can do it quick as a jiffy."

"The paper's perfectly beautiful. You'll streak it if you go tampering with it." Catherine slipped her rubber gloves off, apparently willing to rest for a while. But Rose, not wanting to waste time talking, flew past her down the basement steps, groaning at the descent. At the bottom she yelled ominously up the stairs, "I hope she doesn't come."

Catherine exchanged a sly glance with Simon, then pulled her gloves back on, resuming her work. From the back yard they could hear the not too rhythmical noises Parnell was making as he struck at the rug with a metal beater. Soon the dark old Maytag in the basement began to hum, swishing clean curtains through an unnecessary wash, one that would merely enlarge the sun-eaten holes in them.

"Well!" Rose exclaimed as she climbed to the peak of the basement stairs. "I'll just get my breath for a minute." Her apron was wet and sudsy and her eyes, never still anyway, played over the kitchen, seeking out chores. "I think ... I think she'll have to take the attic room this year," avoiding her sister's name. "There won't be time to get the spare room cleaned."

Though they didn't dare contradict Rose, both Simon and Catherine knew that Cortez could not be directed to share the attic room with the squirrels. She would dance up to her old room, the spare room now, and she would establish herself there even if the Pope of Rome was already sleeping, huddled on the bed in a huge black cloak. Simon, as he studied Rose's face, assumed she meant that she wouldn't have time to pull everything apart in the room—to turn the mattress, polish the cherry finish of the bed, leaving a fine, messy coat of oil on it, tear up the rug and heave it out the window for Parnell to beat, and daub paint on all the woodwork that would, if the new enamel Boyd was now spreading on the bathroom hadn't already done so, sour the whole upstairs for the next week. Well, he thought, it was a relief there was no time for it.

Rose lifted the lid of the small bowl before her on the table and peered in to search for toast crumbs in the quince jelly. She replaced the lid, then carefully adjusted the hairnet around the top of her head. "Between you and me," she said softly, "I'm worried about her."

There was genuine consternation in Catherine's voice. "Cortez? Why, whatever for?"

"Her letter sounded ... don't you think her letter sounded a little homesick?"

Her letters sounded the way her letters and postcards always sounded—unorganized and full of exclamations. A letter sent from New Delhi was no different from letters sent from Santa Barbara or from Shaker Heights: as if she wrote everything while riding a bicycle. But homesick? Now why in hell, Simon thought, would Cortez be homesick for Ventry when she could go anywhere she wanted to in the world?

"I bet she's been unhappy since Aldo died. Don't you think so, Catherine?"

To Simon, who had watched the Boyd sisters nearly all their lives, it had always seemed that Rose could never forgive her sister for being happier than she was. While Rose tended to be headachy and dour most of the time, as she herself admitted, Cortez seldom complained about anything and went through life as though it were an adventure the end of which she alone knew. More than any other person Simon had ever met, she was happy. Rose's suggestion merely revealed her hope that it would be nice if Cortez could only have a little bad luck.

"Cortez has too many things to do to be sad for long, Mother," Catherine answered.

"She should have married again. I've always said that. I suppose you know Gerald Davis always thought the world of her. She could have had him," she snapped her fingers together smartly, "quick as anything."

It was too humiliating even to suggest. Gerald Davis, a widower who owned the Drug and Notion store, was a very plain man indeed, Simon knew—speechless most of the time and, unlike wise and silent men, incapable of anything except platitudes when he did open his mouth. To make matters worse—if a backward personality wasn't enough—a wen had, when he was about fifty, erupted out of the back of his neck at the collar line and was now about the size of a golf ball. About the man, Cortez herself had said the summer before, "Gerald doesn't alter at all," by which, Simon supposed, she meant that old age had merely brought to a head, like the wen itself, a grotesqueness that had always been resident in him.

"She's quite comfortable the way she is," Catherine

143

volunteered. "Gerald Davis ... well, Gerald doesn't have any style to him at all."

"A perfectly nice man," Rose replied.

"I didn't say he wasn't. I just said he isn't Cortez's type. Anyway, I doubt that she really needs anyone very much."

The truth of this startled Simon, and he saw too that Rose's mouth had opened, as if she were going to object, then thought better of it. Cortez needed no one, or so it seemed, not even Rose, who was always waiting for her to get old and to turn to her. But each year it was Rose who got older, not Cortez. Her sister became younger and giddier, more independent and irresponsible than ever. No, she didn't need anyone so much as she needed everyone: people to stare at her on the streets, servants and bellhops and porters, hotel clerks, wine stewards, travel agents, bankers, brokers, attorneys, nephews.

But then she had always been that way, even when she had still lived in Ventry. Cortez had a way of winning people to her side, not so much because she had so many gifts but because she was without them. She had always been and still was helpless, and people were somehow drawn to her because of it. As children, it had been Rose who was the quiet, persevering one who carried home papers from school with small silver or gold stars on them, yet Rose had never been more liked by her teachers. Cortez was loved and marveled at, her messy, arrogant papers hung from the classroom walls like rare butterflies captured once and forever. Although it was Rose who had done the greatest portion of the mean and dirty work around the house, it was Cortez who generally got the credit and the rewards. If there were newly picked flowers on the dining room table, her mother would catch Cortez in her arms and hug her while Rose watched, wide-eyed, her fingers still sticky from the stems. And though Rose was almost two years older than her sister, it was she who inherited Cortez's clothes—too tight, the fabric already thin, the pattern faded—because their mother said Cortez *wore* clothes better than her sister, as if it didn't much matter what Rose had on anyway, or that no matter *what* she had on she would always look headachy and dour anyway.

Yet for all that, Simon knew it was Rose her parents depended on in their old ages. Cortez was horrified by illness. Rose could tote bedpans, give injections, and wash

144

leathery bodies all in a sensible, no-nonsense sort of way, never in good humor but always with a good heart. On those few occasions that Cortez visited her bedridden parents during their last years of life, more often than not she asked Rose to spray the room with eau de cologne before she walked in, and once before them she sometimes didn't know what to say. As with many another beautiful woman, no one had really listened to her, as though the faculty of speech wasn't necessary for someone as precious as she was, and it had become a habit with her to say very little indeed. Back in the days when she used to come home from Cornell for vacations, Simon remembered that sometimes her first exclamations of greeting at the station were almost garbled, unintelligible, as if the words had to be carefully led from a place of unending silence where they'd been held for months. Then, even before Cortez could say much more than how glad she was to be home, her mother and Rose would start talking; Cortez's eyes would jerk from mouth to mouth at the wondrous sounds, keeping her own locked up inside her.

But if she lacked the art of talking—Rose, Simon knew, had perhaps too much in the way of that—she made up for it by the art of her life. What she wore, what she did, what costly paintings or jewelry she bought, all were touched with originality. And it had always seemed to Simon that even the reason she never had children was that children wouldn't fit into the beautiful arrangement of her life, bringing discordant sounds and unpleasant colors and smells. At one time when her husband had implored her to adopt a baby, Simon remembered that she had tramped through welfare wards and adoption agencies and children's homes as if she were shopping for an early Meissen tea set, and that she would hold a baby for a minute—perhaps trying to find herself in its eyes or its mouth—and then run to a washroom and scrub her hands. None of them would do. Rose, upon hearing this, had said, "She'll never change," which was exactly what Cortez had in mind. She never wanted to change; changing was no achievement at all, but a very ugly cheat.

The pity of it was that *Rose* had changed. At the table in the kitchen now, perhaps thinking of the trial before her as soon as her sister arrived, she looked tired. She appeared to have lost interest in the work she had begun all over the house. As Boyd walked through the kitchen to the basement, a can of paint and a wet brush in his hands, his walk jaunty and jazzy, a grin on his face, she seemed to look at him as if she were seeing him for the first time—the animallike vigor, the swagger, the grin of youth. Slowly she brought her face up to meet his eyes, as if to say, "Did I get old?" As if, now that Cortez was about to appear, she was asking the family to pardon her for being crotchety and ill-tempered sometimes, for the confusion she'd created in the house. For scrubbing the porch twice so that Simon would know that he needed her. For no longer being able to expect anything, as they did, from Cortez. For being old. Not getting old, but *being* old.

"I've got a terrible headache," she said. "I think I'll just go lie down for a few minutes."

As she stood up from the chair both Simon and Catherine watched her. Her headaches had happened on schedule before. She would begin to prepare for her sister, somehow convincing herself that this time Cortez would appreciate it and perhaps even say, "Why, Rose, honey, the house has never looked nicer," but then at some point she would realize that Cortez never would and the realization would take all the life out of her.

"I don't want you to try to finish anything by yourself, Catherine," she went on. "I'll be all right after I rest a bit."

"It's the heat," Simon said, lying, watching her leave the kitchen. They heard Rose's footsteps on the stairs, then listened to her tread down the upstairs hall and stop at her bedroom door, pausing there while she removed the small slip of paper between the door and the frame, take the key from her apron pocket, and unlock it.

Three hours later, after Catherine had finished in the kitchen and taken the curtains down from the stretchers, ironed them, and put them back up on their rods, she walked upstairs to listen for any noise of awakening, but there was none. She and Simon then tried to put the house in order again, pushing chairs back in place from the center of the parlor, carried there by Rose, the upholstery shampoo still in its unopened container; removing the bottle of window cleaner from the sill of the bay window where she had left it; laying the carpets on the floors; and trying, without much success, to dirty and smooth over the long, jagged, clean xs on the wallpaper over the radiators that Rose had rubbed there, her finger wet from water, in order to see if the wall needed cleaning.

146

In the basement Boyd dipped his hands into an old coffee can filled with turpentine, trying to dissolve the absurd pink paint his grandmother had chosen for the bathroom walls. Then he went to the back yard to collect Parnell, lying in mock exhaustion on the grass, the rug beater on his belly, fanning himself with a lilac branch. The two of them walked over to the Ventry house and picked up Dewey from the garage floor where he had spent most of the morning in a kind of twilight under the Ford.

As the three of them ambled down the steep, dusty road into the gulf, they kicked stones with their feet, sending them into the bushes at the side. Halfway down the hill, it became cooler—a musty green coolness from the trees that were everywhere, so dense that they nearly choked one another, bearded vines growing from limb to limb. There were deer here, and beavers, chipmunks, possums, and skunks, rabbits, squirrels, and groundhogs, all hidden now, all waiting in the shadows for the sun to set before they went foraging. On the floor of the woods were greens which people in Ventry still picked and cooked in stews: cottonwood, wild lettuce, horse-radish leaves, jowl, dandelion, narrow dock, Johnny-jump-ups, wild beet, and mustard,

At the covered bridge spanning the river, they took turns going over the ravine in the small cable car to one side of it which Boy Scouts from Cleveland had put up several years ago to prove one thing or another—perhaps only that it took longer to pull yourself over a river in a metal basket than it did to walk across a bridge. Each yanked at the cable which drew the scat, sliding, from high bank to high bank, the river far below. In the middle, Boyd leaned crazily over the side, pretending that he was going to faint and fall, but when Parnell, who was next, tried to do it, he became frightened by all the jagged rocks pushing their heads above the water and very quickly began pulling the cable again. Once on the other side, they all threw stones at the brown and weathered siding of the bridge, pockmarked from other stones and from BBs, desecrated by small carved hearts, and by "I love Molly Adams," and by "Easter Sunday, 1871" and a scratchy "Simon, 1893," and even "B. G. and F. V., 1943."

On the other side of the river, the three boys avoided the easy walk along the bank and went crashing through the thick brush, chopping at wild blackberry bushes at their knees, ducking under sumac, and letting the vines from the trees stroke against their faces, Parnell, because he was last in line, getting the full green swing of it in his eyes, but too busy jumping away from imaginary snakes, imaginary yellow jackets, and very real and roused mosquitoes to do much more than wave his hands in front of his sweaty face and hope that he wasn't walking through more poison ivy. *"Criminee,"* he said as his foot sank into a hidden hole and sent him flying to the ground, his fall softened by violets and wild strawberries and—*"Criminee!"* he now yelled—the shiny, tripled leaves of a plant that had special affinity, a fondness, a taste for him, like the Venus fly trap that can't resist its deplorable appetite and what fortune—for-tee-ooon, as Miss Stickney called it—brought its way.

At the wide bend in the river, where the water was deep, Boyd pulled off his white T shirt, kicked off his tennis shoes, dropped his trousers, and slipped out of his shorts, as Dewey did too. Parnell, who had a keener sense of privacy, went behind a bush and furtively began to undress. When he finished, he ran and belly-slammed into the river, hoping that he hadn't been seen, but once he wiped the water from his eyes he looked up and saw Boyd and Dewey laughing at him.

"Sonsabitches," he moaned, watching his brother pretend to double up with laughter.

Dewey said, "Man, we should get old Dorothy down here, and then we could get Parnell laid. You ever been laid, Parnell?"

"Plenty of times. Only I'm not telling you guys."

Which was probably a good thing, because no one knew better than Parnell that his body was too dull to get laid. He was almost tired of waiting for it to get raffish and wicked. Every morning he looked at it to see if something might have happened overnight, but every morning it remained the same.

"Hey!" Dewey yelled, jumping off the bank, then landing on his bottom, slapping the water. When he rose to the surface, his hair in strings over his eyes, he said, "You see old man DeAngelo's house this morning? He's got the American flag flying out the bedroom window like the Fourth of July."

"I saw it," Parnell volunteered from the water, hoping that someone would now ask his very considered opinion of it, but no one did.

148

"How come?"

"You know how he was always so hot for Mussolini back at the beginning?"

It was hard not to remember. The few Italian families in Ventry, and the Germans too, hadn't tried to conceal their partiality for Mussolini and Hitler in the thirties. They were proud of them, as if to say, "By God, you see? They're doing great things over there." Some of the Germans—the Grimms and the Velbingers—had even gone to Bund rallies in Cleveland, coming home on the last train holding small swastika flags in their hands. When Mussolini marched into Ethiopia, the Italians crowed and heaved their chests out. But as the war progressed, they subsided. Finally, when their own sons were drafted, they shut up entirely, ashamed of what was happening in the countries they had left.

"Remember Pete DeAngelo?" Dewey went on. "His pop says he thinks he's over in Sicily. He figured it out from something he said in a V-letter. And old man DeAngelo is from Salerno, so now he thinks Pete might be passing right by there in a little while."

"They crossed the Straits into Italy yesterday," Boyd said.

"That's why the flag's hanging out of the window. Pete's with the 142nd Regiment or something, and his old man says they're going to land them somewhere on the coast around where he used to live. It's crazy, man. Old Pete running up the streets of some old beat-up town and yellin' *'Paisan!'* " It was from Pete, two years older than they were, that they had picked up the sunny greeting.

"Well, I hope he gets through all right."

"The radio says the Italians are going to surrender in the next couple of days," Dewey continued, "so all Pete is going to have to do is walk up the beach and start kissing his greaseball cousins. What a lucky guy! Eatin' the spaghet' and kissin' his fat cousins."

"I sure as hell hope it'll be that easy. He's going to Notre Dame after the war. That's what he told me the last time he was home."

If the Yankees in town—and even the Gavins, there since the middle of the nineteenth century, were not that—were sometimes torpid about improving themselves, perhaps because they had been around long enough to know how hard it was, the non-Yankees did it with

149

passion. Only the very dumbest of the Italian children were content with driving trucks or working on the railroad as their fathers had. After high school they were packed off to Notre Dame or John Carroll in Cleveland or to the University of Detroit, sometimes with not much more in their cardboard suitcases except a change of underwear and an extra pair of socks. Each Monday morning their mothers could be seen walking to the post office, laundry boxes under their arms, the air around them scented with anise seeds from the cookies slipped in on top of the clean clothes.

"We'll march up Italy like we're on fire," Dewey said. "We'll march all the way to Berlin ... in I bet another five months."

"Like hell," Boyd answered. "You know what Roosevelt and Churchill and Stalin decided. Unconditional surrender. The Germans are going to fight right up till there's no one left."

. And that was probably just what F.D.R., Churchill, and Stalin had in mind, Boyd thought. Rather than waiting until after the war to plow Germany under the furrow and spread salt on the land, they were going to let the Germans do it themselves. But the trouble, of course, was that they were forgetting the people who would have to pay for the unconditionality of it all. There was no difference between a conditional surrender and one that wasn't except that the one would cost thousands—perhaps millions—more lives than the other. Neither would bring back the dead. And neither would change the past or the future.

"You know how we could stop this war real quick?" Boyd said. "Instead of killing another half million people, just kill the choice ones. Blow up the White House and Congress, and blow up Downing Street and Parliament, and blow up what's left of the Reichstag and the Chancellery, and the Kremlin, and those places where Hirohito and Mussolini do all their strutting. Churchill and Roosevelt think they're going to make the world better by ridding it of the other guys' tyranny. Well, they're not. It's like dusting. All they're going to do is rearrange it."

"Thank you, H. V. Kaltenborn," Dewey said, bowing in the water, dipping his head all the way in and keeping it under. When he finally emerged, he bubbled and spewed and then asked, "Is the war over yet?"

"Oh, God," Boyd answered. "You never take anything

seriously. If you met Hitler, honest to God, you'd crack some big-assed joke."

"Sure. Why not? 'How-de-do, sahr. What you got cookin' in the pot today? Welsh rabbi? Hey, I hear some of your best Jewish friends aren't. Is that a fact? Well, golly-gee. Gosh-darn. If you aren't a parcel of fun, as we say around Ventry. If you ain't a caution. Oh, ho, my, oh, that old Wagnerian rag.'"

"So?"

"So don't get hopped up about the good guys and the bad guys. The trouble, bub, is that you can't tell the difference. The English are taking potshots at the Jews trying to get into Palestine, don't forget that. And *listen!* You say the big shots are the rotten ones? Did you read in the paper where this pilot in a Flying Fortress saw five buddies bail out near Leipzig or someplace and as soon as they hit the ground the Kraut farmers pitchforked them to death? Little guys. Manure on their shoes. Hayseed in their beards. *Little* guys. And everyone in Washington got in a tizzy because they said it wasn't fair. Fair! For the love of God, those five fliers were dropping bombs on people. On kids and old ladies. Someone should have gone up to them with a bunch of posies and said, 'Welcome to Deutschland, *hombre.*' Or is that the wrong lingo?"

"Welcome to Deutschland, *Schatzi.* Lover, it means."

"*Schatzi* then. And another thing. That guy last week who got the Congressional Medal of Honor for machine-gunning thirty-eight Japs on Guadalcanal. Very big hero. Thirty-eight Japs. We give him a medal. We say, 'Well, pal, you have to forget the rules you learned in Sunday school.' But old Adolf forgets the rules too and knocks off thirty-eight Jews. Or thirty-eight hundred. We say naughty-naughty. How come? Why don't we give him a medal too? Why don't we give medals to the Kraut farmers with the bloody pitchforks? And why the hell not a big, solid gold medal for each one of the thirty-eight Japs?"

"It's not the same thing, Dewey. The soldier in Guadalcanal . . . he was helping to free the place."

"For what?" Dewey quickly asked. "Chasing the Japs out so we can move in and set up Coca-Cola franchises?"

Boyd looked at his friend cautiously. "You're saying that because your old man is an American Firster. He thinks we don't belong there anyway. Hell, you seem to forget they bombed Pearl Harbor."

"Yeah, but there were *reasons*. Who told the Japs they weren't good enough to come to this country? We didn't like their eyes and their skin. They didn't *look* like us. And who raised the tariffs so high they couldn't send any more lousy teacups and firecrackers to the dime stores and had to close all their factories? Hell, those guys are like guys everywhere. They just want to stay alive and make a buck."

"Simon says that Orientals don't have any respect for human life."

Dewey horselaughed. "They don't have any respect for it because so many of them lose it so quick. That's why. They get washed away in tidal waves. They get burned to death in fires and knocked around in earthquakes. Every year a couple hundred thousand die of starvation. But do we care? Hell, no. Now and then maybe the Methodist Church sends a lady missionary over there to tell them it's the will of God. As if they needed to be reminded. But they're getting wise. They're beginning to learn. You know that flat-chested girl from Unionville who went to Moody Bible Institute a couple years ago? They sent her to India or someplace to help put Unguentine on people's sores. To teach the people to brush their teeth and dig latrines and pray. So one day she goes on a pilgrimage up the river a piece with a whole batch of them because every year fifty old ladies or so are pushed under the water in the crush and drowned. She wanted to *help* them. And you know what happened? Those cats began to panic when a fire broke out on shore, and all those fuzzy-wuzzies began running like crazy. They didn't even stop to say pardon us, ma'am, to the lady missionary. They knocked her down and walked over her and broke her back. She's got a cast from her toes to her ears." Dewey shook his finger at Boyd as he was about to make his point. "So now we say Hitler is the bad guy and Stalin is the good guy. Italy has to be wiped out so that we can save the frog-eating French. You know what the Russians and the French are going to give us for our favors? They're going to walk over us and break our backs."

"So what do you do?"

"Nothing is what you do. You go to Oberlin is what you do. Let the other kiddies do the playing."

Maybe he had something. In the absence of public morality—and sometimes there seemed to be almost none—a man would have to content himself with a private one.

Boyd remembered one of the talks he had with his father before he went overseas. Lucas had said that there simply weren't right sides or wrong sides in a war; if the Germans won, they'd be right; if the Allies did, they would. The victors, he said, always had a way of writing history to justify themselves, so much so that Julius Caesar, as ruthless and as cruel a man as history had produced, a man who brought death and the sword to half of Europe, was now lionized by Miss Hilton's tenth-grade Latin class at Ventry High. One hundred years from now, Luke had continued, Hitler might be known as the man who tried to unite Europe to save it from the East or from itself. There was no telling.

But this war was like no other in history, Luke had told him, because it wasn't a war for land or for mere power. Those tired reasons were secondary. Moreover, it didn't make that much difference if Hitler marched into England or Mussolini into Greece. People would still prevail. As long as they had food, men could endure almost any kind of government; they always had and they always would. If you were hungry, Lucas had said, the only freedom you cared about was the freedom to eat. The other freedoms, such as they were, were self-indulgent ones that could be appreciated only by full-bellied people. And what were they anyway? he had asked Boyd. The freedom to elect spokesmen to the town council, the mayor's office, the governor's, to the Congress, and to the Presidency; yet weren't the same unprincipled, swindling, self-aggrandizing men generally drawn to such offices all over the world, whether you lived in a democracy or in a dictatorship with token elections? The freedom of religion as long as you weren't, in some parts of the country, a Catholic, in others a Jew, and almost everywhere that religion of darkness, a Negro? The freedom to die for a nation of businessmen who saw the war as a profitable way out of the sorrowful chaos and depression into which their deceit had thrown the country? The freedom to think of yourself, first and always, and to hell with the others? Hadn't the founding fathers, Luke had asked, the sense to realize that the greatest failing of a democracy was the selfishness it guaranteed its people?

So, Luke had gone on, all wars were pretty much alike; what was gained in one decade was lost the next; a hero one year was next year's enemy of the people. Yet this war, he had said, was a religious war, one like no other in

153

all history, one between the forces of light and those of darkness. And for the first time in almost endless years, man had at last a moral position behind which he could stand. "Think of France," Luke had said, trying to make it clear for Boyd. "France is occupied. But, except for the hardships imposed by war, do you think life is really all that different for the common Frenchman? Isn't he as divided, as ineffectual, as sensual as he's always been? Perhaps—who knows?—occupation might even raise the French from their centuries-old lethargy. But there *is* a difference over there. What is it?"

Boyd hadn't known. He had certainly read as much about the war as his father, insofar as it was possible in the Ohio press that still allowed as much space for a local automobile accident as for a bombing that killed a thousand people. But, no, he didn't know.

"As long as there's a crust of bread and people aren't actively tormented, there's *no* difference," Luke had explained. "None in the world. In France or in Ventry. The only difference in this war—and the moral position you have to fix yourself behind—is that the Germans would carry away Mr. and Mrs. Levinson if they came to Ventry. That is the difference, Boyd."

Even Mr. Roosevelt, Lucas had said, thought of the war as one more foolish territorial contest, and except for a few sanctimonious remarks, fastidiously worded so as not to offend the anti-Semitic element in the country, was moved to say no more than that America *regretted* what was happening to the Jews. But for Lucas this was the last chance man had to justify himself, his last chance to prove himself worthy of life. If men didn't step forward now and raise their hands in disgust and despair, would it matter if they lived or died? More than ever before, men had now to be of the chivalry of Jesus Christ. The world would have to save the Jews.

Well, it was a point of view so utterly unreal that only a Gavin could have created it. Boyd wasn't sure that his father was right. But as he stood in the water in the river, he turned to Dewey and said, "What about the Jews?"

Dewey shrugged his shoulders. "Don't worry about the Jews. That's one thing they know how to do better than anyone else in the world."

But if you didn't worry about them, who would? God knows, if they were all being put to death, they could no longer worry about themselves. Hadn't even Francine said that the finest and kindest gesture one person could bring to another was worrying about him?

"If," Boyd began, "if you didn't have the deferment—I mean, if you didn't have asthma, you wouldn't even go?"

"I don't know. What you have to do is keep things simple, bub. Like Homer Lane, remember him? He used to come to school without breakfasts and wearing a shirt as dirty as the blackboards. You know why he went into the Army? For some good chow and for a clean shirt. You gotta keep things simple." He laughed. "And while you're waiting, what you gotta do is get laid. Piece in our time. That's the only thing that's important. Get laid for all those poor GIs in the trenches. They'd say, 'We're beholden to you, young fella.' "

"Aw, Dewey, you never take anything serious."

"Yeah, and you're too goddamn morose. You're always shopping around for some Holy Grail. Just like your old man. Well, listen, buster, there's none around. We're clean out. Birth, copulation, and death. I think that's what Eliot said. Maybe not. Anyway, he left out evacuation and wet dreams, but he's got the right ticket. You ever thought how good God was when he fixed us up? He could have switched what-you-call toils. He could have let the broad have all her sweet kicks during childbirth. And let the man go through all the pains during the act of love. You ever thought of that? But God is a buddy. The feller gave us a right nice engine. Hey, I ever tell you how I scored with old Dorothy at the school picnic last spring? Man, it was crazy."

Boyd looked at him doubtfully. "I was with you all the time at the picnic."

"Not *all* the time. Old Dorothy and me, we went for a walk, we did. Right under the principal's nose too. She said, 'Now children, if you want to pick flowers, that's perfectly all right, but don't forget we're going to eat in fifteen minutes.' Man, that was the shortest fifteen minutes in the history of the world. I picked me a flower, I did. What a broad."

"Don't talk that way in front of America's youth," he said, indicating Parnell, whose ears had pricked up. "You'll warp him." Boyd dived under the water, grabbed Dewey by the ankles, pulled him under, and held his head until he began to sputter. When Dewey let his breath out entirely, Boyd let him rise to the top.

"My God, you want to drown me?" Dewey yelled,

155

spitting water and driving a finger into each ear. "I saw stars. Honest-to-God stars."

"What is the stars?" Boyd said, hooting, wondering if Dewey remembered the play they had read aloud in English class during senior year.

"The stars ... is big. And they is quiet. Most of all, they is quiet, bub. And ... they never get laid. The stars is lonely and horny, like me."

"That's because they don't know Dorothy."

"Dorothy is now a knocked-up star, you know that? Her old lady had to put her on the bus to Cleveland so no one could see the belly she was beginning to carry around."

After a while Boyd asked, "Did you do it, Dewey?"

"Me?" Dewey leaned back, floated, then kicked water in Boyd's face. "Hell, no. No one can pin that on me. Anyway, a long time ago, I decided I don't want any kids. You know? Why rake them over the coals? I'd make a lousy father anyway."

"You'd make a good one."

Ignoring him, Dewey went on. "Half the old people I know should never have had kids. Me, I should never have been born. That's very interesting, you know? Some guy, in a couple seconds he makes me. He hates my old lady while he's doing it. He hates me even before I'm born. And then all of a sudden I'm alive!"

"Very profound."

"Very. I'm full of it. And you know what else I'm full of?"

"I could suggest something."

"I'm full of ... I don't know. I've got this real sweet thing in me, bub, that comes right up to where my tongue begins. Trouble is, I don't know what the damn thing is. I say, 'Look, God, old guy, what's this sweet thing Dew Ventry is trying to get out? Give a guy a break. A hint.' That's the way I talk to Him. Real informal. No airs. And old God, He goes right back to his workbench, hands all inky, and He don't know Dew Ventry from Stalin. He don't know D. Ventry from Shirley Temple."

"Let me know when you find out what it is. Maybe you're the playboy of the ages. Maybe you're the Glamor Boy of all time."

"Call me that once more and I'll tie you up by your scruffy balls and hang you from that tree." He sank under the water and made for Boyd's knees, pulling him under the surface, keeping his head under his arm like a football until Boyd began hitting at his chest.

When they rose to the surface, blowing water, Dewey yelled, "We still going out to the Lake tonight and have ourselves a hooley?"

"Sure. Shanty Irish Friday night. My Aunt Cortez is supposed to be coming, but I think I can get out."

"Your fancy aunt!"

"My fancy aunt."

"Wow-eeee!" Flapping his arms, Dewey now floated over in the water, his stomach up. He then peed high into the air, into the sun, straight up, ducking as it came splashing down.

"Christ!" Boyd complained. "I'm not going to swim in this cesspool."

"Gotta remember, we're all brothers, brother."

"Yeah, brother." Boyd turned over, floating too, pointing his belly to the sky, then also peed up into the air. "That the real sweet thing you were talking about?"

Parnell, wild with envy, his head filled with their talk of war and girls, moved from where he was leaning against the bank and lay cautiously on his back in the water. But even before he tried to do the awesome thing they had done—a great geyser, a fountain—he felt a watersnake glide against his neck, and as he did he stopped kneading the water and he sank. When he rose to the surface, pink from the sun and his poison ivy, he removed the wet willow leaf from beneath his ear and hoped that no one had seen his cowardice.

"She won't be coming tonight," Catherine said. "She would have let us know if she was coming this late."

Supper had been held over until six-thirty, an hour when most people in town had already finished the dishes and were sitting on their front porches or hosing their lawns. As the clock on the mantel struck the half hour, Rose had announced, "Well, the roast is ruined. We might as well eat," somehow almost gratified that Cortez, wherever she was, had already begun to interrupt the tranquil flow of life in the house, had already ruined the blackmarket roast, bought without red coupons from the man who supplied the Levinsons with kosher meat. "A cow is a cow," Rose had said about it at the table. "He doesn't know if he's a Jew or a Congregationalist. Eat! All they do anyway is baptize it."

Rose had not, of course, noticed that Catherine had

ironed the curtains and put them back up at the windows, or that the kitchen was clean, or even that the roast was in the oven or the potatoes pared. When she had finally left her bedroom, at almost four o'clock, she walked downstairs to resume her work as if nothing had happened.

"She might have waited until after six to leave," Simon observed. "It's the devil's own work to get out of Cleveland when the shifts change at the war plants." Another day of waiting, another day of merciless house cleaning to be lived through would, he knew, be more than a man could bear.

After he had helped Catherine straighten up the house in the afternoon, Simon had walked to the square and looked at the shelves of the Drug and Notion store, hoping that he might find a nice prewar German or French or Italian wine, but there was none. He then vaguely recalled that Frank Ventry had told him it was as hard to find a good Kraut wine as it was to hear Beethoven over the radio, not because there wasn't any to be had but because shopkeepers were afraid to sell what was in their basements for fear of being thought unpatriotic. Simon had finally settled on a bottle of California sherry, the label rather cheap-looking but the bottle itself pretty and European. Because he didn't want Gerald Davis, the druggist, to think that he was planning anything too special, he also picked up a small tin of aspirin. Perhaps people had hangovers on sherry, and they might come in handy. But as he paid the druggist, the man said brightly, "Hear Cortez Boyd is coming to town." The secrecy lost, the gift now seemed a little spoiled. He had meant for it to be a surprise—a little sherry before dinner—but the druggist, he knew, had probably already told every second customer that the Gavins were having sherry in honor of Cortez's visit. The bottle was still unopened, still in its brown paper sack in the hall closet.

"Well, it's just like her not to tell us anything," Rose now said. The second note they received from her, delivered only that afternoon, had said, "My darlings! I arrive on Friday. Don't plan to do a *thing* for me. I intend to wait on *you!* I'm bringing my ration books. Do you need extra sugar? Oceans of love, Cortez." As Catherine said, and truthfully, Friday was twenty-four hours long, and it was a pity she couldn't have narrowed down her arrival more exactly. When Boyd read the note, he said to Parnell, "Oceans of sugar," but the inference, such as it was,

was lost. Of the family, only Boyd and Rose thought that Cortez might be too sweet to be believed.

Simon sat in the parlor waiting. Except for Boyd, who was upstairs sprucing himself up to go out to the Lake, the family was with him, Rose on her lady's chair, Catherine on the sofa, and Parnell on the floor looking through his Russo-Japanese War atrocity pictures with great relish, placing all the pictures of degutted Japs in one pile and those of degutted Russians in a second.

As for Simon, he could scarcely keep his fingers from tapping against the walnut hands of his velvet chair. He always looked forward to having Cortez around the house. She was permissive in a way Rose could never be, actually encouraging his mind to wander and to relive the past. While Rose's conversation was more or less limited to someone's cancer, someone else's hysterectomy, or to the state of moral decay in the world, Cortez would as soon repeat, pretty much verbatim, a talk she had had with Simon perhaps fifty years ago. She would remind him of the afternoon Simon had chiseled their wet footprints into a large boulder in the gulf, footprints that were later discovered by a professor of American History at Western Reserve University and ascribed to the Iroquois Indians. It was a huge joke, though Rose, of course, thought that the two of them were helping to pervert scholarship.

Yes, it would be good to have Cortez around the house for a while. She tended to loosen Simon's memory, to uncover not only the pleasurable things they had done together when they were young, but events that triggered still other adventures of his own. He could remember— "Ah, that was a rare time"—when he was still a man, and not the genderless thing he'd become, the full horror of which hadn't been revealed to him until he was in the veterans' hospital in Erie two years before and found that it was less tiring to squat in order to urinate than to stand. At the time, healing from an operation, Simon had decided that death would be preferable. He had made up his mind to eschew the bedpan once and for all, shocking all the nurses when he told them what they could do with it, pushing them out of his way helter-skelter, telling them he'd give each one of them a good clout if they tried to stop him, and then half falling, gasping for breath, to the lavatory, but *standing* once he got there, the white urinal a shrine, a temple to his youth.

What specifically did Cortez help him recall? Sad to

say, his wantonness mostly, for which his prostate had paid dearly. When Rose suggested that he was surrounded by sporting women on all of his trips, she was wrong, but not entirely. He was surrounded by them at all times. But only the memories of women he'd sported with. Grand, lovely, savage, insatiable women—in San Francisco, in Manila, in Hong Kong. Women whose lust had actually been enlarged, rather than diminished, by time, so that Simon, by himself on the porch swing or in the parlor, would muse, "Well, by God, was that five times between midnight and morning with that Carmencita in Manila, or was it six?" when in fact it had only been twice. What was truly marvelous was that the women in his mind never grew old, and neither did Simon when his fancy brought him to relive episodes. He would, late at night in the parlor, again meet the red-haired girl in San Francisco the night before his ship sailed to the Far East, would strike up yet another provocative conversation with her, would go back to her shabby room, and then—the wonder of it—see himself, not as he now was but as he used to be, strong and strapping and bold, walk into her room with her. Sometimes, as he sat in his chair, he was unable to withhold a short, joyous sigh. At which time Rose, in her bedroom over his head, would begin thumping the floor with her shoe, as if aware that he was keeping company with someone.

As he *was* keeping company. He knew for a fact that an hour spent in the arms of his Filipino girl, dark and smelling as ripe as a musk melon, was better than any medicine Dr. Herron could give him. It brought the wildness back into his eyes and the ginger to his blood.

Yet, during the past year, Simon had found it harder and harder to call up the past. Sometimes, while trying, he would even become confused. Lying in the arms of a woman he had known years ago, he would see that his face had already begun to age—that he had brought a thirty-eight-year-old face to his twenty-year-old task. Or he would watch himself walk again through the lobby of the Palace Hotel in San Francisco, lean and handsome in his uniform, but then notice the rheumatic limp in his right leg which hadn't appeared until he was well past fifty. It almost seemed to Simon that old age was reaching into his dreams. He needed the nourishment and the rebirth and the buoyancy that Cortez could give him.

Rose, reading his thoughts more accurately than the

newspaper, turned to him and said, "Now, I want you to act your age. Don't get any notions that Cortez is coming down here to amuse you and no one else."

"*Mother*," Catherine said in desperation.

"Well, they're thick as thieves."

Catherine said, "Did you hear where the government bought Mr. Hershey's farm out on County Line Road? I heard it down at the store. I can't imagine what the government's thinking."

"It's about time," Rose answered. "I saw the surveyors in town the other day, and I was about to run up to them and ask them when they're going to start digging around here. My property is smack-bang in the path of the canal. But didn't they get into their trucks before I got off the curb?"

Rose's property—the old Boyd farm—was on Phelps Creek about three miles from town, and it lay, so Rose said, in the proposed route of the Lake Erie to Youngstown Canal, a project which had been talked about since the early twenties. Other than the corps of engineers, which periodically received another one hundred thousand dollars to determine if the canal was still practical, the only one who seemed to derive any pleasure from it was Rose. She was going to hold on to her land until she got the right price for it, even if necessary forcing the government to detour *around* it if she thought she was being cheated. When Simon had tried to explain the right of eminent domain to her, she had said, "Eminent domain, shoo! That land is worth a fortune."

"I don't think it's the same thing, Mother," Catherine suggested.

"Of course it is. The *Plain Dealer* printed a map with the canal route as clear as day. And you could see right where Mama's old house is."

"The government's not going to build a canal when there's a war to be won," Simon said.

"I'm not as close to the government as *some* people," Rose said meaningfully to Catherine, "but those mills in Youngstown need water, and they'll have to go right over Mama's house to get it."

"I heard today down on the square that it's not the canal at all. It's going to be some kind of chemical plant. At least, that's what Joe Hershey's been saying." Simon hadn't been able to hide his contempt when he talked to the man. For all his lordly notions of war, he hated for it

161

to bring changes to Ventry. A war plant near town seemed to him to be the first step toward the total destruction of the place.

"This government man drove up one day and began to talk to Joe. He said it was a right nice place Joe had, and then asked him if he'd ever considered selling it. 'Why, no,' Joe said. So the government man said, 'What price do you think you'd want for it if you ever did?' So Joe said the first damn thing that came to his mind—'Enough to buy Public Square in Cleveland'—and the man said, '*Sold.*' It took about five minutes. Of course, they must have been out looking at the place before then."

"I suppose they have to do things in a hurry," Catherine observed, playing with the empty teacup in her hand, listening to Boyd empty the water from the tub upstairs. Parnell was now on the front lawn where anxiety had drawn him; he was sitting high in the tree, dressed in his clean clothes, talking to himself. As soon as the Lincoln turned the corner onto Priest Street, his mother knew that he would shout, "She's here!"

"Well," Rose went on, "I always said that this town would wake up sooner or later. You can't stop progress. A lot of old people around here would just as soon we stay the way we are, fifty years behind the times. I for one think that a change would do us good." She seemed to be reflecting. "Why, take what happened back in the 1860s. My own mama told it again and again. This town was so busy they were sleeping six people to a room at the old hotel—the Coal & Feed store now. The stories of what went on there! A regular boom town it was. Everyone thought it was going to be another Cleveland. Land's sake! And then if four or five old fuddy-duddies who owned most of the land didn't get together and decide not to sell any to the railroad because they didn't want the trains running through their fields. They said the trains would put the cows off their *milk!* Why, this town just died." She stomped her foot on the floor to indicate how quickly it had happened. "And my own mama was the one who said they all expected it to be another Cleveland."

Well, Simon was glad that it wasn't. You could take all your Clevelands in the world, all your New Yorks and Chicagos, and float them out to the middle of some ocean and sink them. Maybe Ventry was old-fashioned and settled in its ways, but at least a man didn't have to look at junk yards filled with wrecked automobiles. The children

162

didn't have to go to schools that rose out of concrete pavements with not even a blade of grass or a tree in sight. When a man died he didn't have to be buried in a city cemetery next to a factory, a fine grit of smoke and dirt covering the very name on his tombstone. Hell, they could have all that. And their chemical plants too. Chemicals to mutilate and maim people? Wasn't life maiming enough without finding new ways to do it? Simon hoped that someone in Washington would realize before it was too late that Ventry, Ohio, was no place for a war plant. It would only bring unhappiness. New people coming to town, the kind of people who lived in houses without front porches. New problems, the kind of problems they'd want to strut down the street. New faces, faces of people who were too busy to stop to talk to a man. No, they could keep all that. Those high and mighty men in Washington asked too much. First to take a man's son away. And then to take his town. No, by God, Simon would ... by God, Simon would tell the President himself. *You ask too much.*

It was Catherine who saw his face whiten. "Are you sick, Father?" She left the sofa and walked toward him.

But Simon recovered himself. "No, not sick."

Rose, too, left her place and nervously adjusted the pictures on the mantel. "Well, if she comes tonight," she began, again avoiding her sister's name, "she can't expect me to feed her."

In the front seat of Dewey's car, its tank half filled with blackmarket gas Dew had bought at a station outside of town at double the price of rationed gasoline, Boyd sat uncomfortably straight, his back away from the seat, holding his knees with his warm hands. Even while he was leaving the house, his legs had begun to tremble. And Francine, whom he talked with for a minute in the Ventry parlor, had been close-mouthed and prim, succeeding, whether it was her intention or not, in making Boyd already feel guilty and increasing the tremor in his knees. As they backed the car out of the gravel driveway, he had seen Tina looking at him through the window, the lace curtain held up to one side by her hand, watching the car until it turned the corner of Priest Street, as if she, too, was aware that she was being left out of something important.

Not until they reached County Line Road, heading north to the Lake, did Boyd even begin to feel at ease.

Next to Dewey, who drove confidently, as if all he needed was a wheel in his hands to assert himself, he watched the farmhouses pass, small, run-down Greek Revival places most of them, yet still noble and lofty, standing in cornfields, wheatfields, and orchards like monuments left by some mad but gifted sculptor. Whoever had designed them had decided that what was fitting for a high hill in Athens was also fitting for Bobcat Valley, through which Dewey drove the car, slowing at the curves and the *Jesus Saves* signs there. And in a curious way the houses were a success. They didn't provide shelter so much as order and grandeur, as if the pioneers had tried to bring these into the wilderness too, an order and grandeur that got no farther west than Ohio, for farmhouses in Indiana and Illinois, Simon had once told Boyd, looked as if they had been pieced together by idiot children.

As they drove north, getting closer to the Lake, the tenor of the countryside changed. New, small, brightly painted houses came into view. It was here, no more than six miles from Ventry, that there were people, Simon said, who put birdbaths and plaster ducks in their front yards, who painted the rocks by the entrance to their driveways a glaring white, and who even—the Lord forbid—strung lighted St. Nicks and bulb-nosed reindeer over the roofs of their houses at Christmas. Here, about two miles from the Lake, lived people cautiously described by Rose as "fast." There were institutions that catered to their fastness. Roadhouses: Pig in the Blanket, Ernie's Chili House, or Chicken Anyway, Anyhow, Any Time. And motels, clusters of cabins; Nitey-Nite, Land o' Dreams, and Rest Yer Tired Bones. Some citizens of Ventry had thought that the latter were used by tired travelers until they read that a married woman had accidentally burned herself to death on a flaming mattress with a dry-goods salesman she had met at Chicken Anyway and carried off to Rest Yer Tired Bones, as she more or less had.

They passed through a small town, about five times the size of Ventry, where, it was commonly said, you couldn't walk down Main Street with your wallet in your back pocket. Here lived the embezzlers who periodically disappeared with Ventry County's tax receipts, and bank clerks who ran away with spotted girls from behind soda fountains. Dentists who waited until young girls were under gas to unbutton their swiss-cotton blouses and then yank bloody teeth from their mouths, fondling with one arm and pulling with the other. Doctors who were alcoholics or dope fiends and who put old ladies to sleep in order to collect their insurance. Grown men who walked down Main Street at midnight in high-heeled shoes and in their wives' discarded house dresses. Women who ran naked through department stores, wearing nothing but the purses in their hands, and were then carted off to state hospitals. A police chief who every day exposed himself before his window at City Hall when the three-thirty school bus paused on the street to make a turn. Mayors and city managers and judges who were involved with the numbers racket, who were living in houses no one making their salaries could afford, and who coaxed drum majorettes into the white slavery trade. There was no end to it. People in Ventry talked often about the northern section of the county, partly because they had so little else to talk about, and they were relieved that hills and cornlands separated them from this land of Cain. Yet as they listened to a description of some newly discovered depravity, generally untrue, their rocking chairs quickened.

No one had expected that even the war would sober the resort town which Dewey and Boyd were now approaching. Three years before, a new county medical officer had reported that his sampling of offshore water at Arcola showed it to be polluted to an unthinkable degree with polio, meningitis, and several other of the viruses that live on the dark side of life. It was enough to frighten any town that made its living on summer tourists. Yet instead of being heaped with rewards, the doctor was called a trouble-maker and lost his job. Ironically, of the four cases of polio that summer, three had been traced to a Baptist Sunday school picnic, far away from the Lake, and the fourth occurred in Ventry to a girl who had never done anything more blameful than read Big Little Books on her porch swing.

Of Arcola Beach, Rose said that it was different from what it used to be, by which she meant it was getting worse. Back in the thirties, those who could afford it sometimes went out there to listen to a band—Harry James had been there when he was still unknown, and it was said rather proudly that a local girl had almost run off with one of his trombonists—and to dance, drink a few orange pops, buy a dozen doughnuts, and return home before midnight. But since the war, said Rose, "the lower orders" discovered the place—white-faced girls who worked as secretaries in Cleveland and Youngstown, or as store clerks, or in war plants, who came to the resort to meet dark-haired, foreign-looking young men, Poles and Czechs from the same cities, who for one reason or another hadn't been drafted. On weekends the cottages along the lake front were always crowded, and on the following Monday the county newspaper printed accounts of motorcyclists who had gone through plate-glass windows, brawls in front of bars, and girls arrested for vagrancy because they were sleeping, not always alone, on the breakwall.

"So with most of the he-men in the Army," Dewey was explaining, "and just these stoop-shouldered little draft dodgers around, the girls have what the French call le pants hot. They work all week in factories, wearing their pinkies to the bone, trying to get another 'E' flag, and then they come out here to sit on the devil's lap. It's the greatest, dad."

"How can you tell ... if they will?" To Boyd it seemed that it must have been a question asked at Delphi. He rather wished that he had enough money to go into Cleveland, the way Howard Foster did when he was feeling horny. He wasn't sure that he could ever talk a girl, especially a stranger, into it.

"You'll know, buddy. They don't wear yeller badges on their chests, but you know," Dewey answered in a quick, sensual way. "Look, you're not chickening out, are you?"

"Christ, no, I'm all for it."

Dewey honked the horn of the car three times, emphasizing his pleasure, then pulled hard at the wheel to round the final curve that led into Arcola.

War or no war, the street wasn't observing the dim-out. It was bright with neon signs and it was singing with noise. Driving slowly down the main street now, looking for a place to park, they could see the crowded dance halls, the shooting galleries, the barbecue stands, souvenir shops, bars with people lined up outside, and the boardwalk heavy with men and women in their twenties and thirties, dressed in shorts or slacks, fancy dresses or suits, a few in zoot suits, and many still wearing their bathing trunks. At the end of the street, under a grove of trees, Dewey brought the car over into a free space and they got out.

On the street, Dewey seemed to become more apprehensive. "How about a drink first, bub? It'll bring out the man in you." Boyd nodded his head, thinking that a drink or two might at least steady his knees—he could bring out the man himself—and Dewey led him toward a bar. Before the war the place had been a Tyrolean chalet, but he saw that it had become Pennsylvania Dutch, even with a few hex signs painted over the still vaguely blue Lowenbrau emblems. A man at the door looked at them without much interest, and either decided that they were old enough to get drunk or that they wouldn't cause any trouble, and waved them in. Once they were inside, an Americanized beer band—in some syndicate's idea of a Pennsylvania Dutch costume—exploded in a polka, and the whole building began to creak and sway. In the confusion Boyd and Dewey inched their way to the end of a long bar where each of them ordered a Tom Collins, the only mixed drink either had heard of, and then turned to look at the dance floor.

There were as many girls dancing with each other as there were men and women, crazily jitterbugging, their teeth shaking in their heads, sweat spilling down their arms, and their feet sliding in and out of huaraches, a kind of squeaky, straw half shoe that had become the rage the spring before because of the leather shortage.

"Who says war is hell?" Dew shouted above the noise.

"Look at 'em. Looks like someone opened the gates of a girls' penitentiary. There are hundreds of them, buddy. It's the Promised Land."

Well, it looked almost too good to be true. He could see that there were girls everywhere, some still white from working in sunless war plants, some with new sunburns shining through their wet faces, all of them apparently happy to forget that they had to go back to work on Monday or even that there was a war. As for the men, they did look runty, as Dewey said, though the runtiness was sometimes covered by wide-shouldered plaid suits, long watch chains falling down past their crotches to their pegged trousers. Not much competition there, he thought. He scanned the room a second time, wondering if he could find someone he knew from town, but there was no one. Ventry was inland only a few miles, already half asleep, people dozing in chairs on their front porches or listening to the nine o'clock news. Here before him were people from the cities whose eyes looked as if they had never known sleep.

"There," Dewey now said, ramming his elbow into Boyd's side. "Over there. See those two chicks?"

"Where?"

"Over there." He pointed with the drink in his hand. "See the one in the white shorts?"

Boyd looked. She was dancing with another girl, her hair was black and long, and her chest was bouncing as she danced, as if she were wearing nothing but skin under her blouse. She may have been a little drunk—at least the stare from her eyes that he now met with his own was aggressive and unashamed—but she didn't look bad. "Nice," he said at last. "You take the other one?"

Dewey watched the two of them silently, as if he were making up his mind, then turned back to the bar. "Maybe we should try another place. Shop around a bit. A man shouldn't put his money on the first thing he sees."

"She looks great to me," Boyd replied, studying the second girl. She was taller than the girl in shorts, brown-haired, rather pretty-faced, with a nice body and nice legs. She jitterbugged less selfconsciously than the other, letting her hands play in the air as she broke away from the black-haired girl and twirled by herself on the crowded dance floor, shaking her behind in the general direction of the bar.

"She's a dog," Dewey said unexpectedly.

"Like hell. She's got a crazy ass."

"Not as crazy as your girl's."

Half impatiently Boyd asked, "You want mine?" then realized that she wasn't his to give away. The look she had given him—well, that was his, he supposed, but it didn't mean that she wasn't with a man back at one of the tables. For some reason, Dewey had decided to play hard to please.

"Naw," he said finally. "Mine's okay. But let's have another drink first. Christ, just lookin at 'em is like walking over a field full of titties. It gives a man a thirst."

Under Dewey's tan, Boyd thought he saw a paleness in his face. Was he, by God, as scared as Boyd was? Maybe, Boyd thought, he was doing it just to bolster Boyd's own confidence. Hell, Dew was an old hand at this.

When their new drinks arrived, they sipped, waiting for the next dance to begin, hoping that it would be a slow Ventry shuffle. And they watched the girls return to their table, where they were, thank God, alone, and where they too began to nurse their drinks. The dark-haired girl occasionally turned to look back at the bar. As another tune struck up—"Sweet and Lovely" it was, jazzed up a bit by the band, but still slow—the girls rose from the table and moved again out onto the dance floor. "Now or never," Boyd said to his friend, and Dew answered, "Now it is," and then heaved a deep breath. They pushed their way past couples dancing, stood behind the two girls for a second, and then asked them if they'd care to dance. They cared. They both smiled and said yes.

In his arms now, Boyd saw that the girl in white shorts had benefited by the diffused lighting in the room. High on her cheek there was a scar, as if she'd been in an accident, close enough to one of her eyes to pull at the bottom lid and give it a surly look. He could also see that the scar was caked with make-up, a lighter shade than her new sunburn. If he had seen her on the street, he wouldn't have looked twice. Still, she had a nice body, and he could feel it against his own as he asked her what her name was.

"Norma. What's yours?"

When she spoke, Boyd knew that he would go to bed with her. Her last name was safe at home in Cleveland or Youngstown. All she had carried with her for the weekend was pressing into Boyd as they danced.

"Simon," he said, not quite knowing why. Then, because he felt obliged to say something else, "You're very pretty, Norma. My friend and I were watching you."

In what seemed to be thanks, the girl moved even closer to him, her body undulating with the music, digging into his. He moved his face into her hair—it smelled nice and clean and full of sun—and then, very quickly, touched her ear with his tongue. Old Dew's trick. There was a kind of half-uttered purr from her throat, so he knew she liked it.

They danced the next dance together too, and then went back to the table. Dewey, looking a little odd, was already there with his girl, and when Boyd saw her up close he wished he'd chosen her instead. On some people you could see sex on their faces, as if in their eyes and on their lips they were exposing some deeper, hidden private part. Dew's girl looked that way. And Dewey must have seen it too, because he had circled his arm around her chair and was resting it on top of her bare shoulders.

After they ordered another round of drinks, Boyd tried to calculate if the money his grandfather had given him would see him through the night. Even as he placed it on the table, he felt a little ashamed of himself for using Simon's pension money on a girl he hoped to go to bed with, and he wondered what Simon would think. But, no, Simon had probably done pretty much the same thing when he was young. Perhaps even Luke had before he got married. Half to soothe his conscience and half to extend what money he had, he ordered a Coke when it was time for another round.

Norma said, "I shouldn't be drinking either. It upsets my stomach."

Boyd thought he might as well see how gamy she was. "Your stomach looks fine from here," he said quietly, then put his hand under the red-checked cloth of the table, resting it on her lap.

"My mother told me about boys like you," she answered, but made no attempt to remove his hand. She looked to Boyd as if she might be able to tell her mother a few things.

"Doris says they have a cottage around here," Dewey said brightly. "They're down here for the whole week."

"We've had our reservations in since last June," Doris explained. "Someone we know in the plant, her folks own it and they let it out. All we could get was a week."

"Talk about war profiteers," Norma said. "We're paying fifty dollars for seven days. Say there are people here every week all summer, what does that add up to? They could pay for the place with the rent they get in one summer. Some favor they did us. And you should have seen how we had to brown-nose around this girl to get a week."

Well, at least her vocabulary was emancipated, Boyd decided. And that wasn't all, because he could now feel her squeeze her legs around his hand where it had fallen into the dip of her lap. He withdrew it, bringing it up higher. Christ-a-mighty, he said to himself, hoping he could calm down before they got up from the table.

"But it's a mess," Doris said. "If our mothers ever saw it, they'd scream."

Norma apparently thought this was very funny, because she now began a laughing jag that ended only when Doris told her that she was drinking too much. It finally occurred to Boyd that she probably was, and that if he didn't get her out of the place pronto she might slip under the table. "How would you girls like to go for a walk along the beach?" he asked. "I mean, if the place is a mess, all we could do is go for a walk."

It took Norma only a few seconds to make up her mind. Over her shoulders she slipped the sweater that had been hanging from the back of her chair, then began to rise, smoothing out her shorts with her hand as soon as Boyd removed his own. Strangely—Boyd couldn't imagine what she expected to find—she looked down to see if everything was in order.

"It's a mess," the other girl repeated, getting up from her own chair. "And all we're going to do is go for a walk. You have to promise not to get fresh or anything."

"Promise," Dew said, winking. "We're in training anyway."

"Norma, ask him what he's in training for."

"That, baby," Dew said, "is strictly confidential. Haven't you heard that the enemy is listening?"

"Some enemy," Doris answered, leaving the table now. "Give us a minute to powder our noses. Norma, do you have to powder your nose?"

"I have to powder my something," Norma replied, giggling again, walking after the other girl. As Boyd followed them, he could see that Norma was either still swaying to the music or giddy from booze.

"We'll get some beer to take with us," Boyd said as the girls made their way toward a door marked *Hers*. "We'll meet you out in front in a couple minutes."

"Roger and out," Doris said, swinging through the door.

The other girl muttered something about keeping Roger where he belonged, giggled a bit more, then went through the door behind her friend. Dewey and Boyd pushed their way through the crowd to the bar where they ordered six bottles of Budweiser to go. "Well, they're not exactly what I'd call the clean-cut Girl Scout type," Boyd observed. They were, he knew, out tonight for the same reason he and Dewey were. They were lonely. Shallow perhaps, but, hell, even shallow people had to get lonely sometimes.

"Boy, do they have class," Dewey replied. "Good breeding all over 'em."

"I like their names. Their mothers must have named them after seeing a Jane Withers movie. By the way, for the rest of the campaign, I'm Simon in case you get confused."

"You think she'll find out you're the prince of Lichtenstein and try to blackmail you?"

"Blackmail, hell. All I want to do is get her home before she passes out. You see how wobbly she is?"

"I thought she was just waving her can. You think she's got a Mexican jumping bean in there? Boy, these broads go wild when they come out here. All by themselves. Not enough stud to go around so they booze it up. They'll make great mothers. PTA and all that jazz. Old Doris says she used to be a pompon twirler with the East High band. How come all pompon twirlers come to evil ends?"

"I'll ask around."

"You see what that cat was doing back there, under the table? She was giving me the old feel. No pig in the poke for her. No Jake Barnes for that broad. She don't go for sentiment."

After the bartender handed them their sacked beer, Dewey said, "It's on me. Courtesy of the old man. He'd be proud of me if he could see me now. Good and depraved. Scatterin' the wild oats. A little oat here, a little oat there. A man's birthright, by gum. 'Doris, old crater, you're everything a man could grope for.' "

"You think we need anything to protect us from a social disease?"

"These girls aren't amateurs. They probably pass out pro kits."

"We better get something. I want to use the Gents anyway."

Inside the head, a poster over the urinal said *Ohio's Vacationland*. Dewey put several coins in a machine and pulled out a package. "They think of everything for a nice vacation," he said, handing Boyd one of the tin-foiled packages. "That's what I call accommodating."

Boyd put the rubber in his pocket, then stepped gingerly over to the urinal, flooded and clogged with cigarettes and last night's vomit. Dew used the second one, and they kept their heads in front of them because it was fruity to look anywhere except at the wall. "Are you okay?" Boyd finally asked.

"Sure. Don't you worry about this guy." He adjusted the bag under his arm and zipped up his pants.

The girls, fresh powder on their sunburned faces, were waiting by the door when they got there, and Norma took Boyd's arm as they began to walk down the street. She seemed to be leading. "God," she said at last, "it's good to be out in the air. Doris and I work at Alcoa in Cleveland, and all we think about all year is going on vacation."

"It must be tough," Boyd said honestly. "I mean, all the guys you know are probably in the Army or Navy."

"You should see the men working with us. Some of them are around sixty years old. They all look like Lionel Barrymore. And if you think that makes them tame, you've got another think coming. There's this one man who works with me, he's always trying to get in a pinch." She giggled a little, then turned down a side street.

"I thought we weren't going to the cottage," Doris said from behind them.

"Don't be a party pooper," Norma replied. "They won't mind if it's messy, will you?" Boyd said nothing, his silence indicating that he wouldn't mind one bit, and behind him Dewey was quiet too. Boyd could make out words that came from time to time from Doris's mouth, but Dewey limited himself to an occasional Yeah or Naw. Probably scared sweatless, Boyd decided, grinning.

As they walked down the unlighted street, passing ugly little cottages with peeling paint, Norma leaned heavily on Boyd's arm, and a few times he prevented her from falling. Most of the places they walked by had names hand-lettered on wooden signs at the steps, all suggestive. *Three Girls in a Bed. Man Reposed.* And *Acres of Belly.* Norma, too, had become quiet. Suddenly she asked, "Do you mind my scar?"

She had asked the question timidly, and it was the first thing she uttered that indicated there might be more to her than giggles. "What scar?" Boyd answered.

"Oh," she replied, then held on to his arm more tightly. "I'm glad you didn't notice it. A lot of people do. A new girl at the plant came up to me once and said, 'Oh, you must have had a terrible accident.' I went into the john and cried."

"You're very pretty, Norma," he said, lying, but not minding the lie this time.

"I *was* in an accident," she went on. "It was when I was fourteen, and I used to date ... well, this will make you mad, but I dated a colored boy. There are a lot of them at East High."

"That doesn't make me mad."

"He had an old Chevy, and we used to go for rides— and things. I liked him a lot. He was very different, do you know what I mean? Some people, they say you should never even talk to them, but he was very nice most of the time. Only he drank a lot. That's how we had the accident."

"In the car?"

"It wasn't even much of an accident. He didn't even get hurt. We just went off the road. He didn't even get hurt, but I broke the windshield. My face. It was all bloody, and there was glass where the scar is now. I just screamed when I felt it. Anyway, he never even came to see me. In the hospital or anything. Did you ever think people could be so mean?"

Oh, God, he wished she hadn't said anything about it. He wished she had stayed the implement he wanted her to be, full of giggles and stupidity. Oh, God, what was he supposed to do now?

"I don't mean you have to be nice to me or anything," she said at last. "I just thought you'd like to know."

And would she do this all her life? Giving her body away but insisting that the scar went with the package? Well, if she did she was barking up the wrong tree. You couldn't get anyone to like you just by parading your infirmities. Hell, he didn't want to know her that way. He didn't want to know what made her an easy lay. Why in hell did she have to apologize for it anyway? She had probably been humping around with the colored fellow even before she went through the windshield, except now she did it with more people. If she had chosen him, as she pretty much had, to help her obliterate things, she sure as hell didn't have to tell him why. Did she expect him to kiss the goddamn thing?

"I didn't even notice it," he said, and they continued to walk along silently, listening to the footsteps behind them.

Norma had apparently decided that she was being too earnest, because she now began to brighten. At a small brick walk, she turned and led them onto the porch of a cottage, then fumbled for a few minutes with her key. "I don't know why we bother locking the place. Doris and I didn't bring anything with us except a few dresses and our bathing suits. It's a mess. We just sat around here last night and got plastered. You'll probably think we're terrible. I'm sort of plastered right now."

"Norma doesn't know how to drink," Doris said from behind her. "I keep telling her you're supposed to sip."

Norma didn't want what you could get from sipping. She wanted what she had. And as Boyd watched her walk

174

into the dark room and snap on a light, he guessed that she had probably been boozing it up since supper, and right now she was flying. As soon as the light was on, she sat down on the sofa.

The place was small, Boyd saw, and it wasn't going to be easy. Dewey's girl said, "The bedroom's mine. That's because I'm paying more rent than Norma. She sleeps on the couch. It pulls out." She went into the kitchen, carrying the paper sack which she had removed from Dewey's arms, leaving the three of them in the tiny room, clothes scattered here and there, movie magazines on the floor, a half-empty bottle of blended whiskey on the maple coffee table, and ash trays spilling over with butts. Dewey had still not said anything, and he didn't move at all until Boyd gave him the sign to go into the kitchen after Doris. But as he did, as though he were sleepwalking, Doris returned to the room, carrying four opened bottles of beer next to her chest. She placed two of them on the ash-strewn table before the couch and then, without saying a word, walked into the bedroom with the remaining two. Dewey shrugged his shoulders once, looked at Boyd, then followed her, closing the door after him.

"I hope you don't think we invite everyone out here," Norma said. She lay back on the couch, and in a minute Boyd went over and sat next to her on the floor, watching her kick off her straw shoes.

"I'm just glad you invited me," he said. "Do you want a beer?"

"Oh, God, no. My head is already spinning."

"I can get it to spin good and proper." That, of course, was probably all she expected. When she told him her goddamn story, maybe what she wanted from him wasn't pity but a good spinning. Well, hell, why not? It takes two to obliterate. He reached up with his arms and rested them around her, then climbed onto the couch beside her. As he bent over to switch off the lamp she pulled back his arm.

"Leave the light on," she said. "I like to see."

If she liked to see, that meant she'd seen it all before. Boyd decided that he didn't have to go slow, and that she didn't want him to. Beside her, he brought his face up to hers, trying to avoid the scar, moving over her mouth, kissing it, then opening it and finding her tongue, tasting the sour, boozy taste there. As he did, he reached down with one arm and slid it up her shorts. She had nothing on, not even panties, beneath them. And she was already wet, as if it had happened back in the bar while his hand was there or while they were walking home. Oh, Christ!

She moved her mouth from his only long enough to say, "Zipper," and he found it on the side of her shorts, drawing it down, pulling her shorts past her knees and off. As he did, a small sound came from her mouth, and then her hand felt him, unbuttoned his trousers, and drew him out. He thought he was going to pop. She stretched back on the couch while he slipped her blouse off, then slid out of his own clothes, throwing them on the floor. Not until then did he remember the package in his pocket. He reached down for it, peeled it open, then got it on. "Do it with your hand more first," she said. She brought his hand back down to her. "Oh, that's so good. You don't know how good that is. Oh, God." In a minute he climbed on her, burying his face in her breasts, and she dug her nails into his back; deliberately he moved inside her. "Wait for me to come. Don't come without me. Don't go too fast. Go slow. I can come. I always come. But don't go too fast. Go slow. Oh, my God."

She moved her legs around him, grabbing him, driving him in farther, and her breath was coming in long aching sounds that could be heard all over the room. She threw back her head, twisted it from side to side, and moved her body with his as he began to ride her slowly, the sounds becoming louder and louder. And then—so quickly that Boyd didn't know what was happening—she became still. "Oh, no. Oh, no," she said, and then a sob came from her throat, as if she were gasping for breath, no longer responding as he stroked her, riding her lifeless body. Suddenly she sat up, pushed Boyd to one side, a sucking noise at her belly as she did, then pulled herself free, fighting for breath, and jumped off the sofa, stumbled over Boyd's clothes on the floor, and ran across the room. Even before the door of the bathroom was slammed shut, he could hear her vomiting.

Boyd felt himself sink every time the retch began in her throat and spewed from her mouth. Sitting on the side of the couch now, he looked down at his own body and saw the useless thing before him. He began to laugh softly, too hurt to do anything else; then the laughter broke wildly from his mouth and he could hear it in the room.

From the bedroom the other girl began to shout. "You

son of a bitch. You cheap, lying son of a bitch." Doris flew through the door and into the living room, naked and half hysterical. Boyd looked at her sullenly, too disappointed to care what the hell was eating her. She seemed crazy, her eyes like eyes he had never seen before. She ran up to him and grabbed the still quivering thing before him, then stooped, rubbing it against her belly. "Please," she said, pulling it toward her, then half falling on the sofa. "Hurry."

"Where's Dewey?"

"Please. Please."

"I said where the hell's Dewey?"

Yelling now, drawing Boyd back onto her, she said, "If you mean your friend, he's in there crying."

Boyd caught his breath as he heard the words. He tried to take the girl's hand away from him, but she wouldn't let go. She grabbed a hold of it with her two hands, and as she did he leaned over and lightly struck her across the face. Then, not knowing why, he struck her again, until she started to scream Norma's name. He picked up his clothes from the floor and went into the bedroom, where he found Dewey, crouched on the bed, bent over as small as he could get, his shoulders shaking.

"Come on, Dew. The hooley's over. We're going home."

He had his pants on before he realized that he was still wearing the condom. He helped Dewey into his clothes, then out of the room, past the bathroom, where Norma was dry-heaving, past the other girl on the edge of the sofa, holding her breasts as if they pained her, yelling at them, screaming, and then onto the street and back to the car.

"She's here!"

The black Lincoln slowly turned onto Priest, moving along at a stately, unhurried pace. Before Parnell scurried down the trunk of the tree, he could see his aunt in the back seat lean over and say something to her driver. A second later and its horn sounded twice. Cortez brought her gloved hands together before her in a silent clap. As for the driver, Parnell had never in his life known anyone more haughty and aristocratic than Harold, a veritable African king. He wore a black Brooks Brothers suit because Cortez thought that a uniform was demeaning, and

177

he always carried a work handkerchief in one of his pockets to wipe smudges off the car when it was at rest.

It stopped halfway up the drive where there were no trees and where no droppings could reach it, and Cortez tumbled out the back door before Harold had left his seat. She stood for a moment on the lawn, looking at the house, stretching out her arms for Parnell to run into them, and shouting, "I'm home, everyone!"

From within the house a painful sound of acknowledgment from Rose's throat could now be heard, and the family ran onto the porch and down the steps to the grass, Rose alone remaining behind the screen door. "Not there, honey," Cortez said to Parnell as he attempted to kiss her. "You'll spoil my lips. You can kiss me up on my forehead though. There! That's a good boy. Simon! Catherine! Oh, my darlings, I'm *home.*"

As she was, and no one—not even the Ventrys, who were watching her through their windows—needed reminding. For less than a minute later she began to assign tasks. Harold was withdrawing luggage from the trunk, and Simon was asked to help him carry it into the hall. Catherine found herself with three furs—two wraps, she supposed they would be called, and one full-length, hot-looking mink. Parnell had reached into the back seat for the large, antique jewelry box which Cortez carried with her everywhere, picked it up, and then felt his aunt raise it from his hands. "No, no, my lamb. Let your foolish old Aunt Cortez carry that. Here, you help get those pretty little boxes into the house."

When Cortez called herself foolish and old, she didn't mean to suggest that she was either; she said it to give her beauty bas-relief. She left the impression of foolishness all right, but if her bank made the unpardonable mistake of charging her account with someone else's five-dollar check, Cortez would storm into the lobby the next day and all hell would break loose. She pretended to know nothing at all about finances, but she probably had as good an understanding of stocks and bonds as the men at Bache & Company, at which place she once had a junior clerk discharged because he had spoken to her, she said, in innuendoes, whatever that meant. As with a good many other rich and seemingly helpless ladies, innuendoes of one type or another did sometimes break into her life, but she was canny enough even then not to be waylaid. When, in Rome three years before the war, a very gallant shopkeeper who had sold her an eighteenth century service for twelve made the mistake of saying, "I'm at your service in all ways, Madame," she went back to her hotel, drew a hot tub, and there dictated a letter to the American Embassy in which she said she'd been importuned. The shopkeeper was scared to death, and to patch things up let her have the silver service for three hundred dollars less than the original price. Cortez, whose intention this had been more or less all along, agreed not to press charges.

She was not, then, a foolish woman. As for her age, her face had been, as they say, fixed. Her eyes, perhaps, were older, lacking those luminous lights of the young, but they were pouchless; the pouches had been incinerated at University Hospital in Cleveland along with much of her cheeks and some of her neck. There were virtually no lines on her face; those that hadn't been doctored were covered with cream and powder that children, ignorant of such arts, sometimes threatened to hug away. Only her neck showed tortuous signs of age, somehow making the young face above it look all the more unlived in. When she had asked her plastic surgeon if something couldn't be done about the folds there, he had told her that nothing short of decapitation would do the trick. Loving life slightly more than beauty, she had demurred. But only partly, because even on this warm summer night she wore a dress with a high collar that almost reached her chin. Her hair, dyed a bright red, was perhaps overly arranged, but it too had its utility, hiding the ears that—treacherous things that they were—had somehow lengthened with age, like melting icicles, drops burgeoning at the bottoms.

Rich, still lovely in a contrived sort of way, expansive, touching, exciting, and always generous of herself, she was also cheap, and no one knew it better than Rose. As with many rich people, it never seemed to occur to her that anyone other than her had any use for money. She was not, for example, prepared to help Boyd with his expenses at college, though she had planned to send him a basket of fruit each month, the messages accompanying which she had already composed and stashed away in lavender in her bedroom desk, to be rationed out, ransomed for thank-you notes, every thirty days. When Luke had gone into the Army, leaving his family in Ventry, Cortez had done nothing more than send down her old Hoover vacuum cleaner and an inexpensive fur lap rug which she had used

179

in her car during the winters until it began to smell of the animal it had once been.

Yet as they helped her up the porch steps and into the parlor, their hearts were in their mouths, already feeling the drama she carried everywhere with her, waiting only for it to open, like the fancy boxes of presents that Parnell looked at in the hall, his eyes hungry and wide.

"Now, Rose, my dear," she said, once in the parlor, "I want you to pretend I'm not here at all. There'll be none of that terrible work you're always doing. The house looks fine just the way it is." She seemed for a second to be engulfed by the emotions she was feeling. "Come here, Parnell, let me kiss you again. Isn't he getting to be the little gentleman?" She bent over and let him kiss—or so it seemed to him—her red hair; then turned to Simon, who had carried the last of her luggage through the door into the hall. "That will do nicely," she said. "Put them by the stairs. Thank you, Simon." Her face deadly white with powder, she went from one corner of the parlor to another. "Everything looks just the way it did when Mama was alive. However do you do it?" Much of the parlor furniture, except for a chair or two and a library table, had come from the old Boyd house; how Rose did it, as Cortez asked, was that she never had enough money to replace anything.

Without waiting for an answer, Cortez now rushed to the horsehair sofa beneath the window. "I *must* sit down. I've never in my life seen so many cars on Route 20. We passed a convoy of Army trucks, and I declare I had to close my eyes. My, but it's good to be home. How sweet you look, Catherine. You'll never get old." She rubbed her hands over the soft mahogany arms of the sofa, as if trying to remember through touch. "Parnell, lamb, do help your Aunt Cortez with her shoes. She's such a helpless old fool. That's a dear."

Parnell walked across the room, knelt as if he were to receive the Host, and then slipped off her shoes, holding them in his hands, wondering what he was expected to do with them.

"It's so late, we thought you'd wait until morning," Simon said, smiling. "Of course, we're mighty glad to see you any time of the night or day."

"Why, thank you, Simon. Isn't he the courtly one, Rose? Why, I remember when you used to come calling on Rose, and I thought I'd never seen a boy with nicer ways. And you haven't changed one bit, have you?"

Rose was standing in the hall, tapping her foot against the bare floor, and looking impatiently down the front steps at the long car parked in the driveway. "Are you going to keep that black man out there all night?"

"Harold? My, you must never let him hear you say that. He's very sensitive about his color." She turned to Catherine. "I've had Harold so long I'm afraid to let him go, even though his eyes are failing. I'm scared to death to ride with him any more.

"Simon, my sweet, would you kindly tell Harold he can scoot home now? And tell him to drive *very* carefully."

Rose walked into the parlor and pulled the shoes from Parnell's hands, looking into them for the label. Predictably—Catherine held her breath as she heard Rose begin—she said, "If Mama could see you now, what do you think she'd say from heaven, not even able to take your own shoes off?"

"Mama?" Cortez looked startled for only a second, then became playful and amused again. "Why, I expect she'd say, 'Whatever does Rose mean, letting her hair get so gray?'" She laughed softly, a high-pitched laugh. "My sister had the prettiest hair. I used to brush it for hours. Do you recollect that, Rose?"

Rose was recollecting nothing. She carelessly tossed the shoes on the floor near one of the bags in the hall, and then, as an afterthought, went up to it and pinched its leather, making a face as she did.

"Is that a Lincoln?" Parnell asked incredulously, watching the car back out of the driveway, hurt that Harold wasn't going to spend the night in his preferred bed, giving it dignity.

"It is, dear, but it's just a small one. Someone as little as your Aunt Cortez would rattle around in a big car. But let me *look* at you!" She studied the faces before her fitfully, first Simon's, then Rose's, Catherine's, and Parnell's, all standing as if they were waiting for her to tell them they could sit. "It's like old times. Why, it's just like our old house. I expect Mama to come down the steps any minute!" She sat back on the sofa, spreading her arms over the old upholstery, feeling the black buttons. "Now tell me all about yourselves!"

It looked for a long moment that no one was prepared to say anything, but soon Simon said, "We don't change

181

much around here. Least so you'd notice it." His speech, usually florid, had become rustic, the speech of a farmer boy in town, and as he noticed it he colored.

"Why, I pray you never do. Any of you." She clapped her hands together before her, as if something shocking had occurred to her. "But where's that wicked Boyd, not even come to see his Aunt Cortez!"

"He should be back soon," Catherine said apologetically. "He went out to the Lake with Frank Ventry's son. You remember the Ventrys."

"The Ventrys! How could I forget? Why, didn't I look after Helen when she was no more than a baby? The summers I was home from Ithaca? Yes, I *did*. She was the prettiest, most adorable child I ever saw. Helen is one of the dearest people I know."

Her eyes became thoughtful, as if she were trying to judge the extent of Helen's dearness, but quickly became playful again. "Well," she began, "I might just punish Boyd for not being here. Yes, I think that's what I'll do." She looked at Parnell, watching the grin come to his face, for this was the moment he was waiting for. "I just might not give him his present."

The presents! A cowboy suit for Parnell with real fur at the chaps! A new car for Simon so they could bury the Terraplane! A solid-gold wristwatch for Boyd! A *necklace* for his mother! A new washing machine for Rose! A . . . A . . .

"Why, did you think I'd forget the presents! Not for the world. Don't I know everyone loves a present? Rose, honey, would you hand me those boxes in the hall?"

Without thinking, Rose retreated into the hall, caught up again in the routine of her youth, but even as she began to pick up the boxes a look of revelation came to her face. She handed them to Simon, and said curtly, "I'll put the kettle on for tea."

"Mama's old kettle! Such a heavy thing. I remember it clear as day. Oh, thank you, Simon." She took the packages from him, placing them artfully next to her on the sofa, watching the impassioned look in Parnell's eyes, trying to draw out the excitement as long as she could, almost teasing him. "Why, it's like Christmas, isn't it, lamb? Now let me see. I *wonder* what we have here. Can you guess, sweet? Tell your Aunt Cortez. Give her a tiny guess."

"A . . . a . . . a . . ." Parnell could scarcely contain

himself. "I don't know," he said at last, feeling his face get red, afraid to say what he hoped, but already seeing that the boxes looked small.

"Well, we'll just have ourselves a surprise then!" She reached for the boxes one by one. "Ah, yes, this is for you, Catherine. And Simon, dear, *you* haven't been forgotten; there's something for you too. Rose! Come here this minute. I've a surprise for you."

No longer surprisable, Rose shook her head in the kitchen, muttered something to herself, and banged the kettle against the stove.

"And Parnell's! We've saved his till last. Here, my love. Now take care you don't hurt the little ribbon as you open it. No, no, not that way. Let me do it."

Parnell's fingers were thick with excitement, unable to slide the ribbon off, and he dutifully handed the box back to his aunt, smelling the rich perfume all around her as he did. Carefully, she removed the pink ribbon, then slowly unfolded the tissue around the box, placing it again in his hands. "It's just a little something," she said as Parnell looked down into the opened box.

Oh, dear, thought Catherine. She had not reminded Parnell to thank his aunt for whatever she brought him, and she watched him fight back the tears. She saw the tie that he held in his hand, and she was pleased and proud of his self-control. The empty box was old and yellowed, and the tie, long out of fashion, would reach Parnell's knees. Simon had one too. They had both apparently been given to Cortez's husband—perhaps by Cortez herself—before his death. Catherine nodded at her son. "Thank you, Aunt Cortez," he said, and ran into the hallway and from there into the kitchen.

"And aren't you going to thank me, Simon?" Cortez now said. "Am I getting to be such a frumpy old woman? Come here—you may have a kiss. A small one, mind."

Simon did what he was told, unaware of Parnell's disappointment. "Would you like . . ." he began. "I thought you might like a little sherry after your long ride."

"Sherry! For me? Why, Simon, how kind." She waved her arms excitedly. "We'll have a little fete, won't we, Catherine? It's just like when Mama was alive."

Catherine sat back in the chair, afraid to look into the kitchen, where she knew Rose would be fuming. The apron in Rose's box—a duplicate of Catherine's own gift and bought, she supposed, at a church sale or in the line of some charitable work—would never be seen. She heard the back door slam shut, and she knew that Rose had already placed her unopened present on top of the garbage can in the back yard. Catherine looked at Cortez. In the soft light from the old-fashioned lamp by the sofa the rings on her hands sputtered with flame as she moved her arms back and forth, unable to keep them still.

Parnell, of course, would be in the kitchen with his face buried in Rose's dress. Catherine told herself that she would have to buy something for him tomorrow to make up for the tie that, because the tears had come too quickly, he hadn't carried with him when he left the room.

"You lousy son of a bitch," Boyd was saying again and again. He was driving the car—too fast, he knew—but he wanted to get home. Beside him, Dewey sat in the seat, still too stunned to speak. He hadn't said a word since Boyd had helped him into his clothes and pulled him out of the girl's room, past the other girl in the bathroom, the place smelling of vomit and hate.

And since then Boyd had repeated the same thing, so that Dewey could almost anticipate the next. "You lousy son of a bitch," he said again.

"I'm sorry."

Boyd pushed his foot harder against the accelerator, to drain his anger in speed. "You're sorry! You've been lying to me all the time. You can take that 'I'm sorry' and shove it."

Dewey bent his head down into his shirt front, saying nothing.

When Boyd had first gone into the bedroom, he had thought, yes, Dewey was drunk and that was why the girl said what she did. But as soon as he saw him, he knew that he wasn't. He was so sober Boyd could almost feel it in the air. "All that was a lie. All that horse manure about Dorothy and Dolly. All that horse manure about the girls you've scored with. All that big sex deal business."

"I guess so," Dewey answered almost inaudibly.

Boyd shut his eyes, opened them again, and reached one arm over and with the back of his fist hit Dewey on the side of his face. Dewey recoiled, then sat up straight again, his eyes very clear now.

"Why did you *lie* all the time?"

"I don't know." He breathed a long breath, and when he next spoke his voice wavered. "I wanted to be like you."

Boyd closed his eyes again. "Oh, Christ!" For a minute he was ready to open the far door and push Dewey out. "What do you mean, like me? I never bull-crapped you. You're the one who got hung up on all this sex maniac business. Christ-a-mighty, who was always telling everyone in school about all the scores he made? Not me, you lousy bastard."

"I know it. I'm sorry."

Boyd slammed on the brakes, not even looking in the rear-view to see if a car was behind him. The tires hissed, the car swerved onto the shoulders, and Boyd and Dewey were yanked from their seats and almost thrown against the dash. Boyd was trying to control his breathing, but as soon as he talked the words came in spasms. "Look," he said after the car had stopped, "if you say you're sorry one more time, so help me God I'm going to take you out into that field and beat you so you won't be able to walk for a week. Do you *hear* me? I mean it. I don't want to hear how goddamn sorry you are."

Dewey continued to look straight ahead, unable to meet his friend's eyes. All he could think, sitting there, was how all his buddies at school would laugh at him once they found out. "Something's wrong with me," he said at last.

Boyd wanted to take another poke at him, but he didn't. He was at that moment revolted by Dewey, not for what hadn't happened to him in the bedroom, but for having told him again and again over the last year how many times it *had* happened and making Boyd himself feel like a foolish child.

"How could I tell you?" Dewey now went on. "If I told you, you'd hate me. Like you do right now."

"Who the hell says I hate you?"

"You did. I got the message. I can still feel it. You throw a nice punch. If you want to, if it makes you feel good, throw another one." He jutted his chin out.

Boyd reached over and pushed his chin down abruptly. At last he was able to breathe without anger. "What the holy hell *hap*pened, Dew?"

"Why do I have to tell you that? You get your rocks off or something if you see me squirm?"

"Lay off. All I want you to do is tell me what happened. For the love of God, you're my best friend. And then something like this comes along and I find out you're not even coming clean with me. I thought I knew you. And now ..." He shook his head, swallowing the rest of his words.

Sullenly, Dewey began to speak. "I was okay. I went in there and I was all ready. We played around for a little while, and I was still okay. And then, as soon as we got going, it stopped. I don't know why. I couldn't do anything. I thought I was going to be okay, but I couldn't do anything. Then she got ... she got mad, and I guess I ... oh, for Christ's sake, you know how easy I cry."

Boyd looked ahead into the dark road for a long time. "That's not the end of the world," he said at last, trying to understand. "What the hell, that probably happens to a lot of people. She was a pig anyway."

"No, she wasn't," he answered. "She would have been all right. A year ago she would have been great. I thought if I tried tonight, maybe I'd be all right again, but I couldn't. My old man, he ... caught me at something. And he whipped hell out of me. I can't do anything since then. I'm dead."

The night Frank Ventry had beat him with the leather belt. Oh, God, so that was why. "The night he went crazy in the locker room and made you go home," Boyd said aloud, remembering. One minute everyone had been slapping everyone else's fannies with towels, and the next someone picked Dewey up on top of his shoulders. It was just joy they had to get out somehow because they had won the game, but Frank Ventry had walked in and pulled Dewey out of the shower room.

"He thought ... hell, I don't know what he thought. *You* know me, Boyd. I don't go for that stuff. I didn't want those apes to pick me up that way. Howie Foster was one of them, and you know how he has half a rod-on most of the time anyway. It probably looked like holy hell. Then, after my old man knocked me around, all you guys saw me bawl. Everyone else got to go to the dance afterwards, but I got shut up in my bedroom instead. I just sat there for a long time—I could even hear the music from the school—and I ... well, I don't know what I felt. The old shaft again. And then I felt like I was going to die if something didn't happen. So I ... I guess I started playing around with myself or something. Pop walked in."

Boyd held his breath for a minute, then said, "But that

happens a lot of times when you're alone. Or when you get scared. Even grown-up men. You take guys, they put them in jail or someplace, and it's the first thing they do. It's nothing to be ashamed about. Hell, everyone does it sometime."

"But your old man doesn't catch you."

"No," Boyd answered slowly, "my old man doesn't catch me."

"I wish . . . I wish I had a busted-up face. I wish I had a scar like that broad had, only it went from my eye to my chin."

"Shut up. There's nothing wrong with your face."

"Well, there's a lot wrong with my something else. Maybe I don't even blame the old man. He sees this kid beating the meat, and he wants to tell me he don't go for it. He tells me, and good. I get the idea. I get the idea so good that the damn thing's dead. You know what I do? I pray to God every night. Isn't that a hell of a thing to pray about? Isn't that a lousy, crappy thing to pray about? But nothing happens."

Christ, maybe it would be better if sons were taken from their fathers. Raised by the state, by strangers, by people who wouldn't ask them to do or be things they couldn't do or couldn't be. Oh, sure, Frank Ventry wanted Dewey to be strong so that no one would dare raise him to their shoulders again. But why? Because he wanted to help Dewey, or because he himself wasn't strong and hated to see his own weakness perpetuated? Fathers should be taken from their sons. All Boyd could think of was the Cuchulainn myth Simon had once told him: Cuchulainn's son who had gone in disguise, as all sons did, to his father to serve him and was instead challenged to a contest of strength and killed. Wasn't that what fathers sought, in one way or another, to do? Having created a vessel with his own imperfections magnified, what else could a father do but kill it?

After a long while Boyd said, "Well, I'm glad you came clean."

"Makes you feel good? Something for a laugh?"

"You know goddamn well that isn't true. You know that girl? You have to watch out for people like that. They're as bad as your old man. Did you think I was on her side? That crazy little slut who couldn't see anything in a man except what he carries between his legs. For the love of God, Dewey, you're a man. People can go all through their lives and never know a man, but, by God, you're a man. And don't forget it. That's straight from the mouth of Wolfe Tone Boyd Gavin, boy sage."

He watched a sad grin on Dewey's face, then leaned over and turned the key in the ignition. "And now we're getting out of here before some car smashes into our tail. When we get down to Oberlin, we can see if someone can help figure out what's killin' you. Just remember, I'm with you, okay? Say it."

The smile half lifted Dewey's lips. "Okay, old sage. I appreciate the company. It was beginning to get mighty lonely where I was."

Parnell, painted with a new coat of calamine lotion, flakes of it falling from his poison ivy like grit onto the sheets, lay on his bed and listened to the sounds in the house. He had come from Simon's room, where he had said good night to his grandfather. Simon had already brought from the closet his best white linen suit—one of his two ice-cream suits, as he called them—and hung it, still in its laundry bag from Levinson's, on the door. His shaving gear was neatly laid out on the dresser, his shoes were polished, and his Panama hat brushed. To Parnell, it seemed almost as if Simon were going on a trip. But he was going nowhere at all except on whatever journey Cortez could bring out in him.

In the spare room next to him, he could now hear his aunt moving slowly across the carpet. She had just returned from the bathroom and when she had closed the door of her room the key had turned in the lock. She would probably be doing womanly things to her small, startled face, putting on creams, rolling her hair, or dusting herself with powder after her bath.

Parnell reached down his leg to make certain that he had put on his white sock and found that it was already there, covering the small brown wing on his foot. Earlier in the evening, when he was in the kitchen with Rose, he had decided that he would never again speak to his Aunt Cortez as long as he lived. An old man's tie! But Catherine had in time coaxed him back into the parlor, where he had cookies and milk, while the grownups had sherry. His Aunt Cortez had said that she wouldn't dare drink more than a sip or two. Then she told them all about her last cruise to South America, taken the winter before and before U-boats made it too dangerous for pleasure ships to use the South Atlantic. Afterward, when Parnell had been scooted off to bed, he had looked at the tie again. It had a Spanish name on its label and it had come all the way from Lima. A fabled city of Peru! It was now tied to the post at the foot of his bed where he could see it and conjure up that country. The noble llama! Machu Picchu! Pizarro! The guano industry. The high and lofty Andes!

In the room on the other side of him, Parnell could hear Simon. There was the ripping noise of paper being torn, quiet, then in another few minutes the creaking of the closet door behind which there was a mirror. Simon was trying on his best suit, probably over his pajamas, to make certain that it hadn't shrunk. He couldn't remember when he had seen Simon so happy. His grandfather hadn't even stayed down in the parlor to read, as his custom was, but had instead gone upstairs when everyone else had. Morning would come more quickly if he got directly to sleep. Rose was in her bedroom too, having said that she was too tired to wait up for Boyd.

Parnell was going to try to wait, but tonight he wasn't certain that he could. Sleep was already stroking at his brain. Listening to Cortez in the next room, he became alert again. The key—the long iron Renaissance key; he had seen it and even once touched it—was now being fitted into her antique jewelry box. He would give just about anything to see what she had in it. Even his self-respect, which, as he slipped out of bed, he could feel flee from him. He went to the ladder-back chair by the door, carefully picked it up, carried it to a place against the wall opposite his bed, then climbed on top of it. Without pride, he slowly removed a pin-up lamp from the wall before him, holding it in one hand, then silently withdrawing a nail that had held it there, tiny shreds of plaster falling to the floor as he did. He would have to remember to clean it up, or someone would notice it in the morning. He had found the hole by accident about a year ago on a rainy day when he had had nothing else to do and had gone around the house looking behind pictures, behind hanging jasper ware and calendars. The hole which appeared as soon as he pulled out the nail allowed him a circular view of the next room. Where a picture of Joan of Arc had once hung on the other side, there was a second hole, across the laths, matching Parnell's perfectly. He struck his eye to the light shining through it and as he did he saw his Aunt Cortez sitting on the edge of her bed, dressed, thank God, and in a pretty nightgown at that. He looked intently, waiting for her to run her fingers through her jewels, the way they did in the movies when the bearded man finally reached the lost treasure room and seconds before he was bitten by the serpent guarding it.

Parnell could see her; there was no denying that. Yet the eye, unless it's a very wise one, uncovers only what is seeable. What was in the woman's mind as she sat at her bed could never be looked at through any hole.

Cortez had, of course, always surrounded herself with things that she loved, fine furniture she had bought in Europe, lovely paintings, and tiny *objets* on the tables in her house in Shaker Heights. She would, while passing them, sometimes bring one to her cheek, remembering the very shop where she had bought it, the very price she had paid, even what she had worn on the day she had found it. And she was surrounded, too, by people who had been chosen with as much care as she chose jewelry. Yet it was less than a week ago, as she had been walking through her house, looking at the beauty she had brought to it, that she had overheard one sentence that made every object ugly. She heard her cook talking to her handy-man, the same cook who had been in her service for almost fifteen years, who had pampered her with food she liked, and who was protective and kind when Cortez was ill or depressed. As she sat on the bed now, perhaps Cortez could no longer even recall the words; no, she could. They were too simple and fundamental. "It's about time for the old battle-ax to die." Upon hearing it, Cortez had gone to her room and hadn't left it for two days. Cortez an old battle-ax? The prettiest girl in Ventry County? What had changed the world so? What could have made it so cruel? She had dismissed the cook with a very generous severance and then written the letter to her sister.

All very much beyond Parnell's vision. As he looked through the hole he saw a woman whose face was shining with cold cream. From the mahogany jewelry box on the night table—she had brought no jewels with her except those she wore—she withdrew a small cut-glass decanter, one of three in the box, and poured liquid from it into a tiny ivory cup. She sipped at the cup silently, then seemed to relax, as if a gentle hand had touched her.

Hoping to have seen the treasure, Parnell saw nothing but the serpent. Criminee! He slowly replaced the lamp

190

and climbed down from the chair, scooping up the plaster dust from the floor and—finding nowhere else to put it— dropped it into his single white sock. He then walked softly back to his bed. Once there he repeated his prayers, already said no more than a half hour ago—for Luke to come home, for Boyd to be a soldier, for a cowboy suit with fur chaps—but now adding a new one. "And forgive me for peeping around at people," he whispered in the quiet room, knowing that he had seen something that perhaps no one else had, and knowing that he could tell no one, not even God.

Walking by the ravine, Boyd looked across the street and saw a single light burning on the second floor, coming from the spare room. Only the small converted oil lamp in the hall was on downstairs, so apparently no one had waited up for him. It was just as well. He didn't especially want to talk to anyone. He would just as soon be alone for a while. To get away from all the poor and perishable people who had claims on him, even Dewey, whom he had left a minute ago on the back porch, a "Help me" look still in his eyes.

To Boyd it seemed that everyone he knew expected to be served in a different way, each one feeding on him, each one sucking something different from him. His grandfather and his father, who wanted him somehow to go look for glory, glory that they themselves had missed; his grandmother, who seemed to be willing to keep him a child all his life so that she could look after him, as she had done with Luke; his mother, who tried, perhaps without realizing it, to be the exclusive holder of his love; Parnell, who sometimes couldn't get to sleep unless Boyd was in the room; Francine, who expected him to carry her away from her home and her father but never out of her own body. And now Dewey. If he wasn't careful, there would be nothing left for Boyd himself.

Each time that he felt someone reach out for him, he remembered the dream—no, nightmare—he had about a month ago, and that woke him with a start. In it, he was sitting on the edge of the river in the gulf, and all around him in the water, heavy from spring rains, were the people he knew, unable to climb the slippery bank to reach safety. A hand would reach up for help. Boyd, in his dream, extended his own, until he felt himself begin to slide down the bank. Then, desperately—it was at this point that he woke up, his chest quaking so that he thought it must wake Parnell—he reached for a stick next to him on the bank and began to beat at the hands, chopping at them. As they reached out for him, he struck at their arms.

There could be allegiance, there could be fealty, but for the love of God there could be no irrevocable claims. Tonight, with Dewey, he felt that Dewey almost wanted to pull Boyd with him, wherever he was going. Or if not that, as if he were saying, "Here, bub, I'm giving you my grief. Now you have to suffer for me." Or Simon, when he talked about the war with Boyd, "Here, I'm giving you my dream. Dream it for me." And Catherine and Parnell, "Here, I'm giving you my love. Hold it for me, and have a care."

But if only people would realize that Boyd needed something too. And who do *I* go to? he wanted to know. Where does my body go? If only it could, he wanted now for his body to leap, to jump as high as the trees.

And when he saw her, dressed in her white pajamas, standing behind the leaves of the low branches, he thought at first it was Francine. But, no, it was only one more person reaching out for him. Well, for God's sake couldn't people realize that he was an animal in the cage of his body like everyone else, and that all he needed . . . all he needed was . . . oh, God. Now, as he looked at the girl, shivering in her pajamas, all he could feel was something tearing at his belly and reaching all the way into his head. He knew what suffocation was, but did the girl before him know what it was to suffocate in yourself, in your own silly fluids, and did she know that a man who can't breathe will do anything for breath?

Oh, please go away. You don't know. There's nothing in you that could know.

"You have no *words*, Tina. Did you come out here for me to help you get words? Well, that's not the way of the world. The only thing I've got . . . the only thing . . . I could hurt you. Go away. Leave me alone.

How long she had been there he didn't know. Perhaps for hours or perhaps she had waited until she heard the car before she sneaked down the stairs. Maybe she was there because she remembered the feel of his arms around her when she had run into them at the party. Or maybe something in the numbness of her mind had sent her out into the ravine. Maybe God Himself had sent her. But a man can't always speak just through his arms, Tina, he wanted to say to her. There comes a time when a man needs . . . some other kind of talk.

"Go home," he said at last. "Can't you leave me alone?"

Walking toward Tina, he raised his hand as if he were going to chop at her, but as he did she reached out and touched his forehead. And when she did, it was as if he were sore all over and wanted to scream, and then he wasn't any more.

"Oh, Tina! You knew that I would!" He took her into his arms, and they fell together into the wet grass.

Six

As quietly as he could, Parnell opened the door of the bedroom and looked at his brother in the bed. An hour earlier at the breakfast table, he saw that something was wrong with Boyd, but when Rose said, "You look sick, child. Do you have a fever?" Boyd had answered, "I guess I have a headache." During the meal he sat before his plate and ate almost nothing, saying only what had to be said, not even bothering to be especially civil to Aunt Cortez, who seemed even more animated than she had been the evening before in the parlor. And at the first opportunity Boyd had excused himself and walked slowly up the stairs to his room. Parnell had looked in for a minute and had then gone across the street to sit next to Tina on the Ventry sofa, but she too seemed dreamy and distracted. And then—he was now waiting to tell Boyd— he had seen what Tina had done.

Sitting in the ladder-back chair next to his brother's bed, Parnell wished that he could crawl next to him, but he knew that Rose would give him a clout if she saw him there. He took from his pocket and held before him what he had found on the dresser, lying there next to some change and a comb, earlier in the morning. He didn't know exactly what it was, but when Simon walked into the room for a second time to march them down the stairs, Parnell had thrust it into his pocket. Rose, he was sure, would start to make the beds even while they were finishing breakfast, and it seemed to be the kind of thing Rose shouldn't see.

He looked at the two newly made beds, Boyd's already wild and wrinkled where his body had tossed on it. What Parnell held in his hand was a small, soft, slippery balloon, tied together at its neck and containing a cloudy, watery substance. Wherever Boyd had used it, he had not wanted to throw it away lest someone find it, and then, Parnell guessed, he had forgotten it. Intuitively, Parnell

194

felt that it would make trouble. It looked strange and foreign, and he had never seen anything like it before.

Well, it would be a secret between the two of them. Things were bad enough already with Aunt Cortez in the house without causing any more hollering. On an impulse he had at first thought of showing it to Tina, but he was so surprised when he discovered what she was doing on the sofa that he hadn't. He put it into his pocket again, the one without the hole.

Frankly, Parnell was at a loss to say what was happening in the Gavin house. When he left his room at dawn to deliver his papers, Simon was already up, and so was Rose, as if neither of them had slept all night. While Parnell was dressing, putting on his underwear backward, and slipping on his shoes without first pulling on his second white sock, he had heard Simon draw water in the tub for a bath. And when Parnell passed Rose's open door, she was standing at the foot of her bed, dressed in one of her old housedresses, her hair looking as if it had been combed, as they said in school about Miss Stickney's, with an egg beater. Yet when he returned a half hour later, the scent of Simon's shaving lotion everywhere in the hall, he saw that Rose had changed clothes again. She was wearing her good Sunday housedress, and her hair had been carefully recombed, the still brownish band at one side brought painstakingly toward the front where it covered some of the gray.

At the breakfast table it had been Parnell who said, "Boy, everyone is all dressed up today," and Rose had answered, "Hush, or I'll wash your mouth out with soap." Nothing more was said about the festive clothes, not even when Aunt Cortez came down, smelling of eau de cologne, full of girlish and silly reminiscences, none of which concealed from Parnell the fact that her fingers were shaking.

After breakfast, Simon and Cortez left the house for the cemetery, where they planned to visit her mother's grave. Parnell had stood behind the screen door next to Catherine and his grandmother, watching the two of them cakewalk down the street, Simon dressed fit to kill, Cortez's shy laughter echoing down the street.

"Why, I honestly believe she's flirting with a seventy-five-year-old man!" Rose said. "Isn't that just like her, Catherine? She hasn't changed at all."

"Oh, I think she has," Catherine had answered. "I think

... well, it looks to me as if she's worrying more than she used to."

"Worry?" Rose had replied. "Goodness, that's one thing you could never accuse Cortez of. Yes, that was one thing she never did." Then with sudden firmness she added, "I just hope she doesn't do anything foolish that would hurt Simon."

Parnell didn't know how she could. Now, as he watched Boyd stir in the bed, he heard a sound escape from his throat. He was having a dream. Perhaps someone was chasing him, the way the man with the hatchet in Parnell's dream sometimes did. He went to the door and closed it all the way and then returned to the bed, carefully resting his body on it, curling up against his brother's back. He remembered how much fun it had been to sleep together in the big double bed they used to have and how they had huddled close together under the blankets to keep each other warm in the winters when the coal furnace went out. But Boyd himself had asked Catherine to buy twin beds after the terrible and depraved thing Parnell had finally done. Either because he had forgotten to go before he went to bed or because he was frightened by his hatchet dream, he had wet the bed. Boyd had known nothing of it until the next morning when he woke up and found himself sopping. He cursed at Parnell, called him a vile pig, and told him he could never sleep with him again.

Boyd began to move and then, apparently feeling Parnell's warm body at his back, opened his eyes. Parnell waited to be shoved out of the bed into a heap on the floor, but Boyd lay next to him, perfectly still.

"Are you sick?" Parnell asked at last, hoping that he might catch it if he was.

"No."

"What's wrong?"

Boyd waited for a long time before answering. "Nothing."

Sweet-mother-Jesus, how could you talk to people if they never *told* you anything? Thinking that it might help if he did the talking, Parnell said, "Did you open the lousy present Aunt Cortez gave you?"

"Why bother? She never gives anything away."

Parnell appeared to be perplexed. "I thought if you're supposed to like people, you give something big."

"Hah. Listen to him. What she does is take something big. The only reason she comes down here is that we're

196

her family and we have to like her whether we want to or not. Just because we've got the same hot-shot blood."

After a while Parnell said timidly, "You mean you don't like any of us either?"

"Sometimes I get sick of everybody."

"Me too," he answered proudly, glad that he could at least share this feeling with his brother. "So does Simon. That's why he runs away. He's going to take me with him the next time."

"You already told me about a thousand times. Hell, he's not going anywhere. He's too old. He should act his age. So should you. Who the hell said you could climb into my sack anyway? What do you think you are, a baby or something?"

"I'm no baby," Parnell replied, bringing his feet over the side of the bed—banished from the Garden, sent flying into space with the other black angels. "I thought you were sick is all."

"Listen to him, will you? He thought I was sick. And what the holy hell would you do to help me, I'd like to know, if I was sick? You climb in my sack. That's what you do. You and that stinky white sock of yours." Even as he said it, he could see the hurt reach into Parnell's eyes. "Aw, forget it."

"Well, you don't have to yell at me. I'm not deaf."

"I wasn't yelling."

"Yes, you were. You said my sock is stinky. Just for that I'm not going to tell you something."

"Oh, God," Boyd said, exasperated. "He's not going to tell me something. And why for the love of God in heaven do you *tell* me you're not going to tell me? Sometimes I honestly think you're a half-wit, you know that?"

Struck to the quick. To his very essence. His whole being at stake. "I'm no half-wit," he said with no great conviction. "Miss Stickney says I'm very smart. And you want to know what else she says?"

"No."

"She said I read more books than almost anyone she knows, and someday I'm going to be very brainy."

"I can hardly wait."

"You wait and see. I'm going to be the smartest guy around here, and when you come to see me and someone'll say, 'There's a Mr. Gavin in dirty pants out here who says he's related to you,' I'll say, 'Never *heard* of him.'"

Boyd began to grin. "You'd do that to me?"

197

"It depends."

"Well, someday I hope you are a very brainy guy, and when I visit you I'll put on clean pants."

"Okay, but don't say I'm a baby."

"Okay, you're not. Now beat it."

"Okay," Parnell said, retreating. He went into the hall, closing the door behind him, then down to the bathroom at the end. Once inside, he took the strange object from his pocket. Whatever it was, it was making Boyd sick. He looked at it once more, wondering how such a little thing could change his brother's eyes and make them so afraid, and then dropped it into the toilet. He flushed it, washed his hands, and went downstairs.

He hadn't even told Boyd what he had seen in the Ventry parlor. As he whispered to Tina on the sofa, he had looked over at the notebook on her lap. She had stopped counting. After her final number, she had written, "That is the last. The End."

Listening to his brother descend the stairs, Boyd heard the piano being played across the street, and it sounded closer than ever before. In the bed he could still smell Tina on his arms and his chest, and his face flushed as he remembered again.

It wasn't his fault. She had waited for him and, not even knowing the name for it, had given herself away as she'd give a piece of candy to Parnell. Oh, my God, Boyd thought. Oh, my *God!* A girl who didn't even know what she was doing. A girl who didn't know why there was blood on her. A booby.

But was she? If only Boyd could say to himself that she was and that what he had done to her didn't matter. But she had shown him something else too—love or gentleness or wisdom, he didn't know which—something so elemental that now, as he remembered it, it almost took his breath away.

Maybe that was the way things were supposed to be. Maybe it was the simple, childlike way people used to be before all the nunnish judges stepped in and put up signposts that said Right and Wrong. For all her remoteness and quiet, maybe she was more of a woman than Francine. What had he been thinking, last night, before he saw her standing by the ravine? He wanted to chop at people's arms when they held them out to him. Yet she hadn't chopped. All she had done was hold on. Afterward, when

198

he had said, "Did I hurt you, Tina? I didn't mean to hurt you," she kissed his cheek again.

He tried to tell himself that it was dirty and the sort of thing the tenant farmers outside of town did. One of them, a cretinous girl Boyd had seen around the square, had even been hauled into court because she was letting everyone diddle her. When he heard about it, Boyd was disgusted. The young men in the country, some of them her cousins, were taking her behind barns or into the woods and then sending her back to her house without a thought in her head, undetected until they made the mistake of gang-banging her, ten or eleven of them, and leaving her to crawl home on her knees. But was Tina that way? Boyd wanted to know. Am *I* that way?

Well, it had happened. It was over now, and that was that. Nothing could be changed. In a way he almost wished Tina was like the other girl, so that he could get off the hook and not feel responsible toward her. It would never happen again. It would never happen again. And Tina, of course, would never tell.

But from his bed Boyd looked across to the dresser and saw again that someone had taken the only thing, if it wasn't destroyed, that could commit him once and for all. He had remembered while he was at the breakfast table, but by the time he returned to the room it was already gone. He felt as if he were drowning, water beginning at his heels and rising along his body to his head. He could do nothing now but wait for someone—his grandfather, Rose, or his mother—to make the accusation, and he would have to tell the truth because they would, each of them, know that he was lying if he tried to conceal the truth. And because of their notions of morality—Oh, my God, he said in his throat—they would hate him as long as he lived.

Please, he said, let them never say anything. Let them not hate me. Even before he drew the pillow around his head, he saw with wonderful clarity that he himself was now in the water and reaching out for them, and that he was asking for them to draw him in. He could feel the shame begin to burn inside him.

Cortez had brought a parasol—actually, one of Rose's summer umbrellas which she used to intimidate butchers and storekeepers more often than to keep off the rain—to protect her head from the sun, and as they walked into

199

the valley, Simon held it over her head. Once under the trees at the bottom, he folded it and carried it under his arm, then led her across the covered bridge to Chestnut Grove cemetery on the other side. They found the graves easily, sitting next to a high monument erected by the citizens of the county for those strangers who had died in the train wreck of 1876—falling, in a winter storm, from the trestle, never to see Ventry except in the few minutes it took them to reach the snowy floor of the ravine. Simon's father, he remembered, had been on the team that had helped old Amos Bennett haul the monument from the horse-drawn wagon and erect it over the mass grave that held those people who were too broken to be sent to their homes for burial.

Standing before the Boyd family plot, Simon could feel the warmth of the sun on his head as it reached through the leaves, and he watched Cortez remove her white gloves and grab at the few weeds in the grass over the graves, and throw them into the dusty path.

"It's funny how the old people picked the spot with the nicest view for the dead," he began. "They don't do that any more. Why, in Cleveland you're lucky if they put you in the ground sitting up, with a view of a highway or the back of a saloon."

"I don't know that Mama is seeing all that much," Cortez answered.

"I wish she could. Your mother was a good woman. I never knew a woman to sacrifice so much for a child as she did for you."

Cortez smiled secretly. "For years I never thought of her as being dead." She backed off to see if she had plucked all the weeds. "You know how she used to go to Cleveland from time to time to buy material for my dresses? She always wanted the best. I think, after she died, I just imagined she was away for the day, picking out fabric or pretty ribbons."

"Oh, she loved to do that," Simon said. "She got the doggonedest pleasure out of doing things for you. And right up to the end she'd talk a man's ear off, telling us about you. It was always Cortez-this, Cortez-that."

"I suppose." She sat on a neighboring tombstone, reading the name on it, a small shiver passing through her as she did. "I don't think," she went on, "I ever had the chance to tell her how . . . how grateful I was."

200

"Oh, she knew. Make no mistake. Some things you don't need words for."

"I could never really talk to her the way I wanted to. Whenever I tried, my tongue would get all twisted."

"Well, she was a strong woman. She knew what she wanted for you, and there was no stopping her. I remember what people said when they heard she was sending you off to Cornell. Why, they thought she was daft. A girl back then was lucky to go to a Normal school, but *Cornell!* Still, your mother always said that the best was none too good for you."

"I've often wondered if she was happy," Cortez said. "You know, Simon, nowadays everyone expects to be happy. They go to analysts because they honestly think they deserve to be happy, but I've wondered about Mama. Do you think she was?"

"People back then had their work to do, and that was enough. I don't think I ever saw your mother off her feet until she was on her deathbed. There was always something that kept her jumping around doing things. No, they don't make people like that any more. Getting up at five in the morning on washdays and boiling all the clothes in pots on the kitchen stove. And still at it when the sun went down again. No, sir, they don't."

"I sometimes think that's what I should have done. Don't you laugh, Simon. You probably think I don't know how to wash my own hands without someone around to push my elbows. But that's acquired, and don't you think it isn't. I sometimes wonder if it wouldn't have been better if I'd stayed right here and . . . and boiled clothes. Mama would never let me. She said I'd ruin my hands."

"Well, your mother saw right away that you were special, and she did everything in the world to give you the things she wanted for you."

With her ungloved hand Cortez ran her finger over the dust on the tombstone where she was sitting, then very carefully wrote her own name. She looked at it for a long time, almost as if she were trying to decide if it would look different—special—even there, and then she slowly erased it. "Did I ever tell you, Simon, how I almost wouldn't go back to Cornell that first Christmas at home?"

Simon's face showed honest surprise. He clearly recalled the holiday, because it was the year Simon had decided to enlist in the Army, hoping that he could see a little bit of

201

the world Cortez herself was seeing. She had been flitting around the house as if driven by joy.

"I don't even think Rose knew," she went on. "Mama made me promise not to tell anyone. I was so unhappy, but Mama made me go back."

To Simon it seemed inconceivable. He could even remember that Christmas Eve, years ago. Before they opened their presents, Cortez had gone upstairs in the old Boyd house and changed into a new dress her mother had made for her, the likes of which Simon had never seen before. And when she came downstairs again, the gaslights so low that they scarcely burned, she had danced for them before the Christmas tree.

"I'm afraid they never liked me at school," she said at last.

"You? Why, everyone loved you! No wonder your mother made you go back. She was right and you were wrong. You were just imagining it."

"Oh, no," Cortez now said. "I knew because I was there. Mama wasn't. They used to . . . the Eastern girls . . . they used to make fun of me. Because I wasn't very polished, I suppose. Or because, well, because I was a hick."

"You!" Simon laughed.

"All those pretty clothes she made for me—did without herself so that I could look nice—they used to laugh at them. Oh, it was terrible. I thought I'd lose my mind. And when I told Mama that Christmas, she wouldn't listen to me."

Yet Cortez had been her mother's happiness. When Simon had said that the old people didn't have time to pause to think if they were happy or not, he wasn't sure that it was a proper description of Cortez's mother. She was happy as long as she was working for Cortez. She seemed to thrive on it. Even now Simon could recall the pains the woman had taken to get her daughter's wardrobe in shape for college, looking through the catalogues that came her way for patterns, always adding a bit more ribbon than was called for, working sometimes late into the night, cutting the expensive silk fabric she had chosen so carefully, her own dress a cheap calico.

"Well, it's a good thing she didn't listen to you," Simon said. "If she had, you'd be living in this funny old town, sitting around, the world out there never knowing who you are."

"She wouldn't let me."

Simon waited before he spoke. "Did you want to?"

"I always felt so *good* here. I honestly believe that everything after one's childhood is a cheat. Because as soon as I left home, I was unhappy. And I was unhappy when I came back to Cleveland and Mama set me up there until I met Aldo. I never liked Aldo. Mama did." Cortez drew her gloves on, stretching them carefully over the rings on her fingers. "You know, I was in Brazil last year after Christmas. It was the last cruise, somebody said, because people were beginning to get worried about submarines. All the way down there, do you know what I hoped?—now don't interrupt me, Simon; I want to finish—I hoped that a submarine would see us and sink us. And when we reached Rio de Janeiro—you'll remember I sent you those lovely cards you still have?—I didn't even get off the ship. I stayed on board all the time we were there and missed the Carnival I told you I saw when I wrote the cards. And do you know what I wished when I was there by myself? I wished that I could be right here, right where Mama is . . ." she could almost not finish, "so I could tell her how much I hate her." She brought gloved hands up to her face.

The "little picnic supper," as Rose described it, was neither little nor a picnic. It was primarily for Boyd and Dewey, who were leaving in three days for freshman orientation at Oberlin, and neighbors, relatives, and friends from all over the county had been invited, filling the house and spilling onto the lawn. For the old people, for whom it was bolshevistic to eat out of doors or on a table without a white linen cloth, a banquet table had been set up in the parlor, and for the younger, more daring ones three homemade picnic tables, two of them borrowed, had been readied in the back lawn. The gathering was, in a way, for Cortez too, because she was to see again many of the people she had grown up with years ago.

While Simon and Cortez were out making calls, Rose and Catherine had spent most of the day in the kitchen. No one in Ventry could get together without eating well, so much so that people would sometimes even say about an impending death, "Well, by God, they'll put on a good feed when *she* dies." A funeral dinner, a wedding dinner, a coming-home or going-away party always included a baked ham, a roast turkey with dressing, baked corn, baked beans, escalloped potatoes, a garden salad, corn bread, country butter, lemon meringue pies, two or three coconut layer cakes, and—depending on the season—hot cherry, peach, or apple cobblers. Because of the war and rationing, it had been harder than ever for Rose to run her supplies to ground. For three days the grocery store in town had a sign in its window that read *No Butter. No Sugar. No Meat until Monday,* and Rose had to beg from friends, using her own complicated bookkeeping system. "Now, I gave you that nice goose for Easter, so that means you should owe me a pound of butter, don't you think, *eh?*" she had said to one woman. And to another, "Suppose you call that cousin of yours in Linesville, the one with the fat pigs, and ask if he's butchered yet. Tell 'im I'll pay good clean cash and throw in two pounds of sugar for extra." Churchill himself, in getting Lend-Lease, hadn't relied on greater improvisation. As for the ham, she got it, and it was a fine one, rubbed in borax and pepper, then smoked over hickory and sassafras, the way the old-fashioned farmers did.

Boyd, Francine, and Dewey were eating off their plates on the steps of the back porch, the only free place they could find. Francine had been talking about Tina, who was in the dining room, scooping ice cream on plates of cake as they were passed to her. The girl had gone to her mother in the kitchen that morning, Francine said, and told her that she wanted to go to the party. For someone who hadn't been out of the house in almost six years, except to go for an occasional ride in the car, it was an incredible achievement.

"I think she's decided she's not going to be afraid any more," Francine now said. "It's funny how things like that can happen."

Boyd wasn't sure that it was all that funny. When, just ten minutes earlier, he had seen Tina in the dining room, he was at first surprised, then very pleased. For one agonizing minute he thought she might do something foolish—run into his arms perhaps—but she seemed very composed. If there was within her any memory of what had happened the night before, it wasn't visible on her face or in the way she reacted to Boyd. She smiled at him warmly, then went back to digging homemade ice cream out of the dish sunk in ice. Maybe, he finally decided, she had just needed someone to draw the shyness out of her, or maybe she had been waiting for someone to find her, to tell her where she was, or to wake her from her sleep, as Simon once said. She still hadn't said a word to Boyd, or to anyone else at the party that he was able to see, but at least she had come out. She had come out from wherever it was she was living, and that was a beginning.

"Oh, she wasn't that sure of herself," Francine continued. "After she got dressed, she changed her mind, but we all persuaded her, even dopey Dewey."

"The day of miracles is here, pals," Dewey said. "First Pop has his man-to-man talk with old father God and swears off the demon booze, and now Tina. Maybe the Ventrys are the Chosen People after all. Maybe, by God, I'm next."

"In the meantime," Francine interrupted, "eat your dessert before the ice cream melts all over you. You already have about half of it on your good pants."

"Impossible," Dewey answered, wiping some of it away with his fist. "I'm a very tidy guy. Boy, this cake is great. Your grandmother sure can cook even if she's a mean old harpy."

Boyd decided to let it pass. Rose wasn't a mean old harpy; she was just working with what she had. Other people were forever touching each other or kissing, but Rose baked what love she had, such as it was, into her cakes and pies and puddings. Even now she was too busy to do any eating herself, instead running from place to place, offering the food she had prepared almost as if she were offering herself, shouting, "Is it *good?*" and then smiling to beat all hell when told that it was. Boyd didn't know what it would be in Latin, but it seemed to him that she was saying, "It is good; therefore I am good." And why not?

"Me, when I get married," Dewey went on, winking carnally at Boyd, "I'm going to marry me a mute. Keep her barefoot, pregnant, and quiet. None of that Carrie Nation stuff for her. She'll get her emancipation in bed, and that is *all*, brother."

"Who would you talk to?" Francine asked, smiling. "I mean, if the only women you like are mutes?"

"Who the hell does Simon talk to? Do you think he can talk to thousand-tongued Rose? My God, no. You have to talk to yourself, that's what. You're alone at all the important times anyway. But the trick is to keep the noise level down so that you can hear what you're saying."

"Simon talks to me," Boyd said. "And to Parnell a lot too. So, you see, it's not as bad as all that. Say he never got married—he's always saying he never should have—then there wouldn't have been Parnell and me. And *that* would have been a loss to mankind."

"Well," said Francine, "it seems to me he's doing most of his talking to your aunt right now. You can't pull him away from her. I went up to her a little while ago, because Mom made me. And I told her that I was going to Cleveland and all, and I hope to see her there. She *didn't* say that she hoped to see me. And Simon was right there, listening to every word."

"Now there's a real woman. She's about the poshest woman I ever saw. What she doesn't know about posh isn't worth knowing."

"She gave me her card," Francine continued, "and she told me to call her. Her card! She probably won't even remember who I am if I do. When I told Mom, she was madder than a wet hen. She said she's going to have a little talky-talk with your aunt. Hey, there she goes now, in fact. Watch for the sparks."

The three of them watched Helen Ventry walk across the lawn to where Cortez was standing under the shade of a tree, the rim of her white hat tipping back and forth over her forehead in the breeze. As the two women met, Boyd watched Parnell jockey for position next to a tree so that he could overhear the conversation. Maybe someday he would write a book to get all the purloined words out of his head.

"I hope I'm as pretty as she is when I'm that old," Francine said, looking at Cortez, standing tall, ageless, and patrician, holding out her hand for Helen Ventry to shake it. Frank Ventry then came up to the two of them, exchanged a few words, then continued to walk among the people scattered over the lawn. He was wearing a blue suit, a little heavy for the summer, but he looked pleased with himself and well. More than that, he seemed to be relaxed.

"Is he still off the gargle?" Boyd asked Francine.

"*He* is," she replied, "but not everyone is. When I talked to your aunt, her breath almost knocked me down. That's one thing I can recognize. I was raised with it. Even when I was so small I wasn't even in school yet, I could tell. Papa would come home from work, and the minute he kissed me I'd know. If I smelled it, I'd always

206

hide because that's when I knew he'd have a fight with Mom."

Suddenly it seemed to Boyd that he really hadn't talked to his aunt since she arrived. Each time that she made overtures, he had excused himself quickly, telling her that he would get back to her in a short while, but he kept putting it off. There was something about her that he had never noticed before. Not the booze, if she was actually drinking, as Francine said. But something about the way she spoke to him that embarrassed Boyd. Still, he would have to talk to her, he reminded himself.

"Well, she's a lovely girl," Parnell heard his aunt say to Helen Ventry. "You can be proud of her."

Why he was following Cortez from place to place he didn't know except perhaps that Tina had said she was too busy to sit with him, and his aunt was the prettiest one at the party to watch. In the morning, after she had returned to the house from the cemetery, he had listened to her draw a tub, then waited for her to pass down the hall in a pale blue kimono, her jewelry box in her hands. She sat in the tub—shameless fellow that he was, he would have watched but there was no decent way—for almost an hour, until he thought perhaps she might have fallen asleep. But at last she had gone back to her room, dressed herself in a high-necked white dress with long frilly sleeves, and a white garden hat, the only one at the party, and had then come downstairs again, her face flushed slightly under new powder.

Watching the two women, he saw that Helen Ventry had also taken pains to look nice, wearing a flowered dress he recognized from visits she made to school during Open House, yet he saw that she had added a just-picked rose to the bodice to make it look newer. Her hair had been waved, perhaps by Francine the night before, and probably with the curling iron he knew they kept in the kitchen. Only her eyes, peering out of their black patches, looked as if they didn't belong, as if something were pressing against them and hurting her.

"You know," he heard his aunt say, "most of the young girls where I live all look alike. One monotonous face repeated again and again. They go to the same schools, they wear the same clothes, and they say the same tiresome things. But I don't think, I seriously don't think I've ever seen a girl as lovely as your daughter. She has a

207

very rememberable face. She'd stand out in any crowd. Of course, how could she be anything else with a mother as pretty as she has?"

The compliment seemed to be a burden to Helen Ventry. "I'm afraid that's not true any more," she said uneasily. "I try to keep myself up, but sometimes I decide that time is catching up with me."

"Why, you're a *young* woman. You should be ashamed of yourself."

"It's different here, Cortez. It's so easy to let yourself go."

Smiling, his aunt replied, "Well, you should just take a day off every now and then and get into Cleveland. It would do you a world of good. I can give you the name of the woman who keeps me from total decay. She's a little Italian woman with a shop near Shaker Square, and though I don't as a rule get on well with Italians, I must say that this woman has very talented hands. After she's worked on my hair and my face for a few hours, I almost feel as if I could go on living for another day."

Parnell watched Helen Ventry nod weakly. She would probably be thinking about the money it would cost. Earlier at the party he had seen Frank slip the four dollars he had borrowed into Simon's hands, and Parnell knew that if you had to borrow money from the Gavins you really *had* to be poor.

"I only hope that Francine will be able to have a nice life," he heard Mrs. Ventry say to his aunt. "I've always dreamed that she could get away from here and ... well, see how they live in the city."

"Secretaries are in great demand. I heard someone say that just the other day. Why, yes, I recollect now. It was one of my lawyers, and he said he'd have a girl in for a month or so, and then she'd fly away and get a job in a war plant. Why, young girls have never in history made more money than they're making now. If I were fffteen years younger, I honestly think, *hon*estly think I'd find a job for myself." She paused. "Of course, there's no room anywhere for a frivolous old woman like me."

"You'll always be young, Cortez. I envy you."

"Why, thank you, Helen. That's so sweet of you."

Parnell could see that Mrs. Ventry was struggling, but he couldn't make out why. She was apparently trying to say something to his aunt. "I wonder," she began in a small, timid voice, "I wonder ... well, we don't know anyone in

Cleveland. We're not very important people, I'm afraid. And I wonder . . . if you could inquire to see if there might be a job for Francine somewhere."

Cortez laughed giddily, touching Helen's arm as she did. "Now, Helen, I've always made it a practice not to interfere in people's lives or to ask favors. I suppose if you make one exception, then there's no end to it. And I really don't know what I could do anyway. You know I'm just a poor little woman living by myself, and I don't get out into the world as much as I used to."

Parnell watched the disappointment come to Tina's mother's face. It seemed almost as if the black patches became larger, as if a dark liquid now seeped from them, covering her skin. "I just thought .. didn't you say one of your lawyers might need a girl? I hate to send Francine to Cleveland without knowing anyone. And I want to make certain she has a nice job. It's hard telling what she might come up with through one of those employment agencies."

Cortez answered that the agencies were now very different from what they used to be. "Why, just this last week I told them I'd be needing a replacement for my cook. She was sick, poor dear, and I had to let her go. And didn't they send me *eight* women, each one more qualified than the last? Why, Helen, it was like trying to find which piece of candy you want in a valentine box." She smiled at her illustration, sure that Helen would know the feeling, though what little candy Helen had ever received was always immediately divided among the children. "But the agencies are *very* good. You won't have to worry about them at all."

If Helen had been disappointed a minute before, she was now angry. Parnell knew the look well, because he had seen it often when she was quarreling with her husband. It was a fighting look, and it now even began to light up her eyes, bringing life to them.

"I thought because we used to be so close that you might be able to do something. I remember . . . how nice you were to me when I was a little girl and you took care of me in the summers when you were home from college."

"Ah, yes," Cortez said happily, "didn't we have the good times?"

Determined, and not at all moved by nostalgia, Helen continued. "I remember it clear as day. How, when my own mother was too busy, you were even kind enough to give me baths. Do you remember, Cortez?"

Parnell watched his aunt's eyes narrow, as if she had begun to smell something bad.

"I remember," Helen pressed on, "how gentle . . . lovable almost, you were to me. How you hugged and kissed me while you were drying me. You were always so kind when you were a girl. I remember . . . how you . . . used to kiss and fondle me and then tell me it was a secret and I ought never to tell my mother."

There seemed to be real revulsion on his aunt's face now, as though she had been confronted by something unpleasant that had slipped from her mind entirely. The memory of it, Parnell saw, made her fingers shake ever so slightly, as if they needed something to anchor them.

"Yes," he heard her say slowly, frantic to end the conversation. "What I could do, Helen, because we've always been so close, I could ask my lawyer if he might know of something. Yes, I could do that for you, Helen."

Simon watched Cortez make her way down the stairs again—it was the second time within the last hour that she had gone to her bedroom—stand for a moment in the hall, looking into the parlor at the people there, and then walk toward them reluctantly. A few minutes before, he had seen her hurry past everyone to reach the stairs, rush up them, and then he had heard her open and close the door to her room. While her face had then looked—how to say it?—as if it were about to break or be crossed by a fissure, he saw now that there was a smile on her lips.

Simon had, at the beginning of the party, brought her up to her old friends, hoping that perhaps they could restore her good humor, but as she listened to them Simon could tell that she was bored. Somehow they weren't saying what she wanted to hear. The old people in Ventry weren't much for discourse anyway and tended to be laconic and short-worded, and now, vaguely aware that Cortez was impatient with them, they were unable to say much at all. Before she had gone into the back yard, Simon had taken her by the arm and led her to Toby Carle, an old suitor of hers, and his wife, a sparse, gray, dumpy woman, but after an accounting of the recent past, there seemed to be nothing to talk about. When Toby had asked her with a real estate agent's kind of geniality if she was still seeing a lot of the world, she hadn't denied it, but neither had she revealed much about it. She seemed almost too bored to speak, or too worried about something that was bothering her to give her attention to anything else. Toby had told her that he had bought part interest in a plot of land next to the Hershey farm, where the plant was going to be built, and she had looked at him as though she were unable to follow his words. At last she had said, "Oh, yes, I recall the place. Those lovely daisied fields where we used to go and pick wild berries," though the land had been plowed in wheat and alfalfa for at least the last twenty years. And, relaxing a bit, she finally reminded the man of something they had done at a picnic when they were still in grade school. He looked at her dumbly, then answered, "The old memory isn't as good as it used to be." He seemed to be embarrassed even to be standing next to the woman whose sweet, flirting words no longer had any relevance, his head bald, and grossness written all over his body.

Simon was almost relieved when he now saw Cortez begin to walk into the kitchen, and through the doorway he watched her begin to wrap an apron over her summer dress. But even before she finished tying the strings, Rose shouted, "Now, no need to get yourself all hot and dirty, poor thing," and scooped the apron off her, sending her on her way again. Cortez stood by herself at the kitchen door, apparently neither willing to go all the way back into the kitchen to be near Rose nor willing to return to the parlor. And the next time Simon looked, only a few seconds later, she was gone. He could hear her footsteps in the upstairs hall.

He was about to follow her when an old friend grabbed him by the arm and pulled him toward a group in the far corner of the parlor. As he approached them he heard one of them say, "Well, if he's a deserter like everyone says, the Army'll catch up with him sooner or later." Lucas. They were talking about Lucas. As Simon listened to the words they now seemed somehow more real, more irrevocable, for having been said in the Gavins' own house. It was what Simon himself had been trying for so long to say. He watched the man who had spoken, waiting for him to continue, but, no, the man now saw Simon. He cleared his throat loudly, as if to cover the words which still rang in the air.

"Any news of Luke?" he asked in embarrassment as Simon joined him.

News? Simon had almost stopped hoping for news. "No, nothing at all," he answered at last.

"Well, it's a shame. I don't know what the world's coming to," the man then said. "Did you hear about the Morrows' son and how they found out just yesterday? The Western Union people must have got in touch with Reverend Hill first, because he was the one who went over to tell Walter Morrow at the store. They say Walter didn't say a thing. Just drew the blinds, locked up the place, and then went home. And as soon as Ada Morrow saw him coming up the sidewalk, they say she broke down. Why, Walter hasn't been home like that in the middle of the day in the thirty years he's had the hardware store. It's a terrible thing to come on people."

"They all seem to happen one right after another," someone said. "First the Leonard boy over on McGovern Street. Then the Thompson boy down on Oak Street. And now the Morrows' son. All in one month. Pretty soon we won't have anyone to come home."

"Well, they should have stopped Hitler back in '38, the way I told you," someone else now volunteered.

"Roosevelt promised to keep us out of war. Just three years back he was still saying that. He said none of our boys would ever have to fight on foreign soil. And between you and me, he was glad the day Pearl Harbor was bombed. Why, I read somewhere that he knew they were going to attack in the Pacific twenty-four hours before. He knew it on Saturday night, and what did he do? He went back and finished his dinner. He was just itching to get into a war. He didn't say a damn thing to the Navy at Pearl Harbor because he knew that the only way Congress would declare war was if American boys were killed. Two thousand of them lost their lives just so F.D.R. could have his war and get his place in history."

It was strange, Simon thought, how a great man could attract so many enemies. He wondered vaguely what the reason was—why some people said that Roosevelt hadn't had polio but syphilis, why some said he was a Jew, and why some said he was in the pay of the British government at one moment and the Russians the next.

"I was reading one of those columnists," one of the men now said, "who has it that when our ambassador to Britain got the call from F.D.R. telling him about Pearl Harbor, what he said was 'Good.' It makes you wonder."

"No," Simon interrupted, "Roosevelt is a very moral

212

man. He loves people. He could never have done anything like that—get us into a war just for his own glory. I have the utmost faith in the man."

"Well, it's not Roosevelt who's making the decisions. It's Harry Hopkins. And he's no better than a Communist. We had to get into the war to help Russia out—after Hitler burned Russia's pact with Nazi Germany. It's a deal Hopkins made with Stalin on one of his trips."

Next they'd be saying that Eleanor Roosevelt was in the pay of the devil himself. "I have great confidence in F.D.R.," Simon answered. "We should all thank God we have a man like that at an hour like this. He knows pain himself. I think that the polio he had . . . well, it brought out the humanity in the man. He knows we all have a little while on earth and that we have to fight like holy hell for what we think is just. I'm sure the man . . . *feels* every time an American soldier is hurt."

"About the way he felt when he tried to hamstring the Supreme Court to get all his Communistic legislation through. That's about how moral that fellow is. He should be impeached."

Yet the man who had spoken, Simon knew, had worked for two years on the WPA, building stone steps down into the gulf that no one ever used because the road was more convenient, taking the government's money when he had none of his own. It was curious all right. Many of the men who had taken handouts from Washington in the thirties hated the government that gave them money for groceries because of the humiliation. Almost no one stopped to think what would have happened to the eleven million unemployed if aid hadn't come their way.

"But it was for the people. He wanted to help the common people. F.D.R. loves the common man. I bet if I went up to the White House and said, 'I'm Simon Gavin from Ventry, Ohio, and I'd like to talk to the President for a spell,' why, I bet he'd say, 'Have a chair.' "

"He'd show you the door right quick. That's what he'd do. The only one he listens to is Sta-leen."

"Why, sometimes when he's giving one of his Fireside Chats," Simon went on, "I have half a notion to call him up. Just to tell him I agree one hundred percent. To tell him that Simon Gavin has confidence that . . . well, by God, that we'll come through, as bad as things look . . . I know . . . I know for a fact he cried when he heard what happened to those boys at Pearl Harbor."

"Wah! Cried! If he cries, he cries solid gold. That's how rare it would be. They say the man has never had less than eight hours of sleep every night of the year, every year of his life. People like that, they don't think of people who are dying. And Churchill! You know, I never saw an Englishman with a face I liked? They all look empty. You can see right through an English face. No character at all. Churchill spends half his day in bed, smoking cigars, and he's up half the night with a wine bottle. He's not much better than a playboy, except he likes wars better'n women."

"He's half American," someone observed, allowing a little character for the man.

"A man needs sleep to make big decisions the next day," Simon said with conviction, defending the sleeping habits of the President, apologizing for his lack of insomnia. "But I know for a fact that F.D.R. loves people. He'll never forget the *people.*"

"Wah!"

The Republicans and farm-country isolationists looked pathetically at Simon, apparently deciding that there was no way he could be enlightened. They then began to move away, to talk among themselves, and it was Frank Ventry who spoke.

"The Gavins will never learn, will they, Simon?"

Well, if it meant doubting everything, believing in nothing, Simon wasn't sure he wanted the Gavins to learn. "No, I expect we never will."

"Wars aren't pretty, Simon, and neither are politicians. That's one thing you'll have to get through your head. It'll save you a lot of trouble later on."

Few things were pretty, Simon supposed, but that wasn't reason enough to believe in the inevitability of unprettiness. There was, even now, a woman upstairs who was suffering—Simon didn't know why or what had brought it on—and no one could say that it was pretty to watch. Yet Simon would somehow have to try to reach her. That he knew. A man couldn't turn his back on people.

"I just hope to God that Dewey will never have to go into the Army," Frank now continued. "No, by God, they'd have to run a tank through my house before I'd let my son go over and fight for those worn-out people in Europe. When the Germans start marching down Priest Street, that's when I'll get out my gun. And that's when I'll let my son fight."

"It's out of your hands, Frank. In a country as big as this one you do what you're told. This isn't the old days." Simon was certain that Frank would now give him his America First views, watered-down Lindbergh and Father Coughlin.

"It's still a democracy, not a police state. Everyone in this country came over here to get away from Europe. Let the goddamn Europeans stew in their own juices. No one can tell me we belong in any foreign war."

"It stopped being a foreign war after Pearl Harbor. We did what we had to do."

"What the empire builders in Washington wanted us to do," Frank replied, angry now. "What you forget, Simon ... what you seem to *want* to forget is that self-interest rules the world. It always has and it always will. You say F.D.R. is a moral man. Then why in hell doesn't he pull our troops out of the Pacific, where they don't belong anyway, and send them to Haiti instead? *That's* where people are suffering. But we don't care about them, and do you know why? There's no money in it for us. We don't have any rubber or oil interests there the way we have in the Pacific. We don't give a damn about people, and you better wake up to that right now. This country is governed by businessmen, money men, and once a man gets the smell of money, that's good-by to scruples."

Self-interest? If self-interest ruled the world, as Frank said, what was the use of even trying to live with other people? "I can't say I've ever even got close to the smell of money," Simon answered, "so maybe I'm no judge of men who have their nostrils filled. But I don't believe that we don't care about the Poles or the French and what's happened to them. No, I just can't believe that."

"Well, I don't know why in hell you can't. France sold out the first chance she could get to protect herself. I wouldn't be surprised if the Vichy government isn't right now trying to get a chunk of England once it's invaded. They're looking after themselves, Simon. And the Poles— hell, the English teamed up to help out the Poles, but *which* Poles? The same goddamn crooks that have been milking people dry all over Europe for the last five hundred years. The nobility, the millionaires, the landowners. I for one think that Hitler's the best thing that ever happened to Europe."

"But it's the way the man's doing things, Frank."

Frank laughed sardonically. "You have to step on some

people to get what you want. F.D.R. did it to get us out of the Depression, didn't he? And Hitler's doing it to get Europe out of the mess and the chaos that's there. Lindbergh calls Nazi Germany 'the wave of the future,' and it *is*. Someone has to be a Nazi Germany to this world to bring a little reason and order to it. If it isn't Germany, then it'll have to be us. Or Russia. Or some other country we don't even know about now. And I say that the Germans would do a pretty good job once they're through with all the killing."

"Yes, they'd do a pretty good job all right. At least the Jews wouldn't have to worry about a homeland in Palestine any more. There won't be any left in a few more years."

Quickly Frank answered, "How much of a fuss did the world put up when the English sat back and let over a million and a half people in Ireland die during the famine? Or who cared when the Turks massacred the Armenians? No one even knows how many thousands or millions of Armenians died. By God, it's hard to *find* an Armenian any more. Hell, Simon, if you want to get mad at someone, get mad at God, not Hitler. *He* let as many as forty million people die in a plague during the Middle Ages—doesn't that stagger the imagination?—and now we're bothered by what Hitler's doing to the Jews."

"I've been mad at God for years, Frank, but a man can't do anything about that. It's just that no man should have the right to say that other men ought to die. What if—now, don't be hurt, Frank; this is for the sake of the argument—what if F.D.R. said tomorrow that the only way we can win this war is to exterminate all the alcoholics in America? Should I let him take you?"

Frank shrugged his shoulders. "I'm already exterminated. The businessmen in this country saw to that when they took everything they could get and then ran out during the Depression."

"It's not the same thing. No one singled you out. Everyone suffered—poor people and rich people, Catholics and Jews. But for the Jews to be killed just *because* they're Jews ... why, that's insupportable. It's the darkest page in history. Next, I suppose you'll say we should go out and shoot the Amish because they're Amish. They're just as different as the Jews."

"No, they're not. They withdraw from the world to be different. The Jews stay out where everyone can see them. They're bankers and merchants; they don't work with

216

their hands except to feel money. They can live in a country for a couple hundred years and still not be a part of the country they're living in. They have no sense of *pride* in being Germans, or English, or Americans. To be a Jew is everything. Well, it's wrong, Simon. They want everything to change, but never themselves. Ten years ago when so many of the intellectuals here were Communists, I bet three out of four were Jews. *Why,* Simon? I wish I knew. Maybe because they have to distrust any place where they find refuge. So they undermine. It's a very ... serious fault in character. An unfortunate one. God knows, if this country ever went Communistic, the Jews would get together and start fidgeting for a monarchy or some damn thing. They hated the Germans long before the Germans hated them."

"But the Levinsons aren't that way. You couldn't ask for nicer people.'

"Hell, Simon, that girl of theirs dated Jimmy Baker all through high school. But do you think the Levinsons would let her marry him? Christ, no. They sent her down to Pittsburgh so that she could meet a Jewish boy. If they're so damn smart, why can't they ever let *go?*"

At last Simon said, "You must hate the Jews."

"I *am* a Jew. Haven't I suffered every bit as much as they have? And did anyone help me?"

"That's very rotten, Frank. To hate people because you see yourself in them. It's all the more reason to help and pity them. Of all the people I've ever known, no one was without hatred as much as Luke. There was almost nothing he didn't love. And he saw that the real peril in this war was that people were hating each other for an altogether new reason. Just because they happened to be a certain way when they were born. And that's why he went."

"Luke was a child and a fool."

Simon looked at him, startled, unable to say anything. "I suppose he was," he at last began. "You might have something. Yes, you might have something."

A child and a fool. Maybe that was what was wrong with people. They could never see how the world made them pay dearly for being children and fools. Even the Jews themselves. To stay in a country like Germany all through the thirties when they must have known what was happening. And still hoping that it wasn't happening to *them* even as they were being carted away. And when it

217

was too late, did they still hope? Oh, my God, they were children and fools.

"And he might have seen that for himself," Simon added. "That's what worries me. He might have *seen* that." Simon spat out the words, as though he had been holding them for a long time. "This is a terrible thing to say, Frank, and God forgive me if I'm wrong, but I think he ran. I think he ran because he saw ... he was a child and a fool. He was running home, Frank."

He had said it. For almost a year he had thought around it, and now it was said. In Frank's eyes he saw the sadness.

Then, quickly, "They can't find him, Frank. They don't know where he is. He's disappeared, just like the Jews. Isn't that terrible? My own son tried to help, but he saw that he couldn't, and he ran instead, and now no one knows where he is."

"I'm not going," Dewey said. He was leaning against a tree in the back yard, his legs spread out before him. A few minutes before, Francine had left to help with the dishes, and the two boys could hear the sounds of plates clinking together in the kitchen. From the parlor, over the low, countrified voices of Gavins and Boyds, they could make out an occasional word that Simon was speaking, first gentle, then argumentative, and now somehow impassioned.

"What do you mean, you're not going?" Boyd asked him.

"You can't tell anyone, because you know what the old man would do. He'd tie my ass to the bedpost." He pulled at the grass beneath him, tossing chunks of it as far as he could into the Victory garden at the side of the lawn. His voice was calm—later Boyd was to wonder at its calmness—when he said, "It's going to sound histrionic or something, and I think maybe I even saw it in a Claudette Colbert movie, but I'm going to enlist."

"Enlist? What the holy hell are you talking about? You're coming to school with me."

"Don't talk so goddamn loud. I made up my mind last night after . . . well, I just made it up. I been thinking about it for a long time. I'm going to take the train with you on Wednesday, only I'm not going to Oberlin. I'm getting off in Cleveland."

"For Christ's sake, that's stupid. They're not even going to *draft* you. They don't want you."

218

"That was sort of a lie too. I guess maybe I'm getting tired of lies. Anyway, it was the old man who was doing the lying that time, not me. All that asthma crap."

"Your pop *bought* a deferment?"

Dewey seemed ashamed. "The Ventrys don't buy. We barter. Pop just asked Doc Herron to help me out, and he's married to a cousin of mine, I suppose you know. He's also an America First buddy of Pop's and doesn't think we should be in the war anyway. The day I went to Cleveland for my physical he gave me ... he gave me some stuff to take that made me breathe like an old man. Don't you remember how I was sick as a dog for two days afterwards? And how I was sick to my stomach on the bus coming home?"

Dewey lowered his face, looking into the grass. "It's not as dirty as it sounds. I guess Pop must have got down on his knees before Doc Herron and said he'd do anything. Isn't that the weirdest thing? I actually think I'm beginning to understand him a little bit. I think he even likes me in a way, and I guess he thought that's what I wanted—to go to college and not into the Army."

"You poor son of a bitch. That's no reason to go out and enlist. Just to show your old man ..."

"To show him I can take it?" Dewey finished for him. "I'm not so sure it isn't. But that's not why I'm doing it. I just think ... last night I decided I better get away from here for a while."

"So you're going to school. Why get into a sweat? I told you I was going to take care of you, didn't I?"

"Oh, boy," Dewey exclaimed, a kind of anger mixed with gratitude filling his eyes. "Someone is always taking care of me. And what's worse is that I'm always ... shopping around for someone to take care of me. It don't go, as the feller says. I guess I have to start taking care of myself."

He watched Boyd's silent face, then continued. "If I stay around here, I'll be a kid all of my life. But if I go away—clean away—and then come back later on, I think maybe I'll change. *You* grew up. But I'm just the way I was five years ago, you know that? Hell, they should use me in a psych casebook or something. 'Young Dew Ventry, everlasting kid.'" He grinned now. "Look. God damn it, look! If I wasn't pinching my lousy fingers together, I'd start bawling right now. That's got to stop. I'm scared sweatless, but I'm going anyway. Pop'll be howling mad for a while, mostly because he'll *know* I'm scared sweatless. But then I think . . . what the hell, you know what I mean."

Sure, Boyd knew. He was going to show his old man that he could take anything the world had to offer, and maybe even show him that he was braver than Frank Ventry was. Oh, hell, what a futile, what a silly gesture.

"He's . . . well, he's different now. He's sort of off the bottle, and half the time he's aching because it hurts him so goddamn much. Well, if he can do that, I can do something too." Then, "Did I tell you we had a talk last night? He honest to God *talked* to me. I guess he heard Tina come in or something; she was out on the porch because it was so hot."

Boyd found it hard to conceal the alarm he felt. For the love of God, the whole house had been awake while he and Tina were in the ravine.

"He heard me popping around the room, so he knocked on the door nice as pie and came in. I think what it was . . . he was really fighting the booze. You could tell how hard he was fighting, and how much he wanted a drink. So maybe it helped to talk to me. Anyway, the funny thing, I told him what happened."

"Out at the Lake with the girl?"

"Yeah," Dewey answered. "He was more embarrassed than I was. Then he told me it was probably partly his fault . . . what he did that time he whipped me and all . . . and he said he was sorry as hell about it. What it was, he said he was mad at everything so he took it out on me because I happened to be around. It was real corny, but I think he meant it. I always used to think he hated me, but what it was, I think, he hated himself. It's funny how things get clear after a while. Anyway, just to shoot the breeze, I asked him why didn't he paint some more pictures for the house or something. I told him they were great, the ones he did a long time ago. And you know what he said? Boy, it really took guts to say. He said . . . he wasn't any good. For a long time he blamed everything on the Depression and on Mom, but what it was, he just wasn't very good. And he didn't even seem mad about it. We laughed like hell."

It was possible all right. A man could be told so often that the world expected things of him that in time he was bound to believe it whether it was true or not. More than one man had come to grief because of inflated promise.

Yes, Boyd supposed, it was probably a hell of a revelation for Frank Ventry. A hell of a one.

"I don't want to go to college anyway," Dewey said. "You know what my old man did last spring? He went down to school and got someone to show him what my lousy IQ is. It's against the rules, but he must have persuaded someone. The old 'Look, do I have a ninny for a son or don't I?' routine. He didn't even know if I was smart or dumb, but he was breaking his balls to send me to Oberlin. You should have seen him when he came home. I was all right! It's a little over 125 or something, which makes it respectable but nothing hot-shot. About twenty points over the boobs. So he thought I could be a doctor, for Christ's sake. If Lew Ayres could do it, why not me? The trouble was that he was doing to me just what the people back in the twenties did to him when he went to art school. I wouldn't be any *good* as a doctor. And I think he'll realize that after a while. In the Army, maybe they'll let me horse around trucks or jeeps or something. Man, I'd like that."

"Jesus," Boyd said at last, "I always thought we were going to room together. That's what I always thought."

Had Dewey told him what he planned to do just the night before when Boyd was pee-oohed at him, Boyd would have been glad, but right now he felt cheated. For all he admired Dewey's motives—wanting to be able to depend on himself—it seemed to him that at least part of their friendship was based on the very thing Dew lacked and wanted now to get for himself. If Dewey fed on Boyd's strength, Boyd also fed on Dewey's weakness. It made for harmony. Yet now, listening to what had been told him, Boyd could see that their world was beginning to tear apart even before he thought it would. Boyd himself to Oberlin. Francine to Cleveland. And Dewey to God knows where.

"Where will they send you?" he asked at last.

"I don't know," he answered. "I think they're sending guys from around here up to Fort Custer in Michigan before basic. Remember Homer Lane? He enlisted in Cleveland, and then they sent him to Custer."

"Hell," Boyd said, "that's a long way from here."

Dewey didn't reply. Perhaps he was thinking what Boyd himself was thinking. Almost any place was a long way from Ventry. Twenty miles outside of town, and you were already a long way from home. And if you got that far, who could say that you would ever come back?

People were leaving, either to go home to milk the cows or to get supper on the table, and at the door Simon said good-by. Too formal, too stuffy, he thought, because he would probably run into most of them in the square in the next few days. After the rooms emptied, he looked around for Cortez but found that she hadn't returned from her bedroom.

He probably should never have said what he had confessed to Frank Ventry because there was no telling what Frank would talk about if he started to drink again. Still, and it pleased Simon, the man had seemed so alert, so interested in what Simon was saying and in what he himself was saying. It was by no means the old Frank, the boy who would come home weekends from art school, his eyes burning with excitement; neither had it been the Frank of only a few days ago. Something had softened him, and Simon pondered what it was.

Walking up the stairs, Simon recalled what Toby Carle had whispered to him as he was leaving the house. "Cortez is just the way she was when she was sixteen years old, isn't she, Simon?" and it was said critically, as if somehow the people who had always been enchanted by her now begrudged her her style, for being younger than they were. Simon had wanted to reply, "I hope to God she'll always stay that way," but he hadn't. He wasn't sure, after all, that he wanted Cortez to remain the way she was. In the morning at the cemetery, after they had left the Boyd plot and walked among the tombstones, what had she said? "When I die, Simon, I hope I can be buried in concrete. I've always felt that way, every day of my life."

Perhaps that was how she had managed to stay so young; perhaps you had to bury yourself in concrete in order to do it. Had Cortez given herself to life, she probably would have lost both her beauty and her rarity, and now when she seemed to want to break out at last, not knowing how, she succeeded only in hating her mother for having given her illusions in the first place. Strange what could happen between a mother and a daughter or a father and a son. No matter how you tried, nine times out of ten you were still unknown to each other.

And Simon—a short while ago so confident, so assured— was now not even certain that he had ever known his own son. All the talks Simon had had with him about the grand things a man could do if only he set his mind to it, yet it might have been that Luke was too small a man to try any of them. If Cortez had nourished her mother's illusions, perhaps Luke had nourished Simon's. Perhaps Luke had never wanted to go to war, but had done it through a sense of duty.

Simon wished that he could have another chance. That the war would stop tomorrow, that Lucas would come home, that no chemical plant would be built in Ventry, that Cortez would be the way she used to be, that Boyd wouldn't have to pay for a sin of his father's. That time could be moved back entirely and people could begin again in a world at peace. If only Simon could tell someone to stop it all.

In the upstairs hall Simon listened at the bedroom door and could hear nothing from within. He knocked softly once, then a second time, and from the other side he heard Cortez ask, "Mama?"

Oh, my God, what was she doing? Could you love and hate the same thing? As he opened the door and walked in, he saw Cortez sitting in a chair by the window, her shoes off, and her hair—as soft now as it was when she was a girl—disheveled, as if she had been running her hands through it. She made no attempt to look up at him.

"Cortez, dear, what's happened? Are you ill?"

She held up one arm, as though to ward him off. "No, nothing is wrong, Simon. I would just as soon be alone though. Be a good boy, Simon."

"I can't leave you sitting here like this," he said, walking toward her.

"Don't come near me," she said, her voice quiet and controlled. "Leave me alone and go about your good Samaritan business somewhere else. I'll be all right in a few minutes."

Simon looked at the ivory cup in her hand which she had not tried to conceal. "If you're feeling bad, Cortez, you shouldn't be drinking. It just tends to depress you more, they say."

She raised her head now, and she spoke as though she were talking to one of her servants. "You have always been such a reader, Simon. Is there anything you don't know? Did you read that in *The Saturday Evening Post?*"

Ashamed because he wasn't as clever as most of the people she knew, he said, "Well, I suppose I read a lot. There isn't much else for me to do around here."

"For your information—and in the event that *The Saturday Evening Post* didn't go into it—alcohol does more than depress one. It kills one. My own doctor told me that. And do you know what I told him? I told him I was getting a new doctor. I don't need anyone to tell me the obvious."

"Have I done something?" he asked, hurt.

"You've done nothing. Just leave me be."

He walked closer to her until she again raised her hand. "I feel very bad to see you this way. I wish I could do something or say something."

"I wish someone could too," she answered. "But I don't know that I can hear voices any more. Isn't that curious? I was downstairs and I couldn't hear people at all."

She appraised him very coolly, looking at him from his feet to the top of his head, as if she were trying to decide. "Simon, you're such a great reader—an admirable reader— you'll be interested in this. It's a vignette. I had . . . I had intended to come down here a day earlier. In fact, I did. Does that confuse you? I had Harold drive me down on Thursday night, not Friday at all. He's such an understanding man. I don't think I could ever find anyone to replace him."

She closed her eyes and leaned back in the chair. "I had him stop in Painesville at Hellriegel's. It's an inn. A very pretty place. Cozy and with a country air. I told him to wait in the car because I needed a little something to eat. That was at six or seven o'clock. I sat at a table and drank, Simon, from then until, I suppose, about midnight. Very quietly. I'm never odious. And then a nice gentleman asked me if he could join me. I told him he could. He was a very nice gentleman. And when he begged me—how can I say what time it was?—one or two, I suppose—begged me to go for a drive, I told him that I'd be charmed. We went out the back way to avoid Harold. He's so good about that. So patient. I think colored people have more patience than we do, don't you? The gentleman took me to his car and for a short drive, as he called it. Can I say he made love? No, you don't make love to someone as old as I am. He attacked me, Simon, and I knew he would. That's why I went with him. I began to scream, and when he'd finished getting his pleasure he pushed me from the car. It was raining that night—remember?—and I walked

224

all the way back to the parking lot. Harold was still there. He took me to a motel where I slept all night and most of the next day. And then I came down here and hugged my nephews. My nephews. In *my* arms." She opened her eyes. "I am now sitting here, wondering why I screamed. Can you tell me, Simon?"

"*Cor-tez.*"

"Don't feel sorry for me. That's one thing I won't have. That's one thing I can't tolerate. My friends in Cleveland don't feel sorry for me. They understand me. People I know put me in cabs when I don't have Harold with me. And there's always a nice gentleman who can't see the screaming in me. And when I get home, Harold is always kind and understanding. Am I shocking you?"

Shocked? Simon could scarcely breathe. "That's no life," he said at last.

"It has to be because it's all I have." She waved her hand in the air before her. "Now go."

But Simon didn't move. If she had to seek out people in bars, if she had to depend on a paid driver to look after her, it was because she wasn't able to find anything in him or any of the family. "Those people," Simon almost shuddered thinking about them, "those people you find in bars, they're not for *you*, for the love of God."

"And what kind of people are for me? Have you ever stopped to consider that? The people I saw here this afternoon—the ugly, grotesque, self-important people I saw downstairs? Are they? Or the people I employ—oh, Simon, they're waiting for me to die, do you know that? Are *you* for me? Is Rose?"

"We care for you a great deal, and we'd be very hurt to see you unhappy."

"My sister cares for me. I know that. She always has. She's very kind. She looks forward every year to my visit. Doesn't she?"

"You should know your sister by now."

"She *hates* me, Simon. And so did all those people downstairs. People with ugly tongues. Helen Ventry. That dreadful Toby what's-his-name. What did I ever do to them? Oh, God, what did I ever do?"

She had never done anything. That's what it was. She had never done anything. If only Simon could tell her to do something for one of them, to forget herself long enough at least to see that there were other people who

225

needed help and understanding too, then maybe they would understand her. If only he could tell her.

Her ivory cup spilled on her lap, and as it did Simon went to her, touching her on the shoulder, trying to bring her some sort of pity. But she pulled back. "Don't *touch* me!"

Her eyes were so full of terror that Simon began to inch his way backward toward the door.

"Don't you *ever* touch me!" Her voice came in small, panting gusts. *"You terrible old man!"*

For Simon it was a hard fist at his face. He knew that he would crumple there on the floor if he couldn't make his legs move out of the room.

Less than half an hour later Simon finally found Parnell and sat him down on the sofa in the parlor. Did he remember how sometimes you had to break a promise, even though you didn't want to, because something very important had changed your plans? When the boy said that he knew of it to happen, Simon told him that he would make it up to him in time, but right now he had to go somewhere by himself and couldn't take Parnell with him. It was to be a secret between the two of them for a little while.

It was not until before supper, as the family was sitting on the front porch fanning themselves, that Rose asked if anyone had seen Simon. No one responded. At last Cortez said that she had talked to him earlier in the afternoon and that he seemed ... well, upset. That was how she put it. Cortez was now composed.

Parnell went to the wicker chair where his mother was sitting and whispered into her ear. She blanched, stood up, and went hurriedly to the screen door, looking into the hall as if for an echo of something she had expected to hear. Silent for a moment, she turned and announced, "Simon's left. He's gone on a trip. He made Parnell promise not to say anything until after he left."

Rose stopped the swing on which she was sitting with Cortez. "But he didn't take his luggage," she said excitedly. "He always takes his luggage!"

"He took a box," Parnell whispered. "He's going to Washington." And Parnell knew with all his heart that Simon was going for Luke. He knew with all his heart, and knowing it he felt the pride burst in him. "He's going to see the President."

"Dear God," Rose said.

Seven

The train was crowded with men in uniform reporting back to camp or going home on leaves before they were sent overseas, and Simon had to stand in the aisle between Painesville and Cleveland. The men were merry, singing songs that seemed off-color, playing poker, exchanging gossip from camp, and swearing at the slow train. At East Cleveland, where the engine stopped for water, he sat on the corner of a suitcase and looked for a long time at a soldier sitting silently beside him. Simon wanted to talk to him because he seemed to be alone, but when he asked him where he was going, the soldier looked up irritably, replied "Frisco," then shut his eyes and settled back in his seat.

At the Cleveland terminal he waited for those who were leaving to push their way from the train before he tried to walk over the outstretched legs in the aisle to the exit. Everyone seemed to be in a hurry; such haste he had never seen before. Once outside on the concrete platform, he put his box down and caught his breath, studying the long, high steps to the station's waiting room that would have to be climbed. He picked up the box—an unsightly Campbell Soup carton he had found in the shed back home, not daring to get his own luggage out—and walked up the first ten steps. Then he stood there and rested, people jostling him as they passed. Not until the lonely-looking soldier brushed against him with a duffel bag on his shoulders, animating him, did he walk another ten steps. Then another, and another until he found himself in the high-ceilinged station.

At the gate Simon had to fight his way through a large crowd of people, poised to run down the steps to the waiting train he had just left, though most of them would have to stand once they reached it. They began to make a small aisle for him, but before he was free the conductor waved them through, and in the confusion Simon's box was knocked from his hands. He held his temper and his tongue, however, knowing that war had somehow made even the simple task of boarding a train an urgent and rude one. He hoped that it wouldn't be like this all the way south.

There was still another line at the information desk, and when Simon finally reached it the attendant was cranky and short in his replies. He sputtered off a long list of train departures, but either because of the noise in the station or because of the excitement he felt, Simon was able to hear only a few of them. When, after the man had finished, Simon again asked what time the next train left for Washington, he looked at Simon with contempt and anger and at last scrawled a time and a gate number in large, underlined letters on a piece of paper and shoved it toward him. Simon was about to thank him, but someone had already pushed him away from the window. He lifted his box once again and walked to the ticket counter, standing there at the end of a line, not remembering until he was halfway to the window that he had forgotten his railroad pass. When in time he reached the counter, he smiled at the man behind it, thinking that the agent might see the joke of it all, and said, "I'm a railroad man myself, and you'll never believe this but . . ." The man interrupted to say, "I don't have all day. Where do you want to go, Grampa?" A few people behind him tittered, and Simon quickly told the man, then pulled a fat bundle of bills from his pants pocket in order to pay for the ticket.

Simon backed away, momentarily forgetting the box he had placed on the floor while he dug for his money. He retrieved it, walked to the center of the station, looked up at the clock at the far end, and saw that it was more than an hour to train time. Only about ten people appeared to be waiting before the gate. Simon, his legs already tired and his head aching from the heat, instead made his way to a bench and sat there, wiping his forehead with his white handkerchief, reminding himself that he would have to keep his eye on the clock. He must have half dozed because when he next looked at the time he had a scant five minutes to reach his train, and an enormous crowd now milled around the metal gate. When the conductor raised it, Simon was the last one down the steps. He walked carefully for fear of falling.

On the lower level he joined a line of hurrying people

moving from coach to coach for places to sit. At the end of the second, too exhausted to go any farther, he rested his box out of the way and let them rush past him. In a few minutes most of them returned, short-tempered and full of complaints, and stationed themselves in the aisle, some standing by the washrooms, others sitting on their luggage. Simon carefully lowered himself onto the side of a duffel bag, hoping that its owner wouldn't object, then waited in all the heat for the train to move. When at last it did, he leaned his head back against the corner of a seat and tried to sleep, awakened every few minutes by legs stepping over him.

Later, in the soft night light of the sleeping coach, he woke up and peered through a window. It was, he could see in the darkness, hilly now and it was raining. Southern Ohio, he supposed, or West Virginia. Hillbilly country. He left his makeshift seat and made his way down the aisle, stepping over twisted bodies, toward the end where he hoped to find a water cooler. He was desperately thirsty, not having had anything to drink since he left home, but he found that the cooler had been drained dry. At the door to the lavatory he could hear dice rolling on the floor. Instead of going in as he wanted to, he returned to his place in the coach, and once there he found that someone was now resting his foot on top of the duffel bag. In the hot and stuffy coach he stood, letting his body sway to the movement of the train, waiting for it to be morning, breathing in the deep, acrid scent of people, watching their sleeping faces. They no longer seemed as hard and cross as they had been only a few hours ago. The people who had impatiently pushed against him in the station and on the stairs now seemed gentle and transfigured by night, far from whatever necessity had sent them on a journey. Standing, rocking, he could hear the rhythmic clackety-clack of the rails, the hooting of the whistle as the train sped past crossings, and the creaking of the coach.

It wasn't his age or his terribleness alone that was sending Simon from Ventry, of that he was sure. Nor did he have any great relish for the trip he now found himself on. To go to Washington—a city already bursting with shouting and ranting politicians, with lobbyists trying to coax war contracts their way, with thousands of soldiers, secretaries, and defense workers—had not even occurred to Simon a week ago. Not even the day before.

Then why was he going? It was hard to say. Perhaps because it was the nation's capital, and it was one of the few places left in the country that still belonged to the people. And it seemed now to be in greater peril than ever before, not because of the perfidious men there who were using it to further their own selfish ambitions, but because of the goodhearted men who had simply forgotten the sounds of people's voices. Even during the worst days of the Civil War, Lincoln had time to talk to mothers who were worried about their sons, but somehow the country had now become too large for that. You could write a letter to your Congressman, and with luck it would be read by an eighteen-year-old girl, the daughter of a heavy-drinking ward politician, who spent most of her time polishing her nails or squeezing her pimples in the washroom. Roosevelt and his staff were even now, according to the newspapers, planning a second front, and F.D.R. was listening to admirals, to generals, and to diplomats. To everyone but the people. Until just that afternoon, Simon had been waiting, hoping for Boyd to follow his father into the Army so that he, too, could be a part of a second front, but now he wanted to stop it like nothing he had ever wanted before. It was no good. The price a man had to pay for glory, the price a *country* had to pay for glory, was too dear.

To Simon it seemed that old men—and he was willing now to admit that he was that—had been given almost no utility at all in this war. Yet perhaps only an old man was able to see what the country was losing, and he alone could bring the war to an amiable conclusion. Perhaps Simon could see F.D.R. and try to explain things to him. To tell him about Ventry, about the family and the way it used to be, and about Lucas and how badly he was needed at home. Simon could even perhaps read a few of the last letters Luke had sent to show F.D.R. what kind of people were being wasted on first fronts and second and third fronts. There was no call for all the killing and all the change. If the President was afraid to sit down and talk the matter over with Hitler, why, hell, Simon would go himself. They could put him in a Flying Fortress and he could parachute out over Berlin, once someone explained the knack of the thing to him. And he could land in the Chancellery, in a billowing cloud of white, like an ancient vision, and tell Hitler that he had come as a personal representative of the people of Ventry to stop the damned war and to learn what the Germans had done to Lucas.

Well, Simon could hope. He had talked to General MacArthur's father, to William Faulkner, and to Robert A. Taft, and that was more than most people had done, by God. He had a way with great men, a way of explaining what was on his mind without using highfalutin words, a way of catching their attention and holding it. And F.D.R. would listen to him, too, if only Simon could get past the nitwits great men always surrounded themselves with. He reminded himself that he'd probably make a better impression if he checked his Campbell Soup box somewhere before he went to the White House. As for his suit, it would be wrinkled and dirty by the time he got there, but F.D.R. must have seen men in wrinkled suits before. If he hadn't, it was about time he did.

Simon watched the people sleeping in the coach: soldiers bent in their seats, traveling toward troopships, too afraid to say more than "Frisco" to a stranger. Stunned-looking wives without husbands pushing from one Army camp to another. Children who ought to be at home in bed and not on a train questing for fathers or brothers. And the old people, like Simon himself, watching what was happening around them and wondering how it had all come to pass. To Simon it seemed that they were all crying for something that had been taken away from them. It seemed that in every heart—and in Simon's own—a child was crying because the world had dealt them all a bad blow. And as the train pushed south, through the quiet, darkened towns, rain splattering at the windows, even the land seemed to be crying.

In the morning the house was soundless and expectant. Even Parnell, who ordinarily ran into the kitchen as if chased by the white-faced bull that was kept in a field at the end of the street, tiptoed in for his peanut butter and jelly sandwich at ten o'clock. There had been, as soon as they left their beds, a second call to Cleveland, but it had produced the same response as the evening before. Everyone was now waiting.

Frank Ventry, the night before, had taken control of the situation. First he had determined which train Simon had taken to Cleveland, then he had talked to the police in that city. When Frank had given them a description of Simon, adding that he was old and likely to become ill, and then told them the circumstances of his disappearance, they had wanted to know what he had done. *Done?* He had done nothing; he had simply run away. The police officer had then asked for his telephone number, told him to hang up, and a minute later called back. "I just wanted to make sure you're not a crank," he had said. "If I understand correctly, a seventy-five-year-old crazy man has run away from home. Is that right?" Frank had gone over it a second time, knowing that nothing would come of his efforts. They could do no more than hope that Simon himself would call before he got too far away.

As they waited up in the Gavin parlor until past midnight, Rose had sat at one end of the horsehair sofa, next to the sleeping Parnell, piecing together parts of a quilt her mother had been working on before her death—small squares and triangles of colors, the lavender of one of her mother's Sunday dresses, the cornflowers-on-white of an old bed jacket, and the green of the robe her father had given her years ago when she was carrying Luke. The quilt would never be completed, not merely because Rose's fingers were less nimble than her mother's or because she lacked "the tasty way with colors" that her mother possessed, but because the dismembered quilt, finer for being undone, was taken out whenever Rose was upset, and the small squares and triangles talked to as if they were the beads of a rosary. Touching them—a graph of the crises the Gavins had seen—seemed to offer solace.

Yet that had been the extent of Rose's outward agitation. At some time in her life she had decided that she worried so well—so extravagantly, so competently, so s*ecretly*—that it was her bounden duty to do the worrying for the entire family. If worry was inevitable, as it apparently was, then it was Rose's task to gather it all to her bosom where it could be hers alone. Thus equipped, she proceeded to pretend that nothing at all was happening. After the call to the Cleveland police, when the family was dispirited and glum, she had suggested that Simon was probably at that moment winking at a scarlet lady sitting across from him on some train. "You can't tell me that a man like that goes around looking at the *country*," she had said. It was false. She knew it was false, and the family knew that it was false. Yet it lifted their spirits as Rose hoped it would. They forgot for a while that Simon had within the last year become old, that at one minute he had been active and full of beans and the next—how suddenly age came! had to fight for his balance when he pulled himself from a chair.

At the Ventry house now, the morning sun shining through the parlor window, Parnell was waiting on the piano stool for Tina to come downstairs, and Frank and Helen Ventry were in the kitchen drinking coffee. Just a few minutes before, Frank had called the engineer on the second crew of the boat and asked him to fill in for the day. "I have to get Simon Gavin," he had said, and when the man asked where he was going, Frank, Helen, and Parnell all realized that they didn't know.

"If he doesn't call between now and six," Helen said to her husband in the kitchen, "you won't be able to get a train out till ten." She rested her dish towel out on the counter, spreading it to dry before the open window. "How much money did you get out of the bank?"

"One hundred," he answered. "I took it out of what Dewey has to have for second semester, but I'll put it back."

"Does anyone know if Simon had any money with him?"

"Mrs. Gavin says that he does. Apparently a lot too, so if I run out we can always use some of his."

Simon had, it was discovered, taken more than a thousand dollars in fifty-dollar bills with him. Catherine had been outraged, saying that it ought to have been in the bank, not in the bottom drawer of his dresser. Yet everyone in the family knew that for all the faith Simon had in America, he had none at all in American banking. When the Farmers' Bank failed during the Depression, he had lost almost three thousand. The money in the dresser was intended for the next Depression.

"Well," Helen said, carefully removing her apron and hanging it behind the kitchen door, "everyone seems to think that Simon is going to call, but wouldn't it be just like him to stay away for a month without saying anything?"

"I hardly think so," Frank answered. "He's getting to be old. Vier Payne down at the station said he had to help him up into the coach. He can't get far this time."

"Well, I just hope nothing happens to him. It would be a pity. He was always such a strong and lively man." She looked through a corner window and saw Cortez walking down Summer, turning onto Priest, dressed in a pale blue, iridescent dress, the color of her eyes.

233

If Cortez was upset about Simon, she kept it to herself. And of her talk with him the day before she had said almost nothing. What Cortez felt now, returning from the gulf where she had spent part of the morning sitting by the river, was that she would be more alone than ever during the next few days. She was vaguely put out with Simon for having helped spoil her little holiday.

"I could see it building up for a long time," Helen Ventry went on.

"You mean Simon?"

There was impatience in her voice. "You'd think Rose Gavin would learn. Isn't it funny how two people can live together for such a long time and still not know how to treat each other?" Embarrassed by what she had said, its relevance to Frank and herself, she turned her head away, pretending work at the sink. "She never allowed the poor man any respect. She made fun of everything he did. I've always felt sorry for Simon."

"Rose is a very strong woman. She doesn't have a nerve in her body."

"I don't know," Helen replied thoughtfully. "Sometimes it seems like a bluff—the way she pretends not to feel anything. Do you remember when Luke's brother had the accident in the tree? Desmond? We must have been in the first or second grade. *You* were at the funeral, because I remember you were. Well, as long as I live I'll remember Rose Gavin and what she did. Before she closed the coffin, she had Vincent Elliott—that photographer who lives in Madison—snapping pictures like nobody's business. Not just of Desmond but of everyone there. All the relatives. All the friends. And the poor little boy himself. It was more like a wedding than a funeral. And Rose didn't shed a single, a solitary tear. She was too busy telling Vincent what pictures he should be getting. My mother said the woman had no feelings at all." She paused now, wetting her lips. "But what I was saying. About part of it being a bluff. The day she got those pictures of Desmond in the coffin, they say she almost went to pieces. As if she had held off until then. As if she hadn't allowed herself to see anything until then. They say she wouldn't leave her room for a week. There's more to her than shows."

Well, the eye was unreliable. That was one thing Frank Ventry had learned, and he hadn't had to go to art school to learn it. "She's a strange one all right. When I was over

234

there a half hour ago, she was going about her work as if nothing in the world was on her mind."

"That's what I mean. I think she feels—actually feels—but she just won't let anyone see her weakness. It was the same way with Lucas. The way she's covered all that up is shameful. No matter what Luke did. It's just that Rose is putting it aside so that she won't have to be . . . confronted with an emotion. Do you see what I mean?"

"I wouldn't be a bit surprised but that Simon is in Washington because of Lucas. To try to get an answer. I think he doesn't know what to believe any more, and he hopes that someone in Washington will be able to tell him. For a man as smart as he is, he's . . . well, he's innocent and unrealistic. He thinks all you have to do is walk up to the White House and ask to see the President and he'll be ushered in. He's so old-fashioned. He doesn't realize that the world has changed. I'm afraid he might be in for a shock."

Helen rinsed the sink, dried her hands on a towel, then finally on her apron to remove the last of the moisture. She stood at the window, listening to the stillness of the morning. Frank had been without a drink for four days now, and under the stress of calling the police and waiting for news of Simon he was chain-smoking cigarettes. She could see that it was taking all of his resources to keep himself from having a drink, when he needed it most. Although she had just washed and dried the coffeepot, she rinsed it in cold water, filled it again, then carefully measured coffee into the percolator.

"I thought you didn't like coffee," he said.

"Isn't it just like me?" she said. "Waiting until it's rationed and as hard to get as cut diamonds, and then developing a taste for it?"

After a while Frank said, "Well, thank you, Helen. I can use it. The coffee helps."

"I only hope Simon has a good breakfast somewhere," she went on. "They'll probably think he's out of his head if he asks for Jell-O. But, you know, Dr. Herron told me in passing one day that he has terribly high blood pressure. I think that's one reason he never ate anything but the blandest of foods. And wasn't it just like him never to tell anyone around the house?"

"I expect he'll be too busy to bother with breakfast. He has . . . well, I think he has a complaint, and he wants to

235

get it off his chest. After that's done, there'll be time enough for eating."

Helen smiled. "There's really nowhere to go any more if you have a complaint. We're getting to be so big. Take my own grandmother. She saw President McKinley when he was campaigning for the Presidency and his train stopped right here in town. Goodness, nowadays no one knows where Ventry is. Anyway, until the day she died she said that it was the prettiest election she ever saw. Because she could remember his speech and the way he'd looked at her, I suppose. But the funny *thing!* When they were going to run that road through Grandma's property, why, didn't she sit herself down and write a long letter to President McKinley as if she were writing to someone in her own family? My, weren't they all innocent?"

Frank began to smile too. "If anyone knew how Simon looked in the Fourth of July parade, stomping down Main Street like Ulysses S. Grant, all dressed up in his Spanish-American War uniform, they'd sure as hell listen to him in Washington. Yes, sir, he was the last of the *old* people around here."

Angry at himself, he slammed his cup hard against the saucer. "Here we're talking about him as if he's dead."

When the train pulled into the Washington station, Simon stood in his place for a long time, waiting for the people to pass. He felt dirty and used up, but at the same time exhilarated. On his head was his Spanish-American War cap, taken from the cardboard box at the last minute and placed over his forehead at a jaunty angle before the cloudy lavatory mirror. After it had been fitted to his satisfaction, and before someone had begun to pound on the door, Simon had snapped a smart salute at his image, practicing what he would do when led before the Commander in Chief.

He was tieless, the tie he had taken off during the night somehow having slipped onto the floor, where it had been walked on by countless feet. His white linen suit was creased and soiled, wet in places from perspiration, and his jacket now possessed grease spots from where he had leaned against the side of the coach to get his balance after descending the few steps to the platform.

He ran his hand over the stubble on his face—it was gray, and it wouldn't be too noticeable—and tried to collect himself. Perhaps he could go for a little walk first

236

to get the feel of the city and then ask someone directions to the White House. The Lincoln Memorial he would like to look at close up, having seen it before only in photographs—that huge, lonely figure sitting in a chair the way country people sat. There was *one* man who never crossed his legs like a fop, thank God. And perhaps while Simon stood before it, he would find the words he wanted to speak to the President.

He walked through the station past a sign that pointed to a bomb shelter, and made his way toward the luggage lockers, but found none vacant. Not knowing how he could dispose of the awkward box he was carrying, he placed it on the floor by his feet and waited for his breathing to catch up with him. When at last it did, he removed from the box the neatly tied bundle of Luke's letters, his change of underwear, his extra socks, and his shaving supplies, stuffing them into the already misshapen and congested coat pockets of his suit. The box he then carried to a litter basket, glad to be rid of the nuisance. He was prepared to venture into the streets. From where he stood in the center of the station, he imagined the spacious city on the other side of the doors—the wide, tree-lined streets, the white domes, the pillars, enduring marble everywhere. French and Greek, yet more American than either, full of a peace and dignity that neither the Greeks nor the French had ever known. As he stood there, already captured by what he was about to see, he was filled with warm familiarity.

When he fought his way through the crowd—the station seemed virtually occupied by a military force—a child who noticed his uncommon hat and his soldierly bearing threw him a sprightly salute, and Simon responded in kind, stuffing his unsightly underwear farther into his pocket with his other hand. He walked proudly toward a desk where, its sign suggested, a hotel room in the crowded city might be found for him. Something not too far from the White House, Simon said to the clerk. "I have business there." Whether he had business or not didn't appear to matter, because the clerk told him that could do no more than put his name on waiting lists at four hotels. He asked Simon if he had any priority. Priority? Hell, he was a veteran of a foreign war, he was seventy-five years old, he knew General MacArthur's father and Robert A. Taft personally. What more priority did they want? The clerk told him that he was sorry, but that it wouldn't do. He looked at Simon's hat for a long time, and as soon as Simon walked away he tore up the four cards Simon had painfully made out, dropping them into a wastebasket at his side.

Simon stepped out smartly and began walking toward the exit, his mind already feeding on the city's vistas of grandeur and order. What was the name of the President's dog? Fala? Yes, that's what it was. "Hello, Fala. How's the world treating you?" And the President's secretary? Missy it was. "Now, Missy, I'd just like to have a word or two with the chief. It has to do with national affairs. I'm Simon Gavin from Ventry, Ohio, and there's something I'd like to talk to F.D.R. about. There's something I want to bring to his attention. *It will bear no delay.*"

He could almost see himself standing in the President's oval study. "Lookee here," he would say, "that's enough of this fiddle-faddle. I'd sure as hell like to know why you haven't found Luke yet with all the manpower and wonderful machines at your dis-posal." Then the President would push a buzzer and say, "Well, by gum, Mr. Gavin, we've been meaning to keep this as a little surprise, but we can't put it off any longer. We've found Lucas. He was right where he was supposed to be all along. And now a grateful nation is returning him to his home." A door would open and Luke would walk into the room, his face contorted with gladness.

Half dizzy from his thoughts, passing busy people who had no notion of his manifest destiny, but feeling the importance of it himself, Simon approached the door leading into the street. As he looked into the glass, he saw himself reflected there, and then something just over his shoulder. Even before he turned to see what it was, the headache that had been bothering him all morning broke all over him, as if a bubble filled with hot blood had split behind his eyes.

Bathroom. Get to the bathroom. Head aching. Spinning. Too hot. Something wrong. Can't breathe. Help me. Please someone help me.

Spasmodically he forced his way to a bench and rested his body there. Sweat broke out on his forehead and his eyes opened wide, as if in revelation; and then he slumped over on the wooden bench.

When, an hour and thirty minutes later, two policemen answered a complaint and came to remove him, one of them kicked at his feet and gave his shoulder a push. He sunk even farther onto the bench. They lifted the outrageous hat which had fallen half over his face. "Looks like the old coot's been having himself a party," one of them said.

An hour before, Parnell had watched his Aunt Cortez walk to the bathroom in her kimono, and heard her draw her second tub for the day. She sat in it for so long that he was sure she was becoming puckered and blue. Finally he saw her pass down the hall and enter her own room, the small antique box partly hidden by a towel in her hands.

Parnell was in his grandfather's room, opening and closing bottles of medicine neatly lined on top of Simon's chiffonier, screwing the caps on tightly after he had inhaled the drugs. He picked up the two straw shoes which Simon kept on the doily, shoes he had bought when his ship had been blown to Hong Kong in a typhoon while he was on his way to fight with Admiral Dewey in Manila. Parnell stroked them, feeling their hot, dry strangeness, then brought them to his nose, searching for the pungent odor of a Chinaman's foot that Simon said could still be found on them after all these years. There! It *was* still there, a ripe Chinese scent, of fish, of typhoons, of pigtails, of rickshaws, of everything Simon had seen!

In the next room Boyd stood by an open trunk, already half filled with clean clothes, still warm from the sun and the iron. Catherine was filling it a few pieces at a time for him to take with him to Oberlin, a journey that even Simon's disappearance couldn't postpone. He pulled off his white T shirt and his sticky pants, tossing them onto the bed, then stretched out on the floor in his jockey shorts next to the open window, letting the wind dry his sweaty body. The house was silent, caught in the torpor of a hot summer afternoon, waiting for a call from Simon.

Boyd half sat up to push the curtain back from the window where it was catching the breeze, then anchored it to the bedpost. Through the window he could see Tina and Francine returning from the square, where they must have been buying things for Francine's trip to Cleveland. A week ago Tina wouldn't have gone that far for anything in the world, but now she seemed even to be carrying a small package of her own, candy perhaps—nigger babies or spearmint leaves—that she had bought at the dime store.

After three days had passed and no one had yet asked him for an explanation of the condom, Boyd had tried to let the entire damned thing fall from his mind. He only hoped that he hadn't awakened in Tina something that had nowhere to go. As he had, he knew, in himself. Maybe the body was a mindless creature unable to remember anything but pleasure, because for the last three days Boyd had been able to think of almost nothing else. It was a feeling that had little to do with Tina. It seemed to him that the feeling could haunt a man until his last breath, could change his life, could make him give up everything else in the world trying to refind it, to act it out again and again. What had the old-timey poets called it? Dying. Yes, it was that all right. Dying without death. The moment it had happened to Boyd he had forgotten everything else in the world. There was no language in his head, no name to himself, no memories, no duties, nothing. Only a newly discovered land.

But the hell of it was that it couldn't be found by yourself. You needed someone to help. Yet no one knew better than Boyd that Francine would hold herself back until the act had been sanctified by marriage. Until she was married, no one could take her a-Maying, no one could show her how round and comely the world was. He wished it was otherwise. His body, he knew, might be too unreliable to wait. And to Boyd, as to all young men, it seemed that this was an affliction no one else had ever known. For old people, whose sex had congealed through disuse or abuse, it would be ludicrous. But for a young man it was a singular torment of the keenest kind.

Still, it was probably no worse than the passion of the old. Like Simon, they simply found substitutes. It seemed to Boyd that some hunger had driven Simon to Washington, a hunger not really all that different from the one Boyd himself felt. Although he wished his grandfather good hunting, he knew already that very little could come of it except disappointment. Only the young could be dreamers; the old had already spent their dreams.

Hearing a noise as he lay on the floor of the bedroom, he opened his eyes, then listened to a short, musical tapping on the door, half open. He hastily snatched his pants from the top of the bed and placed them over his midsection.

"Am I disturbing my favorite nephew?" Cortez asked in a high, distracted voice as she entered the room. "I've been here for ages, my sweet, and you haven't said more than ten words to your silly old aunt. May I come in?"

She was already there. Boyd wasn't able to answer as he would have liked. He instead adjusted his loose pants and his T shirt over his shorts, his uncovered legs spread out before him. "If you give me a minute," he said, "I'll put some clothes on."

Cortez's laugh was shrill and nervous. "My, aren't *we* the modest one? I'll have you know that your Aunt Cortez knows all about you. Didn't she dress you when you were no more than a baby? I *did*."

Boyd could feel his face flush. "I'm not a baby any more," he said curtly.

"Well, you'll always be a little boy to me," she answered, apparently not sensing his antagonism. She now sat on the edge of the bed, smoothing the skirt of her blue dress as she did. "And aren't we the lucky one to be going off to school? I bet your heart is beating like no one else's in the world. Why, the first time I went to Ithaca, it took me two and a half days to get there! And the closer I got, the more my heart thumped. Can you believe that?"

With uncertain enthusiasm, he answered, "Two and a half days is a long time."

"Of course," she continued, giddy and teasing, "this will give away my secret—I'm older than you think, pet—but we went by buggy. A spider buggy, we called it. I bet you've never seen one."

Warming to her a little, aware that she wanted to talk about herself and not about him, he said, "You see them down around Harpersfield and Windsor. The Amish still use them."

She brought her hands up to her face in a theatrical way to show her disdain. "Not *that* kind. Heavens! Ours was the fanciest thing you ever saw—or at least your Aunt Cortez thought so." She paused, her eyes blankly looking inward rather than at Boyd. "Mama didn't want me to go by train. We had *trains* back then; I'm not *that* antique! She said a train was no place for a young girl with no brains in her head. Imagine! She said that about *me*." She laughed self-consciously, a laugh that told Boyd little except that she seemed glad that her mother had said it. "I stayed overnight in Erie, and I thought it was the biggest city in the world. The second night we stopped at Buffalo, and I bet I didn't get a wink of sleep all night. The people and the noise! The hotel was six stories high, and I thought I'd tumble down into the street before the night was over."

She stopped, as though she had re-created the scene so well that it floated before her eyes.

"I bet it seemed like you were going a thousand miles."

"Why, I couldn't keep my eyes still the entire trip. Every time I saw something new, I'd say, 'Papa, stop at once! Stop this instant! We must see this marvelous thing!' And poor Papa always did. We'd get out of the buggy and tramp over the fields to see a view. I've always been taken by views. I love a pretty sight. When I saw Niagara Falls, I trembled like a leaf. Papa had to pull me away. Yes, he did. I was so . . . taken."

Boyd looked at her doubtfully, wondering what she was trying to say. "I don't think there's anything like that around Oberlin. It's sort of flat."

"I've been there!" she said triumphantly. "Name a place and your Aunt Cortez has probably seen it. I once went down there to see a Gilbert and Sullivan operetta. It was a foolish little thing, but I enjoyed the ride. When you're as old as I am, you have to make your own amusements. Oh, yes, I know; you'll say I'm not half as old as I think I am, but . . . let's say I'm older now than when I was . . . *twenty!*" Her eyes seemed to light up as she finished her prankish speech. "I also saw that there are all kinds of forward girls at Oberlin. Someone as handsome as you are will have to fight them off with both arms."

"I doubt that. But they say it's a good school."

For the first time since she came into the room, she allowed her eyes to rest on his body. When she next spoke, there was a very perceptible trembling in her voice, the same trembling that must have gripped her when she had told her father to stop the buggy and to look at the view.

"Why, all the girls will string laurel leaves in your hair. You just wait and see. You'll bring to their minds all the ancient statues of Greece. Yes, I've seen them! Your Aunt Cortez has actually seen them. Phidias and Praxiteles. Oh, I know them well. I've studied them for hours. Can you imagine me doing anything so lustful? It was one of my favorite courses at Cornell, and when I went to Greece I never wanted to leave. Wherever I looked there was beauty. The modern Greeks are ugly wretches—I've seen them too—but the ancients banished ugliness. Nothing less than the beautiful and the eternal would do. Why, do you know that I can tell the difference between a Phidias and

242

a Praxiteles by looking at the tendons of the ankles! Yes, I can. Now, let me see," she said girlishly. "I would say . . . I would say your ankles are . . . Phidian!"

What his ankles were mostly, he knew, was dirty. He had been emptying the year's debris from his dresser drawer into a bonfire in the back yard earlier in the day, and some of the burned and blackened shreds of paper must have settled in his tennis shoes.

"Here," she went on more quietly, "let me see. I must remove . . . your drapery to see if you're . . . fourth century or third century!"

He looked at her uncertainly, but he made no attempt to stop her as she carefully lifted his pants and his T shirt from the top of his body, leaving him with only his shorts.

"Goodness, look at the sweet blush," she said. "You'd think I've never seen a man before. I honestly bet you think your Aunt Cortez is an old prude. And here I've wandered by myself on the Acropolis—at night! Can you think of anything more daring? They say the Acropolis in moonlight is fatal, but I've seen it. Your Aunt Cortez has seen it, and wherever she looked there were beautiful youths."

To Boyd it seemed that she wasn't even talking to him, that she was merely reciting something to herself, perhaps said many times before. It seemed, too, that any minute she would reach over and draw off the only thing that now covered him. Fourth century, hell. She wasn't looking for any third or fourth century.

"Praxiteles," she said once his body had been freed of the clothes he had thrown over it. "Your torso is more Praxiteles. See here." She leaned over and with one finger touched the short spread of muscle beneath his rib cage. "The Greeks found this very lovely in young athletes. No, your silly Aunt Cortez isn't going to tickle you. Don't pull away. Do you see how this muscle here," she ran her fingers over it, "how it adds . . . *move*ment! It's pure Praxiteles. The Greeks thought it very vulgar to rest their weight on both feet. One foot was always half raised, as if they were about to step toward you and fall into your arms. And all the readiness could be seen in this tiny muscle. It's sheer Praxiteles. And your hips." She touched them now. "So lean. So young. A young boy's hips. So precious and guileless."

"You better not," he said, feeling her hand.

"We ought never to be priggish when we look at beauty. It was one of the first things your Aunt Cortez learned. Why, don't you think she had to catch her breath when she first saw young men in all their power and youth, caught in marble for all their lives? Don't you think she wanted to . . . creep inside them? Yes, she did. Such a silly goose she was. But she learned, dear heart, that bodies in marble have none of our vulgarity. One can gaze hours and hours. Yes, your Aunt Cortez has done that, and without shame. No, sit still. Don't be alarmed. She may never see these youths again. She wants . . . to etch them forever in her memory."

What she would have in her hands in another second wouldn't be marble, of that Boyd was certain. And why should he be so revolted by her? She apparently wanted the same things he wanted and was propelled by the same desires, yet he was revolted. He half wondered if she had seen marble youths on the Acropolis, or perhaps just the sweating shoulders of workmen there, shoulders which she hadn't dared to touch. As far as he knew, there *were* no marble youths left on the Acropolis, all of them having been carried back to London by pansy Englishmen. She was grotesque. The old should never expose themselves in this way before the young. Old people were without physical beauty, feeding as they did on their bodies in order to sustain their lives, eating their own youth and flesh as camels drank water from their own springs in order to prolong themselves. Grotesque. Even while Cortez made her outlandish plea through poetry and sentiment, Boyd had been vaguely conscious that her breath was sour.

As she touched him he reached down and slowly drew her arm away, then sat up, pulling his pants over him once more.

She looked at him in terrible surprise, as if the marble had at last spoken. "But you don't understand," she said in a small, quivering voice. "They were all so meaningless. You don't understand at all."

When the telephone downstairs rang, Frank Ventry was out of his chair and into the hall at the second ring, Catherine and Rose right behind him. A calm voice asked him if this was the house of a Mr. Simon Gavin. He answered that it was, and as he did he picked up a slip of paper and a pencil that had been placed next to the telephone the day before. Writing, he limited his responses to a "Yes" and "Oh" and "I've got it now, thank you" and finally, as he hung up, "We'll be right down."

"What did they say?" Rose asked excitedly, pressing close to him. "You should have let me talk to them."

Frank, his face colorless, tried to collect himself. "He's in Washington all right. And I'm afraid ... he's a little sick."

"Sick, *how?*"

"They say he's had ... a heart attack."

The breath escaped from Rose's lungs, a breath that had been held there since Simon had left. "I told you," she shouted. "Didn't I tell you? He has no right to be traveling around at his age."

"Did they say how bad he is?" Catherine interrupted.

With very great effort he answered, "We'll have to go down in an ambulance. I'm going over to see Sam Ducro now and see if we can get enough gas coupons together."

Catherine's face sank, the hope that had been there when he had said "a little sick" now entirely gone. "Then he *is* bad."

"They didn't say much, Catherine. And the connection wasn't what you'd call good. All they said was that they picked him up in the terminal. They thought ... well, they thought at first he was drunk." Catherine closed her eyes as she listened. "But when they got him to the police station they saw he was sick. And that's when they found all that money in his pocket, so they knew he was no bum. I guess ... he looked bad."

Rose became strangely animated, as if talking about it would lessen the seriousness of what had happened. "He always liked to carry big money around. It made him feel important. Remember how I found five hundred dollars staring at me in his overalls pocket once? The ones he uses to dig around the garden? In another minute I would have dropped it into the washing machine." Then, unable to stop, "It made him feel important. Simon always liked to feel important."

Frank looked at her sympathetically, touched her arm, and said, "Well, I better go over and see Sam. I got my clothes all packed, and Helen can fix up a quick lunch for us to eat in the ... the car. No sense you people coming along. With luck, Sam and I can get started in half an hour."

"I'll go," Catherine said. "You have your job, Frank.

245

We can't ask you to take another day off. If Boyd wasn't going away to school on Wednesday, I'd send him."

"No such thing. I've always liked Simon. I'd just as soon go myself. He'd do it for me."

Remote from their words, Rose said, "He probably hasn't had anything to eat since he left. He's so persnickety about food. Do you recall the Rebekah picnic when Mister Gavin wouldn't eat a piece of anyone's pie but my own? Mrs. Snyder—she baked two cherry pies—Mrs. Snyder was mortified to think anyone thought she was dirty, but Simon wouldn't touch them. He'll be starved."

It was almost, but not quite hysteria. Perhaps she was trying to say that she had always been good to Simon, in her way, and that she was blameless for what had happened.

"Mother," Catherine said harshly, squeezing her arm. "He's had a *heart* attack." Rose looked at her as if she were not seeing or hearing her.

"You'll want some money," Catherine said to Frank. "I've got some upstairs I can get."

"Never mind. I've got enough for everything. I'll keep track of expenses. And Simon has his own money for the hospital."

"I hope he's in a clean hospital," Rose then said. "Simon has always lived in a clean house, and it would break his heart if they put him in a dirty room. I hope they took him to a veterans' hospital. He hates to be among strangers. Oh, I know how he's always talking about the people he meets on trips, but Simon is very shy. He's never felt at ease with strangers."

"Shhhhhh," Catherine said. "Simon's going to be all right. I want you to sit down now and get yourself together. We've got work to do. Do you hear me?" She led Rose back into the parlor, where she helped her into a chair. "I just want to say a word to Frank, and then I'll be right back."

"I always prayed he'd never be sick away from home. I always prayed that. Simon always hated to be alone, and now he's with strangers who don't even know who he is. They thought he was drunk."

"Mother, we're going after him."

"He should never have gone away. He kept pretending he was still a young man, and I didn't have the heart to tell him he wasn't. I hope he's in a veterans' hospital where they'll know he was a soldier. He always liked to fancy himself a soldier. Private hospitals are so unfriendly. Oh, dear, he'll never come through that door again, Catherine. I know it. He'll never walk into this house again, Catherine. He should never have left his home."

"Simon is going to be all right. Shhhhh. You sit back and relax and I'll fix you something to drink. I'll put a little whiskey in a glass."

Frank, feeling helpless, began to back out of the room, followed by Catherine. "I'll call," he whispered to her, "as soon as I find out how he is. If Sam and I drive all night I figure we should be down there by late morning."

"You don't know how good you've been, Frank. We'll never forget it, as long as we live."

"It's what anyone would do." He picked up his hat from the commode in the hall and placed it squarely on his head. "And another thing. I didn't want to say anything back there in front of Mrs. Gavin. But they say he's ... part paralyzed. You better fix up the dining room and put the bed down here."

Catherine's face was filled with pain and disbelief. "But, Frank, you said it was a *heart* attack."

"It was a stroke."

As Parnell listened to the words in the upstairs hall, he could feel his head begin to tingle, the way a foot feels when it goes to sleep. Simon was sick. He never saw the President. The police thought he was drunk. He was pair ... he was pair-lized.

Parnell ran down the hall to the door that opened to his and Boyd's room, the straw Hong Kong shoe still in his hand. Bursting in, he saw Boyd on the floor, clothesless except for his shorts, and Aunt Cortez sitting on the edge of the bed doing nothing, touching her hand as if it were sore.

"Simon's got," Parnell shouted, "Simon's got a heart attack!" It was almost a scream. A scream at Aunt Cortez for doing something bad. A scream at his father for not coming home. A scream at Boyd for leaving something wet and evil on his dresser. A scream at people who thought that Simon could ever be drunk. A scream that could be heard throughout the house. *"Simon's got a heart attack!"*

Boyd leaned over and picked him up into his arms as the pale blue dress slithered past him and through the door.

247

Eight

"How come Aunt Cortez is going?"

It was late the next day and Parnell, his hands full of
everyday silverware, was setting the table in the kitchen
for supper. Before each plate he had to establish anew
which was his right hand and which his left, Rose being
fastidious about the arrangement of things, afterward
carefully placing the knives, forks, and spoons on the fresh
tablecloth with incredible precision, hoping that someone
would notice how straight everything was. Except for the
napkins which Rose made him tuck into the water tum-
blers, where they looked like white birds ready to leap
into the air, the table looked very tidy.

The table and the dining room chairs had been moved
from their ordinary places into the kitchen that morning,
and the old oilcloth-covered kitchen table was now on the
back porch. Boyd and Dewey had broken down Simon's
bed, carried it down the stairs in sections, Rose shouting
at them each time the springs came too close to the
wallpaper, and re-erected it in the dining room. Rose, in
turn, had moved her own bedclothes into the parlor,
where she proposed to sleep on the sofa in order to look
after Simon at night.

If she had momentarily lost her reserve the evening
before when Frank took the telephone call, it was perhaps
because there was nothing she could do for Simon. But
her head was strangely clear after she spent a sleepless
night planning the course of Simon's illness. Her hysteria
was given direction. First thing in the morning, she called
the town carpenter and asked what it would cost to have
the doorway between the dining room and the parlor
plastered in, making the place nice and snug. Not content
with that, she next asked how dear it would be to fill in
and plaster the door into the kitchen. It was Catherine
who pointed out that there would be no way to get Simon
into the room, if the work was done before his arrival,

248

and no way to get him out, except through a window, if the work was done after he arrived, not to mention the appalling disorder. Puzzled, Rose went back to her drawings, scribbled on the back of an M. B. King Coal Company calendar, an aid to enlarging the bathroom she planned to have built in a dining room closet, poking out the two narrow windows at one end of the room and replacing them with a large bay that would allow Simon to see his Victory garden, pulling up the rug and refinishing the wide plank floor so that it could be kept antiseptic and clean, and building a monstrous signaling device that would, upon being touched, set a bell in motion over her sofa in the parlor, summoning her to his bedside. Simon's illness had, in fact, become provocation for remodeling the downstairs, a task which had been working in her mind for years. Yet, at lunchtime, when Catherine quietly picked up the scandalous sketch and carried it to the garbage can in the back yard, Rose did not notice its absence, its purpose—the spending of her hysterical fear—already served.

When Frank called around noon, he talked with Catherine and told her that they were going to try to leave Washington in a few minutes. The hospital had at first been reluctant to release Simon because of the seriousness of his condition, but Frank had finally persuaded them if he was that bad he belonged at home, not in a hospital, a point of view held by almost everyone in Ventry but not shared by the world. When Catherine asked him how Simon was, he answered, "He's very sick, Catherine. He's sicker than I thought he would be and it's going to be a long trip home in all this heat. I don't know ... well, I don't know, but I think we better try, don't you?"

Catherine agreed, and afterward attempted to tell Rose in as levelheaded a way as she could how serious it was. Rose, of course, replied that she'd read somewhere that a heart attack was the best thing in the world for someone because it warned a man to be careful. Catherine prevented herself from saying that what it warned, in fact, was that death was closer than one thought; instead, she said that it wasn't a heart attack at all but a stroke. Rose was quiet a minute and then said, "Well, he'll be up and walking around in two or three days, you wait and see. The Gavins have never mollycoddled themselves. He'll be dancing around here in two or three days, Catherine. I bet a dollar." Catherine left it at that, deciding that there was no way one could bend Rose's will, and she had apparently already willed Simon a speedy recovery. She was a match for any stroke, and she would deal with that in time, by God.

"Aunt Cortez is going," Catherine said, pouring steaming water from a pot of fresh string beans, "because she thinks she'll be in the way."

"Thinks, hah! She is," Rose contributed, seldom one to conceal her opinion. For Parnell's edification, she explained to him that his aunt never liked to be around illness and even—"Listen to this, will you?"—went to Miami Beach the week her husband died of a lingering disease. It was the worst kind of fabrication, but no one tried to correct her. "I'll *tell* you," she went on, "on the last day of her own mama's life she wouldn't even go near her bed to kiss her because she saw death on her face. That's as true as I'm standing here. I had to force her up to the bed and say, 'Kiss Mama,' and all she could do was touch her hand."

"That's a terrible thing to tell a child."

"It's God's own truth," Rose continued. "I don't think she's ever been ill herself, except that time she had the black eye after one of those—what do you call 'em? plastic surgeons did something improving to her face. She's always hated to be around sick people or old people." She paused, bringing her hand to her chin. "But now she's old herself. Isn't that strange? Isn't that the queerest thing? She's old herself."

Parnell didn't see what was so strange and queer about being old or why it was stranger and queerer than being young, but he decided to keep the reflection to himself.

"What's more," Rose pressed on, "I think Boyd has had what they call a slight difference with his aunt. Did you notice them at lunch today, Catherine? They were decidedly cool. Boyd scarcely talked to her."

"I was too busy to notice, I expect," she lied.

"Well, one thing you can say about me is that I've got a sharp eye. I noticed them." She seemed unaware that it was her tongue, not her eye, that most people singled out for special attention. "Right after lunch she went up to her room, and she hasn't been down since. Between you and me, she'll probably have to get that man—that darky, that blackamoor—to carry her out to her car."

250

"Hush," Catherine said, knowing now, as Rose herself did, that Cortez drank in her room, but hoping to spare Parnell the sordid details. Hearing the word "hush"—it increased his attention instead of quelling it—Parnell wished that someone might ask him to give his honest opinion of his aunt's fake jewelry box, but no one did. Waiting, he looked at his bent reflection in a spoon, holding it up before his eyes, crossing his eyes at it.

"I think," Catherine said thoughtfully, "I think we all disappointed her. She expected to find something here this time. I don't know what."

"Shoo! She expected to be waited on hand and foot. That's what she expected."

"I think she's lonely."

Rose reacted with surprise. It was perhaps the only thing she had never thought to say of her sister. Lonely? But how could that be? "Why, Cortez isn't alone for more than a half hour every day. Running from one place to another, doing good deeds, doing this for the Episcopal church, doing that for a fund-raising drive, this for a charity . . . she's never alone."

And yet Rose knew that Catherine hadn't said that. She had said "lonely," which was quite a different matter from being alone. "It's a mystery to me," she said at last. "If I went to college, the way Cortez did, I'd probably understand these things, but I don't. I don't know why she's . . . taken up with that terrible habit. For the life of me I don't. She has everything in the world. There isn't a thing she lacks. If she wants something, all she has to do is write a check. She's got a houseful of people to look after her. And yet she does . . . that. It's a mystery to me."

Perhaps even to Cortez. Perhaps she didn't know any longer what it was she wanted, and perhaps that was why she had come back. To take a look at things again, to try to see if she could remember what it was. Well, Catherine knew that there was no helping her now. For someone like Frank Ventry, there might be a way out of the loneliness and the drink, but for poor Cortez there seemed to be no exit at all. Wasn't it a pity, thought Catherine, that God had made her selfish? It was probably the worst affliction of all. Nothing could be done for it.

"But Mama loved her, I'll say that," Rose now said. "I worked for Mama. I took care of her. I did everything. And my sister wouldn't even kiss her before she died. Still and all, you know, I think Mama always loved Cortez more than me. Why is that, do you think?"

No one answered, because no one knew.

"Well, don't quote me, but I've got a feeling she won't be coming back. I don't think she'll visit us any more. I don't think . . . she likes us."

Catherine smiled, marveling at Rose's perception. No, the poor woman didn't. Couldn't. She wanted to, and that was probably what had sent her there, but she couldn't. That was all there was to it.

"I wouldn't change places with her for a hundred billion dollars," Rose went on. "I always used to admire her. I always used to be jealous. She had all those lovely things. That beautiful house. And all those trips she's taken to places you never even heard of. But when you come right down to it," Rose's eyes twinkled now, half maliciously because she was at last glad that she no longer had to feel awed in her sister's presence, "when you come right down to it, all she has is . . . a weakness."

After a moment Catherine answered, "No one's perfect. Cortez. Simon. Myself. You. We all have our frailties." She watched Rose's face, wondering how far she dared go, knowing that what she was about to say had to be said before Simon was carried through the door. "Even you and Simon. You always see Simon as a cross you have to bear. Yet only someone as gentle as Simon is, as weak, could have," she rushed to complete her sentence, "could have put up with you all these years."

Rose now laughed nervously. "Hah! You've read too many books, Catherine. I don't follow what you're trying to say. All I know is that Mister Gavin better not be playing possum this time. Why, I have half a notion there's nothing wrong with him. Yes, I do. Take his malaria. Whoever heard of anyone in Ohio having malaria? I'd like to know. It makes him feel important, that's all. Whoever heard of anyone getting malaria back in 1898 and still having it in 1943, with all the new drugs? I say it's scientifically impossible."

Finished at the stove, having succeeded in shifting the conversation from herself to Simon, and having freed herself from any kind of guilt, she looked at the table that Parnell had just set. "Here, child! How many times do I have to tell you to put the spoons at the top of the plates? It may be old-fashioned, but I think it makes a nicer table."

If Rose thought that, Parnell knew that it was an indisputable fact, not open to interpretation. He watched her seize his carefully arranged spoons—poetry, they were, silver-plated poetry—and scatter them, pointing in all directions, at the tops of the plates. Catherine looked at him knowingly, indicating both that he shouldn't complain and also—he felt very proud and adult—that he was expected to understand why it was necessary for Rose to do it.

Having ravaged the table, Rose now said, "You run upstairs like a good boy and see if your Aunt Cortez is coming down to dinner." The table was now wild-looking and pleasing to her eye.

Parnell's face pinched up. "Do I have to?"

"Run along as you're told. Isn't he getting to be bold? He's getting to be as bold as Mister Gavin."

Cortez did not come downstairs for supper after all, saying instead that she'd stop at Hellriegel's in Painesville for a bite on the way home. The heat, she added, was enough to take away anyone's appetite. After Parnell had repeated all this to the family in the kitchen, ready to sit down at the table, Rose answered, "Well, the heat certainly promotes a thirst. Yes, I'll say that for it." While they ate, Simon still hundreds of miles away and rolling toward them in an ambulance, they seemed curiously light of heart, as if somehow Cortez had, for a brief time, been their enemy, a carrier of discord—how they didn't know—and yet they had managed to stay together, a solid front.

It was Boyd who, at one point, surprised everyone by saying, "What it is, she's really not very nice." It was as fundamental as that. One could pity her. One could even try to like her. One could hope that she would somehow pull herself together. But she really wasn't nice.

When her man, as she called him, drove the long black Lincoln into the driveway, Parnell went to her room, the air freshly sprayed with eau de cologne, and helped carry down some of her bags. She would, she said, carry her antique box and her three furs herself, the furs having made the trip to Ventry apparently only to test their survival in a tropical climate, for she hadn't worn them. She didn't, she added, want a little boy like Parnell to drop her jewels. "You wouldn't want my gems scattered all over the steps, now would you, my pet? You carry the bag over

253

there. That's the one. My, you are the perfect little gentleman!"

After all of her things had been placed in the car, Cortez said good-by to each one. Except for Boyd, who thought it would be hypocritical to act the servile nephew, the family was gathered around her car. "Catherine, I'll fret over you," Cortez said. "I don't want you to kill yourself looking after Simon. Do you hear? You're still a young woman, and don't you forget that. You'll have to get out in the world again after your sons grow up. Why, yes, you can come to Cleveland and keep this silly old woman company."

"You're not that at all, Cortez."

"Isn't she the flatterer? Isn't she the precious one?" Cortez then motioned for Parnell to come to her. "And aren't you going to give your Aunt Cortez an itty-bitty kiss on the forehead before she goes? Come here, you sweet thing. Yes, on the forehead. That's a dear. I don't want you to get my powder on your face. There!" He did as he was instructed, trying not to breathe as he accomplished it; her face was more pallid and funereal than ever. "I'll remember that, my dear. Maybe I won't even wash that tiny spot. Would you like that? Just leave your kiss there forever and ever? Why, I might *do* that."

Suffering greatly, Parnell was relieved when she turned to look again across the lawn, as though she had left something behind.

"Boyd had to run off," Catherine said, knowing that Cortez was looking for him. "It's his last night here, you know, and I told him he could go early."

"His last night! And now he's about to embark on the great adventure! Well, you tell that naughty boy he'll have to behave himself. His Aunt Cortez expects to hear wonderful and inspiring things about him. You tell him that, Catherine, hear?"

Catherine promised to do so, though it was unnecessary because Boyd was at his bedroom window listening to their farewells as he dressed to go out. Cortez walked to her sister, her hands outstretched, and for a moment Rose—who generally hated emotional displays—held her in her arms, neither of them saying a word. When they finally parted, it was Rose's arms that lingered longer. Whatever they had tried to tell each other had apparently been heard. "We've come a long way, Rose," Cortez now said, "haven't we? Why, it seems like yesterday that I kissed you good-by before I went away to school."

"It was such a long time ago, Cortez, but I remember." Then, warming or weakening, "You were the prettiest girl in Ventry County. Then and now. Just you remember that. We were all so proud of you to be going off that way by yourself."

Cortez looked up hopefully, her face soft, almost breaking. "Were you, Rose? I'm so glad. I'm so glad you were. Yes, I think ... I think Mama was right. I didn't belong here. Do you know that, Rose? I didn't belong here, and Mama was right. I belong where I am."

"But you must always come back. It'll always be your home. It's not much, but your room is always spick-and-span, just waiting for you whenever you want to come visit us."

"I'll remember that, Rose." Her voice, which for a moment had seemed honest and sincere under the burden of real sentiment and affection, now became artificial again. "Isn't she the sweetest sister a girl could ask for? Rose, you're too good to me." She kissed her lightly on the cheek, catching Rose unprepared. "Heavens, I must run before I cry. I must run." Then, as she went toward the open door of the car, "Parnell, my lamb, I have something here for you. A little something for being such a perfect gentleman." She dropped an object into the palm of his hand, and sealed his fingers into a fist. "Now, don't let anyone see," she added. She stopped at the door, turning toward them.

"Let me just stand here a brief second and look at my little family," she now said. "So pretty you all are. So lovely. I'll keep this picture in my mind all winter long. All the winters of my life. Yes, I *will*. I'll remember just the way you look, right this minute." Then quickly, urgently, "I must run. Your silly old Aunt Cortez is going to cry if she stands here one more instant."

They watched her fan herself with a palm fan given to her by her driver, and, after other good-bys, she waved at them with her white handkerchief, they waved back, and the car backed out of the drive and into the street.

When the car turned from Priest onto Summer, Rose and the family waved once more, but Cortez had apparently settled back in her seat. Rose shook her head, said something unintelligible—a prayer, an invective, a bit of both—walked to Parnell and unclenched his fist. *"Hah!"*

255

she exclaimed. "Now, doesn't that beat everything? And just when I was beginning to feel sorry for her."

"What is it?" Catherine asked.

"A quarter," Parnell answered shyly. "But it's sort of a new one." Glad that he was old enough no longer to be hurt by such things, happy enough to have a quarter, he laughed. And then they all did.

Boyd and Dewey had for so long promised themselves one last tune, as they called it, on the night before they left town that even Simon's illness didn't seem to justify their putting it off. Dewey had asked the Horse to go with him, and he had also snitched two bottles of bourbon from those his father had laid aside in '41 for a twenty-year war. Boyd insisted only that he get home before midnight, because Frank Ventry had said that they would probably arrive from Washington about that time, and Boyd wanted to see Simon—*had* to—before he went to sleep. "You'll be roaring by then," Dewey had said. "We're going to get so plastered that I'm going to make you climb the church steeple and pray for peace. Tonight is the night old Bacchus rises from his beery grave."

Well, Boyd supposed, the occasion did call for some kind of celebration. Dewey had already told him what he planned to do on the following day: he would go as far as Cleveland with him, send his luggage home by Railway Express from the terminal, then cross the street and enlist at a booth in Public Square. It was the only way it could be done without revealing his intentions to his father, who would otherwise prevent it. Because he was over eighteen, Dewey was his own man and could do what he pleased in all places except in his home.

Although it was still illegal for him to drink at that age in Ohio, the nation had providentially made it possible for him to go to war. But where to drink without leaving the southern part of the county was another matter entirely. Only one roadhouse in the area served the underaged, but the place was so sinister and dirty that only the desperate used it. It generally smelled, as Dewey said, of cat pee and sweaty underarms. They settled instead on a hamburger and beer roadhouse near Walden Creek, about six miles south of Ventry, used largely by farmers' sons and their dates when they weren't wrestling with each other in the back seats of their beat-up cars. Though Walden Creek was dry—the town, and the stream, because that too had petered out by August—the people in the village looked on the saloon with a degree of tolerance, glad that there was a place where their children could work off steam. Here came Wanda, Jeanette, and Brenda with Chester, Buck, and Leroy to order hamburgers and 3.2 beer, to feel each other under the tables, to play the juke box, and sometimes even to wander by mistake, they said, into a storeroom that had once housed homing pigeons and there gain their ease, so to speak, not at all bothered by the absence of hygiene. The building had once housed an antique and trading shop; the name of the saloon became, predictably, Walden Pawn.

Be that as it may, it was on its best behavior on this night, and Boyd and Dewey had brought their dates to the middle of the floor and were dancing to the music coming from the juke. Despite the surroundings, no one could have been less venal and provocative than Betty Jo, Dewey's date, and Dewey was much aware of it. He had already whispered to Boyd that the Horse could be led through a French whorehouse and come out thinking that she'd visited a convent. She had no capacity for sin.

"Hell," he said, leading her back to the table. "I'm not physically fit to fight a war. Who taught you how to dance anyway? Jesse Owens?"

Betty Jo was not amused. She was the sort of girl who liked Hawaiian music, who did all her homework every night while she was in school, and who dutifully told her mother whenever she didn't have her daily bowel movement. "As a matter of fact, no one taught me," she answered, stating a truth which was by this time obvious. As they reached the table where Boyd and Francine were sitting, she added under her breath, "If you do that once more, I'm going to leave."

Honestly puzzled, Dewey asked, "Do what once more?"

"You know. Feel me that way. This is a public place."

The public in the place had seen worse, but Dewey chose not to pursue it. "Well, by Gawd, I'd be glad to take you somewhere else."

"You can take me home is where you can take me."

Dewey shrugged his shoulders and helped her into her chair. As he did, he leaned over and whispered to Boyd, "Betty Jo wants me to take her home. She says I felt her."

Grinning, Boyd asked, "For the love of God, what was it like?"

"She's wearing dry ice under her brassiere."

257

The girl pretended to be outraged. "I heard that, Dew Ventry, and I don't like it one bit. If you're going to be dirty . . ."

"And how *can* I be dirty?" Dewey interrupted. "I get too close to one of your upside-down nipples, and you start yelling that you've been raped."

The girl was speechlessly angry. Francine, who had heard only part of their argument, said, "What's wrong? Has something happened that I should know about?"

Curtly the girl now answered, "I told your brother to take me home. He's being vulgar."

"I'm sorry for breathing. 'Scuse me. Just pretend I'm not here. You two go on and talk about Albert Schweitzer. I'll sit here and think vulgar."

"Now he's making fun of me!" Betty Jo exclaimed, ready to rise from her chair. But Boyd, not wanting the evening to begin badly, reached out and held her down by the shoulder. "Sit down," he said. "I'll get you something to drink. Relax."

"If she does," Dewey said, *sotto voce,* "her cold tits'll melt and roll down her belly."

"What did he say?"

Fortunately she hadn't heard; a reference to her breasts upset her terribly, but any talk of her belly would have driven her well-nigh mad. "Just relax," Dewey said to her. "Do what the man asks." He watched her restore herself to her chair, resting her legs primly under the table, as close together as they could go. The sight was apparently too much for him to bear, because he now stood up. "I'm going out to the car to see if the good fairy has left me anything for the tooth I put in the glove compartment. I asked for booze."

"If you have one more drink, I'm going home in a cab," his date said.

Ignoring her, Dewey said to Boyd, "Are you coming with me into the forests of prime-heevil, buddy? A promise is a promise. Tonight we get screwed." Quickly adding: "Sorry, Betty Jo. An old Irish expression. From out of the bogs. No offense. Plastered it means, oiling the machinery. A bit on the drunk side."

"In a minute," Boyd answered.

"A promise is a promise. The bourbon is eight years old and aging by the minute. One must nip it in the bud. The moment it reaches its peak."

"Okay, so start nipping."

"I shall test its fragrant bouquet," he said. "I shall drink to our companions at arms, the valiant Rooskies. I shall drink to slit-skirted, yaller-eyed Madame Chiang, the poor people's advocate and our good buddy. And to my own sweet youth, about to give itself to the highest cause. The brooding Achilles ventures from his tent! Onward! Sound the alarums! Up democracy! Up the Rooskies! Up Madame Chiang! Up F.D.R.! The King! The Pope!" And he went out, demonstrating.

"Revolting," Betty Jo managed to say, not aware that what Dewey had said constituted the most spirited kind of Irish praise and had been borrowed from Simon's own lips. It meant merely "F.D.R. forever!" and so on, and had nothing at all to do with great anatomies.

"He's so juvenile," she said, sipping her Coke, having declined beer for fear of losing her head.

"Juvenile! For God's sake, that's what he's supposed to be! So am I a juvenile. When did that break a law?"

"She didn't mean it that way, honey," Francine said, trying to mediate.

"Well, then what did she mean?"

"You don't have to be so aggressive," the girl replied. "I just meant, well, he's doing what any juvenile would do. Trying to get drunk on his last night in town."

Hell, it was the romantic and chivalric thing to do, Boyd knew. A hero's last night. Some American girls, by God, had a gift for not having fun. "All he wants is to have a good time," he said to her. "What the holy hell is wrong with having a good time? I'd like to know."

"*I* didn't say anything was wrong with it," Francine declared.

"No, but she did. She's sitting there with her legs so tight you couldn't work a thread between her knees, and she says Dew is juvenile."

It was clearly the wrong thing to say. "Boyd Gavin! You better apologize. No one has ever in all my life talked to me that way."

"Oh, hell, Betty Jo, give the guy a break. Here, he asks you out on his last night in town. He's going away tomorrow and no one ... really knows what's going to happen to him. So he tries to give you a little feel, and you get all hopped up. God-a-mighty, I'm sick of prudes."

Francine looked offended. "I suppose that means you're sick of me too. I *told* you this would happen. You've been drinking too much."

"I didn't mean that, Francine. It's just ... can't you people for once in your lives try to be natural? Just for once? Can't you remember that Dewey ... well, that every time some broad gets mad because Dew feels her, he ... loses something, and I don't mean a feel." He saw that Betty Jo was close to tears. "I'm sorry, Betty Jo. It's not just you. You can't ... do something you can't do. It's as simple as that. I guess I was just feeling sorry for Dewey."

To give the girl her due, it wasn't all her fault. Dewey happened to be different from most people, and he took special handling. He needed reassurance, not the perpetual questioning he always got. Every time Betty Jo held herself back, Boyd knew, she helped annihilate Dewey a little more, and it seemed stupid and ludicrous. Hell, if you were someplace where no one would give you food, you shag-assed to where the giving was, no matter what the risks were. If only a girl could understand that. Dewey was in more real peril than even he knew. He was going into the Army without a political thought in his head, going off to war not to crusade against tyranny and injustice, not to hunt for the scent of blood most men sought, but to get his manhood back. He was going to offer the mutilated remains—whipped by leather belts and walked on by spiked, high-heeled shoes—to the nation in hope that the nation would heal it. But what if the nation was too busy?

Looking now at the girl across from him at the table, Boyd seriously wondered if it was worth it. She was a Sad Sack; that's all he could say about her. Dewey had never even tried to like her, and it must have taken real effort on his part to feel around for what little she had. As she now returned his look, she said, "Dewey isn't even nice to me. You didn't go to the Senior Prom with him, but *I* did."

The spell was broken. No longer did Boyd have to worry about what was going to happen to Dewey. Anyone that goofy simply couldn't come to harm; God couldn't be so base, so without humor. And as each one at the table remembered what Dewey had done after the Prom, they began to smile, first Boyd, then Francine, finally Betty Jo herself.

"That was the funniest damn thing," Boyd said at last. "I don't even think Dew knew what he was doing."

"Funny?" screeched Betty Jo. "I was wearing a new

formal, and I'd sent all the way to Bonwit's in Cleveland to get it. It was ruined!"

At this auspicious moment Dewey returned to the table, more glassy-eyed than he had been when he left. He looked guardedly at his friends, wondering what their angle was, then said, "You guys laughing at me?"

"We were talking about the Prom," Boyd explained. "And what a gallant guy you were when you took Betty Jo home in the rain."

Perplexed, Dewey muttered, "So I took her home. So what?"

"So it was pouring, is what. It was raining so hard you couldn't see out the windshield of the car. And you were wearing that rented tuxedo from Levinson's, and you said if you got it wet you'd have to pay them another three dollars."

Francine finished the story. The four of them had double-dated, using Dewey's precious Ford, and late at night as Dewey left the car to take his date up to her front porch, he removed the umbrella from the floor. Once outside, he held it over his head, careful to keep the rain off his rented tuxedo, walked in front of the car to Betty Jo's door, opened it for her, and the moment she stepped out, he dashed up the sidewalk to the porch, over the puddles, the umbrella still over his head. Alone. "The only trouble," Francine concluded, "was that she was ten feet behind you all the way."

Dewey appeared to be properly mystified. "Did I do that? Son of a gun. Must have had the foe on my mind." To Betty Jo: "How come you didn't say anything, pal?"

"Say anything! I would have drowned if I opened my mouth. And what *I* hated, as soon as I got to the porch, you kissed me on the nose and said, 'Gawd, you're all *wet.*' "

"You slammed the door in my face."

"I had to. I was soaked to my drawers."

Dewey now poked her arm playfully. "Now don't talk vulgar," he said, grinning at last, sliding his chair closer to Betty Jo's. "By God, things are looking up. We might have us a little tune after all."

"We will," she answered with great control, "if you get your hand off my leg. Otherwise, I call a cab."

Dewey pulled back, shrugging his shoulders.

An hour later Boyd and Francine were spread out on

the wet grass next to the river, holding each other, the empty car behind them at the end of a dirt road. Dewey and Betty Jo were quarreling somewhere in the distance. Every now and then they heard her say, scolding and put out, "If you do that one more time, I'm going to walk home."

"I wonder who's winning," Francine asked at last.

"Virtue," Boyd answered blandly. "And it's too bad. I wasn't kidding when I said a while back about Dewey needing someone. Someone to cuddle up with, the way we're doing. But Betty Jo is the kind of girl who listens to everything these runty little preachers say. She thinks it's dirty to be close to someone. Girls like that kill people like Dewey." He waited, adding, "Not to mention me."

Francine half groaned, apparently anticipating the line their talk was about to take, because it had happened so many times before. "How many times do I have to tell you, Boyd? With a girl it's different."

"Different how? You're alive right now and someday you're going to be dead. *Tonight* you could be dead. Dewey is half drunk, and he could run the car off the hill up there before we get you home. And then who would you live with in your coffin, Francine? You'd live with virtue. It don't talk to you, as the feller says. It's got no tongue. I've got a tongue. Dewey has a tongue. See what I mean?"

"If all the people we know went around thinking this was the last day of their lives, what kind of world would it be? No one would ever get out of bed."

"It would probably be a hell of a lot better than the way things are."

"I'm serious. You said something just now about runty little preachers. Well, it so happens I don't particularly like preachers. Their heads are so full of divinity that they have no time for people. They keep saying 'God' and we keep saying 'Me.' But the whole idea of religion is that we shouldn't hurt each other. That's all. And if . . . we did something, you could hurt me. You know you could."

"I wouldn't."

"That's what you say, but no one can tell. Did you know I had a long talk with Dorothy Larson before they made her leave school?"

"Dorothy was too goddamn dumb to know what she was doing. I don't mean people like that. She got knocked

262

up, and she deserved to get knocked up. Every second guy in the senior class got a little piece of it."

Hurt at the reminder, Francine added, "And you too."

"I told you about that. I could have, but I didn't. We started, and you know what? I told you that the bell rang for classes to change, but you want to know the truth? She smelled of all the other guys she'd ever been with, so I stopped. I'd rather . . . do it to myself than with some . . . public convenience like that. I was talking about love, or don't you know what that means?"

"I know what it means. I could write you a fat book about it. But what I was trying to say is that she did too. The man who did it—I mean made her pregnant—works at a bar in Conneaut. And she really loved him. I'm not saying she was smart enough to know, but I'm saying she thought so. She told me. And what she also told me was that the two of them used to take walks together right here in the gulf, and then he'd push her into the bushes. And she couldn't stop him. That's what I mean. You don't think when that's happening. Sex has a mind all of its own. It does its own thinking. And now she's going to have a baby. That's very commendable, I guess, but it's not going to have any father because the man is already married. She didn't even know that. She loved him, but she didn't even know that. So now she has to go through everything all by herself. Her own father won't even let her get near their front door."

"She doesn't count. She's been the town pump ever since I can remember."

"She's a *girl*. And what happened to her could happen to me or anyone else. You don't have to be dumb to get knocked up, as you put it. Ask around Oberlin when you get down there. No one gives you an IQ test before you start having a baby."

Boyd was impatient, exasperated, unable to cope with Francine's undeniable rationality. "But you don't have to. I've been telling you for the last year. We're getting married, aren't we? *Aren't* we? Well, then what's wrong with it? You say girls are different. I say so are men. A man needs that, Francine. Sometimes . . . oh, hell."

"Sometimes what?"

After a while he said, "Sometimes it's like I'm going off my rocker. I've already told you about that. For the love of God, I'm eighteen years old. Do you want to get real shocked? Yesterday . . . something happened in the house.

263

Something that made me sick to my stomach to watch. And then a couple minutes later I found out about Simon. I should have gone somewhere and cried, but do you want to know what I did? I went to the head and I almost ... well, you know what I almost did. Instead, I put on my track shoes and ran for around five miles, right here in the gulf."

"You shouldn't feel ... ashamed because of that."

"I'm not, for the love of God. I'm ashamed because no one lets me act like a man. I have to *run* my sex off. That's all."

"But how do I know you're going to marry me, Boyd? You're going away. Anything could happen."

"You know because I told you. Maybe I'm mixed up, and maybe I do things sometimes that ... don't sound very nice, but I'm no heel. Do you want to get married right now? Do you want me to borrow Dew's car and take you somewhere and get married now? Is that the only way you'll believe me?"

"You know that you can't, and neither can I. You're going to college and I have to get a job."

"People don't *have* to do anything, Francine. No one can make you do anything. I could enlist in the Army tomorrow and we could get married the next day."

If Francine had earlier been upset by the turn of their conversation, he saw that she was now damned well alarmed. She sat up quickly on the grass. "Don't you ever! Where would that get you?"

Boyd pulled her back down next to him, leaving his hand on her shoulder. "It could get us married, that's where. That's what I'm talking about. We could stop being kids and get married."

"It could also get you killed. That's a high price to pay just to get through adolescence."

She had such order in her mind. He loved her for it, because it tended to lessen the confusion in his own, but at the same time he was angry that she would never loosen up, never surrender her good sense. He wanted something that had nothing to do with sense. The world was cracking open, cities were being bombed, people were being killed, and Francine was talking sense. Was she right or wrong? Hell, he admitted, she was probably right, and that was the toughest thing of all to swallow. "I shouldn't be going to college anyway, Francine. I'm doing it because Rose and Mom want me to. They want me to turn my back on

264

the world because of what happened to Luke. They never even asked me what I wanted to do. And it's about time I started to do things my own way, my own style. Like Simon says. He'd be proud of me if I went into the Army, and you know why? Because he thinks there are some things more important than life. And honor is one of them, cornball as that sounds. Rose doesn't know what it means. And, honest to God, sometimes I don't think you do either."

"Please don't quarrel on your last night, Boyd. Anyway, isn't that what I'm trying to say too? Don't *I* . . . aren't I expected to have any honor, or does that belong exclusively to men? If I did something with you, the way you're always asking me . . . the way I want to, where would my own honor be? If something ever happened to you—you just *said* we could be killed any time—could I ever be someone else's wife and have someone else's children?"

"Oh, for God's sake," Boyd said, genuinely angry now. "American girls have such a goddamn exaggerated notion of what their maidenheads are worth. It's about as holy as a fingernail. It hasn't been put there by some angel. It's not gilted and jewel-studded like some damn Persian painting. It's just a piece of membrane. It means nothing. Absolutely nothing."

Catching his anger, she now said, "If it means nothing, then suppose I give it away to everyone I meet? Suppose I do what Dorothy did? Would that please you?"

Oh, my God, she had him. "Damn it!" he said, turning away from her. "Let's not even talk about it then. Every time we do, you always end up by saying that you'd feel dirty. And what you're saying is that *I'm* dirty. I'd have to be to make you feel that way. And if that's what you think, well, then I feel sorry for you. The runty preachers have won. You can carry your virginity to heaven with you and one of the runty preachers can make a wing out of it."

A faint smile broke over her face. "It wouldn't fly," she said.

"Oh, hell, it would fly. It would fly to Mars and back."

"No, it wouldn't, because I don't even think I have it any more. You remember a year ago when we used to get horses from the Spragues and come riding here in the gulf? And then I had to give it up? Well, this is something I never intend to tell my children, but I think I lost what you call my maidenhead on a horse's back. So it's not that that I'm trying to save."

"Francine," Boyd said laughing, "you didn't!"

"I'm not even strictly speaking a virgin. I don't think I could pass the wing test."

"What a waste."

"And I have lewd thoughts about you almost all the time. Now you know how depraved I am." She paused for a moment. "I sleep with you. I go to bed with you every night. And I wake up with you every morning. Still, I don't want . . . I don't want you to do anything like that, Boyd. I'm saving myself for you, until you know what you want. That's all. I already know what I want."

"But so do I."

"No, you don't. Not yet. I can tell. I wasn't valedictorian of my class for nothing. I'm a wizard that way. I think . . . you don't really know yet. But I'll wait around, Boyd."

"And how will I know when I know?"

"You'll know. And right now I want you to lie down next to me."

Boyd smiled weakly. "We'll just have another big-assed dialectic if we do."

"Lie down! That's the class valedictorian talking. She's decided that she wants you to lie down next to her."

Boyd obeyed. Hell, he was unworthy of her. Doing what he had done to her own sister when he wasn't in possession of any of the reason and sanity Francine herself possessed, doing what he had almost done to the girl at the Lake, doing to himself in the quietness of his room what he thought had to be done lest he go crazy. No, there was no one else like Francine, and he was unworthy of her.

Yet when she came to him now, playing the aggressor in order to remove some of his rage and hunger, his hunger and rage were only increased. Something else in him—not reason—something that had been planted there when he was conceived, took over his mind. As she bent over him, kissing him, his anger subsided entirely and was replaced by the old yearning, and he was unable to hold it back. She played with his lips, moving her own over them, and brought her tongue into his mouth, softly touching his teeth and his tongue, as if to quell once and forever his violent talk.

Boyd carefully lifted her body from him, then stretched

266

her out on the grass, returning her kisses until he heard her breathing quicken. He locked his mouth on hers, touching her neck and her shoulders with his hands, and then with a daring he had never had before he brought his hand into the V of her blouse, feeling her pull back as he did, unable and unwilling to leave her mouth for fear she would call out. *Oh, God, Francine, you have to let me be my own man. You have to let me do it in my own style. What you say about my not knowing myself isn't true. I do. I know.* And as though she was finally willing to offer him some small gift, she stopped struggling, letting him now touch her flesh beneath her blouse, letting him draw her brassiere up and over, freeing what was there, and then letting his lips play over them. She ran her hands through his hair as he did, and it was she who at last reached down and brought his face back up to meet hers, as if the touch of him on her body was too much for her to bear. But Boyd couldn't see it that way, as no man could. He found her tongue again, feeling her breathing become faster and shorter now, and slowly with one hand he stroked her hip, pushing his face hard into hers now because she was fighting back. He tried to reassure her with his mouth, tried to tell her without words that it would all be fine and wonderful, and then he brought his hand beneath her dress until he found her pants and quickly—so quickly that much later when he tried to remember it, there was little recollection of what he had touched—dug into them, resting his warm and quiet hand now on the soft, furry covering he found, trying to make her understand that it was a way of love, a passage to love, and the only way the two of them could speak, until with one gigantic effort she pulled herself free.

"*No!*"

Boyd drew his hand away and sat up straight, his breath coming in short painful jerks, full of shame. They sat on the grass for two minutes, three minutes, five minutes, saying nothing, listening only to their own heavy breathing. After a while, knowing that there were no words, feeling dirty and disadvantaged, exposed, as though Francine had seen him and was revolted, he said sadly, "We better go now. I'll rouse Dew."

On the way home they maintained their silence, Dewey and his date in the front seat every bit as quiet as Francine and Boyd in the back. At the Ventry house

Francine scarcely waited for the car to stop before she opened the door and without saying good night to anyone walked up to the porch. Dewey remarked, "Looks like it's getting a little cool," then turned the car around to drive Betty Jo home on the other side of town.

As they drove, Boyd considered again what had happened. Yes, he would have to know himself, and it would be uphill work all the way, but Francine would have to give it a try too. For all her talk of morality and goodness, what Boyd remembered most of what had happened in the gulf was that she had let him down. If she loved him, she would have extended her notions of morality to include what he had asked of her. It was wrong to be too reasonable, to try to subject everything to analysis. If, at this very moment, there was an accident and if the damned car caught fire and Boyd were trapped in the back seat, he knew with certainty that Dewey would come barrel-assing through the door to help him even if it was impossible to help, even if it was unreasonable. But Francine? He wasn't so sure. For all he knew, she would judge it with her mind first. She would let him down.

Well, it was a hell of a way, an empty way to leave town. He had the feeling that Francine probably wouldn't even see him off tomorrow, somehow afraid or ashamed to stand before him now that he had touched her. God-a-mighty, that was wrong. If it was a fault of Boyd's in not being able to hold himself back, then Francine was equally at fault for not being able to let herself go.

Boyd now watched Dewey walk Betty Jo to her front porch, straight and unbending as a stick. She landed a kiss on Dewey's forehead, said something about having had a good time, which she obviously hadn't had, then vanished quickly through the door. If Dewey was prepared for one last try, he was too late. His hand, poised before her dry chest, touched wood.

"God, but the Horse is ardent," Dewey said, climbing back into the car, inviting Boyd to hop over into the front seat. "By the time she gets married I hope they have a new way to make babies. No man's ever going to get it from her unless he shoots her full of cocaine first. Whew! Look where she kept pinching me."

As Dewey backed the car out of the drive, turning down the street and heading back to the gulf for the bombing they'd promised themselves, he showed Boyd his bruised neck. "Every time I kissed her and tried to give her a friendly little feel, she pinched the hell out of me. My neck's raw."

Well, it was a manly bruise, as Boyd's own was. Boyd took the bottle from the glove compartment and held it to his mouth, then handed it to Dewey, who lifted it high, keeping his other hand on the wheel.

Dewey said, "Is she a pig or is she a pig? A *bona fide* pig."

"She comes pretty close." He looked behind Dewey's collar again. "You better put some iodine on that when you get home."

"She could have rabies? Do horses get rabies? How about handing me that bottle again? I'll disinfect myself from the inside out." He pulled at the bottle again, then returned it to Boyd's lap, where Boyd did the same, half afraid that he'd be sick if he didn't proceed more slowly. He watched Dewey steer the car back down Tannery Hill to the place in the gulf they had just left. "Can you get rejected by the Army because you're drunk?" Dewey finally asked. "Because I'm still going to be drunk tomorrow."

"All good Americans get drunk before they enlist. It's compulsory."

"It damned well better be. I just hope no wise guy asks me to read one of those little-assed signs that begin with an E as big as your face and end with an ant's Bible." Dewey brought the car off the dirt road, parked it under a grove of trees, and cut the motor. "Hey, get out, bub. We're here. Back in the forests of Bacchus. Old Bac here—if you ask him the right way—will do his rutting dance amongst the trees for you, goosing every little sapling, every little maple, el-um, and mighty oak, blood running down his beautiful neck."

"Up your beautiful neck," Boyd said, getting out of the car.

"Up your beautiful navel ... Hell, man, you got your own bottle under the seat. This here is mine. Part of my inheritance. The fatted calf. 'Lad,' my pop says to me, 'you're a meathead and a disappointment, but you might as well live it up. The booze is on the house. The fallen house of Ventry.' You think a fifth apiece is enough or is that niggardly? Christ, just don't get sick and vomit it. That there's expensive gargle, bub."

They left the car, each carrying a bottle, and walked toward the river's edge, Boyd carefully avoiding the place where he and Francine had been stretched out only a few minutes before. He could see where the grass was matted, and he stepped around it gingerly. Once by the river, they plopped on the ground, each with a tree behind his back, their legs inverted V's before them.

Settled, Dewey said, "You and Francine had a fight."

"Yup."

"Bad one?"

"Sort of. She's very pee-oohed."

"Can a feller ask what it was about?"

"A feller can guess."

"The feller already has." Dewey played with the bottle in front of him and raised it once more to his mouth. "Go easy on her. Remember that Mom has been working on her for almost eighteen years. Francine has a lot of forgetting to do before she can grow up. This is what you call gratuitous advice. I've got a feeling I don't have to tell you."

"I guess you don't. Hell, I suppose I shouldn't even be talking to you about it. She's your sister."

"But you're my asshole buddy, buddy."

"Asshole buddy," Boyd repeated.

"Mom has put the fear of God into her. You know— and this is something *only* an asshole buddy would tell you—you know that Francine keeps her Tampax under lock and key? She's got the box locked in her desk dresser. When she needs it, she goes to it like a dog who's buried a bone. I saw her put it there once. I think ... she has the other thing under lock and key too."

"It'll work out," Boyd said after a while. "I think we just have some things to think over."

"I sure as hell hope it turns out all right. An erectionless man likes to see his buddies happy in feather beds. I'll be best man at your wedding."

Boyd laughed, and instantly wondered if he should have. "Is that ... still eating you?"

"I'll be okay as soon as I get away from home. I tried to get something out of the library the other day about it, but you know how pickled-faced Miss Douglas is, always sitting behind her varnishy desk so you can't get in without passing her. 'Why, Dew Ventry, is there anything I can help you with?' she says. I couldn't very well ask her where the erection section was, so I just tooled around home medicine, but what I found ... I found, well it happens. They even make little things to help you out.

270

Erector sets, only they're not called that. The thing is, I'm not . . . I don't think I'm what you call impotent permanently or anything. I just can't . . ."

"Sure," Boyd finished for him. What he couldn't do just happened to be about everything. It was a raw deal. "Drink up. What you need is good American bourbon surging through your balls, Dewey boy."

"You're not just a-talkin'." Dewey now stretched out away from the tree, his head in the high grass, looking up at the sky. "By God, I'm off to hunt the bloody Hun. Teach 'em manners. Tell 'em to get back to making beer and good sausage—and each other, of course—and leave all the important policy decisions in the world to old Dew Ventry, junior-grade Harry Hopkins. Doesn't it get you in the gut?"

To Boyd it still seemed unreal. "Your mom and dad are going to be mad as hell when they find out you're not in Oberlin."

"No, they're not. They're going to be worried is all. And you know why? Because they'll think maybe I can't take it. My pop knows me good. Maybe I can't."

There was real doubt in his voice. "Hell, you can take anything, Dewey. How about the knocking around you got for four years playing football? Well, three years anyway. Not counting the year you busted your arm."

"I was scared crapless most of the time," he answered. "Just like I'm scared crapless now." Dewey sipped at his bottle again, then shook his head, finally waving his hand in front of his mouth and throat, cooling the bourbon. "Remember how froze up I got in that game with Fairport Harbor last fall? I was supposed to bulldoze this big Finn, their guard, remember? And every time I saw his face I got scared. He was always breaking through and stopping you before you could get hopping. I couldn't hurt him. He was this big dumb guy with weepy eyes. But then that one time he got through, he threw one at you around the knees and brought you down, and before the son of a bitch got up I saw him dig his elbow into your gut. Did old Dew Ventry get mad! Let me tell you. I near killed the feller. I bet his balls still ache."

"You almost got yourself thrown out of the game."

"So what? They had to carry old Jean Sibelius off, didn't they? A compound fracture of the gonads. Put there by old Dew Ventry's dancing knee."

Boyd, remembering it, smiled. "It sure as hell made things easier for me. We won the game."

They were both conscious of, and a little embarrassed by, the "we." Just the two of them had won the game? Maybe. The other guys helped, but it was Gavin and Ventry who got all the razmahtaz in the newspaper the next day. And in the final quarter when Boyd went over to give Ventry High a six-point lead, he knew that Dew's eyes were wet and that his feet were running with him all the way.

"Weren't we the two hot shots? Now I *ask* you," Dewey said, grinning, then sinking into silence for a few seconds. "Sometimes, you know, sometimes I thought we could always stick together. Just the two of us could stick together like that. Real funny."

"Funny." Yet Boyd himself had once thought the same thing. Well, what the hell, there had to be an end to the Huckleberry Finning. If you didn't stop being a kid, the psychiatrists would say naughty-naughty.

"But I think I'm going to grow up quick once I get in the Army," Dewey went on. "You probably won't even recognize me, I'll be such a big deal."

"I'd recognize you at the bottom of a twenty-gallon barrel of motor oil, meathead."

"You would? Son of a gun. How you like that! Asshole buddies for life." Dewey now tried to raise himself from the ground, patting it first with his hands to make it stop moving. "Hey, I tell you what. What say I race you to the bridge over there to see which one of us is top dog? How about that? Settle it once and for all." With difficulty he managed to get himself in a standing position. "Christ," he said, "someone must be trying to get me drunk. Where did the ruttin' bridge go?"

"That-a-way," Boyd said, pointing, then stood up. "Look, whoever wins gets to toss the guy who isn't a big deal into the river. The little deal gets dunked. That okay?"

"I'd drown. I've got too much ballast. I'm veering to the larboard, as us nautical fellers say."

Boyd leaned over, picked up a small twig from the ground, and drew what was, everything considered, a remarkably straight line. "This is the starting point. Put your balls up to it and spring when I whistle. We shag-ass."

"Boy, of all the cheats. Of all the unfair practices. Of

272

all the ... by God, of all the mean-mouthed, dirty tricks. The feller who whistles *knows* when the whistle's coming. He's already sprung away. You're a cheat."

"Pardon," Boyd said a little drunkenly. "My humble, heartfelt apologies. Mustn't let it happen again. Must be a gentleman. My Aunt Cortez says I must be that at *tall* costs. Now where were we?" He looked stupidly at the mark he had just drawn. "Tell you what. I'll give you my best one-two-three. The way it works, bub, when you hear the three ring out, you run your bushy tail over to that tree by the bridge. You see that what-you-call sycamore?"

"The article with the slippery trunk?"

"Roger. The first one there is the winnah. The best deal of all."

Doubt again came to Dewey's face. "Unfair! You're taking advantage of the lame. I got a busted neck. I been mauled by a virgin. What you call the virgin maul. Who ever heard of a guy with a busted neck running a race without a headstart?"

"I'll headstart you in the gut, lad. This is an honest race. No thieves can enter. It's between you, me, and old Father God."

Dewey looked pathetically at the grass. "Who's going to carry the bottles? We leave them here and some wily old coon's going to come along and stick his nose in them."

"I carry one. You carry one."

"What if I fall? What if I bust my beautiful face? The face that's going to launch a thousand slips. The face that's going to bring Tabasco to the blood of countless girls. The face of a saint, as he's painted by my good buddy Michael the Angelo. A face, when you see it, you want to jump out of your clothes. A face that brings tears to the eyes of old men with boggy prostates, yearning for their lost youth. A face ..."

"I get the idea," Boyd answered. "I'll bust mine too. We'll do the old Damon and Pythias. Just keep it unqueer."

"Keep it unqueer. Roger and over." Dewey now stooped over, poised at the mark, holding his half-emptied bottle in one hand, the other scratching at the ground. "Ready?" He watched Boyd next to him shake his head up and down.

"One!"

"Uno!"

"Two!"

273

"Duo!"

"Thr . . ."

"Stop the show!" Dewey now shouted. "A calamity. I got to take a leak. Un leakissimo. A guy with a floating bladder is bound to come in last."

"Time to pour the water off the potatoes." Boyd stood up, unzipped, moved toward a tree, and said, "I piddle on thee, old sumac tree," as he did.

"I piddle on thee, virgins of the world."

"Shake it once or twice, but no more; you'll turn into a dwarf."

"I'll find me a nice virgin dwarf if I do. To bite me on the neck," Dewey answered, zipping up. "I'm ready to give you my all. My very all. I'll race the hell out of you. I'll show you who has brave balls and who doesn't. *One!*" He fell down to his position.

"Hey, wait a minute. I have to get in my official Olympic stance. I want to cut a figure. I have to arrange my Greek muscles here in my belly. There. How I look now? Pretty good? You ever see anything like it?"

"You look crazy drunk. Your ass hangs low."

"One!"

"Two!"

"Thu-*reee!*"

And they were off, falling over the grass, running through the darkness, stumbling over branches, into holes, kicking up leaves, yelling their heads off, two madmen racing in the night.

"You son of a bitch," Dewey yelled. "You've been practicing."

"Hurry up, meathead. Last one in gets a dunking."

"Son of a bitch," Dewey said again, half running, half falling over the ground. With a superhuman push he tried to make his legs move faster, but they didn't seem to belong to him. They couldn't do what his befuddled, be-bourboned mind was telling them to do. He could feel his wind begin to give way, and then a sharp pain in his stomach. "You lousy guy. You cheat. You been practicing."

Running along the edge of the river, Boyd kept his distance from Dew, listening to his outrage fill the night air. Sweating, puffing, he raced toward the tree next to the bridge, feeling full and exhilarated and happy and drunk.

"You mean . . . lying son . . . bitch." Dewey looked

ahead and saw Boyd closing in on the sycamore, shining in the light from the sky, and he could almost feel his eyes begin to get wet as he hoped for some miracle to work his legs. Then, so quickly that he scarcely knew how, he saw Boyd slow down, cut the steam, and as Dew caught up with him, reach out with one arm and lock it around his shoulders, holding him tight as they passed the tree; then they fell to the ground, heaving for breath, arms and legs scattered over one another.

"You won."

"*You* won."

"We both won. We're both top dogs."

And as they lay there, half drunk, fighting for breath, already feeling the loneliness that was about to begin, a new life that would change them, kill their youth and their silliness, their childhood, their games, they said not a word. It was almost the sleep of children they were trying to prolong. In all the stillness of the valley, they could already feel something begin to leave. Boyd, as he looked up at the dark sky from the wet grass, could feel his youth pass from him like a shadow that had crossed his face for a moment and then disappeared.

Simon lay on the bed in the dining room, his head propped up against three pillows. The toes of his left foot ached and smarted, his leg felt stony, his arm heavy. His chest was sore from coughing, yet he was unable to bring up the phlegm there. His eyes were watery and his ribs hurt from forcing air in and out of his lungs.

He had been in the bed since eleven, and even now, an hour later, he still felt the suffocating hotness inside the ambulance during the long ride from Washington. He would have liked a glass of water, but the decanter was, he saw, on the night table to the left of the bed, and if he rolled over toward it he was afraid he might upset the glass and awaken Rose. Instead, he lay on his pillows, his eyes open, the lid of one of them leaden, unable to be entirely opened or shut.

It had been a solemn homecoming, unlike any that Simon had ever known. When Parnell first saw him being lifted from the ambulance, Simon could tell that the boy was frightened, but a minute later he threw himself on Simon's chest, almost upsetting the stretcher. Catherine had looked as if she were carrying the burdens of the world, yet she tried her best to cheer him up, talking to him optimistically as she washed his face in cool water, telling him that Ed Burd, who lived on the other side of the Humpback Bridge, was getting along nicely after a stroke a year ago that had crippled his legs and in some incredible way left him blind but otherwise still functioning. She seemed then to wait for Simon to say something equally reassuring—"Well, I may look bad, but I feel finely," or whatever—but he said nothing at all. He was unable to make the chords in his throat work, and it was a minute or two before Catherine realized that his quiet did not derive from the fatigue of the journey.

Rose, when she first saw him, had been unwilling to meet his eyes. During the painful ride from Washington he had wondered how he would be able to confront her, but he now saw that she was not going to allow for any confrontation. She had busied herself with all the sickroom paraphernalia and when Simon asked for a slip of paper so that he could write a message to her, she had hastily shoved both of his arms—his good one and his bad one—under the summer blanket. Whether she knew what he was thinking he couldn't say. She sometimes had uncanny intuitive powers, and it occurred to Simon that perhaps Rose could see what he had stumbled onto in the Washington station.

Even before he heard Boyd enter the hallway, Simon thought that he could smell the manly and youthful scent. Boyd must have been running. As he tiptoed into the room Simon saw that his clothes were sticking to his body and his eyes were fired by some great effort. Simon tried to work his own face into a smile, but only half of his sunken cheek responded, the other half lying loose and relaxed.

"Hello, Simon," he heard Boyd whisper as he came close to the bed. "I'm glad you're home."

Simon looked at his grandson's face for signs of Luke—looked now in a way that he had never looked before, because he knew now that Lucas was dead. Just as Rose knew.

He had gone to Washington for Lucas, and instead he had found Rose. Just two mornings before, as Simon had begun to push his way through the exit in Washington, he had noticed a reflection in the glass; the reflection itself was of no account—it was merely a woman, whose face he hadn't even seen, who at that moment raised something, a ticket perhaps, close to her face to study it. His hand had already begun to push open the door when the reflection struck somewhere in his mind, taking all the breath out of him. And then the headache had broken all over him.

It was Rose he had seen. Reading the telegram to the family more than a year ago, then carrying it to her bedroom and hiding it, and finally on the same afternoon buying the banner with the blue star for the parlor window. *She hadn't read the telegram at all.* Simon had seen that in the glass door in the station. She had read words that weren't there.

Lucas was dead, and Rose had known it from that first day. She had known for over a year, bearing all the suffering by herself in her bedroom. Oh, it was a terrible thing for her to have done, Simon knew, defying truth that way, putting herself between grief and the people she loved, as a man would shield another from a bullet, and all the while having to live alone with the truth. And through her own misunderstood valor, she had allowed the town to conclude that Lucas was a coward and had run.

If only he could tell Boyd; but there was no telling left in his throat. If only he could reveal to Boyd that his father had died an honorable death and that he had been doing what he thought he had to do until the life was taken from him. But, no, there were no words.

Yet even as Simon had misread his own son, he now gravely underestimated his son's son. Boyd needed no such reassurance. Though he didn't know that Lucas was dead or that Rose had concealed it, he had half suspected it, which was a damned sight more than Simon had. It was his father who had told him that a man had always to follow the chivalry of Jesus Christ, and he knew that Luke would never betray that chivalry, even though he was a dreamer. Boyd had never doubted Lucas. His dreams, yes, but not the man.

"You're going to be all right now," he said to Simon. "We're all going to take care of you."

Simon could see the understanding on Boyd's face, and he saw, too, that a change had just within the last few days worked itself there. It was no longer a boy's face. It was full of glory and exaltation that he had somehow just found.

Ill as he was, a machine perhaps too broken even to try

to piece together again, he was strangely proud. Of Luke, of Boyd, and even of Rose. When Boyd kissed him lightly on the forehead, he knew that the world was not so evil that he couldn't sleep in it for at least one more night.

The next day, a hangover headache beating against the back of his eyes, Boyd told the family that it would be best if Dewey and he went to the station by themselves. They could say their good-bys in the privacy of the house. Rose, who at farewells tended to be less weepy than she was full of last-minute instructions, felt left out of things, even going so far as saying that he was ashamed to be seen with his own grandmother. After he put her mind to rest, he finished packing and went across the street to say good-by to Francine, but just as he thought, she was still in her bedroom—coming down with the flu, Mrs. Ventry said, though Boyd knew that she was too shaken to stand before him.

After an early lunch, and after Rose again told him what he would have to do once he arrived in Cleveland— "Don't mosey in the terminal. Get in line for your train as soon as you can. Don't be ashamed to assert yourself. If someone pushes you, you push back twice as hard"—he kissed everyone good-by, received their many God blesses, and he and Dewey made their way down Priest Street to the station. Parnell, who had been told that his brother didn't want anyone to see him off, ran behind the houses along Satin, following them. Once at the smoke-encrusted Romanesque station, Parnell hid behind a mail cart piled high with canvas bags and packages, watching Dewey and Boyd as they waited on the platform. As soon as the train pulled in and the two of them climbed up to a coach, suitcases in their hands, Parnell ran from behind the cart, waving at all the windows as he flew past them, looking for their faces. The engine hooted once, then twice, and the train began slowly to move. It was then that Boyd saw his brother racing along beside it. "So long, old buddy," he shouted through the open old-fashioned window. "You're the man of the house now—so you better be good and smart."

Parnell stood on the platform and waved, and even after the train had gone over the trestle, even after he could no longer hear its whistle, he continued to stand there, waving down the tracks. After a while he began to walk home, changing his walk to a swagger as he crossed the square.

At the Cleveland terminal, where Boyd was to wait an hour and a half for his train to Oberlin, he helped Dewey Ventry with his luggage, carrying it to the Railway Express office and putting tags on it for it to be shipped back home. Dewey kept nothing but a shaving kit and a small canvas bag. Afterward they walked into the Fred Harvey restaurant on the lower level and had a sandwich and a malted, neither of them saying much.

When they had finished, they walked out into the center of the high-ceilinged marbled station. "You take care of yourself, bub. Write me long letters and everything, okay?"

"Sure," Dewey answered. "And you write me too. Tell me all about the tail down at Oberlin."

"You'll get every rutting detail. You *are* still going to do what you said?"

"Me? Why, you're goddamn right. I just walk out of this Taj Mahal, out to the street, and right smack there on the square is an enlistment booth. All I do is go up, snap a salute, and say, 'Gen'ral Dewey Decimal Ventry reporting as ordered, Sahr.' Sound good?"

"Perfect. You son of a gun." They shook hands once more, Boyd feeling the tremors that were already in Dewey's fingers. "Take care. Be gung-ho. Love it up. Be a credit to your nation, your family, and your sex. Not necessarily in that order. Keep alive, Dewey."

"You too. Keep alive. I'll write."

"Look, you got everything you need? Birth certificate and all?"

"Yup. Everything. I'm all ready for them. All they have to do is give me a short-arm. And quick like that I'm a sol-jer."

"Write."

"I will. You too. So long, meathead."

"So long, Dewey. Take care."

Boyd watched him climb the long ramp to the street, then disappear in the crowd. When he saw the last of him, he went over to a telephone booth and made a call. He then tagged and checked his luggage, as Dewey had done fifteen minutes before, keeping back only the things he would need for the next few days. When he made his way out of the station, a little over half an hour had passed since Dewey had gone.

He waited for the traffic to pass, then crossed Euclid

279

and up the curb to Public Square. In the middle, he saw a small white booth, emblazoned with flags and insistent posters. Dewey was standing in front of it, looking, as he must have been doing for the last thirty minutes.

Coming up from behind, Boyd could feel the grin begin to slide over his face. He went up to Dewey, gave him a punch on the arm, said, "You forget something, bub?" and then the two of them walked into the booth.

Nine

In the half dark of a late October afternoon, Boyd sat beneath a desk lamp in his room and finished a letter to Francine, the third that week, then rose from his chair and walked to the small washbasin against the wall where he turned on both faucets and splashed water on his face. Drying himself with Dewey's faintly sour olive-drab towel, he returned to the chair, still rubbing his face, wondering what it was that had overcome him as he sat writing.

Francine had written first, more than a month ago, breaking the ice, apologizing for not having said good-by, and he had quickly answered. In a while, after the awkward exchanges of guilt and self-recrimination, they seemed to have refound the easy familiarity that, as long as he had known her, had been strained only on the night he tried to make love to her. Her letters were now full of excitement. She was in Cleveland, not in college at all, having told her parents that it was too late to be accepted at a good one even if they were willing to let her use the money that had been set aside for Dewey. They were written on the letterhead stationery of an insurance company where she had managed to get a job, through no effort of Cortez, who seemed to have vanished, and they were concerned with new restaurants with foreign names, with new people, and with events that Boyd couldn't follow. He read hungrily for news of Ventry, but what he found—the DeAngelo boy had been killed at Salerno, the new war plant was being built on a twenty-four-hour-a-day work schedule, and at least three hundred construction workers were now living in or near town—provided more unrest than solace.

Outside, the chimes of Burton Tower tolled seven, and as Boyd looked through the window at the inner courtyard of the quadrangle he saw four men in the Program walk from one of the lounges, books under their arms, toward the Union or the library. Four residential houses in West Quadrangle had been usurped by the Army Specialized Training Program, housing perhaps a thousand men enrolled in the corps, men who represented the bulk of male students on campus. The place gave the appearance of a women's college under siege, most of the students who would ordinarily have been there now in the Army or the Navy. As the soldiers in the Program were often enough reminded, they never had it so good, living, except for the required GI discipline, in comparative luxury, studying in walnut-paneled libraries, eating in high-ceilinged rooms behind fake Gothic windows, and relaxing in red leather club chairs in smoking lounges donated by Chicago or Detroit millionaires for the comfort of languorous scholars.

It was lunacy. Somehow, someone in Washington had decided that the war would, after all, be won by intellect, and the Program had come into being, training men, as its name implied, for specialized tasks. In Boyd's case and in Dewey's too, it was in chemical warfare. In lecture halls still echoing with the lessons of Kant and John Donne, they learned how to kill with a modernity that left Boyd stunned. Others in the Program learned more gentlemanly roles: there was a huge group studying Japanese, another German, still others Serbo-Croatian and Russian; a small pocket of men were learning Portuguese in order to be sent to the Azores or to the refueling bases in Brazil, and a few more were at work on Chinese so that they could be flown over to the Burma Road.

Boyd and Dewey had thus far even avoided basic, such was the haste with which the government sought to put their minds to work. After they had enlisted in Cleveland, they had been sent with a large group to Fort Custer for reassignment. There they had been given batteries of tests and interviews and had first learned that what was most expected of a U.S. soldier was patience. For two weeks they had done nothing but police the area for cigarette butts, work in the mess halls, and scrub the barracks. Every third day, after their area was clean beyond belief, the troops were trucked into the countryside, where they hid while a cigar-smoking colonel inspected the place, presumably for signs of life. They were issued wooden rifles because the real articles were still in short supply, they shined their boots and their brass, and they wrote letters. In sections of thirty or more, the original body of men gradually thinned out, sent to one basic training camp or another, until only six remained. It was thought that something out of the way had been planned for them, and they hadn't been disappointed. Two were shipped to Purdue, two to the University of Kentucky, and Boyd and Dewey to Ann Arbor. It had been found that they were smart. When Dewey learned it, all he said was, "For the love of God, do they mean *me?*" They did.

While they had waited at Fort Custer for the Army to make up its mind, Boyd and Dewey had got to know each other. It was one thing to know a buddy only at his best, but it was quite another to spend twenty-four hours a day with him, to sleep in the next sack, to sit next to him in poisonous community cans, to stand for hours by him beginning at five in the morning while a fat-headed, illiterate set of stripes mispronounced the roll call ("Gayvin . . ." "Yo!" "Vintry . . ." "Yo!"), to help him wash pots and pans with a two-year-old crust of grease, to try to make a game out of which one could shred Lucky Strikes in the neater way while policing the lawns, or just to sit and shoot the bull, the only shooting at the moment they were permitted.

Away from home, Dewey had become shyer than ever. Boyd, easy and outgoing, had made new buddies at Fort Custer, joking around with them, glad to listen to their city talk. But Dewey, when he wasn't with Boyd, would take out a paperback Edith Hamilton and reread the same page for a half hour while sitting on top of his foot locker. Still, almost everyone liked Dewey. It was just that he seemed a little too timid, too unaggressive to like anyone in return, as if somehow he didn't want to get too close to anyone because he knew that it was the fruitcaky thing to do and something that wars brought out in all men. Boyd could know him, because Boyd had been around for a long time, but let anyone else try to get too familiar and Dewey was the next minute back in Edith Hamilton's classical arms. One buddy of Boyd's, a fellow named Olson from Gary, Indiana, which he described as Chicago's whorehouse, had called Dewey "a stuck-up bastard," but Boyd knew that he was all wet. Dewey was still scared. That was all.

Of course, at times he wondered if it wouldn't have been better had he let Dewey go his own way. To try to work out for himself whatever it was that was eating him. Yet when he considered it, he pretty much decided that Dewey would crumple entirely if he was left alone. At least with Boyd around, he now and then still had good times. He was, for one thing, the funniest guy in the barracks, though some of his jokes were lost on the men around him. On one night when they were allowed to leave the area and go over to the PX and drink it up, Dewey had been the life of the party. The same Olson, who had earlier attributed Dewey's stand-offishness to a wild hair in the wrong place, said now that he was the greatest. "All you have to do is get to know him," he added, implying that he did, though he didn't at all, nor did Boyd, really, or even perhaps Dewey himself.

On the train to Ann Arbor, by themselves again, both glad and disappointed to be away from Fort Custer, Dewey had been ebullient. If the men back at the camp didn't have a word for Dewey, he had several for them. "Apes," he had said, "Cro-Magnon men." To Boyd it seemed that Dewey had to hate people before they hated him, giving him an advantage at least in timing, and it didn't seem fair. Underneath, most of the apes were scared kids just like Dewey, but he never took the trouble to find that out. It was on the train trip that Dewey had almost set up a test of Boyd's allegiance. The train had stopped in Detroit for a few minutes to discharge and pick up passengers, and Dewey ran into the station to get a few beers, telling Boyd before he left not, for the love of God, to let the train leave without him, knowing that if he didn't arrive at Program headquarters in Ann Arbor on time he'd be AWOL. When the train began to move out of the station and Dewey had not yet returned, Boyd didn't know what to do. He half wanted Dewey to be AWOL to see what he would do under the stress, to let him finally break out for himself if he could, correcting what was probably an error in judgment that Boyd had made when he enlisted with him. But at last he sprinted to a conductor and told him that his buddy back at the terminal would be in a hell of a lot of trouble if the train wasn't stopped. Even before the conductor could explain to him that trains weren't delayed for friends who went over the hill to buy beer, Dewey had materialized from the end of the coach, a sack of beer under his arms, a grin on his face, as though he had waited there to see what Boyd would do, teasing him. By the time they arrived in Ann Arbor, they were both a little high, each having downed five bottles of beer during the hour's ride, each drinking for a different reason.

Now, almost two months later, Dewey was in real trouble for the first time in his life.

Although the Army had spent perhaps thousands of dollars on IQ and psychological tests to weed the chaff from the golden grain, they might have saved themselves a hell of a lot of trouble had they made a two-dollar telephone call to Miss Agnes Stickney in the Ventry grade school. She would have told them that Dewey was the smartest thing to walk on two feet, and then added forlornly, "But he's crazy." She of course would have been wrong, too quick to explain Dewey, but at least the Army wouldn't have put him in chemical warfare. He was a truck and jeep man. Didn't they *know?*

They were learning. The course at Michigan was a hurry-up one, almost breath-taking at times, and though no one was more interested in lab work than Dewey—it gave him a chance to use his hands—when it came to writing lab reports he merely said they were a bore and asked Boyd to do them for him. Boyd hated them every bit as much as Dewey did, and though he was himself swamped with work he always came to his rescue. Yet because of the cruel mechanics of the alphabet, he wasn't able to help Dewey in classes, as he had in high school. Dewey sat on the other side of the room from him in most of them, and he was on his own. Even so, it was still Boyd who drilled him every night back at the dorm, even hitting him as he shouted facts Dewey was expected to learn. *"Learn,* you lousy meathead!" he'd yell at him. "Do you want to get shot?" To which Dewey would generally reply, "I'm tired, man." Then he'd look at Boyd with that "What's the use?" look in his eyes. Boyd would ignore it, punch him some more to keep him awake, and continue with the cramming session.

What *was* the use? Christ, the use was survival. If Dewey was axed from the Program now, God knows what would happen to him. He seemed more helpless and confused than ever, and more dependent on Boyd. If in the middle of the night Boyd jumped up from his bunk in the overcrowded, sweaty room designed for two and occupied by four, Dewey would say, "Hey, where you going?" and Boyd would answer, "For God's sake, I'm going to the can. Is that all right?" Dewey wasn't being kept in Ann Arbor by the skin of his teeth, but by the skin of Boyd's.

You could con the Army for a while, but not forever.

285

Dewey was already in a serious mess in two of his classes, and he no longer seemed to care much about them except . . . well, it was a big Except. It sometimes appeared to Boyd, as it had once before back in Ventry, that Dewey would be happy only if he could bring Boyd down too. After Boyd had received a barely passing grade in an important Physics test, having spent most of the previous night helping Dewey to bone up, Dewey hadn't concealed his amusement. "You're in the same boat, fella," he had said happily.

Leaving the addressed envelope on the desk in the room, Boyd now put on his OD tie and looked around for his coat. He'd go out and drop the letter in a mailbox, he decided, then come back to the dorm to study some more for a test the next day. He knew where Dewey was. He was at the movies. And when the movie was out, he'd come back and hit the sack until eleven or twelve o'clock, the middle of the goddamn night, and then, and not until then, would he expect Boyd to go over every mother-lovin' detail that might appear in tomorrow's Inorganic Chem exam. Even at that, Boyd would have to pummel hell out of him to get him out of his bunk, then slap at his face with a wet washcloth to wake him up.

Dewey walked into the room, leaving the door open, throwing his cap on the desk. "Good movie," he said, stretching out on his bunk.

"I bet," Boyd said sulkily. "I was studying."

"For the chem test? It'll be a snap."

"Yeah, like the last one. You know what happens if you flub this one up?"

"I get my ass transferred to the Infantry."

Boyd looked at him impatiently. "Well, then hit the books. For Christ's sake, what are you doing in the sack, man?"

"I'm going to get a little shut-eye first. Where are you going?"

"For a goddamn walk. I have to mail a letter anyway."

"What's the news from Francine?"

"Same as always. She's living it up in Cleveland. She wants to know if we get home for Christmas. How the hell am I supposed to know?"

"I heard some guy at the movies say they were going to disband the whole mother-friggin' Program here. You hear that?"

286

"It's a rumor. They keep it circulating so everyone can run scared."

"Christ," Dewey said smiling, "the war'll be over by the time they think I'm smart enough to fight."

"No such luck. One of these days, some bird-brain in Washington is going to find a lot of missing 201s, and he's going to say, 'Where the hell *are* these guys?' Someone'll tell him we're all in college, for Christ's sake, and then he'll shove all our asses into the Infantry."

"It can't be worse than Inorganic Chem. Look, you going to play school with me later on?"

"Sure," Boyd said without any enthusiasm, reconciled to it.

"Wake me up at midnight."

Angry now, Boyd answered, "God damn it, Dew, I'll be *beat* by then. I've been hitting the books all day."

"We'll just give it a couple hours. I'm in pretty good shape for this one."

"Yeah, I know what kind of shape you're in. But if you think I'm going to pound you for a half hour before you wake up, you're ... " He stopped, unable to think what Dewey would be under the circumstances. "For the love of God, can't you *help?*"

"I sleep heavy."

"Christ, I wish I could sleep. You never give a guy a chance."

"Cheer up, old fella. I'll save your life one of these days. Someone'll toss a bomb at you and I'll say, 'Not my old buddy Boyd,' and then I'll throw my bosom on top of it. How's that for gratitude?"

"I'll believe it when I see it. I'll believe it when your goddamn bosom lands in my lap."

"It'll be too late to believe then, bub. A man, he has to believe before the bosom flies." He looked wisely at Boyd. "And a man also has to have sleep. You wake me at midnight?"

The trouble with Dewey was that Boyd couldn't tell when he was in earnest and when he wasn't. What he had just said in his jazzy, goofy way seemed to offer allegiance in return for a little more help, but Boyd wasn't sure any more that he could tell what Dewey meant. "I'll wake you up," he said at last, walking to the door.

"Okay, old buddy. But don't get the clap out there, hear? There's a dance tonight at the League. A lot of the uglies are out to console the GIs."

"How come you're not going?"

The smart-aleck grin reappeared. "I'm sacrificing. I have to study. Nighty-night."

Boyd left the room, closing the door behind him. Christ, it looked as if Dewey was trying to see how far he could push him. In a curious way it seemed also that perhaps he had just discovered that he hated Boyd because he was so dependent on him. Could that be? Was Dewey at last able to see that he couldn't do anything without Boyd's help, half hating Boyd for it, no longer caring if he passed or flunked his courses if only he could make things hot for his benefactor? Or was Boyd imagining it all?

Yes, maybe Dewey was changing after all. Maybe he knew his own life was in danger and he now wanted to bring that danger to Boyd's.

Boyd kicked at the dry leaves at his feet. The air around him was filled with blue-white smoke from countless bonfires. He made his way across the Diag to Hill Auditorium. Cast-iron lamps threw a somber, wavering light on the pavement where he walked, bringing into focus a half-washed-out, hand-lettered sign painted there before the war. *Beat Stanford*. It had been walked on, rained on, and snowed on for so long that little of it remained. Boyd wondered vaguely if Stanford had been beaten, and wondered too what Ann Arbor had been like when people thought that those things were important, when they could still write hope on a sidewalk.

The library was blazing with lights, and now a stunned, tired girl emerged through its doors, looked in wonderment at the smoke in the air, drew it into her lungs, and then quickly walked by herself somewhere for coffee or a sandwich. There were no men, as there must have been before the war, waiting for them on the steps to take their books and to talk about T. S. Eliot as they passed beneath the dark trees. The girls Boyd had seen on campus seemed sobered, sheafs of V-letters from lovers or brothers sticking out from the pages of the books they carried, the no-nonsense "We are at war" look on their faces.

Boyd had already decided that after the war he would come back to Ann Arbor and not go to Oberlin at all. The place was fantastically pretty. On the train coming in, he had thought for a few minutes that it was going to be Venetian; the train followed a river, then ponds, and tiny English lakes, and finally stopped at the bottom of a steep hill, town and campus hidden at the top. There were wide lawns, gigantic elms, and prosperous-looking nineteenth-century houses; and the campus itself—white Early American, ashen Greek, gray and gold Gothic, at one moment rich, at the next down at the heels through an excess of scholarship—and on the other side of the campus the large houses of fraternities and sororities, lost in trees and vines and magnificence. Everywhere there was quiet. Except for the chimes from the carillon, it seemed to Boyd that all he could hear was the turning of pages.

And the libraries and study lounges! When Boyd first made his way into one building at the end of a mall, he scarcely dared sit down in the opulent surroundings, marble mantels, decadent-looking chairs, and downy sofas all around him. How could a man settle his behind on such finery and go about the mean task of studying? Each time that Boyd tried, he found his eyes rising from his books again and again to look at where he was. Shy girls curled up on leather sofas, their shoes on the thick carpet, their notebooks illuminated by chandeliers that must have weighed a quarter ton, small, apologetic table lamps at their sides as concessions to eyesight. For someone who had done most of his studying back home in a straight, hard-as-nails ladder-back chair in his bedroom, it was a revelation. Boyd, sitting in one of those disgracefully luxurious armchairs, felt both rich and wise. Perhaps that had been the intention of those who built the place. Perhaps if a man studied in shabby surroundings, his knowledge, too, would tend to the cheap and shabby.

As for girls, Boyd hadn't had time to think much about them. He was generally too spent after a day of classes and studying to get to know any of the girls on campus. He had, shortly after arriving in September, attended a mixer at Stockwell Hall and had met a girl from Laguna Beach, California. When he talked to her, all he could think was that she must have spent most of her life at the edges of swimming pools and in the front seats of pale blue convertibles. At one point when Boyd stupidly made some reference to what he thought was the splendor of her dormitory, an enormous, hundred-windowed Tudor mansion high on a hill, she had said in a matter-of-fact way that her own home was rather like it. "Only smaller," she had added while he caught his breath, but by that time he felt too intimidated to press on. It had never before occurred to him that some people in the world lived in houses that weren't like those on Priest Street or Satin.

Boyd had excused himself from her to fetch a glass of punch, then sheepishly walked out of the place, afraid that he might be asked where he lived.

Now, at the end of his walk, he dropped his letter in a box outside Hill Auditorium where only the week before he had heard for the first time in his life what he imagined was a symphony—it hadn't been; it was a symphonic arrangement of *Tosca*—and after he overheard two girls in front of him say that it was a poor performance, he tried to contain his emotions, his childlike pleasure, although by then he was sure that everyone had already seen through him. Not until he got back to West Quad did he dare, in the privacy of a shower, to whistle all he could remember of it.

As he walked past the boarded-up fountain near the League, he heard not *Tosca* but Tommy Dorsey. Well, even someone from Ventry could savvy Dorsey, at least. The music was coming from a record on the second floor of the brightly lighted building. He sat down on the concrete bank of the fountain, breathed in cold air and sweet-scented smoke, brought the collar of his coat up closer around his neck, and looked at the windows.

What made him turn his eyes he didn't know. Even long afterward he didn't know, unless it was a feeling that someone had been watching him. He looked to one side in the darkness and saw a girl standing by the curb in front of the League, caught there almost between steps, pausing as though she didn't know which direction she should take. In a minute she continued walking until she reached the door directly across from where Boyd was sitting, where she again paused uncertainly, then pushed through the dark oak doors and walked in. Her face had looked very fresh and clean, and also—what was it?—full of hesitation, as if at the last minute she might have turned from the door and hurried toward the women's dormitories.

Without quite knowing why—she hadn't looked at him once he brought his head up—Boyd rose from his uncomfortable seat and followed her. Once inside the building, he saw her walk up the stairs at the far end of a long hall, still hesitantly. At the cloakroom—cloakroom, he said to himself; whenever he heard the word he thought of the musty, wet-wool smell of the tiny rooms off the classrooms back in Ventry—he checked his coat, watching the girl behind the counter first hang up a green, water-

290

repellent coat with a furry lining. "There's a dance upstairs, isn't there?" he asked, and the girl, moving back to an open book before her at the counter, told him in what sounded like an English accent that there was, the accent probably coming from having read too much poetry. Boyd went up, imagining that he could still smell perfume on the stairs, paid his fifty cents, let someone at the entrance to the ballroom stamp the back of his hand with ink, and then moved into the large room from which the music was coming.

He stood against the wall for what seemed an unbearably long time, looking for the face. When he found it he continued to stand where he was. Except for perhaps fifteen men in suits, each one, to be nasty, more gnomish, bespectacled, and 4-F-ish than the last, all the men were in the Program and in uniform. Boyd recognized several of them from classes, but made no attempt to join them.

The girl was standing by herself a few feet from the entrance, as though she had gone as far as she intended to go. When the record on the machine ended, Boyd walked up to her, his knees unsteady, and stood next to her without saying a word. Another record began; he was still unable to say anything. At last, mustering up his courage, he turned and said, "I'm a lousy dancer but would you like to dance?" For a while he thought she was going to say no, or that she was waiting for someone, but then she smiled, stepped out onto the floor, and waited for him there.

She did not look like most of the girls back home. She wasn't wearing any make-up that he could see, not even any lipstick, and the color of her cheeks was startling. It wasn't until later that he learned she never washed her face—using creams instead—and that much of the color was put there by rubbing her cheeks with a terry-cloth towel. Her hair was braided, the two thick braids brought to the top of her head and pinned down, giving her the look of a Scandinavian milkmaid except that the face beneath the braids was rich and complicated, every second something new happening in it, and not at all vacant as a cow-girl's face would be. It was corny perhaps, but Boyd thought that she looked more medieval than anything else, somehow having stepped out of a tenth-century illuminated manuscript. In part, it was because of the way she walked. She looked as if she were striding across marble while everyone else in the world walked on gravel. Much

291

later still, he learned that her walk was mostly the result of having had to live with a volume of the Harvard Classics on top of her head from her thirteenth to her nineteenth birthday, but even that knowledge didn't spoil the effect.

"I saw you come in," he said at last. "I was out there freezing my ears off, and then I saw you come in. I guess I must have followed you."

"I saw you too," she answered quietly. "I was wondering if you would."

Boyd had never in his life thought that he could be that lucky. "You did?"

"I walked behind you all the way from the library. Then I watched you sit by a fountain that's been boarded up for more than a month. The poor soldier, I said to myself. He needs cheering up. So I came in here, very conspicuously waving my behind as I passed you. I hope you noticed."

Boyd grinned, liking the unmedieval way she talked. "I noticed. But I'm not really a soldier."

"And I don't ordinarily wave my behind. Are you in the Program?"

"Until someone finds out how dumb I am."

"It was rather backward of you to be sitting out there in the cold. Don't you like dances?"

"They're all right," he answered. "When I was little, my grandmother used to make me help her carry food and things to square dances. I used to stand over by the cakes and watch a lot."

"Well, you can't stand by the cakes all your life, can you, Private Gavin?"

"How did you know my name?"

"I'm psychic. Also, it's written on the tag on your shirt. I have all kinds of accomplishments, among which is being able to read scratchy writing. You're from around here, aren't you? Indiana, I'd say."

"You're close. Ohio."

"I could tell by the way you talk. It's a beautiful way to talk. I can hear dusty roads and swimming holes."

Boyd had never considered it before, but he supposed he did have a rural twang. There was nothing at all rural about the way she spoke. Weeks later, after he had been given her photograph, it seemed that she spoke in a way that only someone who had been photographed by Bradford Bachrach could speak. Quick, impatient, elegant, as if her tongue had never spoken a dirty word.

Boyd laughed. "I'm sort of a hick."

"It's the best way to be. I used to have an aunt who lived in Vermont. She was rather a hick too. No, what she was, she *became* one. She'd lived in New York most of her life, and then one day decided oh-what-the-hell, and moved up there and bought a house. I loved it. Everyone else in the family was scandalized because she subscribed to *The New Republic,* and the house didn't even have running water. But I loved it."

"We're not exactly savages," Boyd replied. "We have running water and all."

"And swimming holes," she added. Then, "Would there be a barefoot girl back home next to one of them?"

My God, Francine *did* go barefoot most of the summer. "It's worse. It's even more *Tom Sawyer* than that. She lives across the street. Only she doesn't have a picket fence."

"Well, I'm glad she's at home working needlepoint, or whatever it is they do." They danced, waited through a change of record, danced again to Glenn Miller. "I came up here tonight because I rather hoped you'd follow me. You still haven't told me if it shocks you."

"No."

"That's good. Sometimes people take me the wrong way."

"I'm not much for analyzing people."

"Well, don't change. Don't ever let anyone take you in tow and polish you. Once you start worrying about people's motives, you get a little jaded. And you're not at all. You're very innocent, aren't you?"

"How do you mean?"

She looked straight into his eyes. "I told you I wanted you to follow me up here, and you still haven't made a pass."

Boyd found it hard to keep up with her. "I didn't know that you wanted me to."

The self-confidence on her face left her and she again looked alone and undecided, as she had when she first walked into the building. "I really don't know what I want," she said at last. "Look, do you really like to dance?"

"No, not particularly. I already told you. I'm the cake man."

"It shows a bit," she said amiably. "We haven't moved from this one spot in the last two records."

"Back home we call it the dusty road shuffle."

"Would you like to go?"

"With you?"

"Don't worry. I'm not making a pass at you. I just thought maybe we could go for a walk. I've been in the library with Maxim Gorki since four o'clock. There's a war on, I keep telling myself, and people I know are actually getting killed, and where am I? I'm in the library with Gorki, trying to finish a paper that's going to bore the living daylights out of Professor Barrows."

"Was he a poet? Maxim Gor . . . ?"

"You are innocent. Don't they let you read books back in Ohio?"

"We read *Ivanhoe* and *A Tale of Two Cities* in high school. And an O'Casey play and some things like that. But no . . . no foreign people."

"Well, my God, you might use a little polishing after all."

Boyd wondered if that was what he needed. It seemed— was it possible?—almost as if she was offering to help him in some way, but she hadn't told him how yet.

"I don't even know your name."

"Pris Bollinger," she replied. "Only my friends call me Pipsi." She took his arm and began to lead him off the floor. "Consider yourself my friend."

Boyd couldn't remember when he had talked to some-one so much. Back at the dorm, after the men in the Program learned where everyone else was from, most of the talk had to do with the Program or with snatch. As pleasant and good-natured as many of them were, it seemed to Boyd that some kind of physiological error in their construction made it necessary for most of their thoughts to pass through their gonads en route from their brains. They sat at their desks with slide rules rising from their crotches and reminisced about their last lays. One funny fellow, the day before, had got everyone in the dorm to sign a birthday card for a nurse he was dating in Detroit, accompanying a giant-size jar of Vaseline. Still others went up to Windsor in Canada to sport with the tarts there because of the favorable rate of exchange, and talked afterward about Canadian amity. But about them-selves they said almost nothing. They wore their private parts on their sleeves like chevrons, but that was all they revealed, and, everything considered, this wasn't really half the distinction most of them thought it was.

Walking across campus toward Hill Street, Pipsi Bollinger and Boyd managed to give each other capsule histories of themselves, and—at least Boyd thought—with surprisingly little concealed. Maybe because she was from New York, where Freud's spirit had first settled and loosened everyone's tongue, there seemed to be nothing so confidential that it had to be withheld. She had gone to Brearley, then up to Smith for a year where she had one weekend met a Williams senior who was going to enroll in Michigan Law School the following term. "No one invited me," she said, "but I came with him. I'm a great follower of men, you see." She explained that they had continued to date each other for a year, and then everything had gone wrong. "I'd like to say he was queer. I like to believe —because it's good for my self-esteem—that any man who doesn't fall in love with me has to be queer. And God knows, I know half a hundred in New York where there's one behind every ginkgo tree. But I don't think he was. He was from Toledo, and it just so happened he liked a girl back there more than he liked me, the fool."

Boyd had never heard a girl say "queer" before. And he had never heard a girl, or imagined there *was* one, who could admit quite frankly that she had come in second place. There was more to come. He now listened to her tell him that she had, while she was getting over her lawyer, fallen in love with a junior in the College of Engineering but that he had been drafted the year before. Since then she had apparently spent most of her time with Max Gorki.

Their backgrounds couldn't have been less alike. "I live wherever my mother and father live, taking turns. My father lives in Rye, only he's in Washington now, and my mother lives in New York, only she's almost never there. They're separated. So as an added bonus, I have *that*." She laughed outright. "I like your *David Copperfield* past better. I spent almost all my time alone when I was growing up, or with people I didn't like. When I came out here, I decided I wouldn't even have anything to do with my parents any more. I don't feel anything toward them, and I expect they don't feel much toward me. Anyway, I don't even write letters to them any more. My mother calls me once a week if she has the time, but all she does is talk about herself. So we're different that way. I don't really have any family, the way you do."

Boyd had told her about Ventry, and how his own family had lived in Cleveland during the Depression, moving in with his grandparents when his father went into the Army. He told her that what he remembered most about the Depression—apart from Frank Ventry's empty sandwiches—was that his mother and father had moved in and out of three different houses in Cleveland between 1930 and 1936, each one less nice than the last, each one with a lower rent. And how a neighbor woman near one of them had every second day called Boyd and Parnell over to her house when the bake truck came around and bought a lemon-filled cupcake apiece. It wasn't, he said, until he was in high school that he realized the woman had bought them cupcakes because the Gavins themselves had no money for them. Strangely enough, Boyd didn't mind telling the girl he was with that his family was broke and always had been.

"Well," Pipsi said, upon hearing it, "I think we're both fairly lucky. I pity all those people who grew up in the early twenties or even back at the turn of the century. They're all so goddamn shallow. Do you know when I was *really* born? October, 1929. Isn't that incredible? I came in with the new world. All I can remember is that girls I was going to school with would just disappear, and then my mother or father would say, 'Oh, didn't you know? They lost their money.' And that's about all we ever thought about. The Depression and losing our money. And then, as soon as that was over, we started to talk about the war. It was a very—how can I say it?—*adult* childhood. I was born in 1925, when all those revolting people were marathon-dancing and drinking bathtub gin, but I didn't get going til '29."

Boyd was not ashamed, as he had been with Laguna Beach at the mixer in September, to tell her about his home. He was vaguely aware that her family must have had money in order to be able to worry about losing it, yet she listened to him with eagerness, not disapproval. If anything, she appeared to be almost envious when he described the town he was from.

"And do you still live in the little country town?" she asked.

"Since my father went into the Army in '41." Boyd waited, wondering if he dared say the words to a girl who was no more than a stranger. What he then said hadn't even been said to Francine. "For a long time we thought he was missing," he went on, "but I'm pretty sure he's dead."

"Oh." She held his arm tight. "What rotten luck."

"My grampa says it's the way of the world. If you don't get killed one way, you get killed another. It was very hard at first, but I think we're okay now. I mean, we're all reconciled to it. All except my grandmother and my kid brother. And they'll wake up one of these days too."

They made their way slowly up Hill Street, passing darkened fraternities, many of them closed since the war, the leaded windows of first a French château, then an English country house, then a red-brick Georgian place vacant and lightless. It was hard to imagine that people had once grown up in them, had made preposterous displays for Homecoming games, had sneaked beer through the back doors for illicit parties, or whistled at passing girls from their terraces or sun decks. For Boyd, it was the strangest dim-out he was to encounter during the war. There were no lights in the houses, not because electricity was being conserved, but because there were no hands to pull the metal strings of bridge lamps in the deserted rooms.

"The boy I used to date, the engineer, used to live there," she said, pointing to a brick Williamsburg place as they crossed Washtenaw Avenue. Unlike the others, it seemed to have a use, probably because of its prominent position at the intersection. A Red Cross sign over its door announced that it was a Blood Bank office. "It was all so silly," she said.

"Why silly?"

"Silly because he was so ... stupid." She turned her eyes from the house, then continued to steer Boyd down the street. "I told you he was drafted, didn't I? Well, I went down to see him once at Fort Breckinridge—that's in Kentucky—while he was in basic. For all practical purposes, we were engaged. We were pinned. I went down there, I think, to prove something to him. We took a room in a hotel, and we spent the night together. Only he never touched me. We just lay there next to each other and talked all night. He knew he was going overseas, and I don't think he wanted to hurt me or anything. Anyway, I got letters up to around Easter of last year, and then they stopped. When I went home for vacation, I'm afraid

297

I made a fool of myself. No one had ever *told* me anything. No one even knew who I was. I called his home in Maryland, half frantic, and his mother, as cool as a cucumber, said, 'Billy's dead.' I just about screamed."

"I'm sorry."

"Don't ever say that. You can't be sorry unless you know someone. Just say ... well, what was it you just said? It's the way of the world." She took her arm away from where it was entwined with his and stuck it into the pocket of her coat. "But there's more to the story. It gets more squalid. After I found out, I did something terrible. I left Mother's apartment and went out to a bar. It was the first time in my life I was in a bar by myself. And I picked up a sailor. I suppose I wanted to tell God or someone that two could play the game. I made the sailor happy, I think. As for me, all I got from it was crabs. Is that what they're called? Sex fleas. I used the flea powder that belongs to my mother's corgi. And after that, it's happened four more times. Not crabs—but the other thing. You're the lucky sixth. So now you know why I picked you up. I spent the afternoon reading Gorki in the library, and all I thought about was picking someone up. Don't for the love of God feel sorry for me. You'll be doing me a favor. And I don't want to hear any moralizing either."

"Shut up. Don't talk that way."

"I thought you better know. It's better if you know when you can't expect anything. I don't think you'll be able to get anything from me, if you know what I mean."

"You've already given me a hell of a lot."

"Well, at least you know. And now you're invited back to where I live. Are you coming?"

Boyd stopped her at the corner and turned her so that he could see into her face. "You won't solve anything by doing that."

"But you can't solve anything by not doing it, either."

"Are you really so tough?"

She waited a long time before answering. "No, I'm shivering."

Then they walked on, kicking at the leaves falling at their feet, making their way down the dark street.

Pipsi lived at the Chi Omega house, she said, but she had taken a room in a private home about two blocks away where she could work in quiet and where she could go when she wanted to be alone. It was a pleasant place, half-timbered and many-chimneyed, and occupied by a professor's widow who had, before the war, let out several rooms on the third floor to medical students. Pipsi had a bed, a desk, a bathroom, a femur bone which had been left and was now used as a paperweight, and a full-sized drawing exposing the human nervous system, for all of which she paid ten dollars a week. It was here, as she put it, that she was at home with her dark-browed Russian lovers, as she was majoring in Russian Lit.

But when they arrived, quietly opening and closing the front door, Pipsi alone went up the stairs, first motioning for Boyd to sit down in a tiny, book-lined study off the hall. When, a few minutes later, and after Boyd had heard the gurgling of a john at the top of the high house, she finally returned, he saw that she had pulled off the sweater from over her blouse and that she was carrying a box of crackers and a half-filled bottle of liquor. She went to the kitchen and reappeared a second later with two opened tins of something and a wedge of cheese.

"A feast before the slaughter of the innocents," she said, putting it all down on the table before Boyd, then closing the door that led into the hallway. "The anchovy paste my mother sends me from S. S. Pierce. The other tin has pink caviar; it's just salmon caviar, the cheap kind. If you don't like fishy things—do you?—the cheese is Camembert, and a little stale. But the Drambuie is faultless."

Boyd had never known anyone who deliberately ate fish. He now smelled the anchovy paste and was properly revolted by it, unable to think why a girl as lovely and wonderful as Pipsi could contaminate herself in such a way. "I think the cheese is about as far as I can go," he said, and after he tasted it he realized that even that was too far. What incredibly rank things New Yorkers ate. But the Drambuie he liked. It was honeyed and rather thick.

She was perfectly at ease. She sat across from him in a chair like the Victorian chair Rose sat in at home. All the furniture in the room, in fact, was like the furniture in the house in Ventry, yet it wasn't. It was a while before Boyd realized that the pieces must have passed through antique shops and expensive refinishing and reupholstering.

Her room upstairs had been carefully chosen, she now told him. She had seen perhaps as many as eight rooms in

299

eight houses until she found the right one. "When I told the woman here my name and had to repeat it three times, I knew I'd found just what I wanted. She's stony deaf." Boyd laughed at what she said, and as he did she kicked off her shoes and walked to him, sitting down on the sofa. "You're too far away," she said.

He was thankful that she had come to him, because he would never have been able to go to her, though he wanted it more than anything he'd ever wanted. He took her into his arms, then kissed her, tasting the Drambuie on her lips. When they'd finished, she leaned over and snapped out a light on the table next to them. "It's easier to find yourself when it's entirely dark."

"Something you read?"

"Experience," she answered. "You can forget everything in the dark. It's the poor man's narcotic. And while you're forgetting, if you're lucky you discover something in yourself."

"I thought . . . the idea was to find something in someone else?"

She considered what he had said. "I know what I can feel, and I can't go beyond that. I have limitations, I'm afraid. Sometimes . . . I think Freud has given us a standard of excellence no one can reach."

"It hasn't helped him much either. He's in London now, dying."

"I know," she said. "*That* I did read. I'm a promiscuous reader too. Where his jaw should be there's a great cancerous hole, and his dog won't even go into the room because of the smell. There's some kind of lesson there, but I'm not sure that I know what it is. All that talk about love and sex, and all he wants now is for someone to be *near* him, and no one will." She made a small sound in her throat, almost the beginning of laughter. "So maybe we all have a Freud's jaw, Private Gavin. And all we want is for someone to be near us."

She hadn't put it in a particularly amiable way, but he thought he understood what she was trying to say. "You never . . . when you were with those other people, you never felt anything?"

"I felt myself. I just told you. I felt a touch, and then I felt myself."

"That's too bad. It's not the way I figure it."

He was sure she must have smiled in the darkness.

"I like that 'I figure it.' I think if you keep talking that way, I'll fall in love with you."

"Is that a good reason?"

"It's one."

Boyd slowly stroked her fingers, then kissed each one. "You know what I can see?"

"Didn't I tell you that people can see better in the dark?"

"I can see that you're hating something." As he said it, he felt her fingers go limp, and then her body move away from his. "Do you hate me because I'm not the man who was supposed to be here?"

"That's not fair. You weren't supposed to say that."

"But I can't . . . stay with you if you go on hating something. It wouldn't work out, would it?"

"Do you want to leave?"

"No." He didn't. He couldn't bear to leave her now, even if she said she despised him. "I'm lucky as hell to be here. I'm beholden to you, as they say. Even if it's not very important to you."

"I'm just a girl who picked you up."

"No, you're not. The minute I saw you, I said, there's someone I'm going to know."

"But not this way?"

"I don't think we know what way it's going to be. That's all I'm trying to say. Just forget all the other people. Can you do that?"

Maybe she couldn't, but she was going to try. As he kissed her again, he wondered if Francine could ever give herself as this girl was doing, merely because she wanted someone to touch and reassure her, to be *near* her. If Pipsi was a little spoiled by hating too many things—her family, her utilitarian lovers—at least she didn't lock up what love there was left. Perhaps all she wanted him to do was to take the hatred from her, but even that was a *gift*, wasn't it? At least she had something to give away as a start. What Boyd had done with Francine was like stealing.

"Here," she said, "let me help you with your clothes. Do you mind if we do it this way? It seems so stupid to go through all the fuss and bother of working things off bit by bit. Let me unbutton your shirt. I'm a good unbuttoner. And don't . . . worry about anything. I'm not a little girl. I used part of my Christmas money to buy a dia-

301

phragm. I only wish we had clean sheets. I love the feel of clean sheets when I'm naked."

She *wasn't* ashamed.

"Will anyone hear?"

"Does it make any difference?"

"No."

"But no one will. I told you that the woman who owns the house is deaf."

They began to undress each other, carefully, marveling at what they uncovered, until there was a pile of clothes on the floor. Pipsi let herself slide from the sofa onto them.

"You have to help me," Boyd said. "Forget everything else and just help me."

"I will."

"And I'll think of you. Do you see? That's all you have to do."

Boyd straightened her out in the confusion in which she lay on the floor, her legs already moving apart in the clothes they had thrown there. They found each other's bodies, stroking and kissing what they found, touching each other with their tongues, and when they were ready she reached down and helped him, moved him into her. A short cry came from her mouth—no, from somewhere far within her, some dark place—as he settled in deeply.

Very slowly, because he wanted it to last a long time, Boyd moved his body; and she met each one of his thrusts with one of her own. He could feel the gentleness of her all around him, and it was a feeling like none he had ever felt before—different from Tina, and different from the girl at the Lake. And then, as he looked into her face, her eyes closed, her mouth flung open, he saw that she could feel it too. In time, as he wrung himself out in the smooth flesh beneath him, it was more than just an unborn child draining from him, but loneliness as well. And then something else came and took its place.

When a sound—a scream almost, as if it had been buried inside her all her life—came from her lips, Boyd covered her mouth quickly with his own so that only he, and no one else in the world, could hear it.

When he returned to the dorm, tired and at the same time exhilarated, he could think of nothing except what had happened to him. His lips were sore and the light beard that had broken through his skin felt like so many

302

pinpricks from having been stroked by the girl's hands. He unwound his tie, throwing it on top of a chair, and slipped out of his shirt. Not until he sat on the edge of his bunk to remove his shoes did he remember Dewey.

He walked in his stocking feet to the desk and lifted the books and papers until he found the alarm clock, then held it close to the window so that the light from the courtyard would fall on it. For the love of God, it was after two o'clock. Trying not to wake up the other two men in the room, he went to Dewey's bunk, over his own, and began to shake him. He seemed irretrievably asleep. But as Boyd lightly slapped his face, his eyes finally opened.

"Look," Boyd said, "it's two o'clock. I just got back. I'll meet you in the hall in five minutes, okay? We can study in the can. *Dew*, are you awake?"

"Sure-sure," Dewey answered. "A min-ute."

Already hating himself for the fatigue he would feel in the morning, just when he most needed to be alert, Boyd picked up Dewey's books and notes from the floor where he always kept them, then walked into the lighted hallway, leaving the door slightly ajar so that Dewey would be able to find his way around in the room.

At the end of the hall he pushed through a swinging door into the head, heavy with cigarette smoke. Two buddies of his were sitting in two cubicles, reading their notes, underlining with pencils, drawing on cigarettes. The doors to the cubicles had been there during the first week of classes, but had later been yanked off by a colonel who was outraged that soldiers could sit in privacy while a war was going on.

"Boning up?" Boyd asked, moving into the room.

"Where's God's gift to science? We miss him."

"He's in the sack, but he's due in here in a couple minutes." Boyd walked to a urinal, somehow the mere availability of one bringing on the urge, rested Dewey's books on its top, and unzipped. All over his belly he could still feel Pipsi's warmth.

"I keep telling myself," one of the men behind him now said, "if Ventry can pass this test, so can I. Only I'm having a hard time convincing myself."

"The trouble with *you*, hot shot," the other said, "is that you evolved too fast. Just phftttt! And you're supposed to be a genius. Your old man's a bricklayer, *his* old man was a saloonkeeper, and—phftttt!—you're supposed to be a

303

genius. You're forcing it. You don't have the breeding yet."

"Screw off," the first one said. To Boyd, "What about Glamor Boy? Is he getting the shaft or is he getting the shaft?"

Boyd, through at the urinal, winced at the nickname. Somehow, God knows how, the men in the Program had stumbled onto the same name that had tormented Dewey all through high school.

"He missed two classes in Trig last week, or didn't he tell you? Lieutenant Zell didn't even bother with innuendo this time. Said he's going to get that goldbrick and stick a rifle up his butt."

No, Dewey hadn't told him. The Trig class was the only one they didn't share. "He's all right," he heard himself say. "He's just . . . he sleeps a lot."

"I been trying to get him to share my sack, but old Glamor Boy says no-go," the first one laughed wildly.

"Christ, I could go for that," the other said. "Hell, I ever tell you I been blown in eight red-blooded American cities, including Laramie, Wyoming? I'm fixin' to set a record. Of course, it's just a little sideline."

Boyd turned to them, confusion on his face. "Lay off it, will you?"

It was apparently the remark the second one needed. "I'd like to lay on it," he replied. "Jesus, that boy is all sex, you ever notice? You sit down next to him and—ping!—you get an electric shock. And those weepy eyes. You know what I see there? I see jazzing. That's what I see. Christ, that guy is all sex. But ask him when he got laid the last time, and he clams up like nothin'."

Boyd shook his head. "You guys are really sick."

"Yeah?" the first one said. "So what does your buddy do when he's supposed to be at the library? You know where he hangs out? Rice's is where he hangs out."

"So?"

"So he's always down there by himself. Isn't that right? A guy, he never gets laid and he hangs around bars by himself, nine times out of ten he's a pansy."

Boyd recoiled at the word. "You know," Boyd said, "I don't get you guys." He pointed to the second one. "Bragging about all the times you've been blown, and then calling Ventry a pansy because he doesn't get laid. Maybe there's a reason he doesn't get laid, you assholes. And if you're collecting votes, you son of a bitch, you get my vote as the pansy around here."

"Hey, wait a goddamn minute. I don't go for that crap."

"Go pull it off. All the way," Boyd said, then pushed through the door into the hallway, walking loudly back to the room. Once inside, he looked for Dewey, but saw that he was still in the sack.

"Damn it, you got to study," he said to the sleeping figure, waiting for a response that didn't come.

For a long time Boyd stood by the bunk and watched the face before him. You're *dying,* he said to himself. Do you know that you're dying? You so goddamn fragile that you can't fight back? Is that why you're skipping classes, Dewey? You don't want to be near these half-wits because they're going to ask you when was the last time you were laid? Are they screwing you up? Am *I* screwing you up, kid? Is that what's wrong? Am I screwing you up?

No, maybe it wasn't that Dewey had changed at all. Maybe he was just the way he had always been. But the world had changed and become meaner. Now there were people who had quick, ready-made explanations for everything, who could look at a guy and the dead welts on his back and not ask him why they were there, but who could remember the shock they felt when they sat down beside him, a shock generated by their own sodden shoes. And who could distrust a man because he reminded them of what they had been before their fall from grace. Well, hell, no wonder Dewey slept all the time.

Sleep good, Boyd said to the still figure. There are some things a man has to work out for himself. Sleep good.

The next morning, after a wiseacre sergeant stormed into the room and bellowed at the four men to drop their socks and grab their frocks, a new variation, Boyd looked out of his tired eyes into the bunk above him and he knew that Dewey was still asleep. When another man asked, "Aren't you going to pound him awake?" Boyd answered, not knowing exactly why: "Let him sleep."

At breakfast he ate powdered eggs and Spam with a surprisingly good appetite and then made his way to Angell Hall, where he took his exam, trying to keep his eyes off the vacant desk. At lunchtime, when he returned to the room, Dewey was just getting out of the sack. "What happened?" he said.

Boyd looked everywhere but at his friend, afraid that the betrayal would be visible in his eyes. "I tried to get you up."

"Oh," Dewey answered, and slid slowly from his bunk to the floor. "That's okay, Boyd; don't worry about it."

The son of a bitch, Boyd thought. Did he always have to be so goddamn kind? Who said I was worrying anyway?

Two days later the boom was lowered on Private Ventry, and to Boyd it seemed that Dewey was almost relieved. On the morning when Dewey was to report for his calling-down from Program headquarters, Boyd walked with him over to the building. He wanted to tell him why he had let him sleep through his test, but he wasn't able to, at least partly because he didn't know. As for the words spoken by the two men in the head that night, he now realized that they meant almost nothing. The same fellow who had boasted of an intrigue in Laramie, Wyoming, had in the dining hall the next evening pointed through the window at a huge St. Bernard, an orphan of war left on campus by one of the fraternities, and said that he could *go* for that. All Boyd could think was that he had axed his best friend because of something a nitwit had said.

Yet, truthfully, Boyd also knew that he wasn't spending all that much time thinking about Dewey or his problems. On the day after he met Pipsi, his body had burned from the moment he woke up until he saw her again that night, and he could think of little other than the pleasure he knew was waiting for him. If, back home in Ventry, he had ached all over because of unfulfillment, the ache was now much keener because he knew that it would soon be lifted, and apprehension made it worse than ever. He sat through the day in his classes and brought his penciled hand close to his mouth, kissing it with his tongue the way Pipsi had, trying to recall the sensation until the touch itself could be met with again. Met again it was. That night and the next night. He had waited for her at the library, then the two of them had walked back to her place, where, as soon as they determined that the woman upstairs was asleep, they had made love. And once he had left her, the ache in Boyd began again, anticipating the next time.

Dewey had been pulled out of classes entirely and spent most of the day lying on his bunk, waiting for his new assignment. On those occasions when Boyd was with him, neither did he try to apologize for what he had done nor did he tell him anything about the girl. If Dewey were told, then Francine would have to be told, and Boyd wanted to put that off for as long as he could. For the time being he had decided to luxuriate in his new-found position and leave it at that.

Dewey, of course, already knew. On the night after the colonel had told him that he would be transferred as soon as they found a suitably abject place for him, Dewey had looked all over the dorm and then the Union for Boyd but was unable to find him. He went downtown, where he'd been before, and sat in a bar for two hours, boozing it up. Later, as he was lying in his bunk in the room, he woke up when Boyd came in, and as Boyd stripped he imagined that he could smell the scent of a girl on him, a heavy wet sex-scent. For one moment Dewey was about to hop out of his sack, grab Boyd's hand, and shake it, but he then realized that perhaps Boyd wanted to keep it a secret. Lying there in the darkness, he wanted to leave the place more than ever, if it was now necessary to keep secrets.

And he remembered what he had heard that morning. "Let him sleep." When he first heard the sergeant's whistle, he was vaguely aware that he had missed the cramming session the night before, but he was still reasonably confident that he could get through the test. Yet even before he opened his eyes, he had heard Boyd say, "Let him sleep." As he lay on the bunk, listening to the three men in the room dress and leave for breakfast, he wondered what in hell he had done. For some reason—and it must have been a good one—Boyd wanted him out of his hair. Dewey knew that he couldn't show up for the test because Boyd didn't want him there. Instead, he continued to lie where he was, looking up at the celing, until lunchtime when Boyd returned. And then he had heard Boyd's lie.

Well, maybe Dewey slept too much and maybe he didn't study as much as he was expected to, but that wasn't justification enough for Boyd to give him the ax. Half the time when he pretended he was sleeping he just wanted to get away from the men in the Program anyway. They weren't bad guys, actually, but it was hard for Dewey to talk to them. They were, for the most part, city men, tough as nails, cynical as all hell, and on the few occasions that Dewey tried to carry on conversations with them, they generally changed the topic from Ventry, the only thing Dewey liked to talk about, to the number of times they'd scored in Windsor over the weekend. They would expect Dewey to contribute something. He had at first played along with them, repeating some of the lurid tales he used to tell Boyd, but one day Boyd happened to overhear him and said, "Watch out for him. He's got a yeasty imagination." Everyone had laughed. As for their other pranks, well, hell, Dewey was used to a different kind. The guy in the room next door would step out of the showers and walk down the hall, still wet, and there stoop over, light a match, bring it back to his tail, and blow it out by breaking wind. It was a great feat, and everyone clapped except Dewey, and everyone urged the star to do it again. He generally obliged.

If the other men in the Program thought that Dewey was the only child in their midst, he was even more convinced that he was the only one who wasn't. Dewey had always been under the impression that farting was an amusement for ten-year-olds and for fifty-year old Rotarians with prostate trouble, but that somewhere between those two ages a man was supposed to accept it as a not cspecially noteworthy phenomenon. Once, the Big Wind had also paraded around the dorm showing off a lipsticked private part, describing for the benefit of everyone the girl who had done it, he said. To Dewey it seemed that lovemaking for most men was about as exalted as blowing out matches, and he was almost glad that for the time being he wasn't a participant. The very next time that the Wind set himself up in the hallway for his display, Dewey had to restrain himself from bringing his GI boot up to the bare behind and driving the lighted match up as far as his liver.

As for what Boyd had done, Dewey was upset primarily because he knew that he must have let Boyd down in some way, provided him with provocation. What it was he didn't know, unless Boyd was now ashamed of him for some reason, ashamed of his helplessness and ineffectuality. Yet Dewey knew for a fact that he was no more helpless and ineffectual now than he had been two months ago. The only explanation he could imagine was that Boyd had grown up and now had a girl—no, a woman—and that when that happened a man could no longer have buddies. To hell with both of them, he thought.

Yet for all that, after supper on Thursday night, Dewey had followed Boyd across campus because he knew that he was probably going to meet the girl. Dewey wanted to

see what she was like, and whether she was worth a ...
well, he almost said friendship, but then he decided not to.
And when, standing behind Angell Hall in the darkness, he
finally saw the girl leave the library and walk down the
steps where Boyd was waiting, he thought she looked fine.
He watched her lean her books against Boyd's chest and
kiss him; he wasn't sure that he went for that, because
back home in Ventry it was a man's job to do the kissing.
But she was very pretty and somehow worldly. She looked
smart and fine and rich.

If Boyd was growing up to be a man who could have a
woman, Dewey was pretty sure that all he was growing up
to be was alone. He had been alone almost since he had
left home. Well, what the hell, he'd tie one on. Get drunk
in honor of being transferred to the Infantry. Get roaring
drunk like the old man used to do. He turned and headed
away from the campus now, making his way toward
downtown Ann Arbor. Maybe the hardest thing in the
world for a man to learn was that his only company was
himself, and that all the rest was self-deception.

"You look tired," Pipsi Bollinger was saying as they
walked away from the library. "I don't know what the
Army thinks you are. They expect you to take a four-year
course in a year. It's mad."

"I guess I'm a little tired."

Boyd hadn't had much sleep the night before. It wasn't
until after two that he got back to the dorm, and though
all the tingling had left his body and he felt relaxed, he
knew that Dewey was on the top bunk, and he knew that
his eyes were wide open. Every time he began to feel sleep
wash against him, he heard Dewey carefully change his
position or try to find a softer spot in his pillow.

"I've got a buddy who's getting the shaft," he finally
said.

"Kicked out of the Program?"

"Yeah. I knew him back home."

"Is that the one called Dewey? The one you told me
about the night I met you?"

"Did I? I forget." So much had happened so quickly
that Boyd had no way of remembering. The night before
when Pipsi had gone up to her room for a few minutes, he
had opened a book of hers he had been carrying and read
her name written on the fly sheet. My God, he was in love
with a girl, and he didn't even know how to spell her last

name. All that day he had written "Pipsi Bolinger" on the tops of his note paper, and not until he opened her book did he see that it had a double *l*.

"You said you had this friend you've known for a long time. And I asked you if he's from—what do you call it?—Ventry, and you said that's his *name*. I said, how chic to have a town named after you. And how incredible that there are *two* people from Ventry."

"There are a lot more than you think," Boyd answered, smiling. "It's not that small. They're even building a war plant in town."

Pipsi laughed in a good-natured way. "Heavens! Who's going to work in it? Women and children? I mean, with the town's two youths here . . ."

Boyd punched her arm playfully. "Farmers mostly. They're just itching for an excuse to make money. And there'll probably be a lot of people moving in from Cleveland. My grampa says," Boyd paused, wondering again at the strangeness of a God who would take Simon's speech from him, "he said that all the Youngstown racketeers will be moving in next. He's an optimist."

"Are there any other optimists? Girls maybe?"

"Do you mean, do I have a girl? Sort of. I already told you."

"Sort of a girl?"

Boyd couldn't suppress his grin. "No, there's no doubt about that. I mean, we were going steady up until the week I left."

"And are you still?"

He waited for a long time before answering. "I don't know. I expect not. If you're . . . very far away, it's hard. That business about absence making the heart grow fonder is for the birds. What it does, it leaves a hole. So then it's easier," he turned to the girl, "for someone else to crawl in."

"But I never crawl. I came in on my own two legs."

"They're great legs too," he said, leaning over now and pretending to study them. "I watched you come down the steps of the library. Did you see how I watched you?"

"I thought I'd never get to the bottom. My God! I said to myself, is this fellow lascivious or is he just sentimentally interested in architecture?"

"Both. Actually, the girl back home . . . do you want to know her name?"

She seemed to consider it. "No," she said at last.

He was grateful for that. "I don't think I ever really looked at her legs," he resumed. "Isn't that crazy?"

"What in the world *did* you look at?"

"Oh, I saw them all right, but it was like," he grinned again, "my orientation was different. They were good running legs and all. She used to win the potato-sack race every year on the Fourth of July. Yours are different."

Pipsi heaved her elbow into his ribs. "There *is* no Fourth of July where I come from. Isn't that when they make little boys play fifes and drums? I mean, no one pays any attention to it in New York. And it's just as well, because I'd be lousy in a potato sack."

"Who said I wanted you in one? I just said your legs are different. When I see yours . . . will you laugh if I tell you?"

"Not if you don't want me to."

"When I see yours, I break into a sweat. Honest to God. Now you can laugh all you want to."

"I don't think I will. It's about the nicest thing anyone has ever said to me. It's even nicer than getting an A on my Gorki paper. Did I tell you that? Professor Barrows said I must have been inspired. I didn't have the courage to tell him how."

Boyd guffawed. "When did you finish it?"

"The next day. After I met you. My mind was so clear. It's a funny reaction, I suppose. I've been all mixed up for the last year, and now everything seems all right. If you help me with all my papers, I might even make Phi Beta Kappa."

"I'd love to, as long as we can do it on your couch."

"You're depraved. Still, I rather like you."

"Is that all?"

"I rather like you a lot."

"All?"

She grabbed his arm. "I'm sick with love. I can hardly breathe. Let's hurry home."

Later, much later, while they were still on the couch, hidden in the darkness, Pipsi said, "And when is your friend going?"

"Who? Dewey?"

"If that's his name."

"He's waiting for orders."

"What's he doing in the meantime?"

"What's he doing? He's sleeping is what he's doing." As he said it, Boyd felt the guilt rise in him again.

But Dewey was very much awake. As he walked toward downtown Ann Arbor, he felt as if he had enough sleep to last him for the next five years. The loneliness inside him was almost palpable, almost a substance, if only it could be brought up to his mouth, that could be touched by his tongue. He passed several girls on the street, watching them approach, then walk by him, wondering if there was a way of stopping them, but knowing that they would only run or laugh if he went up to one of them and said, "I know this sounds goofy, but could you talk to me or something?" They'd have him in the psych ward of University Hospital before the words were out of his mouth.

Ann Arbor was for Dewey, unlike Boyd, a place where all he could hear was his own silence, where he could walk three or four blocks past hundreds of people and not see a face he knew, and where no one knew his name or anything about him. As he continued down the street, he paused before a beat-up Ford, the same model as his own, parked in front of a sandwich shop, and before he went on he let his hand reach out and stroke its fender. For a moment he thought that he might go into the place, sit down at the counter next to the person most likely to own a '36, and say "I know that model better than Henry Ford. I bet it has a slippery clutch. Right or wrong?" But having said it in his imagination, he no longer felt any need to say it aloud.

He had spent almost two hours that afternoon at Headquarters, where he turned in all his books, then waited to be interviewed by a lieutenant in Personnel. When, in time, the colonel came in, the same one who had told him two days before that he was washed up in the Program, he had the mad notion that the man was going to stand him up before everyone, pull off his brass, and then rip the insignia off his arm; the way martinet French generals in the movies did when confronted with traitors. The colonel, however, had looked at Dewey as if he had never seen him before.

Well, by God, Dewey now murmured to himself, making his way down the street, I'll get so stinking drunk I'll vomit over the side of the bunk right on my old buddy's head. Where does he get off anyway? "Let him sleep," he had said. "Let him *sleep!*"

He passed the Pretzel Bell, smelling of steak and beer, and as he did he furtively looked through its windows. It was crowded with senior girls who had waited four years for the ritual of getting drunk with impunity and being girlish and silly, and with a few pale 4-Fs, and two or three men in the Program. Dewey didn't like the place because everyone in it was so goddamn smily. Rice's, down the street, was a sadder, smileless bar that catered to tweed-jacketed, leather-elbowed men on the faculty who went there to wail over Melville and Nietzsche, and by town drunks who went there to wail over the degeneration of the university and the faculty.

Well, at least Rice's would be sufficiently dark so that no one would bother Dewey. The other bars in town had apparently been lighted by someone who had won a contest to see which kind of fluorescent could expose the most burst blood vessels in bartenders' noses. As he pushed through the door, he waited for a few seconds while his eyes adjusted to the shadows, then walked to the bar, sat on a stool, and said, "A double bourbon. And water."

The bartender looked at him with scrutiny. "How old are you, kid?" he finally asked in the resigned tone of a man who had been lied to more often than he could remember.

Dewey had been through it before, and each time he wondered if it would ever stop. Why does it always have to be *me?* he wanted to say. "I'm twenty-one, and you know goddamn well I'm twenty-one. I've been in here before, for Christ's sake."

"Okay, so you're twenty-one. Do you have any identification?"

Dewey could almost feel his knees buckle. Other guys could walk into bars when they were fifteen and get anything they wanted, but as soon as bartenders took a look at Dewey's face they seemed to read the liquor laws printed on his forehead.

"I'll vouch for him," someone now said from the other end of the bar. "He's twenty-one."

It was said with authority, and the bartender apparently decided that it would be no good to resist. "Whatever you say, sir," he said, then walked halfway down the bar and upended a bottle of bourbon.

Dewey looked to see who his benefactor was, already vaguely recognizing the voice. He wouldn't have come into the place had he been able to see him from the street. It was the same Lieutenant Anthony in Personnel who had been at his guts all afternoon. Dewey hugged the stool with his buttocks, and when his drink came he asked for another, taking advantage of the lieutenant's testimonial.

Anthony had moved slowly along the bar until he was now on the next stool. "You're tying one on."

"It looks that way," Dewey answered, not even bothering to honor him with the required "sir." He brought his eyes up to the mirror over the bar to see if Lieutenant Anthony's face showed signs that he was aware of the omission, but Dewey found none. Under his crewcut hair, his face was taut and tanned, strong, half collegiate and half West Point. He sat ramrod straight at the bar, apparently the way they had taught gentleman warriors to drink at the Academy.

"I wouldn't take it too hard," he said. "You might not be transferred to a bad outfit after all. What did the colonel say?"

"Infantry. Probably to Kansas. That's where Fort Riley is, isn't it? About six weeks there, and then he hopes I'll get my ass sent overseas. A nice fella."

"He's on the spot whenever we have to report casualties here. They get in a flap in Washington."

"I'm getting tired of this place anyway," Dewey said truthfully.

What was almost a smile broke over the lieutenant's face. "A gent in Tennessee makes a great drink for people who think they're tired. It'll give you back your will to live. Ever tried Jack Daniels?"

Dewey looked up, then shook his head.

"You can't do better. Take it from a man who was weaned from milk at an early age and switched to Tennessee whiskey. The next round, I'll buy you a shot. It's best to drink it neat. I'm something of a missionary that way, spreading the light."

To Dewey it seemed that he must have been spreading a little in his own direction. His words were thicker than they had been in the afternoon, and because he spoke in a curious dialect—Southern, Dewey supposed—it was hard to follow him. Still, he didn't appear antagonistic, nor did he seem particularly embarrassed because he was an officer and Dewey an enlisted man.

"Are you from the South?" Dewey now asked. "You sound that way."

"A small-assed town near Memphis. You can always tell when someone's from Memphis because we say impor-

314

dand instead of impor . . . hell, I can't say it the right way."

Dewey grinned. "I'm from a small town too."

"This your first time away from home?"

Well, it probably showed, so there was no sense lying. "I've been to Cleveland a couple times. Christ, when I went to Cleveland it was like going about four hundred miles away. But what it is, it's about fifty."

"Are you going back there when all this is over?"

Either Lieutenant Anthony had taken a course in how to win friends—the easiest way was to ask questions—or he was genuinely interested. Dewey decided to believe the latter. "I think so," he answered, pleased that he could talk about his home. "I'd sort of like to open a garage back there. I like to play around cars and things, and I figure I might open a garage in Ventry. That's the name of the place I'm from."

"That's your last name too. Some deal. Getting a town named after you."

"That's only because we were the first ones there." He studied the lieutenant's face to see if he was interested in hearing more. "Back in the 1840s some guy came along and offered us five gallons of good corn whiskey a year for as long as we lived if we'd name the town after him. But we didn't buy it. We didn't begin to drink seriously until the last couple generations. The first Ventrys were cabinetmakers, then we branched out into coffins and finally opened a funeral parlor. After we buried just about everyone, we went into Ornamental Iron, only we lost that during the Depression. My old man, he . . . well, he just works on the lakes."

"That's funny as hell," Lieutenant Anthony observed. "My old man is in the body business too. He has a funeral parlor. One thing he doesn't do is whistle while he works. But you know what he gave my wife and me for a wedding present? He gave us two cemetery plots."

"He sounds like a real sentimental guy."

"And when my kid was born, he was a landowner before he was christened. I've got one in the oven down there now, and I expect he'll get his plot of ground in about three months."

The lucky guy was married. "It's tough that they're all down in Tennessee and not here."

"You're not just a-talking," he replied, then ordered another round. "Hell, there's no law that says a man can't

315

buy a drink for someone he's just helped bulldoze out of the Program."

"I guess I deserved it," Dewey said, unwilling to tell him about Boyd's role in it.

The lieutenant raised his glass, said, "Well, here's to," and then watched the pleasure reach Dewey's face as he tasted his own. "You're a real son of the South, I see," he went on. "We have a *virtu* for bourbon down there. It's probably the only thing we do well." Then, as if it had just occurred to him, "You remind me of someone I used to know back home."

Dewey felt vaguely uncomfortable, but he said nothing.

"We went to high school together, and he went up to Great Lakes about the time I got my appointment. He's in the Pacific now, on a destroyer. He said the hardest damn thing about training at Great Lakes was that they made him learn how to swim. Hell, he thought that's why they built ships—to keep you *out* of water."

"You have to in the Navy. In the Army all they make certain you can do is breathe." He discovered that he was eager to talk more about home. "I used to swim a lot in high school. We didn't even have a pool, but we had a team. They used to bus us to a town about six miles away where there was a Y. Anyway, we came in third place in the All-Ohio swimming meet, and when some wiseguy reporter found out we were from the sticks and asked us where the hell we *swam,* we told him we lowered ourselves down the wells in our back yards every morning."

After three more drinks, difference in rank was largely set aside. Each tried to outdo the other in maintaining that he was a hayseed, but the lieutenant, who came from a village of four hundred or so, finally won out. He had got his appointment to the Academy, he said, because his father had buried a senator's mother with such distinction that it was the only way the senator could show his gratitude. As for the Army, Anthony said that he was a career man and that he didn't mind the sit-down job he'd been assigned to, though he expected to lose it in a short while. He intimated that the Program was on the rocks, and that it was only a matter of time before it folded entirely. The Army, he said, would need anyone who could carry a rifle for the big push in Europe that everyone knew was going to take place the following year. It helped to console Dewey. He hated to think that he was

316

the only one in the outfit who was going to be transferred to the Infantry.

Later, when the bartender blinked what few lights there were in the place and shouted, "Last call," the lieutenant said, "Look, do you want to come back to my place and help me finish a bottle? These Quaker bastards are closing up shop."

It sounded all right to Dewey. "I set out to get drunk tonight, and I'm not halfway there. Where do you live?"

"I've got an apartment around the corner. It's a good place to get drunk because the colonel lives on the top floor. You're right under the eagle himself."

"Sounds fine. Let's shove."

"Help yourself to a chair," Lieutenant Anthony said about five minutes later in a furnished apartment a few blocks from the bar. He took off his coat and threw it on one end of a sofa and then added, "That's my wife you have in your hands."

Dewey studied the photograph he had picked up from a table. "She's damn pretty," he said at last.

The lieutenant neither denied it nor agreed. "I'll fix you a couple funeral parlor specials. If we had White Lightning, they'd be better, but the stuff is hard to come by up North." He disappeared into the kitchen, a minute later poking his head out to say, "You can put something on the phonograph if you want to. What kind of music do you like? There's a lot of Dixieland there."

Dewey bent over the record cabinet and pulled out a few records at random. He was about to place one on the turntable when he realized he didn't know how to operate it. Rather than asking and showing his ignorance, he stuffed the records back into the cabinet and looked around the room. It was a cheerless place, and the few prints on the walls didn't help much. He supposed they were European; one appeared to be of sunflowers, the other a portrait, but they were both twisted and contorted almost beyond recognition. He then glanced at a group photograph of the West Point class, trying to find the lieutenant, but he was unable to. Everyone looked like everyone else, tight-lipped, alert, and tough in a phony way, as if someone had held cold knives next to their skin while the picture was being snapped.

From the kitchen, Dewey heard the sound of ice being removed from a tray. "What I was going to tell you back at the bar," Anthony said, "is that I know some people in

Washington. We might be able to keep you out of the Infantry if we play our cards the right way."

Dewey could scarcely believe it. "Jesus," he said, "you think you could swing it?"

"I don't know, but it's worth a try." He returned to the room, carrying two glasses, handing one of them to Dewey. "I'll see what I can do in the morning. One thing about the Army. Know the right people and anything is possible. I've got a buddy who pulls some mighty heavy strings."

"Jesus," Dewey repeated, "that'd be great. Son of a gun! Do you think you could get me assigned to someplace near home? Ohio or Kentucky?"

"Hey, hold on. I said I'd give it a try. Hell, I don't know General Marshall."

"Well, if you could—*Jesus*, that'd be great." Dewey wondered why in hell he hadn't liked Lieutenant Anthony before. He was actually going to try to help him. Son of a gun. What an ass Dewey had been, mouthing off the way he did at Headquarters that afternoon.

"Drink up. I'll be back in a minute."

"Sure," Dewey answered, watching him leave, then enter another room off the small foyer. Son of a gun! Wait until old Boyd hears. He thought Dewey was all busted up, that he was getting the shaft, but Dewey had a better deal working for him than Boyd did. Anthony said he knew someone in Washington, for Christ's sake. And if Dewey could get a good assignment now, before the Army got in a bind for the invasion, hell, he'd be sitting in clover. It would mean that he'd pulled off something that even Boyd hadn't been able to do.

In the middle of his thoughts the lieutenant walked back into the room. Dewey stared at him in disbelief.

"What's wrong?" Anthony asked.

Dewey put his drink down and moved to the edge of the sofa, about to get up, knowing now that he had made a mistake. "I . . . it's a hell of a time to take a shower is all."

The lieutenant, clothesless, laughed a little, then snapped off the ceiling light.

"Hey, what the hell are you doing?" Dewey rose from the sofa and tried in the darkness to make his way to where he thought the door was.

In a second he heard the answer. "Christ, man you *are* playing hard to get." As it was said, Dewey felt him brush against his side, then reach down and touch him on the fly.

"You get your goddamn hands off me, buster."

"Take it easy, take it easy," he said soothingly, then with his hand began to unzip Dewey. Dewey reached out in the dark with his fist and brought it hard into the face in front of him. But even before he felt the sting of his knuckles, his own head reeled back, sharp and quick, from a punch the lieutenant landed.

Breathing heavily, Anthony said, "If you don't want to play, you don't want to play. Why the hell did you come back here then?"

Dewey shook his head, stupefied that this was happening to him. Oh, for the love of God, he should have known. He had heard about guys like this, and he'd walked right into it. But all he could say was, "For Christ's sake, you're *married.*"

In the half darkness he could see that Anthony had somehow managed to get himself aroused. Dewey felt nothing but repugnance as he watched him bring his hand to the white thing before him and hold it at its root, then reach out once more with his other hand for Dewey.

"Don't be so goddamn naïve. You'd think you never did this before."

What moved Dewey then was an anger and humiliation deeper than any he had ever felt. He lunged at the man a second time, and as he did the lieutenant's fist caught him squarely in the face, sending him back across the room, knocking over the coffee table and onto the floor. He felt blood rush into his mouth even before he felt any hurt.

"You dirty fuckin' son of a bitch," he said, his chest heaving. "You dirty fuckin' son of a bitch." He wiped his hand over his mouth, picked himself off the floor, and began to make his way to the door.

"Look, kid, you don't get anything for nothing in this world. I thought you knew."

Dewey opened the door, uncertain whether what he tasted in his mouth was tears or blood. "I'm getting the idea."

When, a little after midnight, Boyd returned to his room at the dorm, he saw that two of his roommates were sacked out but that Dewey's bunk was empty. Strangely, Boyd missed him. There was no one to scold, no one to call a meathead, no one to pound awake in order to study.

He had already taken off his shirt and his shoes before he decided that he wasn't ready, as tired as he was, to go to sleep. He slipped his shoes back on, picked up a book and some paper, and walked downstairs.

Once in the lounge—filled with bogus English furniture and what someone must have decided were manly paintings of warships and battles—he dropped into a chair opposite the door and opened his book. He read two or three pages, and closed it. Using the book as a desk, he placed a piece of paper on it and for the sixth or seventh time that week tried to write a letter to Francine.

He didn't know what to say to her any more. Whatever he wrote seemed cold and flat, and he knew that Francine would read between the lines. Yet when he tried to write an honest letter that would explain what had happened to him, he couldn't get anywhere with that either. He would no more than begin to tell her about Pipsi, and then his loins would cry out, and all he could think about was Pipsi. He wrote a foolish, superficial note, at the end of which he said that he hoped she was meeting new people in Cleveland. He read it over a few times, then ripped it up and stuffed its pieces into his pocket.

He must have fallen asleep, because when he heard the outside door bang open and shut again, he was startled to find himself in a chair and not in bed. He rose from it, went to the French doors that opened into the hall, and as he did he saw Dewey. His face was streaked with blood, trailing down the front of his coat onto his shoes, and he looked at Boyd with loathing.

"For the love of God, Dewey, what happened!"

Dewey held on to the banister, and slowly began to mount the stairs. "I ran into a train is what happened. What the hell does it look like?"

Boyd rushed after him, trying to take his arm and help him up the steps, but Dewey pulled away. At the landing he turned quickly, looked into Boyd's eyes, and each saw that he was looking at a stranger. "Will you leave me alone? Will you for once and for all leave me *alone!*" He continued up the stairs to the second floor, Boyd following.

"At least I can help you clean up your face, can't I?"

"I can clean my own fuckin' face. I can even crap by myself. I can do *every*thing by myself, buddy boy."

At the entrance to the lavatory, Boyd ran before him to

go in first, reached out to help him, but Dewey struggled free. "Don't *touch* me, for Christ's sake, or I'll kill you."

"Sure, Dewey, anything you say." Boyd watched him enter the room and lean against the tile wall, not even making an attempt to walk to a washbowl. Boyd then pulled a fistful of paper towels from a container, held them under a faucet for a second, and turned toward Dewey. Dewey merely brought his hand up before his face as Boyd tried to wipe away the clotted blood, then swiped at his arm, sending the wet papers slapping against the floor.

"You're drunk, Dewey. You don't know what the hell you're doing."

"I'm as sober as you are," he answered, and Boyd knew that it was true. "I stopped being drunk on the way home."

"Well, damn it, you can't hit the sack that way. You look like a stuck pig. At least get some of the blood off your face. Jesus, your eye looks bad."

"Fine. That's the way I like it."

"I don't know what the hell happened to you, and you don't have to tell me if you don't want to. But it's not my fault, you asshole."

After a long wait, during which they could both hear themselves breathing under stress, Dewey said quietly, "When you look into my face tomorrow morning, you can say, 'Let him sleep,' and, by God, this eye won't even see you."

Boyd let the breath out of his lungs. He could feel his face color with shame. "I wanted to tell you, Dewey. That's why I stayed up. So I could tell you. Honest to God. I didn't mean to fuck you up." He reached out for one of Dewey's bloody hands to guide him to a basin, but Dewey struck at his face with his open palm.

"I said I'd kill you if you touch me, and I mean it."

If Dewey had a knife on him, Boyd would have been afraid. "Did you think I wanted to hurt you, Dewey? I *didn't.* I honest to God didn't. I wanted to help you get on your own feet."

"You wanted to get me off your ass is what you wanted."

"I *didn't.* I swear to God, as I'm standing here, I didn't. I wanted . . . hell, I don't know what I wanted. I wanted you to do something by yourself." As he spoke his voice lowered, so that the last words were almost inaudible.

"So I ran into a train by myself. I'm a big boy now. I'm in your league."

"I wanted to help you, Dew."

"You sure as hell did." Very slowly, as if he couldn't stand any more, Dewey let his back slide down the tile until he rested on the floor, and the tears came. "Thanks, buddy. You're my old buddy all right."

"I wanted to help you. God strike me dead if there was another reason."

"You did me a favor all right."

"For God's sake, what happened?"

It was a minute before Dewey could control himself enough to answer. "There are a lot of people in the world ready to do a guy a favor. Honest to Christ, you don't know how many. You do me a favor so I know who I'm not. Someone else does me a favor so I know who I am. Oh, my God, old buddy, what a night! Old Dew Ventry is beginning to see who he is!"

"You're not making any sense."

"Who the fuck says that things are supposed to make sense? That was back home. We're not back home any more."

"Look, Dew," Boyd implored, "please for Christ's sake don't hate me because I made a mistake."

"Who says I hate you? You got it all wrong, bub. I hate myself. I hate my face. I hate my arms. And I hate my body. I hate who I am!"

"Dewey, you're crazy! You're going to wake everyone up."

"*You never let me know!*"

To Boyd it seemed like the worst betrayal of all, but he didn't know what it was. Never let him know what? That the world was base? Or that Dewey, like everyone else, was base too? With the wet towels in his hand now, he bent over the shaking figure on the floor and began to wipe the blood from his face.

Ten

Lieutenant Anthony had been as good as his word—you couldn't get anything for nothing—for toward the middle of November Dewey at last received his orders to report to Fort Riley, Kansas. The sloppy season of cold rain and gray days had arrived in Ann Arbor, matching Dewey's mood entirely, and he was more than anxious to leave. He and Boyd wisely limited their conversation to comments on the weather, working out all their rage and impatience on the rain and the cold, not the first time that the tedium of sunlessness has allowed two people to talk together, more or less, without saying anything.

They did not see much of each other. In the weeks preceding Dewey's departure Boyd spent most of his time, when he wasn't in classes, with Pipsi. Before the rains set in, and during the last few days of crazy and unexpected Indian summer, they were as daring as the season. They had late one night gone into the Arboretum and there made love on the dry ground, rolling each other into huge banks of oak leaves. On another night they walked to the top of Beer Mountain, breathless by the time they reached it, then raced under the trees and finally fell into the high grass. And on the weekend before Dewey left, they went on an impulse into Detroit to see the Museum; they registered as Mr. and Mrs. Gavin at a hotel at two on Saturday afternoon, and there for the first time they made love in a bed and on sheets which Pipsi said any self-respecting girl had a right to covet. Their supper was sent up to them, and as they ate they searched the *Free Press* for amusements that might help them pass the night, finally deciding on a movie. The decision made, they fell back on the bed. The next morning, after breakfast had been brought to them, Pipsi went into the shower to correct what she called her disarray so that they could at last visit the Museum, but Boyd followed her and made love to her, the shower beating on their heads as they lay sprawled in the tub, both laughing at their wantonness. Afterward, as they returned to campus, Pipsi said, "We ought to have seen their Breughel. They have a perfectly lovely Breughel."

On the day Dewey was to leave, Boyd got up at five in the morning to help him get his things down to the station for the early morning train to Chicago where he was to make a connection for Kansas City. They took turns carrying the duffel bag—agreeing that greater punishment man has never known—and walked slowly down the hill while the town still slept. It was different from any walk they had ever taken before. There was no small talk, no bullshooting tall tales. Grief or relief, whichever it was, kept them silent.

"You'll probably get home for Christmas anyway," Boyd said at last, coasting down the steep hill. "I'll see you then."

"Yeah," Dewey answered. "They'll let me go home for Christmas just like they're letting me have a day's stopover in Ohio." His face twisted in contempt for all the people from whom comforts could be coaxed or bought. "What the hell difference does it make if I go south from Cleveland or Chicago? Those fatheads at HQ said that Chicago was shorter. I've been sitting on my tail for the last two weeks, doing nothing, and all of a sudden I'm indispensable to the war effort."

It was a raw deal, and to Boyd it seemed that someone in Headquarters was out to make things as uncomfortable as possible for Dewey. A day or two at home in Ventry would have helped him a lot. As it was, Dewey was going into the unknown even without the renewed succor of Ventry, and with only the recollection of having made a scandalous mess of things at school.

"Someone said you guys are getting leaves over Thanksgiving," Dewey said petulantly. "Isn't that just my luck? I wait around here for two weeks, and then they ship me out right before Thanksgiving. Christ-a-mighty, I'm beginning to think Goering is calling the signals in Washington."

Boyd waited, and in another minute said, "I'm not going home." He watched Dewey's face to see what his reaction was, but he was unable to read what he saw. "I'm going to New York with . . . this girl I know. I guess I didn't tell you about her."

"Hell," Dewey answered shortly, "everyone knows you have a girl."

Boyd didn't know if he was more exasperated with himself or with Dewey. "For the love of God, if you knew why didn't you ask me about her?"

Shrugging his shoulders, he replied, "If you want to keep secrets, keep secrets."

"It was no goddamn secret. I just ... I didn't want Francine to know about it just yet."

"And you thought I'd tell her? My God, but your confidence in me is impressive, bub. If you really want to know, Francine wrote me a letter a week or so ago. So other guys can have secrets too, see? All she wanted to know was, was anything wrong up here. Girls can tell. I told her that everything was honky-dory. I still lie pretty good."

Damn him and his everlasting sacrifices, covering for Boyd even after what had happened. "I tried to write her. Only I didn't know what to say."

"You might try telling her the first thing that comes to your mind. You might try that. All this—devious crap gets me in the gut."

Boyd felt it was unnecessary to point out that first things, as Dewey called them, almost never came to anyone's mind without being cheek-and-jowl with second, third, and fourth things. Francine herself was a walking testimonial to that.

"What's she like anyway?" Dew asked shyly. "Isn't her name Bollinger or something?"

"She's very different," he answered. Maybe that wasn't the most suitable way to abridge Pipsi, but it was the best he could do. She was a place as much as she was a girl, but he couldn't very well tell Dewey that. She was a refuge where he could bury his body, she was a million pleasures, she was someone he could talk to while they held each other. Even now as he walked, he was conscious of the large blue love-mark she had made low on his neck so that he could touch it while he was in classes and know that her lips were with him even then. She was, at one and the same time, a cannibal gorging herself on Boyd, and food for a starving man.

"I gathered she was different," Dewey said, ambiguously. "One of the guys in the dorm said she's loaded too. She has loot. By God, you can't do better than that. That old

Horatio Alger business—getting up in the world the hard way—is for the birds."

Pipsi never lacked money, to be sure, even going so far as paying their expenses in Detroit, but it never occurred to Boyd that she had anything other than the allowance all middle-class girls at college received. "I guess I never asked her."

"This guy in the dorm—he's from New York, so he should know—said that her old man's a very big deal. What's the law firm Roosevelt was with before he had his vision? Your girl's old man is a partner or something, I think. Nice going, lad. Stay alive until the war is over, and you'll have it made. You can visit me in my little old shack down in the gulf. Park your Bentley next to the privy."

"Cut it, Dew."

He laughed easily. "Anything you say, dad. Maybe I'm just pee-oohed because ... well, because it sounds so great. Did I tell you I saw her once? Your girl?"

"Where?"

"One day when you were waiting for her in front of the library. I had myself a look-see. You have good taste, *amigo.*"

"You should have come up and I would have introduced you."

"Hell, I'm just a country boy. I don't feel good unless I have cow manure on my shoes. I don't know how to talk to posh people."

"She's not posh." And yet Boyd knew, of course, that people back home would probably think she was. She wasn't, thank God, like Aunt Cortez, who didn't come into her kind of poshness until late in life and who guarded it like a condor guarding reeking flesh. Once, while they were making love in the Arboretum, Pipsi had thrown a cashmere Peck & Peck sweater under her on the grass, even though she knew it would be grass-stained before they had finished, and to Boyd it seemed the most elegant thing a girl could do.

They walked in silence for a minute, each thinking his own thoughts. "Do you want me to write a letter to Francine? Make it easier? Get you off the hook?"

"I can do it myself, Dewey. Like I say, I hope I can see her over Christmas. I'd like to talk to her, if you know what I mean." He paused, trying to get the words out the right way. "I also hope I can see you over Christmas, because I'd like to talk to you too. I don't think we can talk here any more. I don't know what the hell happened. We always used to be able to talk so easy."

"Yeah," Dewey answered.

They waited at the gray stone station, and neither spoke again until they heard the train far down on one side of the Huron River. They watched it pull into the station.

"Well, that's the way things go," Dewey said, about nothing and about everything, then boosted his heavy duffel bag to his shoulders. "Look. Forget what I told you that night in the can, will you? I was drunk."

"I already forgot. It just . . . didn't sound like you."

For a minute it appeared that Dewey might now ask what he was supposed to sound like, but instead he walked to a coach where a conductor stood. *"Look.* If . . . I don't see you at Christmsa, Jesus, I hope you get all the breaks, buddy. I really do. Sometimes you gripe my ass—you know that—because you're such a great guy and I'm such a little slob. But I want you to know that you've helped this little slob a lot. No crap. I mean it. Shake." He held out the hand that wasn't being used to steady his duffel bag.

"Dewey, you crazy guy. Take care, will you?"

"My God, I *will.* And you be nice to that girl, hear? I expect to throw rose petals at your wedding."

"I'll see you at Christmas, fella. We'll go down to the gulf and chop us down a twenty-foot pine, oKay?"

"Sure, sure, Boyd. So long. I'll write."

"Write, for God's sake. Don't just sit around and sulk."

"I'll write. My sulking days are over. I'm off to be a hero, lad. So long, Boyd, take care."

"God bless."

Christ, Boyd said to himself, watching Dewey mount the steps to the coach, he's crying again. Look at the goddamn fool. Grinning his head off, and his eyes are all wet. What a guy for getting choked up. Honest to God, there wasn't another guy in the world who was man enough to get choked up the way Dewey could.

Poor mucked-up Dewey, Boyd said as the train began to move from the station. May the world never hear you crying. May it never discover you. May the world leave you alone.

It was another week and a half before Boyd heard from him, and then it was a postcard. "Did you know there are goddamn *Alps* in Kansas?" it said. "My ass is broke from climbing hills. The guy who said Kansas is flat was lying dead-drunk in bed." Next paragraph: "Basic is killing me. Guys here are Missouri hillbillies. Witty, cultured, full of repartee. The meathead who bunks over me is a great talker. All he says is Shee-ittt. When he gets really expansive, he says Chicken Shee-ittt. On thus rests the hope of the Western World." Finally, in words so tiny Boyd had trouble making them out, "It looks like Christmas will be spent at home on the rifle range—unless I go over the hill. How are you, buddy? I got honest-to-God laid my first Saturday night in town! I'm all right! Will tell you lurid details in a letter. There *is* a God." His address followed, most of it written in the square intended for a postage stamp, and half blurred by water.

As soon as Boyd received the card, he coaxed a confused girl at Western Union to send a telegram to Dewey, even though the wires were supposed to be restricted to grave military matters. "GEN EISENHOWER EXTREMELY PLEASED ABOUT BREAKTHROUGH ON PECKER FRONT YOU DO YOUR COUNTRY PROUD DRIVE ON FULL BLOODY ACCOUNT AWAITED." Whether or not Dewey received it, Boyd didn't know, because in a subsequent card he made no reference to his accomplishment and how it came to pass. Then, two days before Thanksgiving, Boyd got a third card: "The sobering news is that I have the clap. Oh, woe is me. I go into the brig for a week because they say I'm a threat to the American way of life. They'd bust me but I hear I'm already at rock bottom, a minus-private. At least I'll get out of training for a while, and that's killing me. This clappy guy doth weep and carry on. I miss you. Be good. D."

Oh, Jesus! Even Job had it easier than poor Dewey. Boyd borrowed a few dollars from Pipsi, telling her that he'd pay her back as soon as he could, and bought some candy and cookies, stuffed them into a box, and sent it out Special Delivery, hoping that it would reach him while he was still in the brig. On a card he wrote: "To a fallen comrade. Mend quickly. Don't despair."

On the same afternoon, two days before the Thanksgiving recess, Boyd called home, using the telephone at Pipsi's place in order to help justify the lie he would have to tell. When he revealed to Catherine—God! how his throat caught when he heard her voice and Parnell's yelling in the background!—when he revealed that he wouldn't be able to get home for the holiday because

328

everyone had been restricted to the dorm, he could almost see her face sink in disappointment.

"But that's terrible," Catherine finally replied. "We've all been expecting you. Oh, *my*."

"I'm sorry, Mom," he said, hating himself for the lie he had told, but knowing that they would be even more hurt if they knew he was going to New York, that he had chosen to spend the holiday with someone else. "But it's not long till Christmas," he added, "and I should be able to see you then."

After she had recovered enough to speak, Catherine then said, "It'll be the first Thanksgiving this way."

Even as Boyd talked to Parnell and Rose, he wondered what his mother had meant. Had she, instinctively, felt his lie and meant that this would be the first Thanksgiving soiled in such a way? Or had she meant merely that his place at the table would be vacant, and that with Luke's also empty, and Simon's, it would be terrible lonely? He didn't know. Perhaps a little of both.

Afterward Pipsi said to him, "You better hang up the telephone the right way. You've got an apron string caught in the wire."

Boyd foolishly replaced the receiver a second time before he realized what she had said. Pipsi had rather advanced views about families—that they should be used while a use could be given them, after which they should be chucked, pretty much as she had done—and Boyd was also aware that she was more than a little bit jealous even without having met any of the Gavins back home. On those occasions when she told him that it was childish still to be that attached to his family, he had replied that it was equally childish for her to be uncomfortable because he was. She was a fierce opponent of momism, a word she'd picked up in a Psych class, almost evangelical about it, but Boyd ascribed it mostly to the fact that Pipsi's mother, if she'd been described correctly, deserved every bit of hatred she allotted her.

When he left the telephone, Pipsi circled her arms around his waist, apparently to reassure him. "I suppose it's selfish of me to want you to come home with me. But, my God, I don't think I could bear it by myself."

"Have you told anyone I'm coming? Your mother?"

"She knows, but don't expect too much from her. She never likes any of my friends, and she's probably already made up her mind she doesn't like you. She thinks I'm a libertine. But I promise that we won't have to spend much time with her, so it shouldn't be too painful."

Boyd felt more than a little bit uneasy about the prospects of going into a house—or what was probably a crowded New York apartment—where he wasn't welcome. "I honest to God wish I could stay in a hotel or someplace instead."

"Impossible. New York is crawling with people. Dirty little Jewish war profiteers. Thousands and thousands of soldiers on leaves. Half the streetwalkers in America. You couldn't *get* a hotel room."

Boyd grimaced at her description, but let it pass. Pipsi was irrational when she spoke of Jews. She even once told him that she had blackballed a girl from Grosse Pointe who was being rushed by Chi Omega, and for no apparent reason except that she looked Jewish, whatever that look encompassed. And on one Sunday afternoon, after dragging Boyd to a chamber concert in the Rackham building, they had no more than sat down in their seats when she punched his arm and said, "Let's go. They're all Jews. They'll only make the music depressing." What sort of tricks Jews had at their disposal which enabled them to make Bach more depressing than gentiles could, Boyd didn't know, but then he was no judge of such things.

He said, "We could always go somewhere else. Some of the guys at the dorm who live too far away to go home are going up to Iron Mountain to ski. I've never done that. It sounds like fun."

"But so is New York. New York is where the fun *begins,* Boyd. It takes years for it to trickle out to the Midwest." Then, observing his indecision, "Don't you honestly think it'll be better for us to stay together? I mean, rather than your going off to that dreary place in Ohio and me to . . . ?"

"It's not dreary," Boyd interrupted, angry that anyone would come to this conclusion about the town just because smart and clever people didn't live there.

"I didn't mean that, pet. I mean it's so isolated. Don't you think we'd have a better time with my family even if they are terrible?"

"Only if you stay with me all the time."

"All right. I promise. I won't leave you for a minute." She brought her head close to his and said, whispering, "I've managed to get us into a sleeper. That's supposed to be a surprise. It's my Thanksgiving gift to you."

"What a way to give thanks! How the hell did you manage a sleeper?" Most Pullmans, he knew, were used for troop trains. And if a stray Pullman now and then found itself a part of a civilian train, it was generally reserved for industrialists touring war plants or for high-ranking military officers moving from camp to camp.

"I broke down and asked Daddy. And, of course, he asked the right people. That's one thing I can say for him. He doesn't know many of the wrong ones." She laughed, apparently at a private joke. "He'd be furious if he knew we were only to use one of them. He's very patriotic."

"I don't mind sitting up in a coach," Boyd said half defensively.

"Oh, God, don't be a spoilsport. I've already got the tickets. If we don't use them, what'll I do with them? I'm sorry now I told you that Daddy got them for me."

"You said you don't even like him."

"Oh, hell, I don't know. I suppose I ought to, oughtn't I? But I think I'm a little indifferent. Daddy tries to be nice, but he's not an emotional man. Sort of a stuffed shirt. Sort of a stick-in-the-mud. But he probably won't even be in New York, except perhaps for a few hours on Thanksgiving Day. He'll be in Washington."

"He sounds very busy." Boyd imagined what it would be like to have a father who was important and who had so much to do in Washington that he could spare only a few hours to celebrate Thanksgiving. Somehow, it seemed to Boyd that it was the way he used to think of Simon in his dreams—running from place to place, meeting interesting people, and making interesting decisions. Perhaps it was just as well that Simon was what he was. Perhaps had Simon been a Big Man, as Mr. Bollinger apparently was, Boyd would now be saying about him that he was a stick-in-the-mud.

"Oh, God, he's busy all right. He's so busy he doesn't even have time to notice that Mother is having an affair with my godfather. It's hard to imagine that the old thing is still up to it, but apparently she has resources I can't see. Anyway, the hanky-panky has been going on for about three years. We're a real nest of gentlefolk." She ran her fingers over his lips. "Still want to come home with me?"

Boyd could feel her against his body, and all he knew was that he didn't want to be away from her for four days. "More than ever," he finally said. "Someone has to be there to love you."

Late in the afternoon on the day before Thanksgiving, they boarded a train for Detroit, Pipsi looking incredible and stunning in what Boyd took to be a New York costume. He had only once before seen her in high heels—he ruefully admitted that they had seldom done anything together that required them—and as for the broad-brimmed hat now on her head, it made her look grand and worldly. When they left the train in Detroit and changed for the train to New York, she carefully placed a pair of sunglasses on her nose. "So I'll look wicked," she said, to which Boyd replied, guardedly, "Or so no one will recognize you when I climb into your berth?" She persisted, however, in keeping the glasses on even when they went into the dining car for supper. Not until the train sped south across the Michigan border into the farmlands of Ohio did he say to her, "You'll have to take those glasses off so I can see your eyes. I want to see your eyes when you look at Ohio."

"Do we pass through Ventry?"

"I think so," Boyd answered. "The sky lights up and firecrackers go off."

"Goodness! Like what Joan of Arc saw!"

At eleven they asked the porter to make up their berths, and after they were prepared Boyd read in his own for perhaps another hour. Then, when the coach seemed quiet, he turned off his reading light and slipped below into Pipsi's. She flicked off her own light and pulled him under the covers with her.

"God," she whispered, "I thought you'd never come. I thought people would never go to sleep."

They rocked and pitched each time the train did, and Boyd slowly removed the top of Pipsi's pajamas, then the bottoms. "Impostor," he said. "These are boy's pajamas."

"Always. I used to be a tomboy. I even once had a crush on a teacher of mine at Brearley. But I think I've passed through it, don't you?"

"You're doing nicely." He slipped out of his GI shorts and his T shirt, pushing them under the blankets down by their feet, and then held her in his arms.

Each time he found her body, it was as though he were finding it for the first time. No matter how often he had kissed the tiny appendectomy scar, the mole above her

332

navel, and the soft down on her belly, each time he discovered something new: a touch that pleased her, or the different ways that her breasts would feel on different days, sometimes soft and vastly pillowy, other times almost hard and inanimate. Their mouths had searched each other in preposterous, unkissable places, and he had even once—drunk with what she offered him—kissed each of her toes, then worked up her body slowly with his lips until he reached her forehead, leaving behind a slippery, wet coat as he made his journey, and then she had done the same, shamelessly, no part of him excluded from her, no part unworthy, after which they had made a slapping, singing kind of love with their tongue-wetted bodies.

"How fine it is to make love on a train," she said. "All my life I'll remember how you loved me all the way from Detroit to New York. Let's not even sleep."

"Who said I was going to let you?"

"It'll have to last us a while. We won't be able to do anything while we're at home. There are always people around."

"I'll make it last until the minute we pull into Grand Central."

"You'll have to give me ten minutes to repair the damage before we get off the train. Otherwise, I'll look like a tart."

"That's okay with me. Anyway, tarts don't wear boy's pajamas. They wear silky black negligees."

"How do you know?"

"I have a rich imagination."

"Then don't waste it. Pass it around."

When, in time, Boyd went into her, he held it longer than he ever thought he could, trying to make it as endless and as good as his body would let him, Pipsi whimpering in pleasure beneath him. And when he finally let go, it was only because the word came from her drowning mouth, asking him to, and then slowly he pumped himself out.

As he lay resting in the berth, the window shade half up, their two naked bodies hit from time to time by the moon and by flashing lights at crossings, Boyd could feel a warm wave begin to wash over him. As the train pulled up the grade, then slithered over the trestle high above the river, he saw the first lights of town. And at the top of the hill—in a second so brief it passed almost before he felt it—he imagined he saw himself as he was long ago, looking at the train as it sped through Ventry, screaming its

333

whistle, the white steeple of the Congregational church pointing into the sky behind him, the empty square, Satin Street, Summer, Priest, and home. Oh, my God, he said to himself.

"Are you cold?" Pipsi said as Boyd brought the blanket up over his body, then hers.

"No," he answered, not willing to share what he had felt. "It's nothing."

In the morning Pipsi was the first to awake from the third nap they had taken during the night, and she roused Boyd by saying, "Hurry. We're past Tarrytown. You better scoot. I have to make myself a decent woman."

Boyd looked through the window and saw a wide river, then waited until the corridor seemed unoccupied before he climbed up to his own berth and partially dressed. When the men's lavatory was free, he washed and shaved, returned his toilet kit to his berth, and waited for Pipsi at the end of the coach, looking at the land they were passing as he waited. In a while the train left a final tree behind and slowly made its way past the squalor of what Boyd supposed was Harlem: dirty-windowed tenements, shuttered warehouses, dark streets burdened by thousands of garbage cans. The pavements and sidewalks seemed to have been made only to accommodate debris; what hadn't been heaped into the cans was blowing around the asphalt in the November wind. There were no faces that he could see. Only wretched buildings and cans. He wondered vaguely if the city fathers had put these small metal caskets before every stoop so that Negroes, when they felt the swoon of death in them, could lower themselves, too, into them, their last and most abominable bag of filth and sorrow, and then be carted away in grinding trucks before their cooling bodies offended anyone.

As the train began to pull into a tunnel, he was almost relieved that perhaps the worst had been hidden. And when he saw Pipsi approach him from the other end of the coach, he was glad that he was no longer alone in this new world where she was carrying him. She had, he saw, installed her sunglasses on her nose again so that she looked almost like a stranger, but it no longer bothered him. He listened to her tell him that they would probably soon be passing directly under her mother's place, and all he could think was that the Bollingers, too, lived in a tenement. "We don't live on the right side of the tracks," she said, "or the wrong side. We live right on them."

As soon as the train came to a stop, and with a good bit more authority than Boyd could bring to the task, Pipsi grabbed a redcap and pointed out the bags he was expected to carry. He was an old man, yet when Boyd told him that he could carry his own canvas overnight bag without any trouble, Pipsi hurriedly stuck it under the man's already busy arms, whispering to Boyd that he was depriving him of his livelihood. The three of them then walked into the enormous station, Boyd marveling at what he saw, and stupidly asking the man if he liked his work, if he had a family, and where he lived, to all of which the redcap responded with astonished grunts. Pipsi then slowed her pace and explained to Boyd that he didn't have to be *that* friendly, and that the redcap probably thought he was insane. "Oh" was Boyd's thoughtful observation, embarrassed that he had broken an unwritten New York rule.

At the door to the cab Pipsi finally removed her sunglasses, threw herself onto the seat, and told the driver, "The corner of Sixty-fourth and Park." Boyd sat back, next to her, his hands on his knees, and looked through the windows. Watching him, Pipsi asked, "Well, is it big?"

"Bigger than Ventry," he answered. "Also, there's a lot of concrete and bricks. Aren't there any wooden houses here?"

"You can't build wooden skyscrapers, pet, as pretty as one would be. They'd all tumble down." She pointed. "This is Vanderbilt Avenue. Named after them when they still had money. That's the Yale Club over there. Sometimes Daddy sleeps there when he's in the city or when he's been drinking. And down at the end and around the corner is where Park begins."

Boyd looked everywhere for signs of greenery and a park, but saw nothing but a miserable mall of withered grass in the middle of the street. "I thought it was supposed to be on Central Park?"

"Well, you've got me there," she replied. "I don't know why it's called Park. Fifth is next to Central Park. And of course Central Park West, but no one lives there any more."

Boyd accepted her word for it, not even bothering to ask her why Central Park West was unused, then occupied himself with looking up at the buildings they passed. From the outside, they looked vaguely like the tenements he had

335

seen earlier in the day, except that these were wider and higher, their bricks were cleaner, and each had a canopy before its door. "Are those offices?" he then asked.

"No, sweetheart, people actually live and breathe in them, as surprising as that may seem."

It sure as hell didn't look as if anyone could. But he made up his mind that he had uttered his last dumbfounded country-bumpkin question. He remained quiet, peering through the windows of the taxi; when they stopped at a corner building, he wasn't ready by half to get out. He was about to open the door when it was opened for him by a man who appeared miraculously from the darkness of the canopy and who had a tight, professional smile on his face as though there were a slice of lemon peel under one of his lips. "Welcome home, Miss Priscilla," the man said. What a curious thing to call her, Boyd thought. A mixture of friendliness and officiousness.

From where he stood on the pavement, the building before him looked like all the other sorrowful ones they had passed, and only the polished brass holding up the canopy and on the hardware of the door distinguished it from the Glidden Paint Factory in Cleveland. He stepped carefully up to the sidewalk, avoiding what looked to be ordure left by dogs—he had noticed it coming up from the station, but it seemed too absurd to ask Pipsi what it all meant in the middle of a large city—and into the building. The floor he found himself on appeared to be black and white marble, and a many-prismed chandelier illuminated the chief ornament of the room, a green-uniformed elevator man. "Good morning, Miss Priscilla," the man said, then shepherded them into his climbing box.

"You didn't tell me you lived in this kind of place," he whispered, once inside. "You said you lived on the railroad tracks."

"We do. They're under the street. Now don't you get intimidated."

"I'm not."

When Pipsi rang the bell at one of the doors on the twelfth floor—she told Boyd that all they had was half a floor, which seemed to him plenty—he was surprised to see a man who seemed to be dressed for a church wedding open it. "Good morning, Miss Priscilla," he said in a faintly foreign tongue. "It's good to have you home. Your mother said that the gentleman can occupy your sister's room. She won't be coming home."

"Thank God," Pipsi roared, and led Boyd into the foyer. "Is Mother up?"

"I'm to wake her at eleven. Cook has breakfast ready for you. We've been expecting you."

"Good. I'm famished." To Boyd, who was trying to make himself as inconspicuous as he could, she said: "I'd love Eggs Benedict, would you?"

Boyd indicated that he would love them to death, whatever they were, then listened to Pipsi tell Jean-P.—it seemed to be the handle by which the gent in black went—that they would have that. Jean-P. slid away over the marble floor, leaving them alone.

"You never told me you had a sister either," Boyd said at last.

"She's not. She's my half sister, and she's an ass. She's at Sarah Lawrence, which isn't surprising. Come on." Pipsi took his arm and led him into a second hall, far larger than the Gavin parlor and dining room together. It was heavy with paintings. Boyd leaned over now to read a brass plate on one. "Is it real?" he asked with proper reverence.

"Probably not," Pipsi responded, "but I expect Mother paid for the real article, and you can't quibble with *her*. If it wasn't a Goya before, it is now. But most of the art is perfectly awful. My grandmother and grandfather lived in Paris part of the time back in the eighties and nineties when all those fabulous things were going on in French art. But do you know what the fools bought? Murillos. There's one in the dining room that will scare you half to death. And one in a bedroom, I think. And Riberas! There are a couple of those. Also a Rubens, but it's absolutely ghastly. The poor dears just didn't have any taste. Think of all those Cézannes and Van Goghs they could have bought for half nothing."

It seemed to Boyd that they had done very well indeed. If they had no taste, they made up for it in bulk.

Pipsi waved her arm at the entrance and said, "Small sitting room." It was in no way small. Somehow—Boyd couldn't fathom the architecture of the place—the ceiling had leaped, and it was here two stories high. The walls were paneled in the French manner, he supposed, painted an aging white, and met a ceiling with large plaster rosettes. One entire wall was given to high windows, dressed in crimson hangings. As for the furniture which confirmed it as a sitting room, Boyd had never before seen anything like it. The room was large enough to be divided into about four or five separate sitting areas, each with its chairs and sofas, but built for the most part around Gallic-looking furniture. The upholstery on some of these latter pieces appeared to be the original, almost thread-bare in places. Noticing his interest, Pipsi told him that they were Louis XV, indicating that they were earlier, rarer, and more monstrous than Louis XVI. "Mother wanted to have that thing recovered," she pointed contemptuously at a love seat, "but when the people at French and Company—it's sort of a shop—heard about it, the man there said he'd commit suicide as an act of protest, so she's left it alone. I hate all of it."

Boyd calculated that Louis and his buddies must have had tiny fannies; if not that they must have spent most of their time slipping out of their seats onto the floor. Not that it would be much of a hardship in this room. The floor was covered in a pale yellow rug about which Pipsi said, "Aubusson. Not Audubon. He's the chap who paint-ed birds. The other people made these abominable rugs."

At the entrance to the next room she said nothing but, "Big sitting room. It's nice for parties, but otherwise it's a tomb." If it was a tomb, it was a commodious one, about three times as large as the small room and running along the entire front of the building, a rose-colored marble mantel at each end. A grand piano in one corner looked tiny and dwarfed, and on the walls were still more paint-ings, the walls themselves covered in what he thought might be damask or silk. Of all the riches his eyes met, nothing impressed him more than a small five-inch-square painting, a Chardin if its brass tag was to be believed, that merely sat, slightly upended, on the top of an inlaid desk, as if it had been carelessly forgotten.

After he saw the library ("Lots of books, but you can't read them because the print is so wretched," she said about the calf-bound volumes which lined the room) and the large, oval dining room, the main feature of which was a gigantic painting of St. Sebastian ("As punishment when I was little, Mother always made me sit facing it when I wouldn't eat my dinner"), Boyd turned to her and declared, "Whew! I didn't think you'd live in this kind of place."

"Well, as a matter of fact, this is only about the fourth or fifth time I've been here. We used to live on the corner of Seventy-sixth. Not a cooperative; just an apartment.

Then Mother got the idea that a Jewish family had moved into the building. That sort of thing makes her break out in hives."

Boyd squinted. "I suppose there are a lot of Jews in New York."

"Millions. And now more than ever with all the refugees. They've ruined Riverside Drive. I'll have to get Mother to tell you all about it. She considers herself an authority on the Jewish threat. She's sort of the original anti-Semite."

At last Boyd said, "I don't think I'm going to get along with her."

"But of course you're not. I told you."

Boyd found the place oppressive. All he wanted to do was to get out. "Why don't we shower and change and then go somewhere for breakfast? Leave the Eggs-whatever-they-are for your mother. After she's eaten them, I'll tell her they were laid by Jewish chickens."

"Hens, silly." Then, "Poor fellow, the climate doesn't agree with you, does it? All right, I'll tell Jean-P. Here, you can use this room. The plumbing is on the other side of the closet, last door to the right. I just hope my half sister doesn't come home. You'd hate her."

"Do you?"

"I told you I do."

"Isn't there anyone around here you like?"

"Absolutely no one. Except you. That's why I've carried you, lock, stock, and barrel, all the way from the cornfields. Now go in and wash. Get nice and clean. I have to show you off to everyone. I'm so proud of you."

Boyd pretended to hit her on the chin.

"And then we can go out for breakfast. We can stay out all day. Only I'm afraid we'll have to have dinner here. Otherwise, Mother will be bearish. Did you bring black tie?"

"Black tie?"

"All right, a dinner jacket. A tuxedo."

"Hell, why would I have a tuxedo?"

"Mother dresses for dinner, and I think it's fun too. I'd like to see you out of that uniform. Maybe I can get Jean-P. to round up something. I have a pimply cousin at Choate who uses this place to change clothes sometimes during the rutting season—the deb parties and all—and he's about your size."

Boyd half closed his eyes. "Do I have to?"

"I don't want you to look too rustic. I want you to look beautiful."

"You're asking the impossible."

"You *are* the impossible. I never thought I'd meet anyone like you." As she said it, she went to him and he folded his arms around her.

"Hey," Boyd said in a minute, feeling—surprised when he did—the desire rise in him again, "you better go now or you might be in danger. Right here at the fountainhead."

"I love that kind of danger."

While Boyd was in the shower, there was a knock at the door, and as he stepped out onto the tile floor he saw Jean-P. look past him as if he had trained eyes not to see unclothed bodies, mumble an apology, hang something in the closet, and disappear. After Boyd dried himself with a monogramed towel that seemed about eight feet long, he went to the closet, removed the tuxedo from its hanger, and tried it on even without first drawing on his underwear. Expectantly he walked to the mirror on the back of the bathroom door, where he studied himself. He looked like a perfect fool. He slowly removed it, put on his wrinkled OD uniform, and waited for Pipsi, too afraid to walk out into the hall by himself for fear of running into her late-sleeping mother. As he waited, he bent over at one of the high windows and peered down into the street, then brought his hands up in horror and dismay when his fingers touched the white marble which had been placed over the wooden sill. What in hell am I doing in a place like this?

When Pipsi was ready, they went down in the elevator to the street level, where the man in uniform ran before them to the door and opened it as if his life depended on it. They turned the corner and walked in what Pipsi said was the direction of the Park. Breakfast, she told him, would be on her. "We'll put it on tick," she said. "You can feed me after the war." She said that they were going to the Pierre, where they were bound to run into some people she knew. "I want to show you off," she repeated. All Boyd wanted to do was to have a quiet breakfast, then sit down somewhere and take off his shoes.

It appeared to Boyd that many of the people in the restaurant hadn't yet gone home from parties of the evening before. Here and there he saw men who were still in the hateful black tie, and at least a half-dozen women in their evening dresses. Before several tables were ice buckets in which Boyd supposed champagne was cooling. Not unexpectedly, Pipsi knew the people behind one of the ice buckets, and she steered him toward them. Though three were still in evening clothes, one girl seemed to be dressed in jodhpurs.

"Do we have to sit with them?" he asked as they approached the table.

"Don't be a recluse," she answered. "They're my friends."

Well, it was at least a comfort to learn that she liked some people in New York. But after he met them, Pipsi kissing the two boys at the table, grabbing the hands of the two girls, he couldn't imagine why. Of the people there, the only one who was half bearable was a fellow named Phil. His eyes bloodshot, and still a bit drunk, he asked Boyd about the Program, saying that he would himself probably be drafted in another few months. He had known Pipsi since they were children, he said, but he couldn't remember much because he had recently gone through shock therapy. The latter was said in a somber, matter-of-fact way, and was not meant to be amusing. He was apparently with the girl in jodhpurs, who, he explained, had scooted home to change in order that she could go riding in Central Park. As for the girl herself, after Boyd heard her announce to the table at large that three separate men had tried to hump her—her descriptive word—the evening before, he decided he didn't like her. He couldn't imagine what had compelled her to say it, especially in front of her date, who had probably been one of them.

As soon as Boyd and Pipsi ordered their Eggs Benedict, Boyd asked Phil if there was a head nearby he could use, and Phil answered that he was just going there himself. As they rose from the table, Pipsi leaned over to Boyd and whispered, "Better keep your back against the wall," which he presumed was a private joke, because he wasn't able to make anything out of it. The two of them then walked through the dining room, and as they did, the boy asked, "Have you known Pipsi for a long time?"

Going into the lavatory, Boyd gave a swift account of their meeting, Phil listening attentively. "She's a very sweet and troubled kid," he said sympathetically to Boyd. "She's one of my favorite people."

Boyd looked at the mouth that could utter such a

341

preposterous and meaningless thing, and as he did he watched a smile form on it, then quickly disappear. It was a terrible, secretive, man-to-man look, and Boyd couldn't at first figure it out. It was almost a look that said "I've been there too." Good Christ, was the boy trying to tell him that he had slept with Pipsi? The son of a bitch. Why would he want to tell anyone?

Boyd used the urinal fully and lavishly, Phil next to him forcing himself. On the way out, he asked Boyd if anyone was putting him up in New York. When Boyd said that he was staying at the Bollingers', the boy took a piece of paper from his pocket, apparently scribbled his address on it, then handed it to Boyd. "If Mama Bollinger pitches you out, give a ring. I've got my own place. Pipsi knows where it is."

Back at the table, Boyd had trouble getting his food down his throat. Pipsi's friends talked about what they had done last summer in East Hampton, the girl in jodhpurs revealing that someone named Wendell had tried to hump her during the entire month of August. She was the first to leave, saying that she was going riding for a spell, after which she was due at a hospital for volunteer work. Phil made arrangements to pick her up there for a cocktail party late in the afternoon. Boyd half wondered if she did her volunteer work in her riding habit. She sure as hell wasn't volunteering much humping.

Five minutes later the other three prepared to leave, first saying that what they needed now was a little nap. Boyd may have misinterpreted, but he had the feeling that the three of them planned to nap together. Phil again urged him to give a ring if he needed refuge, and then they left, leaving Pipsi and Boyd at the table, the empty champagne bucket at their side.

"Your friend Phil," Boyd began, "what does he do?"

Pipsi smiled. "I suppose he's just charming."

Boyd couldn't deny it, but it didn't seem to him that it could be a lifelong profession. "Is that all he *does?*"

"There are a lot of people in New York who spend all their time being charming," she answered. "He has a little bit of money, and he goes to parties and things."

Boyd put his coffee cup down. "He's also slept with you," he said at last.

Pipsi's face was at first confused, as if she were searching for a way out of the accusation. Then it became angry. "Did he tell you that?"

342

"No, he didn't," Boyd replied. "I guessed it."

"Well, it happened a long time ago."

"I thought you said . . . the first time it happened to you was when you picked up a sailor in a bar."

She was frankly antagonistic now. "I didn't *say* that. I said it was the first time I was in a bar by myself. I didn't *say* I was a virgin."

"Oh, God!"

She reached across the table and placed her hand over his. "You don't have to worry," she then said. "Phil's mostly a fairy anyway."

Mostly a fairy. Oh, my God! So that's what she had meant by her admonition as they left for the lavatory, and that's why Boyd got the invitation to put up at his apartment. Mostly a fairy! Boyd didn't even want to know what it meant or how it could be.

"And have you also slept around with people who mostly aren't?"

Pipsi reached for her purse, then signaled the waiter. "Don't spoil things," she said.

"And where, Mr. Gavin, did you say you were from?" Pipsi's mother was sitting on one of the fragile love seats in the small drawing room, her feet held up by a matching footstool. She had, in the New York fashion, put her hand languidly in Boyd's when they were introduced, then pushed the two of them into the room, yelling at Jean-P. that drinks could now be served, resting herself on the settee, commanding it and the entire room. For Boyd, whose notions of gentility derived primarily from having twice seen *Gone with the Wind*, she was a surprising woman, her face full of shrewdness as she appraised Boyd, a cigarette waving in her hand as she talked. It had been Pipsi, during a strained conversation that followed their breakfast, who told him that her mother, like many of the women of her set and generation, had before she settled down passed through what she called the Europe cycle, implying that most American girls back then had gone to Paris not for free verse but for free love. Boyd, who had dutifully read Scott Fitzgerald because Dewey had urged him to, now thought that he knew what had happened to all those rich and vulgar people. They merely got older, though they remained, most of them, rich and vulgar. It wasn't entirely farfetched, for Mrs. Bollinger, Pipsi said, had known Fitzgerald from parties.

343

Her way of speaking in fact, might have been acquired at one of Gatsby's crowded gatherings, because even in this quiet room she shouted. She shouted at Jean-P. when he glided onto the carpet with a tray in his arms, she shouted at Pipsi and at what she regarded as the unsuitable way Pipsi was wearing her hair, and she had just shouted her question at Boyd.

Boyd sat back in his chair and removed the last drink from Jean-P.'s tray, still dressed in his ODs, having told Pipsi in the hall that he felt phony enough without being dressed in a tuxedo.

"His name is Boyd," Pipsi addressed her mother, "and I already told you where he's from."

As she had, but apparently the woman hadn't listened. "A little place called Ventry, in Ohio," he answered at last. "No one's heard of it, and it's just as well."

"It sounds very amusing," the woman said, successfully concealing whatever amusement she might have felt.

Pipsi asked in exasperation, "Mother, why are we waiting? Didn't you say we'd be eating at eight?"

"I'm expecting a few people. The Hales. And also Irene. She particularly wanted to see you."

"Is *she* still around? Goodness, I thought she'd be a paratrooper or something by now. Irene is a cousin of Daddy's. And she's very excited about the war. Actually, she's the only really nice one in the family."

"Priscilla!"

Nonplused, Pipsi said, "And Daddy won't be here at all?"

Pipsi had already explained it to Boyd. Jean-P. had taken a call from Mr. Bollinger in the afternoon, at which time he had said that he'd been trying since morning to get out of Washington but it looked as if he wouldn't be able to make it. Upon hearing it, Pipsi merely shook her head and said, "The old story." When Boyd learned that the Hales were coming to dinner, he thought that Mr. Bollinger was a very sensible man indeed to remain in Washington. Hale, Pipsi's godfather, was the one who was also her mother's lover. Boyd thought that it was astonishing that New Yorkers could keep everything so friendly. As for Mrs. Bollinger, it was hard to imagine her as anyone's lover. She appeared to be the sort who would smoke cigarette after cigarette while it was going on, leaving the last to burn into a night table while she smokelessly stole her pleasure.

"Your father is a demon for work," the woman said. "I've told him there are limits to one's enthusiasm, but he likes to believe that his is endless." She turned to Boyd again, studying him carefully. "I've been to Ohio on several occasions. I have friends in Gates Mills. The Devereaus. Did you know them from Murray Bay, Priscilla?"

"Perfectly horrid people."

"Not at all. Does your father work in Ven . . . ?" She seemed to be unable to free the rural name from her tongue.

"Ventry," he answered, this time a trifle militantly, deciding that it was foolish to be civil to the ignorant woman. "He was . . ." no, he would not tell her anything about his father, "born and raised there. We're living with my grandparents."

"I've always thought it was healthy to live on a farm." Somehow her manner of saying it seemed to suggest that there were piles of manure before the front doors of all farms. "Gavin would be an Irish name, wouldn't it?"

"Yes," Boyd replied, wanting to add that he wasn't a Catholic, but at the same time not wanting to give Mrs. Bollinger the satisfaction of knowing it.

"Your father has many Irish friends," she said to Pipsi, indicating, Boyd supposed, that she did not. "I used to know the Wingfields, I think they were called, but I suppose they were Anglo-Irish. A girl who came out the year I did married one of them who lived in a very wet house in Wicklow. She put in central heating, and then left him. Later she married a French jockey. What *was* her name?"

Boyd felt stupid for not being able to provide it. "We're not all that Irish any more," he said. He looked imploringly at Pipsi, but she didn't seem to notice his discomfort.

"Yes, I suppose," the woman answered, glancing at the doorway in a gesture of tedium.

Later at the table, the light from the candles shrouding the agony of St. Sebastian in his frame, Mrs. Bollinger crushed her last cigarette into a small silver ash tray before her and pointed a finger at Jean-P., who began to pour from a large, napkin-wrapped bottle, moving from glass to glass. "I've broken into your champagne, Priscilla," she said. "Your father and I bought it the year you were born, and I'd planned to use it for your coming out.

But I'm afraid we'll have to delay that until this nasty war is over."

A sacrifice, Boyd wanted to say, but instead sipped at his glass. It tasted rather like white vinegar.

"It's too barbaric anyway," Pipsi replied. To Boyd she had once described a New York debutante as a scared-silly girl standing around while young men pinched her flesh to see if she was ready for copulation and breeding. Boyd had pretty much decided that most debutantes, like spring forsythia brought into a warm house, forced themselves into an early bloom.

Behind him he felt Jean-P. approach with a serving dish that had been carried into the dining room by a red-coated gent whose utility seemed to end there. Jean-P. lifted a fish and rested it luxuriously on Boyd's plate, somehow managing to place it in a perfectly harmonious position. Boyd picked up what he later concluded must have been a salad or dessert fork, saw his error, but continued to use it, Mrs. Bollinger's eyes on him all the time.

"It's lovely," the woman called Irene said, apparently about the champagne. "It's awfully hard to come by good champagne any more. I read somewhere where Goering—isn't he the fat one?—had all that heavenly '39 vintage packed off to the Fatherland."

She turned to Boyd, winked in a conspiratorial way, and waited for the people at the table to begin to talk to each other. When the noise level—sustained by Mrs. Bollinger's shouting—was loud enough, she leaned over and said softly, "So you're what Pipsi has caught. I must say she has impeccable taste. Much better than Cousin Frederick's."

"Her father?" Boyd asked.

"Yes," the woman said smiling. "I suppose Pipsi's mother has already asked for your dossier?"

"Orally. I don't think I scored very high."

"Don't be too hurt. She wasn't even able to *walk* past the Colony Club until Frederick married her." She seemed to be pleased at the surprise she'd created on his face. "Oh, she has the wherewithal now," she continued, "but between you and me her grandfather sold newspapers on the corner of Canal Street until he'd saved enough money for his first fling on the market."

Well, at least that explained some of her animosity toward Boyd. He didn't know where Canal Street was, but he had the feeling that anyone there was in the wrong place. As wrong as Ventry. "I did reasonably well," he went on, "until she found out that I'm Irish. I think she has visions of a papal seizure, though actually I'm not even a Catholic."

"Don't let that get you down," Irene answered. "She'd give her false eyetooth for a *bona fide* Catholic. Aren't they the ones who put plaster Infants of Prague on top of their radios?"

"You've got me. I guess I'm just a Congregationalist."

With what Boyd now thought was maliciousness, Irene put her fork down and said, "What a wonderful stroke of luck for Pipsi!"

Boyd watched her face, trying to fathom her meaning. "That's a strange thing to say," he whispered.

"Not about someone who's Jewish."

Boyd felt as if the woman had struck him. He tried to swallow the bite of fish in his mouth, and he thought for a moment that he would have to spit it out in his napkin.

In a while he said, "Are the Bollingers?"

"Only Pipsi's mother. I'm surprised she hasn't told you. Pipsi, I mean to say. As you can probably guess, her mother isn't terribly proud of it. Isn't she frightful? I was on a committee to help Jewish refugees resettle here in New York—good God, I'm not even Jewish—and all she said about them when I asked for a contribution was that it was unfortunate. I asked for money, and I got a judgment instead. She hates being a Jew, and so does Pipsi. I honestly think that the Jews in Europe weren't able to do anything to stop Hitler because of the same kind of terrible self-hatred."

Boyd began to breathe again, and as he did he said, "I'm surprised that you're telling me all this."

"You shouldn't be. I'm not really very fond of the family. And what I was *expect*ing you to say . . . I was waiting for you to say, How curious Pipsi didn't say anything. You haven't said it yet."

"So?"

"So Pipsi isn't all that unlike her mother, my friend. Do be on guard. I'm very interested in genetics. I happen to believe if a python breeds with a lamb, you're going to have a lamb that isn't happy until it tightens itself around someone's neck. You can't shed genes, I'm afraid."

"What a very unusual thing to say."

"It's an unusual family. There's enough hatred in this

room to build a skyscraper if only it could be pressed into stone. When I found out that Pipsi was bringing someone home, all I could think was, *poor* fellow."

"I still don't follow you."

"You will in time. You know, if someone hates himself it's almost impossible for him not to hate everyone else. Just be on guard. Watch for signs of irritation around your neck." Then, because the conversation around the table seemed to have stopped, she said in a strong, ringing voice, "The Dover sole is marvelous. How ever do they get it over here? Submarines?"

Boyd sat before his plate, feeling cheated and broken, half choking on the fish, unable even to look across at Pipsi.

The group was sitting or standing in the large drawing room while Jean-P. passed around brandy and offered cigars to Boyd and to Hale. Upon being asked, Hale had answered that he worked on the Street, a reply which pretty much ended any kind of conversation Boyd might have wanted to have with him. He didn't even have the interest or novelty of lecherousness. He was merely a pompous old man who now talked about corn products, whatever they were, and the bundle one could make now that all animal fats had gone to war. It seemed to Boyd that Wall Streeters lost what little distinction they must once have had when they stopped marrying chorus girls. From Mrs. Bollinger, the man couldn't have got much more than accommodating animal fat.

When, at last, Boyd saw Pipsi leave her mother, he excused himself from Hale and walked toward her, taking her arm as they met, leading her into a corner. "Are you having a good time?" she asked once they were alone.

"No."

"Well, maybe we can get away in a few minutes."

Even before the last word had left her mouth, he said, "You're Jewish."

Her eyes shone with anger and disappointment. "Who told you that?" She looked across the immense room. "*Irene!* Irene told you! Damn her all to hell. What does she mean, going around like that, pretending to like me on the one hand, and on the other . . ."

"Why are you so goddamn ashamed about it?"

"I'm not ashamed." She seemed to have collected herself. "I'm only half Jewish anyway."

New York was strangely a place of halves—where people could elect to be half fairies, where people could elect to be half Jews. "But why did you say those things about the Jews? So I wouldn't think that you were one? Oh, for Christ's sake, you sure as hell misjudge me."

"You don't understand."

"I don't know why it's so goddamn hard to. You get the idea you don't like being Jewish—pardon me; half Jewish —but you don't just hide it. You knock the Jews. You do the little stormtrooper routine." Boyd waited. "Do you know that you even called someone a dirty little Jew? I never heard anyone say that before, Pipsi. And then it turns out you're part Jewish yourself."

"It's all automatic now," she said. "I don't even think any more. All I know is that I used to . . . get in trouble if I told the truth. In school—at Brearley here—I once had to read a paper about my family, and I was naïve enough to say that my grandfather's name was Julius Friedman. Good God, never again. I was cut. I was absolutely cut. I ended up with two friends, both of them Jewish. And do you think I could have got into a sorority in Ann Arbor if Chi Omega knew about Julius Friedman? Hell, no. My grandfather's name is Joseph Franklin and has been since the day I changed it when I was fourteen."

"But you're not answering my question. Why did you say those things?"

When she looked at him, it was a look of resignation. "I hate them because they expect everyone to suffer. Why should I have to suffer?"

"Because they are." He waited for her to raise her eyes, but she didn't. She stood directly before him, and she was looking into his chest. "If I were a Jew, or if I were part Jew, and there were all those people getting killed, I wouldn't be ashamed of them. I wouldn't call them dirty little Jews."

"They could have *run*, Boyd. Did you ever ask why they didn't run? Well, I have! I know a Jewish girl who came over here with her family in '37, and I'd be glad to introduce you. *She* could tell you, because she told *me*. All her relatives stayed over there. And do you know why? Because they valued money more than they valued their lives. They wouldn't leave their businesses. Their windows were broken, the Nazis wrote 'JEW' on their doors, and they still wouldn't leave because for a Jew, to be without money is to die anyway. Well, it so happens I hate that."

Oh, God, Boyd couldn't listen to it. She *did* hate them. Very quickly he said, "Let's go. Let's get out of here."

"Let's go where? I can't just leave."

"Go get a coat. We can go somewhere. A hotel or something. I don't like it here. It's beginning to stink. Your pretentious, bigoted mother and everything. She's the one who's taught you all that, Pipsi. That's not you talking."

Pipsi seemed hurt, as though it were permissible for her to say these things about her mother, but she resented hearing the words from Boyd's lips. "Boyd, I *can't*. You know that I can't go to a hotel with you."

"Do you mean you're also ashamed because you're sleeping with me? Is that what you mean?"

"I never said that. It's just that there are *some* social requirements, and you know that as well as I do. For God's sake, I can't just move out of here and into a hotel with you."

"Well, get your coat and we can go somewhere else. Hell, we can go to a synagogue."

She looked at him in disbelief. "Boyd, are you crazy! I've never in my life been in a synagogue."

"Neither have I. So it can be a first time for both of us. Isn't the God just about the same? Or is theirs a dirty little God?" He took her arm and began to lead her out of the corner toward the hall. "You can tell God that you're part Jew and ask Him to forgive you for saying those things you've said, and I can tell Him we've been sleeping together, and ask Him to forgive me for that."

She pulled her arm free. "Boyd, you're out of your mind. It's Thanksgiving. Synagogues probably aren't even open."

"We can do it on the steps. It's the same thing."

"That's cheap and dramatic. That's silly and theatrical."

"I just want to be honest. You said you won't go to a hotel with me because you're thinking about your reputation. So I asked you to come to a synagogue with me because I'm thinking about mine."

There were tears in her eyes. As she broke away, she said, "I'll put something on," and walked from the room.

Had he been fair? No, probably not. Could you tell a white man whose grandfather was a Negro that he was a coward and reprehensible for not living in Harlem? You could, providing you weren't yourself a Negro; if you were, you would give your lifeblood to change places with him. And could Boyd, who wasn't a Jew, ask a girl to become one because Luke had long ago tried to teach him to pity and love them? Yet Boyd had never had to tell his friends that his grandfather's name was Julius Friedman. He had never suffered the isolation and terror that the world had heaped on the Jews since the beginning of time.

When Pipsi didn't return, he knew that she never would. The choice was too final, the promises too risky. And when, after he had waited by himself at the end of the room for five or six minutes, the butler came up to him and handed him a note on a small tray, Boyd knew what it contained even before he opened it. "I have a terrible headache. I'm sorry. Love, Pipsi."

Without excusing himself, Boyd went to his room, not even stopping as he passed Pipsi's door, and began to toss his clothes into his bag. He hadn't even known her, and he had asked her to make a sacrifice greater than any he had ever made. All he had known was her body.

Before he left the room he went to the telephone, placed a collect call to Ventry, and talked to his folks. He told them he was in New York over Thanksgiving—oh, God, help me be honest—and that he'd see them all at Christmas.

As Boyd walked through the hallway to the door, the stuffed-shirt butler looked through him as if it were the most commonplace thing in the world for a guest to be leaving in a huff, then told him that a Mr. Philip Something-or-other had called during dinner to say that the key to his place was under the doormat. Boyd shook his head, wondering at a city which expected its people, even transients, to have hearts and bodies of such versatility. "If he calls again," Boyd said to the man, "tell him . . . tell him that I'm mostly gone." "Mostly gone, sir?" "Mostly gone."

While Jean-P. disappeared toward Mrs. Bollinger's shouts, Irene walked into the foyer. "My, but you're an impetuous boy. You aren't leaving, are you?"

"I have a train to catch."

"But how sad. It's Thanksgiving. You're being silly. Have you and Pipsi had a quarrel?"

"I'd just as soon not talk about it."

"Well, hold on for a minute and I'll come too. We can share a cab. And don't be hostile, my Irish-American

351

friend. This is Thanksgiving, and even the Indians are nice to the Pilgrims on Thanksgiving. I'll just be a second."

She couldn't have bothered to say good-by to anyone, because she appeared a minute later in her coat, notched her arm in his, and led him to the elevator. "Tell you what," she said. "We can get a hansom. I'll take you for a ride, so to speak. Are you in mortal terror?"

Nothing could scare him any more. "Not in the least."

"Well, come on then. And just between us, my friend, you're well to be out of *that*. They'd pick you to the bone."

Boyd felt that he was expected to make some observation about the family which would substantiate what she had just said, but he was unable to. Instead, he looked at his watch. "There should be a train around midnight," he said.

"Well, we have two hours to restore your spirits. In two hours anything can happen."

Boyd supposed that it could but that it was unlikely. He felt tired as hell, partly because he had almost no sleep the night before and partly because of what had happened. Worse, he already missed Pipsi.

As they walked down the street, it seemed to him that the city was still living in the peace of 1938. If there was a war, it hadn't yet touched most of the people he passed. Some were arriving at apartment houses in cabs while going the round of parties, tall and beautiful women with black-coated men. There were foreign-looking young men, presumably from liquor shops, rushing through the night to deliver packages. There were lonely men with dogs paused before the windows of art galleries, looking in as if they were trying to remember something. Neglected-looking middle-aged women who had perhaps just left the movies, their legs unsteady from having been sitting down, lingering too long at green lights and looking up at the faces of strangers. There was the whistling of doormen for taxis, the bellowing of a hundred horns, and the low, windy, maniacal sounds of a subway beneath the sidewalks. Nowhere at all was there a sign of war. Out at sea, no more than fifteen miles from this coast, tankers and merchant ships slid through the dark waters, men praying that they wouldn't be visible to submarines in the hot, pink light from Manhattan that lit up the sky, silhouetting them, zeroing them in. Perhaps even as Irene climbed into a horse-drawn hansom, putting a match to a cigarette, enough light was at last given the sky so that the ships could be seen. Christ, thought Boyd; all those superfluous people living in light while the rest of the world lives in darkness.

"I may have had ulterior motives," Irene began once the hansom was in motion. "I never really *know* why I do what I do. I suppose, well, perhaps I said, 'Now there's a boy who needs looking after.' "

"You may have something," Boyd answered.

"I wish someone had looked after me when I came here for the first time. Did Pipsi tell you that we're from Pennsylvania? The Bollingers? Well, we are, and poor as church mice, but with slightly better credentials. We didn't know what money *was* until my cousin married Pipsi's mother. But no, I suppose it really wasn't a marriage. It was a trade. She made him rich, and he made an honest woman out of her. He got her into St. James' Church. I must say I had as much morning dew in my eyes when I came to this city as you have right now. Fresh out of Swarthmore, and I thought the world was my oyster. Well, my friend, the world is very perilous if you don't know your sea creatures. The place is more like a man-eating stingray.

"What do you do?" Boyd asked.

Irene pointed at her head. "The floppy hat should give me away. I've been on *Vogue* since I left college, but be a gent and don't ask me when that happened. I'm a kind of professional girl, only it's getting harder and harder every year. We try to tell dumpy women what to do with themselves to look chic. How to make the most of nothing. Still, it's not a bad way to pass the time, except one *does* get sick of being with women all the time."

"Maybe you'll feel better if you take off your hat."

"My God, you *are* a man. Just what I'd love to do. Here in New York every second man has a mother problem—or a problem mother, I don't know which—and they like hats. They covet them, I think." She slipped her hat off and placed it on her lap. "Am I cheering you up?"

Boyd nodded his head to indicate that at least she wasn't depressing him, and then wondered how old she was. In her early forties perhaps, but he couldn't be sure. She was so smartly done up that whatever age she had wasn't on display. What she was, first, was a very attractive woman; what she was next, was a very attractive forty-year-old woman. And, strangely, he didn't mind

353

being with her now. He was almost glad that he didn't have to be alone while he waited for the train.

"Do you have to go back tonight?" she asked at last.

"I don't have much money," he answered truthfully. "I sure as hell don't have enough to pay for a hotel room for the next two days and a train ticket too." Pipsi had their return tickets, so he would have to buy his own. Coach this time.

"It *would* be a pity for you to leave now. New York is perfectly lovely at this time of year. I think I might know a friend who can put you up for a few days."

Boyd considered it. It was Thursday night, and he didn't have to be back on campus until Sunday afternoon. If he arrived before then, those few men who had stayed in the dorm would know that something had happened between Pipsi and him, because they had all been told that he planned to spend Thanksgiving with her. As for going home, it was too late for that. He would have to leave the same day he arrived because of the lousy train service to Ventry. "Sure," he said. "Why not?"

In a minute she leaned over to the driver and gave him an address. "Three East Eighty-second," she said.

"Shouldn't you call first? To make certain he's home?"

"Oh, someone's bound to be around."

When they reached the place—it was the ground floor of a town house—Boyd was surprised to see her open first a black wrought-iron gate and then a red door with a key. "You must know these people pretty good," he said.

"Very."

Once in the step-down living room—white walls, white carpeting, and even a few pieces of white upholstered furniture—she turned to him and said. "*Now*. Make yourself at home. The tenant is very understanding."

Then and only then did Boyd ask, "Do you live here?" He was beginning to think that if Dewey was Job, then he himself was Candide. The affliction was becoming apparent.

"Yes, but don't panic. I won't bite you. I love young people. Sit down and we can talk." She removed her coat and walked back to the foyer with it, stopping once she was there to watch Boyd settle himself in a downy sofa. "You're the most incredible-looking young man I've seen in a long time. The people at the office won't believe I've chanced on someone so incredible-looking."

"It's sort of a lousy way to put it."

She smiled at his embarrassment, then returned to the room, where she touched his hand as she passed him. "By the way," she said, "I put something in your pocket when we were in the cab. I don't like to see an impoverished youth. You'll certainly have some expenses back at school."

Well, at least she was being realistic about it. Practical. He wondered how often she had done it before. While Irene left the room for a second time, he reached into his pocket and withdrew a bill—good Christ!—a crumpled fifty-dollar bill. He had never seen one before. A handsome stud fee indeed. Hell, Boyd wouldn't have to go back to college after the war to learn a vocation after all. He apparently already had one. God, what stupidity! Before she returned to the room, he smoothed the bill out, placed it on the table next to him, and put an ash tray over it. He rose from the sofa.

"You're probably angry now," she said, seeing him get to his feet. "But I do want you to stay. I didn't . . . know how else to do it. I don't think you're buyable, so I probably made a mistake. But, as you can see, a woman has to work all the angles. Are you put out with me?" When he didn't answer, she continued, "All I could think when I saw you a few hours ago was, dear God, let him like me a little bit."

Like her? Pity her maybe. What did the woman think she was going to get for fifty dollars? Hell, with that she could buy her weight in stingrays if she really wanted to wrestle. In him now, Boyd had about fifty cents' worth of love, and he doubted that he could even get that out, penny by penny. All those poor and wretched people he had met. First a guy in a men's room who had already made love to Pipsi. And now Pipsi's own cousin. Both of them hoping to sustain themselves for a few minutes on what was left of Boyd. Well, you couldn't say that New York didn't make people resourceful.

"Look," he now said, "I'm sorry. I'm not a prig or anything. I just didn't think you wanted anything like this. It's just that . . . well, I've had a big day. I think I better go."

"Please stay."

And if he did, would there be even more discoveries? Hell, he didn't want to discover anything else. About other people or about himself. "Did you," he began, "did you tell me all that about Pipsi because you thought we might have a fight?"

She waited, perhaps studying her answer. "I don't think so. But maybe I hoped."

"I really better not stay."

"No one's forcing you."

"I better go." He drew on his coat, then reached down for his bag.

"Is it because I'm old? Is that why you're repelled?"

"Good God, no. Get that out of your head."

"Then why are you leaving?" She stood in the doorway to the hall, blocking his way out.

Could he say it? Could he say that he had just been trying to tell a girl that the only way to salvation was through honor, and that now, this minute, he learned that he would never even have had the occasion to talk about honor to Pipsi had this woman before him not dishonorably set him up for it? "I don't know," he said. "Maybe I'm a little sick. I feel a little sick is all."

"I could doctor you."

"I better get back to school." He walked toward the door, and as he did he added, "I didn't take the money. It's back there on the table. But thanks anyway."

She looked older now. Her eyes looked tired, and as she held her hand up to her mouth, he could see the blue veins in it throbbing. "They *are* making them scrupulous out in Ohio these days. Take the money. It's yours. You can use it to buy a nice young girl. I'll even tell you where to go. Go to Times Square. You'll have one in five minutes." Then, quickly, "You'll need more than candy bars here. You don't get in on the candy bar trade until you're overseas."

Boyd saw that her face was working in anger. Scruples? Hell, he didn't have many left. But it seemed to him that she was trying to tell him that he was odious because he retained a nostalgia for them. "I guess we don't understand each other. I'm sorry about that."

"I bet you are," she said, holding the door open for him, "you little shit."

Boyd recoiled. He had never heard a woman say it before. He looked back at her once more as he left, and she was still holding on to her floppy hat.

Back in Ann Arbor, Boyd finally let his body make his decision for him and five days later he called the house where Pipsi had her room. The woman who answered the telephone said, "Miss Bollinger didn't come back after Thanksgiving. I got a very nice note from her that said she's transferring to Barnard next semester."

That night he took the train into Detroit, where he walked around the streets for a few hours, had a few drinks, and finally got into a cab and asked the driver if he knew where he could find a woman. "It'll cost you plenty," the driver answered, "but I know a place."

"Fine," Boyd said, anxious for the pleasure he was going to give himself, and at the same time disgusted with himself for being anxious.

When the cabbie drove up to a seedy-looking building— it appeared to be a small hotel—Boyd moved to the edge of the seat and reached into his pocket for his wallet. And as he did, the neon of the hotel's sign shining across his legs, he saw Francine's face for the first time in over two months. And he felt, by God, as though she had seen him too, had been looking everywhere for him, and had now found him in a strange city before an even stranger hotel. He removed his hand from his pocket and slowly sat back in the seat, wondering why and how it had come to him. He felt soiled and dirty from all the abuse he had given his body. All he wanted to do now was to take a bath. Not a shower, but a bath. To soak in it for about five hours until the stink was gone.

"Look," he said at last. "I've changed my mind. You can take me back to the station."

Eleven

Fort Riley, Kansas, hadn't been established for the intention of breaking men, though it sometimes did that, but to prepare them to be broken elsewhere. A better site could not have been chosen; even Private Ventry had to concede that. It sat at the foot of tall, treeless, and—if you happened to be climbing one—almost topless hills, at one moment hot, and at the next cold in such a way that the manmade device to cope with it had not yet been invented. When the last of the original prairie grass had been ground away by tanks and by huge, loping trucks, there remained the soil. Only it didn't. It blew. As fine as sand, as red as blood, it blew even when it was heavy with rain. It lodged in food, in nostrils, between the toes, at the convoluted bottoms of navels, in pockets, in foreskins, in hair, and, though rarely, on the ground.

In the midst of this floating land were long, one-story barracks housing men who woke every morning to find a gritty layer of red on their faces. Not that they noticed it; a veritable avalanche of mud wouldn't have awakened them during the few hours of sleep they were allowed. As part of their training they were on what the Army called sleep discipline, and which was characterized largely by the absence of it. Very often they didn't return from field exercises until nine or ten at night, having been awake since four-thirty in the morning. And at nine or ten the red sand had again to be scrubbed from the barracks, the mess halls had to be cleaned for the next meal, and the regalia of war had to be prepared for the following day. Sometimes they didn't get to sleep until one in the morning, only to be hauled out of their bunks four hours later. For most of them the war—the real war, not the Kansas war—was to offer respite. In time many of their lives would be lost, but at least most of them, not all, met death after having had more than four hours of sleep the night before.

358

If the First World War was the last to be fought by gentlemen—Dewey felt there was some doubt about that—then the Second was the first to be fought by kids. In his barracks no one was over twenty. There were, as he had written to Boyd, a great many Missouri hillbillies, speechless, stunned fellows who had grown up with shotguns in their hands and who were accustomed to the indignities of nature and to fathers who were bullies. Without the shy help that they gave Dewey, he wouldn't have been able to get through the first weeks of basic. The laconic fellow in the bunk over him polished his boots and laid out his gear for him on more than one occasion. With another of them, he had disarmed a live land mine, the farm boy going about it as though he were setting a bear trap, though Dewey would have blown his head off had he done it himself. They taught him to sleep standing up, eyes open, and on the top of a foot locker while oiling a rifle. They taught him to run for all he was worth out the rear door when the company sergeant approached the barracks late at night recruiting men for details. Finally, they taught him to hate the Army, though he didn't need much coaching. For them, and for Dewey too, the real enemy was not Hitler but the company sergeant, a monumentally ignorant man, a career soldier who had three times been busted from ranks, and whose favorite form of punishment was to drag a recruit out to the sand and kick his butt while he did fifty push-ups, generally biting the dust at forty. Kobiak was his name, and it would be remembered by all of them, long after they had forgotten Tojo or Goebbels. He boasted that at least two of the men in his company could expect to get their asses shot off during training. During the previous training period, it was said, one GI had drowned while on a forced march across a swollen river and one had had the most desirable part of his arm blown off while on grenade practice. In peacetime it would have raised a furor. In war it was called patriotism.

And it was Kobiak who escorted Dewey to the brig several days after his first twenty-four-hour pass from the base. As for the pass, Dewey had no idea how he got it, because all but four men in the company had been restricted to barracks over the weekend. His name had apparently been chosen at random, and afterward—it was his only pass while at Fort Riley—he wished that it hadn't been.

Near all Army camps there are towns whose only industry it is to get soldiers drunk and to get soldiers laid. Sometimes, because of terrible zeal, the former was achieved without the latter, the omission remembered only after the worst of the hangover wore off. At Fort Riley the men lived for boozing it up and for tail, both in plentiful supply, at inflationary prices, and of dubious quality. The booze was watered down and bad. The girls were painted up and not good—hustlers from the streets of Chicago, St. Louis, and little Southern towns, all out to make a fast buck while the war lasted. They went about their business like nothing before or since. To descend from the bus at the station in Junction City, as Dewey did late one Saturday afternoon, without being given an amiable goosing by one of the pack of girls waiting there was a salutation denied no soldier in this man's Army. Not even Private Ventry.

He accepted the goosing in the good-natured spirit with which it was offered, but he wasn't ready for anything just yet, thank you. Dewey, of course, had very special reasons for wanting to get laid, and he had decided that he would go about it slowly. He first went to a hotel where he ordered a beefsteak, home-fried potatoes, a salad, pie and ice cream, and three bottles of beer. His stomach fed, he then went across the street and sat through a Deanna Durbin film which bored the hell out of him. By ten at night, when he finally ventured out, the best of the girls, at no time choice, had been picked over, and only the maimed or the rejected were available. Yet when he stationed himself on a corner, and when the first woman to walk by said, "What are you doing, soldier?" he answered, "I'm going home with you." And so he did.

She took him to a house where friends of hers, as she called them, also lived, though there were as many visiting GIs as there were friends. As they went into her room, another woman left it, whom Dewey's girl described as her oldest, even dearest friend, adding once she had gone, "But don't go near her. She hates soldiers just now." It seemed a strange place for a woman who hated soldiers, but Dewey let it pass. His own woman undressed in less than ten seconds, as Dewey did too, after which she led him to a washbasin, apparently to wash him but perhaps merely to make certain that he was free of the lovemaking disease. And then they had sprawled in bed. Away from home and all the doubts he had grown up with,

Dewey gave his all, which the woman seemed to think was quite enough, even once going so far as asking him to take it easy. He did take it easy. It was the easiest thing in the world. Her body was flabby and she smelled of cheap perfume and hastily washed-off sex, but she was a woman, and Dewey liked it fine. She tried to be nice, even pretending to have an orgasm, which must have been hard considering the frequency with which she had to bring one off, and he was grateful for it. Afterward he felt as if he could lick the world. He dressed, told the woman she was great, paid her, and then went into the hall while she arranged herself for her next client. Just before he began to walk down the stairs, he saw the other woman. She smiled at him, and he smiled back, thinking it the friendly thing to do. She had been drinking, he could tell, and apparently wasn't on duty that night. She walked up to him, put her arms around him, and kissed him, holding it for about three minutes, opening his mouth and getting at his tongue, making his lips good and wet. Finished, he thanked her for what he thought was a very nice bonus, said good night, and caught the last bus back to camp. Three days later he thought that he might have the clap. Four days later he knew he did. And five days later, after a short-arm, Sergeant Kobiak knew too, and took him to the brig. All Dewey could conclude was that the woman in the hall, made sick by a soldier, had decided to return the gift and had chosen Dewey. But why *me?* was all he could say to himself.

Why Dewey? Because he looked the cleanest and most hurtable of the lot? There was no telling. A major at the base hospital, put Dewey on penicillin—a new drug in limited supply—and told him that soldiers who used penicillin while others were dying for lack of it ought to be shot. Dewey was amenable to the suggestion. In the brig, more uncertain of himself than ever, more confused by the ways of the world, he would gladly have changed his place with the dead.

But the dead stayed dead, and Dewey stayed in the brig. He slept on bare springs with a blanket as a mattress, used a slop jar that he was required to empty twice a day, and was pulled out of his cubicle early every morning to scrub an already spotless latrine that no one was permitted to use because it was the first place the CO looked at when he inspected the area. He wasn't allowed to read anything, and he wasn't allowed to lie down on his springs until lights-out. The man in the next cubicle had knifed another soldier; the one beyond him had drunkenly run a truck into a barracks; and another had lost his temper and taken a punch at Sergeant Kobiak during training. Yet Dewey was the most abject and miserable of the group. Each time that he was led out of his cell to get penicillin shot into his behind, they laughed their heads off at him.

Then, at the end of the fifth day, Sergeant Kobiak reprieved him. He told Dewey that he was going back to training and that several surprises had been arranged for him. The surprises, in the order given, were that Dewey was to be pulled out of his sack at three-thirty every morning, not at four-thirty with the others, to go to the kitchen and clean the grease trap. When he returned to the barracks at night, after a day in the field, he was expected to scrub down the latrine so that Kobiak, as he worded it, could eat a fried egg off the floor. And, finally, he was to leave the barracks for no reason, *no* how, without first getting permission from Kobiak. Dewey did all that and more. He even stole a cold fried egg from the mess hall and placed it on the clean latrine floor for Kobiak to find in the morning, but providentially a hillbilly buddy with a weak bladder picked it up at night when he went to use the place, saw it staring at him, and flushed it down the john. After a week of rationed sleep, about three hours a night, Dewey would not have been able to recite his serial number had anyone taken the trouble to ask him. He was not able to remember anything that had happened to him the day before. To make matters worse, he had by this time a head cold that had settled in his chest and that was so severe that he thought sometimes he wouldn't be able to get his next breath. He lived in a kind of twilight, neither entirely alive nor entirely dead.

Then, as quickly as the punishment had started, it stopped. Kobiak had apparently got tired of sticking Dewey's head halfway into a toilet bowl and telling him to rescrub it until the water in it was pure enough to mix with bourbon, got tired of finding neglected corners in the grease trap, got tired of Dewey. And none too soon. During the two weeks Dewey had lost about eighteen pounds, there were black shadows under his eyes, and his fingers shook. He still had his cold—back in Ventry they would have foolishly called it pneumonia—but he was too afraid to report on sick call.

Late on a Saturday night a week before Christmas, Dewey was sitting in the post library next to a skinny and deformed Christmas tree, finishing a letter to his parents, telling them that no one was being given leave to spend Christmas at home. He folded the two sheets of paper, drew them into an envelope, keeping his hands close to the desk as he did so that no one would see that they were shaking, then ran his tongue over the gluey section, sealing it.

No one had given him permission to go to the library. He had given the order to himself. By the time the company returned to the barracks that night, it was already after eight o'clock, yet he thought he might still have time to run over to the post office before it closed at eight-thirty. But as the men were being discharged to file into the mess hall, they were told that they were expected to GI the barracks for an inspection early Sunday morning. Added to which—and it seemed to Dewey that the Army had surpassed itself in choosing a Christmas present—they learned that on the following day they would leave the campsite and go on bivouac for the next seven days. They'd be there over Christmas. Dewey said to hell with the supper and to hell with the Army. Instead of eating chow, he went back to the barracks and showered, then high-tailed it over to the post office, where he got a money order for a gift he wanted to send his folks. He went to the library, where he wrote a note to a Cleveland department store and a letter to his family. He was for all practical purposes AWOL, but he knew that even the Army had limits to its imagination, such as it was. There was simply no greater way to punish a man than to send him on bivouac over Christmas.

Behind him at the other end of the room he could hear a uniformed girl librarian explain to a group of nodding soldiers the intricacies of—what had she called it?—Beethoven's Ninth. She began by saying that she wouldn't play the beginning section just now, half confessing that no one would listen. Instead, she said, "We'll start with the Chorale, the Schiller poem Beethoven set to music. Does anyone know who Schiller was?" Dewey turned around as the question was asked, but none of the GIs sitting near her seemed to be able to respond. Each soldier was lost in his own longing, undressing the young girl in his mind as she bent over and placed a record on the turntable.

But, no, someone sitting in a chair directly next to the

Music Appreciation group, but not a part of it, was grinning. Dewey recognized him. He was in the same company, but lived in a different barracks, and he too must have walked away in order to avoid the GI party. In the second that Dewey's eyes met his, they gave him a "What a lot of horse manure, eh?" look.

Dewey rose from his straight chair, sticking his two letters into the pocket of his fatigues, and walked to a shelf of books. He looked at them sleepily, not knowing where to begin even if he could keep his eyes open. Since five-thirty in the morning, an hour after reveille, the company had been on the rifle range, and Dewey had spent most of the day in the pouring rain in the pits, drawing targets. When it came his turn to fire, his hands shook so much it was only with real effort that he could hold his rifle steady. His cough was worse than ever. Now, as he stood by the books, the phlegm collected in his throat so that he wondered if his next breath could work through it. He coughed—a long, loud, pestilential hacking that could be heard over the music from the phonograph.

"That's some Hymn to Joy you have," the soldier who had grinned a little earlier said, coming up from behind. "All you need is for someone to set it to a tune, and Rat Brain back there can give a lecture on you."

Dewey figured that it was a reference to Schiller, but his mind was too cloudy to make anything of it. It had been such a long time since he had heard anyone say anything even halfway literate that he didn't know how to respond. Most of the talk back at the barracks was of the "If I have to eat one more fucking piece of this fucking Spam I'm going to fucking throw it in someone's fucking face, and they can fucking well fuck it" sort. "What a crock," he answered. "Did you see that guy back there? As soon as the broad bent over, he almost stuck his head under her skirt."

"For better acoustics," the soldier replied. "I see you skipped playing house tonight too."

"What's there to lose? The next seven days can't be worse. All they can do is sink me back in the grease trap."

"It was getting to be your home away from home. I was wondering when Kobiak was going to lay off."

"He's a goddamn maniac."

"They make the best soldiers. You should have heard him a couple days ago. After we got the lecture on

364

concentration camps. He said the only mistake the Krauts made was that they're roasting Jews and not niggers. You ever see what he does when we pass that colored outfit over at Company C? He waits until he has a mouthful and we're marching right next to them, and then he spits."

As part of the Army's campaign to make the recruits hate the enemy, they were given talks two times a week on various of the more documentable German and Japanese atrocities. But it was self-defeating. For any GI who had half a mind—some had less, to be sure—it merely called to their attention the lesser atrocities around them. As for putting Negroes in concentration camps, it wasn't the first time Dewey had heard it suggested. Some of the men in the barracks said they'd go over the hill before they'd fight anywhere near a coon outfit. It was even said by some that the Army was rushing Negro units to the beaches in Italy as quickly as landing craft could be found for them, because bodies alone were needed, the most expendable ones, to eat up German fire. This was false, but their telling of it was wishful. To Dewey it more than ever made clear that the only difference between Germans and Americans was geography. The hillbillies and Southerners he had met would dance in the streets if the Negroes in their home towns were quietly collected at night and carted off to camps. What was especially surprising was that the Southerners and hillbillies were in most other ways kind and generous. They simply misplaced their generosity and kindness when anyone mentioned Negroes.

"If I ever get overseas," Dewey said, "the first guy I'm going to kill is Kobiak."

"You're going to be too late," the other replied. "I'm going to kill the bastard on the way over. He's going to get his on the high seas."

Dewey wondered if he should now tell him what Kobiak had said to him the day he left the brig, the few words that had started Dewey's hands shaking. It was too fantastic. Kobiak had told him that he was going to get him. That was all. Get him. He said he hated these smart-aleck college kids who thought they knew everything, and that he'd have Dewey's ass before training was over. Dewey hadn't been able to forget it or to figure it out. He had done nothing but meet up with the case of the clap, and that alone didn't seem to justify Kobiak's threat.

The longer he was in the Army and living a life where

women played almost no part, the more it seemed to Dewey that men's sex drove them to action far more than their intellects. Kobiak hadn't even noticed Dewey until he got into trouble at the cat house in town, and then he had put the screws on tight. Not until Dewey discovered that the girls in town called Kobiak the Thin Line Pencil was he able to understand even part of it. Kobiak ran blind when he thought that a weaker man was getting rewards that he had been deprived of. To complicate matters—or perhaps to cinch them—the soldier who had replaced Dewey as Kobiak's special object of abuse just happened to be a hillbilly with the most spectacular set of genitals Dewey had ever seen, yet the guy said he was a virgin. When the troops showered, Kobiak would walk in and out of the latrine like old Ahab stumping over the deck of his ship, the weight of the world on his shoulders, never showering himself—he stank to the skies—because of his hairlessness and thin-linedness. Dewey supposed that Great White Whales came in different forms, and he wondered if it wasn't true that all men hated and distrusted weaker men because they were reminded of their own weakness. It was okay with Dewey as long as Kobiak kept off his back, but when he said he was going to get him it frightened Dewey because he didn't know what Kobiak wanted to get.

The GI next to him peered at the shelf before which Dewey was standing. "What are you reading? I hear they've got a complete *Chicken Little.*"

Dewey hated to admit that he hadn't read anything other than letters for the last two weeks. "I'm just window-shopping. It feels good just to look at these books. You've been to college?"

"Two years at Princeton. Then I heard my country calling. Actually, what it was, my draft board heard first."

"I was up in Ann Arbor for about a month until they found out how dumb I was. I got busted out of ASTP."

"It's supposed to be a good school."

For a second Dewey compared him to Boyd. In some ways he was very much like him. Clean-cut, decent-looking, and a gentle way of talking even when he was shooting the bull. Or, no, maybe he was more like Dewey himself. Yes, that was it. Dewey felt at ease with him, almost as if he were talking to himself and not to a stranger.

"Are you from the East?" he asked.

"Georgia. But I went up to Massachusetts to go to school. And then to New Jersey. So I've got a fucked-up accent. I'm sort of stateless, but I'm working on a Kansas drawl right now. Christ, isn't this place the asshole of the world? Someone would do Kansas a favor if they moved all the people out and used it for an automobile graveyard."

Dewey's sentiments exactly. He smiled. "My name's Dew Ventry." He held out his hand and shook the one before him.

"Hank Berkheimer," the other answered. "World's greatest authority on Schiller. Hell, I'm surprised they haven't arrested our musical librarian. Playing Nazi music."

"Are you German?"

"That's what they say. My grandparents were anyway, and I've got a lot of cousins over there. Or I used to."

Dewey waited, then said, "Jesus, you're the first real German I think I've ever met."

"Calls for a celebration. I'll treat you to a bottle of AWOL beer. The next German you meet may shoot off your head."

"It's hard to understand," Dewey said.

At the PX bar the two of them reconnoitered the place to make certain that Kobiak wasn't there, then settled down at a table as far away from the juke box as they could get. Berkheimer told him that he missed being a priest by a hair, having spent two years in a seminary before he went to Princeton, and finding not, as he put it, that he had no vocation for the priesthood but that the world had no time for priests. He talked about his being Catholic—he still was—in a dispassionate, unheated way. He had left the seminary, he continued, after first having stolen away for a weekend and going to New York to look sin squarely in the eye, hoping that in the process God would be more clearly revealed. As it was, he said, God was more standoffish than ever and sin alone had been revealed. He had spent the weekend with a colored girl, his first, in a sleazy hotel on upper Broadway, where in time a priest from the seminary found him. The man explained to a guilt-stricken Hank, not only a fallen man but a fallen Southerner, that St. Martin himself was colored and that he shouldn't feel too cut up about having been with a Negro girl; he then asked Hank to recite fifteen Holy Marys. Hank got as far as the fifth one, and went out into the streets to look for the girl to tell her the good news about St. Martin. It seemed to him, he said, that she needed the reassurance more than he did. "After that," he said, "I found out that everyone was pretty much alone, just the way I was, and that I could help them and also help myself more by touching them than by preaching. The funny thing about it is that God *is* love. Only we have to do it for Him. But I got more than I counted on. The road to heaven, as you damned well ought to know, is paved with cases of clap. Once when I was with a girl, one weekend while I was at Princeton, I honest to God got out of bed and went down on my knees to pray. She asked me if I was praying for her and I said, 'Hell, no, I'm praying for myself.' Because by that time I'd decided that whoring around that way wasn't my cup of java. I could give but I couldn't take. And after a while— I won't go into the fancy details—I found out what God had known all along I'd find. I didn't take to feeding birds, like St. Francis. I took to feeding myself. I found out that you are what you are, and the most religious thing in the world is to *be* it, as kindly as you can. End of story. As instructive as it is, it's not being read at apostolic missions."

It was a kind of inverted confessional. And Hank Berkheimer, for all his irreverent talk about the Church, seemed still to be priestly, and an honest priest at that. He noticed—perhaps only someone who had spent a long time studying himself could see tremors in others—that Dewey's hands were shaking, and he seemed even to know why. He told him that Kobiak wasn't a man, but a carry-over from the days when savages rubbed dung in their hair, painted their faces with ash, and set out to disembowel people in the next tribe. "Don't worry if you think you're not suited for war," he said. "It's the highest praise that can be given a man. And as for Kobiak and all his buddies, don't turn your cheek; you'll just regret it. There's a kind of German proverb that says more or less 'He who has faith in God and also defends himself will always triumph.' A little bit of God and a little self-defense."

Kobiak and his buddies were everywhere, Dewey knew. They were fathers who struck out at sons with leather belts, girls at resort towns who didn't take the trouble to look at a man, friends who knifed you when you needed

368

help, and still other girls who planted the clap in strangers. Yet Berkheimer seemed to be a man who not only accepted Dewey for what he was, but was trying to tell him that it was a noble and lofty way to be.

"Look," Dewey said, "you tenting with anyone out on bivouac?"

Berkheimer answered that Kobiak had already assigned tentmates, but that he would try to get a buddy of his to switch. Dewey felt protected for the first time since he had left Ventry. He knew now that nothing could happen to him and that no harm would come his way.

As punishment for having disappeared from the GI party, the two of them got to dig latrines at the bivouac site. They were trucked out at five in the morning in pouring, half-frozen rain, laughing at Kobiak and the rest of the company because they would have to march, full pack, to the bivouac area over roads that were ankle deep in mud.

It was only after they were still working on the latrines— "Dig them like graves," they were told—that they saw they had twice as much work to do as the rest. When the other men arrived, they went to work in pairs to set up their tents; once finished, they had time to chow-down on K rations. Dewey and Hank were still on their grave detail, and it was almost another hour before they were ready to pitch their own tent. They had no time to eat. "Back to the pigs," Hank said when Dewey came over with wet leaves to soak up some of the muck on the ground where they would have to sleep. "This is going to play hell with your cold. With luck, you'll get pneumonia."

"I think I already have it."

"Cheer up. The end is in sight. Just remember all the Krauts you can kill. I'll give you the addresses of two cousins of mine over there in Hitler Youth. Hitler *Jugend*. They're probably ass-deep in mud too. They talk Schiller. They whistle Beethoven. Kill 'em all."

"Dry up," Dewey said.

"I wish like hell I could. I'm wet to the balls."

At this moment Kobiak walked by, inspecting the area, and as he passed Dewey, half bent over and pounding a stake into the ground with an entrenching tool, he kicked him in the rump and sent him sprawling in the mud. Dewey was up in a second. He grabbed the field knife from its holster around his waist and said, "If you do that once more, you fat-assed ape, you're going to feel this knife in the middle of your gut, so help me God."

Kobiak smiled, as if he were pleased that he had at last been able to provoke something like this. He stepped up to Dewey, took a fistful of Dewey's soaking poncho in his hand, and said, the smile gone, "You'll get a fuckin' court-martial for this when we get back to camp."

Berkheimer was standing right next to Dewey. "If you have something to say to a man, say it. Don't kick him. And if you're really hot for a court-martial, I'll be glad to say my little piece."

Kobiak looked at both of them with loathing. "You fuckin' college kids," he said. "You'll get yours yet. Pull the tent down and put it up the right way. It looks like a shit house."

Kobiak said it about almost everything that displeased him, even about shoes that weren't polished or unshined brass. Hank Berkheimer replied, "We already dug that for you, Sarge. You're in the wrong place. Just follow the signs and look for the holes."

Dewey began to scrape the mud off his fatigues with his fingers, watching the two men before him as he did. They seemed to be trying to outstare each other, and it was Kobiak who first turned his face away. "You've got five minutes to pull this shit house down and put it up again. That's an order." With that, he walked away.

After he left, Hank shrugged his shoulders, looked at Dewey to see if he was all right, and then said, "Just keep away from him. He's out for you or something."

"I keep away from him all right. Tell the fucker to keep away from me. God *damn* him anyway."

"Take it easy. He's not important."

The two of them pulled up the stakes they had driven into the ground, rolled up the canvas, and removed the poles. They then re-erected the tent in the same spot in the same way. When they had finished a second time, they stood by it in the rain, waiting for Kobiak's whistle to call them to assemble. Suddenly Dewey turned to Berkheimer and said, "Why don't we go over the hill, Hank?" He moved his eyes slowly over his friend's face. "This buddy of mine from back home, everyone says his old man went over the hill. They don't even know where the hell he is. So why don't we get lost? Then when the smoke clears, five years from now, we can come down again and start to live."

"You think you could?"

Dewey's face twisted in self-contempt and anger. "No," he said at last. "And you know why? My father. I have to show him I can kill as many guys as the next fella. Then maybe he'll get off my neck."

As they now listened to the whistle calling them to fall in, Hank said, "There are a lot of different ways of going over the hill. I went over two years ago. I don't even write letters to my family any more. The only reason I'm here is that there's no other place for me to go."

Dewey watched the rain stream down Berkheimer's face and tried to read what he saw there, but Hank quickly reached into the tent for his rifle, avoiding Dewey's eyes. Dewey grabbed his own rifle, set it over the shoulders with the bore down to keep it dry, and they began to walk to the assembly area. Not until they were almost there did Dewey ask, "What did you mean when you said that about going over the hill?"

"Just what I said. There are hills all around you can go over. There are all kinds of ways to spit in the world's eye." He left it at that.

The week passed in mud, in cold rain, and in snow squalls. As the red clay finally froze, so did the layers of mud on the men's uniforms, so did the afternoon sweat under their arms, and so did their raunchy underwear. By the end of the second day the last face had been washed and shaved in the icy stream at the bottom of the hill or in the bucket by the latrine; by the third, even the brushing of teeth had ceased. Wet socks were removed from white-blue feet and replaced by other socks still soaking from earlier wettings. Beards collected ice, mud, and various of the body fluids from nostrils, eyes, and mouths, freezing as it met the air. Breaths were foul. Bellies were laden with frozen, razor-edged pieces of K rations. Backs ached from sleeping on the ground. Heads ached from spending days in the wind on the firing range. And hearts, the most achable of all, went to pieces as Christmas Eve approached.

The Army, in planning the bivouac, had closely duplicated what many of the men were later to run into during the winter's push across Europe in 1945. They duplicated everything but the killing. And that—or a facsimile—was planned to take place on the night before Christmas. The men in the White Army would be actively engaged in the phony slaughter of men in the Blue, or the other way around, depending on who was first able to place his finger on the frozen metal of his trigger.

On that day a driving, freezing rain began in the morning and lasted until nightfall. Fake charges had been placed here and there on the ground, and when these exploded all men within fake shrapnel range were required to throw themselves in the mud and become fake dead. A parachute unit from another outfit was flown behind Blue Army's lines, ejected from planes, only to fall into trees four miles from enemy territory. Tanks rumbled across the frozen wasteland with an incredible show of force and became stuck in the boggy red clay by the river. Howitzers and bazookas were pulled into the battle, sending dummy shells screaming through the air, silenced only after the frantic, tree-locked parachuters walky-talked to Headquarters to report that the damned things were falling on them. Toward evening, flares were set off, mostly to illuminate the terrible confusion. Tracer bullets lit up the sky, and the battle was still under contest. Dewey's White Army platoon had captured a lieutenant colonel from Washington who was serving as an observer, but let him go when he told them it would probably cost him a promotion. Dewey's platoon, in turn, was momentarily captured single-handedly by an eighteen-year-old kid who surprised them as he walked from behind a clump of bushes where he had gone to take a leak. They jumped him, took two packs of Chesterfields, and then high-tailed it through the woods to freedom. It was silly. That was the only word Dewey had for the war games. If they set out to prove that war was a science, they forgot that man was not. If they set out to prove that war was stupid, they succeeded.

That war was both—not merely stupid, not merely unscientific, but scientifically stupid—was already understood by Private Ventry. Everywhere he looked, he saw nothing but degenerate children being led by other degenerate children. Worst of all, it somehow seemed that degeneracy had become the ideal. It was Kobiak, not Christ, who was Boss Man now, the only commandment that could leave his befuddled mind the word "Hate!"—a word that men were expected to live with much as the "Kill! Kill!" they'd been taught to shout when they drove

372

their bayonets into sandbags, simulated bodies, urged to twist thrice before removing.

Dewey hated all right. He hated their war. Long ago his sister Francine had said that it would change nothing, that it would simply rearrange evil for a few years, and Dewey could already see the new evil replacing the old. Half the world could be killed, but the Kobiaks would always survive. In whatever peace that might come, after the last body had been buried, the Kobiaks would prevail. They would be Jew-hating Germans, German-hating Jews, Negro-hating whites, white-hating Negroes, yellow skins hating pink skins, black skins hating yellow skins, blue eyes hating brown eyes, brown eyes hating blue, beef eaters hating pork eaters, rice eaters hating beef eaters, ant eaters hating nit eaters, and cannibals—the only honest ones in the batch—liking whatever luck brought their way.

In this frame of mind, Dewey was now lying in the darkness in his pup tent, wrapped in his sleeping bag, the rain beating down on the canvas over his head. The sweat was rolling down his face, and yet he was cold. He had never in his life felt so cold before. An hour ago, when a truce had been called to feed K rations to the war's victims, Dewey hadn't even bothered to eat. He stretched out in the tent instead, even declining the food that Hank brought him, not even responding with a wise crack to his "Look at the little treat Sergeant Kobiak's fixed up for us. A box supper for Christmas Eve." Hank had then gone on guard duty for an hour and was due back in a few minutes; in another hour's time Dewey himself would have to leave his sleeping bag and do the same. After that, at eleven, White Army was to infiltrate through the night course, crawling on their bellies to Blue Army's positions. All Dewey wanted was to be free of it. He didn't want to kill anyone. He didn't even want to play at killing anyone. He wanted to go home.

A little after nine Hank stuck his head through the flap of the tent and slithered in, soaking wet. He was carrying a preposterous winter's branch from a tree. From where Dewey was lying, he watched him pull two pairs of wet socks from his pack, take his metal knife, spoon, and fork from his mess kit, and carefully tie them to the branch with an extra shoestring he'd broken in pieces. He then stuck it upright into the soft leaves and hard mud on the floor of the tent.

"Great." Dewey coughed. "Just like home. When do we open the presents?"

Hank sat on his sleeping bag and began to untie the muddy laces of his boots. "Don't knock it. This turncoat priest had to look all over the goddamn place to find just the right branch. It's from a sentimental German. After a while, if you ask the right way, I may even sing *O Tannenbaum*."

"I'll come in on the chorus. I'll make like a tin whistle with my teeth."

Hank saw that he was shivering. "You're going to shake yourself into a fit," he said, beginning to rise. "I'm going to tell Kobiak you're sick."

"You tell that bastard anything and you'll get a bayonet up your behind. I don't want any favors from that guy."

"What the hell you trying to prove?"

Even if it was tellable, Dewey wasn't sure he could get it out of his throat. He figured he must have a temperature of 102 or so, and with that kind of body heat it was no use to try to scrutinize himself, what he was, or what he was doing. Instead, he comforted himself by recalling all the times he had been sick back home, lying in his warm bed next to the radiator, eating chicken noodle soup and sandwiches for lunch, and listening to the radio serials, from "Pepper Young's Family to "Light of the World," Tina and Francine and Boyd coming in every now and then to keep him company. By Christ, that was a long time ago. The guy who said there was light in the world had never spent Christmas Eve in a tent in twenty-degree weather.

"You think they'll let us call home tomorrow?"

"If you have a voice that carries," Hank replied. "Those sons of bitches, dragging us out here in the middle of nowhere on Christmas."

"A lot of guys have it worse. Will we get leaves before we go overseas?"

"They'll give us leaves if they want to. And if they don't want to, they won't. We'll probably be in England by February. Then they'll drop us off in France for the shooting season. And after that we chase the bastards into Germany and hunt up my cousins. I'll point them out to you—they've got distinctive Berkheimer noses—and you can do the firing. I'll sit it out."

"They'll have to stand mighty still for me to hit them."

"Christ, you *are* shaking. Here." Hank pulled the sleeping bag from under him, his head hitting against the top of the tent as he did, then placed it over Dewey. "When we get to Germany, and after we've shot up my whiskered old aunts, we can steal their blankets. They've got real sexy blankets. These chicken-feather-filled things that they stick out the windows every morning to get the sun. I've seen pictures of them."

"I'll do my sleeping on the ground without any blanket," Dewey replied. "Where are you going to sack out?"

"After we cut up the Berkheimers?"

"No, right now."

"I'll just sit here." Hank studied the wet, matted-down slop where his sleeping bag had been. "On second thought I'm sacking out in your sleeping bag. Move over. Big smelly Hank is climbing in. Unfrocked priest and watered-down Kraut."

"Kobiak'll come in and pin a morals rap on us."

"Let him try. What do those guys know about morals? Let someone just try. I'll pin a morals rap on F.D.R. and Hitler. Move over. Sorry for the fragrant body."

Hank crawled in, zipping up as much of it as he could, then rearranging his own bag on top of it. "Nice and cozy. This here is what you call a crowded tenement. If it gets too crowded, speak to your priest."

"That's okay. Thanks. That helps."

"It antedates blankets. Men knew about it even before the Chinks discovered firecrackers. Great Christmas, eh? It's as warm as St. Patrick's Cathedral on the seventeenth of March. What we'll make us here is a little-assed church."

"Yeah, and you'll also get my fuckin' cold."

"So? Two can suffer easier than one. That's why churches are *built,* man."

Maybe he had something. Maybe when two people could help each other, they made their own religion as they went along. The rest of the world didn't matter. "When you said what you did," he said, "about going over the hill, did you mean what I thought you meant?"

"Probably."

"That's what I thought. I had this feeling."

"Should I get out of your church?"

After a long while Dewey answered, "No." He would make his peace with the Germans now. The rest of the world could make its own on whatever terms it wanted. Lying next to Hank, he could feel Hank's sex grow and, in

375

fever and fatigue, his own. With one hand Hank reached down and freed himself, then Dewey. And as they rose and fell against each other, it seemed to Dewey that for the first time he could see the world in all its clarity. People were born in certain ways and had to live in certain ways. There could be no rules made by some to exclude others from life. For the world now to tell Dewey that he was wrong was for it to tell a Jew that he was wrong, or a black man, or a leper. If he was an outlaw now, a source of ridicule for other people, it was because the rest of the world happened to go out of the law in a different way. If they felt that their way was better and richer, then all they had to do was take a room in a hotel next to a copulating couple and listen to the groans and creaking springs for a while. Their way was no better, Dewey was finally able to admit to himself; it was just theirs.

And when it happened for the two of them, it happened at almost the same time, the same second, and to Dewey it seemed to drive away all the sorrow outside the tent and even in himself. Afterward they lay in the dark, listening to the rain on the canvas, neither of them saying anything. When they were ready, they did it again, this time more carefully, pulling off most of their clothing and finding each other's body. And when it was over, they were in the dark again.

A little before ten, Dewey sat up and tried to draw on his clothes that were heaped everywhere inside the sleeping bag. "Thanks," he said at last.

"I can stand guard for you if you feel lousy."

"I'm okay," Dewey answered, sliding out of the bag. "I want to clean up a little anyway."

"Put on your poncho. It's raining to beat all hell."

"I will." Dewey brought it over his head onto his shoulders, then picked up his rifle.

"Look, Hank," he said, "Merry Christmas."

"Merry Christmas to you." He waited for a minute, as if it were hard for him to speak. "I had the feeling this was the first time for you. Just remember that what we did is all right. I've had long talks with God about it, and He said that all God's chillun is the same. We just have to work things out in special ways."

"Thanks for telling me. I guess I'm lucky it happened with someone who's on good terms with the brass."

Outside, the rain had turned to light snow, and Dewey

376

watched it fall as he made his way to the latrine. At a half-frozen bucket of water there, he scooped up enough to douse his face, gasped as it met his skin, then dried himself with the sleeve of his field jacket. As he turned and began to walk down the path toward his guard post, his boots sucking at the snow on the ground, he almost walked into Kobiak. He stood directly before him, gross and threatening, and Dewey unconsciously stepped back to let him pass. But Kobiak did not move. He stood there.

What Dewey saw in the darkness on the path was not Kobiak at all, but his father, waiting for him now because he had caught him at something heinous. In all his rationalization while he was in the tent, Dewey had considered the world but had forgotten his father—who was five steps away, looking at him with revulsion. It was the same look Frank Ventry had given him on the night he had pulled him out of the locker room after the game, the same look Dewey had seen as he beat him with his belt. A look that told Dewey he *knew*, and that he hated him for the knowledge.

Even as he realized that it was only Kobiak, he was unable to rid himself of his father's eyes. When Kobiak passed by him on the path, Dewey cringed, waiting for a blow that never came, bringing his head close to his chest. Eyes closed, he heard feet continuing up the hill behind him toward the latrine.

He stood on the path, as alone as a child, almost too afraid to move. No, maybe there wasn't a hill big enough to go over. And there was no going back to Ventry. You could kill a man and be forgiven by a father, but you couldn't do this. This was the one sin for which there was no pity, the one shame for which there was no understanding. Dewey could feel his father's repugnance, and in time it became his own. There could be no going home now. He had failed his father, and he had failed his own dreams.

Instead of walking to HQ tent to report for guard duty, he slowly made his way down the hill behind the bivouac to the flooded stream at the bottom. Above and around him in the night sky he could see the stars, the tracer bullets burning in the darkness, smoke curling up from fires. He stood on the bank for a long time—a half hour, then an hour—trying to remember all the good things in life and forgetting the bad, the trusts he had kept and the trusts he had broken, the promises made to himself and the promises that now could never be made. A step at a time, he lowered himself into the water, feeling its iciness over his legs, his hips, and soon his chest. In his mind was the only prayer he knew any more, and before he slipped under water his gray face was washed in tears. He reached out, first struggling, his hands closing around water, and then he let himself relax, praying to God that his father and all fathers would understand that he had tried.

Twelve

A light snow was falling on Ventry, Ohio, covering the walks, the wooden benches in the park, and the frosted grass, drifting at the spindles of porch railings, on steps, and at the sills of windows. It fell on bottles of milk left near cellar doors, frozen and heaved into the air, on Christmas wreaths, and on the cap, the shoulders, and the already beaked nose of the Civil War statue. It fell on hedges of children standing outside the Drug and Notion store before dolls that ma-maahed and toy trains that tooted and rock candy that had been in stock since last summer. It fell on the backs of shivering dogs and on humorless sparrows. It fell on sliding old ladies who ventured out for tea or cookies from the store, on resolute mailmen, and on the egg man as he made deliveries from his Model T Ford. It fell even on a deer that had walked up Tannery Hill early in the morning and stood in front of the Casto Theater on Main Street only to be frightened away by Parnell Gavin drawing his sled through the square on his paper route, telling it to "git."

Now, at noon on this day before Christmas, it fell again on Parnell as he made his way across the square, plowing through the drifts, the back of his half-unbuttoned blue mackinaw white with snow from where he had just plopped down to make a very comely angel. His face was scarlet, because of good circulation, the cold, and the inadequate dye of his red muffler which he was in the habit of chewing. His open arctics flapped at his feet. One hand was covered by an ice-encrusted mitten, the other naked, its mitten vagrant, passing the winter under a snowbank somewhere to pop up in March with the violets. At the end of these two hands was a tree—a prodigious tree, an outrageous tree, a tree twelve feet high but otherwise with little character. He had bought it, paying a cold quarter, from the sidewalk in front of the hardware

379

store, and it was the first he had ever bought by himself. A scandalously shaped tree, but a lot for the money.

He dragged it behind him over the soft snow, first with his mittened hand, then with his bare hand, sitting down on top of its bushy branches every now and then to catch his breath. He made his way slowly down Satin, looking up at the windows he passed to compare Christmas decorations with his own at home, saying hello to people with shovels and brooms, and then turned onto Summer. There he met two friends and gave each of them a ride on his tree, pulling them along in the snow until they toppled off. By the time he reached Priest Street, his burden had somewhat diminished, a trail of green branches and needles stretching all the way back to the square, diminishing the wrong way, in width and fullness, not in height.

On Priest, even the falling snow was unable to cover the rape of the street by construction workers. Between the Gavins' desolate Victory garden and the corner the ground had been scooped up and tossed in huge piles, maples had been chopped down, and in what had been an open field were six long, wretched new houses, built not even of lumber, for that was scarce, but of cold gray concrete blocks which would later be stuccoed. For the new families that would be coming to town to work at the chemical plant, similar developments—one was not much more than a barracks—had been erected in other corners of the town. The steeple of the church in the square, hitherto the only intrusion in the sky, now competed with three giant smokestacks which could be seen from all over Ventry, lacking even the apology of the cross on the steeple.

As Parnell pulled his precious cargo down the middle of the street, he counted seventeen cars and two trucks parked at either side, more cars than he had ever seen there before. From within the new houses he could hear pounding and grinding, and before him on the clean snow he saw waxed paper from sandwiches and from nickel pies, debris from the workers' lunches, blowing around in the wind. The men themselves were too formidable to speak to—men from Cleveland who were angry because they had to work in a small, isolated town, or men from the hills of West Virginia who spoke in a peppery way that Parnell could not understand—and he knew none of them except by sight. Their cars he passed every morning on the way to school, and the cars seemed very sophisticated. In the windows of some were rabbit feet, in others were dangling, saintly-looking figures hung from rear-view windows, and in one was stuck a sign that read *Don't look in! The girl may be your daughter!*

He tugged at the remains of his tree, bringing it over the lawn and around to the back of the house, where he stood it against the porch, then studied it once more, pleased that he had an eye for beauty. He would have to fit the tree into its standard, made by Boyd three years ago in his manual training class at school, carry it into the parlor, and help decorate before Boyd arrived later in the afternoon. He leaned over and removed from a branch one withered and crumpled Lucky Strike wrapper, fastidiously dropping it in the wastebasket as he walked into the kitchen, his face burning as it met the heat.

Later, after Rose had told him that she asked for a *tree* and not a sequoia, and instructed him to cut it clean in half, he moved it into the parlor before the bay window, setting four *Liberty* magazines under one corner of the wooden standard to compensate for a certain crookedness that had escaped his keen scrutiny. He placed holly-wreathed wrapping paper at the foot of it, sprinkled artificial snow over the paper, and finally, even before the tinsel and ornaments were up, arranged his costly presents on the floor under the branches. There was a long, hundred-toothed comb for Rose, a pink vase from the dime store for his mother, a mouth organ for Simon, a jack-knife for Boyd to use in the Army, and—the last present he had made in school, showing it to no one at home—in the box marked *Daddy* a handmade, real Indian belt.

When he finished, and knowing that Rose and his mother were too busy to help decorate the tree at the moment, he went into the kitchen, where it smelled yeasty and good. Rose had been baking the Gavin Christmas bread—brown and raisined sticky rolls—all morning, and he saw that she had brown sugar on her chin. Her face, however, remained unsweetened, perhaps because Parnell was wearing Boyd's track shoes over her kitchen linoleum.

"Young man," she began, "if you think you're going to prance around my house with those spikes on, you're very much mistaken." To add emphasis, she shook a brown-coated tablespoon at him. "I don't know how you can keep them on anyway," she continued. "Your brother wears a size-eleven shoe. All the Gavins are that way. Big feet, small brains."

Parnell made no attempt to hide his outrage. "Who has a small brain?" he asked, offended.

"Now, don't you be bold. I'm at sixes and sevens as it is. Dr. Herron arriving at five, and Boyd coming in on the six o'clock train. If you ask me, I'm the one who should be there in bed, and not your grandfather."

Parnell was unable to figure out people who were always threatening to throw themselves into sickbeds. He bit his chapped lip and surveyed his grandmother, wondering if she really was in good humor or bad. "What exactly does Simon have wrong?" he asked. "What is pair-lized?"

"Run off now. You see what you made me do? You made me empty the dishwater, and I didn't even do the baking pans."

Why Parnell was relevant to the dishwater, he didn't know; he stuck on. "Is it when your tongue stops?"

Rose closed her eyes and prayed to one of her secret Catholic saints. "Lord have mercy on me. They'll all put me in an early grave." She attacked the hot water faucet in the sink, turning it on until it was steaming, drawing enough for her neglected pans. "What it is," she said, musing, "it's a heart attack of the brain." Having delivered her medical opinion, she saw that Parnell's face was more confused than ever. "Do you remember when you cut your knee so bad? Where the scar is?"

Parnell was able to feel it even under his corduroy pants—Simon, when he had speech, used to call it "a blackguardy scar indeed"—and he even remembered what had caused it. "That's when I fell on the barbed wire," he answered at last. "When someone was chasing me."

"*That* is a one-hundred-percent lie. If you came home at night when we call you, you wouldn't get caught way over on the next street in the dark. Mrs. Sprague clearly said she saw you from her front porch, running down Summer Street like a rabid dog, and then she saw you go kerplunk on the sidewalk and tumble over on the fence she set up for her new grass. No one was chasing you."

"How would you know? You weren't even there. There was too someone."

"Who, may I ask?"

Parnell had answered the question before, and he hadn't been believed then either. "It was a big gray man."

"Well, honey," Rose began, in another tone, "that's

because it was getting dark and you couldn't see very well. That's why we always make you come home as soon as the sun goes down."

"He had a hatchet."

Rose was now exasperated. "Well, Mrs. Sprague didn't see any big gray man with a hatchet. Or any little gray one either. That's what you get for seeing those terrible motion pictures with all those killers."

"What terrible mosh-pictures did I see?"

"That Fu Manchu. Why, do you remember that Saturday last July when I gave you enough money to go to the movies because you said they were showing kiddy cartoons? And I asked you to buy a quart of strawberry ice cream from McMorris's on the way home? You re*call?* Well, I never in my life saw anyone run into this house the way you did. Like someone had poured gasoline on you and set you on fire. 'And where, Parnell Gavin, is my ice cream?' I says, and you just run past me up the stairs to your bedroom and lock the door. *Well!"* Agitated, she wiped the corner of her apron over her forehead. "And didn't Guy Rogers come to the back porch ten minutes later with the ice cream—why, it was a puddle by then— and didn't he say he saw you throw it up into the air on Main Street, give a whoop, and then run? Just toss it into the sky and run because you had to walk *past* the Fu Manchu picture you'd just come *out* of. That's what I mean."

"I don't remember that," Parnell said, remembering.

"Hah!"

It was often difficult to carry on a conversation with Rose because she tended to meander. Parnell had almost forgotten what they had been talking about. Putting the threads together again, he asked, "Do you mean pair-lized like a scar?"

Rose, who had also misplaced the topic, looked at Parnell as if he were getting a little daft, refound the point she had been trying to make, and said: "What I was saying before you got me all wound up, I was saying, you recall the blood on your knee and how we put cold water on it to clot it? Well, that's what a clot is. And when you have a heart attack sometimes it sets in motion a small, tiny clot that runs lickety-split through your veins and takes root in your brain. That's when you have a stroke."

It may not have done for the Surgeon General, but it

seemed to do for Parnell. "And that's when you can't talk any more? Like Simon?"

"It's the general idea, if I understand correctly," she said, leaving no doubt that she did. "But your grandfather isn't half as bad as he's putting on, mark my words. I asked Dr. Herron for his candid opinion, and he said he's seen plenty worse. Plenty. You have to will yourself better. It's all in the will. I expect I'll have Mister Gavin up and dancing around before spring."

Parnell hoped so, but he didn't know how she could. Every afternoon after school he went in to sit with Simon and help him exercise with the red rubber ball. Parnell would place it in Simon's limp right hand, close his fist over it as much as he could, and tell Simon to keep squeezing. More often than not, the ball slid out of his hand onto the floor. Far from being able to dance, as Rose said, Simon could barely keep a spoon in his left hand to eat. As he fed himself—he was at last off his Jell-O and on a meat and potatoes diet—he often hit the spoon against his chin, and always spilled food on what everyone called his extra-large napkin, but which was in fact a bib. About the only thing that Simon was able to do well was sit in his wheel chair in the dining room or the parlor, looking out the windows hour after hour, watching the men build the new houses, shaking his head sadly.

"Will those people in the new houses have kids?" Parnell asked. He was sitting at the table, counting the packages of Juicy Fruit gum that Boyd had sent him as an early Christmas present.

"Those miserable houses?" Rose shouted, pointing her spoon at the street with vengeance. "What they're going to have is *prob*lems. They're going to bring all their problems right with them. You can't tell me different. There'll be drinking and carousing and every sin known to man and beast. If I had my way I'd sell out and move as far away as human legs can carry me. The deserts of Arizona!" She looked down at her grandson as he arranged his packages of Juicy Fruit on the table. "If you don't stop fingering that chewing gum, you'll have it all melted together. I can't imagine why your brother sent you fifty packs of gum anyway. You'll have gum in your jaw on the day you die."

Parnell knew why Boyd had sent them; it was because Parnell had never, in all his life, had so much of one thing before. "I have two hundred and fifty sticks," he said proudly, then looked at the clock on top of the icebox. Only three o'clock! A whole afternoon before Boyd got home.

"How far actually is Michigan? Is it far from the war?"

"Goodness, child, one of these days you'll drive me screaming from the house with all your questions." She collected herself, apparently deciding that the day before Christmas wasn't the appropriate time for it. "Your brother is in college, and you know that as well as I do. The Army saw right away he was smart."

Parnell struck. "I thought you said we all have small brains."

"Well, they're small but they're adaptable. Poor Dewey Ventry had to leave school because he couldn't settle down to his studies, and Helen told me yesterday he won't even be getting home for Christmas. It's the first time he's ever been away from home too."

Francine was already in town, Parnell knew. He had seen her on Main Street earlier in the day, and she had been with Howard Foster, who had a deferment because he was working in his father's plant. Each time during the last month that Francine had come home, in fact, the Foster car was always parked in the Ventry driveway. Not that Parnell went over there as much as he used to. Tina, who had given up counting, was now keeping a written history of the Second World War. In a new set of black notebooks from the dime store, she copied at least fifty per cent of every *Plain Dealer* Parnell delivered, even the day's weather and the price of grain. If he walked in while she was at work, her pale forehead furrowed, she would say, "Hush," and continue writing: "Wheat was nominally higher Friday; basis steady; corn easier; receipts 91 cars." Such was the scope of her task that she had little time for playing the piano and none at all to sit and talk with Parnell. When, the summer before, she had begun to go out into the world for the first time, people hoped that she might be getting well. As it was, her unwellness appeared merely to have found a new outlet. Parnell had lost his only friend to history. He had already decided that he was going to enlist in the Army.

"How old am I anyway?" he now asked Rose.

"You'd forget your name if we didn't remind you every day. You're nine."

He screwed up his face. "Ugh-hhh! My name."

"It's a perfectly lovely name. You take some names,

385

they're common. Like John. Or James. If you have a name like that, someone'll say, 'Well, I ran into John downtown today,' and the first thing you have to ask is, 'John who?' Now, you'll never have any trouble with Parnell."

Probably, he thought, because no one would want to run into somebody named Parnell. "Tell me about him again."

"Who? Parnell? Can't you see I've got work to do? Anyway, you've heard it, I bet, a hundred times." She paused, apparently wondering if it was right for her to deprive him of his heritage. "Parnell was a liberator of Ireland," she said importantly. "There were several because it took Ireland a long time to be liberated. He's a national hero, put to death by the murderous English." Although Charles Parnell had died snug in his bed, perhaps in the arms of his sweetheart, Mrs. O'Shea, the Gavins had never acknowledged it.

"That means I'm named after someone who's dead." As Parnell uttered it, he felt his heart swell.

"Well, sweetie," she answered patiently, "it's pretty hard not to be."

He wished that Rose would *talk* more. She was too telegraphic for his taste, accustomed as he was to Simon's old oratory. She used words in the same way she served her plate at the table—enough to get by on and with no waste. If only Simon could speak, he could help Parnell pass the time while he waited for Boyd, perhaps even tell him a swashbuckling story. "Tell me about the man in Cleveland," he said, "who was eating soup and found a gold tooth in it."

It was too much for Rose to bear. She could look after Simon and even nurse him, but she couldn't speak for him. "You shoo! Out of the kitchen!" she yelled. "I don't have all day to tell you stories. Do you think I'm the public library? Anyway, I never approved of Mister Gavin telling you those murder stories."

Disappointed, Parnell began to rise from his chair. The tooth-in-the-soup story, one of his favorites, he had heard many times, though he didn't know if it was true or if Simon had made it up. It concerned a Greek restaurant owner in Cleveland who killed his wife and then made soup out of her in order to dispose of the body.

He hobbled on his toes to the closet by the basement door, sat on the top step, and drew his arctics over the track shoes, buckling only the bottom metal clasps. Not until they were on did he remember the peril his chewing gum was in; Rose had threatened to throw it all into the furnace. He returned to the table, picked up the box, carried it into the hall and up the stairs to his bedroom where he locked it in his dresser. Even before he was halfway down the stairs, he heard her shouting at him.

"You have your *dirty* boots on, and you're walking all over my clean house! I honestly believe that you're trying to drive me out of my mind."

"Is Gramp ready to go outside?" Parnell asked, unperturbed, his ears inured to her abuse.

The two of them then went into the dining room to get Simon ready. His face was calm, numbed. Parnell helped his grandmother slip his overcoat over him, then wrap him in a blanket. They rolled the wheel chair through the kitchen, down the new ramp on the back steps, and into the winter air.

As Simon was wheeled over the snow in the driveway toward the front of the house, he waited for Parnell to rearrange the stuffing around him, as he always did. Once on the slippery front walk, Parnell stopped pushing the chair long enough to lean over and pull Simon's hands from under the blanket where Rose had thrust them. He placed them artfully on Simon's lap, one over the other, in the reverential position used by undertakers in their work. "There," he said. "That looks nicer. If I don't put your arms out, all anyone can see is your head."

Which was probably true enough, but it nonetheless bothered Simon. He sometimes had the feeling that his grandson and Rose thought of him as a wordless doll that could be manipulated in whatever way they chose, that would wet when they told it to, and slumber when laid down. To have his face washed and shaved by Rose was torture, not because she used the razor brutally, but because of the foppery she subjected him to. He had never in his life used after-shaving talc, but he was always heaped with it by the time his face met her esthetic standards. As for his hair, which Rose trimmed every two weeks, it was entirely out of control. Cutting it, she would say, "Why, I just think I'll let this little bit curl over your forehead—like so!" and forcefully pull a curl-less strand of his hair into his eyes, making him look like a Central European gigolo.

Yet she was kind, too, in her way; he couldn't deny that. Every night she was up from her makeshift bed in the parlor three or four times to look into the dining room to make certain that he was sleeping and not dead, half the time pinching him awake to determine it. For his part, Simon had given up all thoughts of dying. During his first weeks at home he had sometimes hoped that he might slip away at night, another stroke, but he knew that Rose would merely run to his bedside, tug one way while Death tugged the other, and even Death would falter under her sharp tongue. He would outlive Rose, perhaps just barely; it would have to be his sacrifice. However dependent he was on her, she needed him even more. To work for him, to cook for him, to make him feel comfortable. For Simon to die would be for him to bring unemployment to Rose, and it would kill her in a painfully lingering way. Yes, he would have to outlive her in return for all the favors—weren't favors sweetness and love too?—she had given him.

As a large green truck from a department store turned the corner onto Priest Street, Simon felt Parnell's hands at the back of his wheel chair grow limp, and he knew that Parnell would be fixed to the spot where he stood until he learned who was getting something new. They watched it move slowly down the street, a bumping noise from within as it went over the hump in the pavement where sewers for the new houses had been laid, to stop in front of the Ventry house. A man stepped out on the running board to look again for numbers—there were none—and then walked up to the Ventry front porch. In a minute Helen Ventry came to the door, nodding her head in surprise to a question she had been asked.

"Rats!" Parnell said. "There's a truck from Higbee's in Cleveland, and it isn't even for us. I thought Aunt Cortez might be sending us a surprise."

Simon felt his grandson put the chair in motion again, sorry and ashamed that Cortez had sent nothing but a card with a five-dollar bill in it. Even if she had bought only a two-dollar gift, as long as it arrived in a box it would have pleased Parnell more than money. Simon hoped that the family's gift to him would make up for it. Everyone had chipped in—Rose, Simon, Catherine, and Boyd—to buy him the almost legendary cowboy suit with fur chaps. It, along with the other gifts, wouldn't be opened until Christmas night, after service at the church and after the pageant Parnell was to appear in as a Wise man. It was an old rule, excruciating for children, made by Simon's father who thought that presents ought first to be offered to Christ, after which, and only after which, could the family open their own.

"This is Priest Street where we are right now, Simon," he now heard Parnell say, rolling him through the snow. "It's where you live. Up here where we turn is Summer Street. Then comes Spring. And after that Satin." He paused, apparently lost in thought. "What I always think pecul-er is that there's no Winter Street or Fall Street."

What Simon thought even more peculiar was that Parnell had somehow decided that Simon was unable to see or think for himself. To go for a walk with his grandson involved listening to a running account of whatever they passed. He heard him say that they were going by the new houses.

It was inconceivable, he thought, that people could live in one-story houses. Degrading. Moreover, there wasn't a front porch on the lot of them, no place for a man to sit on summer nights. Only windows. Big, ugly, unfriendly windows that would probably have curtains behind them which could be drawn.

The town was changing all right. Simon had read in the Ventry County *Sentinel* a few days before that the housing developer from Cleveland who was putting up these abominations had said he expected the place to grow by leaps and bounds. He even had the effrontery to say that what the new people would like most about Ventry was its quaintness and Early American charm. Hell, thought Simon, what they were bringing to town was Late American charm.

Simon had already seen it in small towns closer to Cleveland, and it would happen in Ventry too. In time there would be people who spent half their lives in automobiles. People who packed their elderly parents off to nursing homes as soon as their breaths began to turn sour. People who played golf instead of working around the house or the lawn. People who arrived in enormous yellow Allied moving vans from all over America, following jobs as they arose, without any kind of pasts, without any kind of histories worth talking about except continual motion. People who would come to town to make a living, not to live. Mothers who would spend more time at new country clubs and beauty parlors and psychiatrists than they would

389

with their children. Fathers who wouldn't know or care what their sons or daughters did. Children who would be bored because they couldn't smoke marijuana or drop their pants whenever they felt like it. People who wouldn't even remember that there had been a war, and that men had died. Selfish, self-centered, pleasure-driven people. Late American people.

Well, he was almost glad that Lucas would never have to see it. The war was changing the country too much. It no longer mattered who won, because the old peace had already been lost. All the place needed now was a war of national liberation to free the country of its people. Yes, he was glad that Lucas wouldn't have to see it.

Parnell said, "Do you know what I dreamed last night? I dreamed that Daddy is coming home tomorrow. Do you think he will, Simon?"

Oh, my God, he still believes! He still thinks Lucas is coming home.

No, Simon wanted to say, he won't be coming home this Christmas or next Christmas or the one after that. And Rose would have to tell him. To delude Parnell any more was only to punish him, to offer him hope when there was none. Every man had to die, once and for all, and Rose could hold it back no longer. She would have to tell. And if she wouldn't, then Simon himself would.

Now, from deep within his throat, Simon made a sound, as if he were straining with all his might to say a word.

Hearing it, Parnell stopped. "What's wrong, Simon? Do you have to go to the bathroom?" He looked into Simon's face, and finding no ready answer began to turn the wheel chair back to the house. Simon sat sick and humiliated as Parnell pushed him toward home.

In the house again, Simon was brought into the parlor where he could watch Rose and Catherine decorate the tree. With his one good hand, his left, he was able to lift a cup of hot soup that had been placed on a table at his side. Parnell had run outside to wander through the half-finished rooms of the new houses as soon as the workers began to drive away in their cars, urged by Rose to pay especial attention to the bathrooms because she had heard they were no larger than broom closets and fit only for circus midgets. The Gavins' bathroom, a bedroom before plumbing had been introduced to town, was splendid, majestic, and half vacant, most of it unused floor space.

Before the window, the tree began to take shape. Catherine and Rose were tying popcorn balls on its branches, draping colored strands from limb to limb, throwing tinsel over it, and covering its defects with prewar ornaments.

"Well," Rose said, "I'll be glad when Christmas is over. This is the worst Christmas I've ever had. My hip is killing me." It was a refrain the house had heard before, said about almost all holidays, the "worst" varied to fit the date, the Fourth of July, her birthday, Easter, or Thanksgiving.

"I'm just glad that Boyd is getting home," Catherine replied. "The Ventrys are heartbroken because Dewey is down in Kansas. Frank painted the living room and the dining room, and Helen's been getting the house ready for the last two weeks, but now they find he can't even get home."

Like anyone who worked on the lakes, Frank Ventry had a forced vacation, payless, from November, when the lakes froze over, until March, when they began to thaw. In past years little indeed had been done around the house in the way of repairs. But everyone in town knew now that he hadn't touched a drop since last summer. He had, as Catherine said, painted part of the downstairs, and he had also sanded and revarnished all the bedroom floors, and even made a ten-story-high birdhouse—the most magnificent thing Parnell had ever seen; it was shaped like a castle!—which he intended to put on a pole in the back yard as soon as the weather permitted. When Rose saw it, she said you could tell that Frank still had artistic hands, and that it would be good to see if not peacocks, at least fancy birds on the Ventrys' lawn again.

"I was always partial to Dewey," Rose said. "It's pitiful that the Army has to take boys when they're still almost children."

She bent over and searched through the box marked *Xmas Decorations* which was stored most of the year on a shelf in the fruit cellar. "Now what did we do with that Santa Claus face Parnell made in school last year? Or did you think it looked cheap?"

Catherine said, "Cheap! I just hope Parnell doesn't hear you say that. He wouldn't talk to us for a week if we don't use it."

"I suppose," Rose replied, flicking her finger against a small shiny red ball she had taken from the box. "Just look at these," she went on, holding up another. "They're all made in Japan. Here we are killing each other—goodness, the man who made these may this very minute be breathing his last breath—and I'm hanging them up on a tree. Isn't that the queerest thing?"

Catherine nodded her head, indicating perhaps that the irony of it had already occurred to her. This still left her totally unprepared for what Rose next said.

"Between you and me, I've said my last prayer. I'm not going to pray any more. I took the Pope out of the drawer this morning and rested him in the wastebasket."

The tinsel fell from Catherine's hands. She turned and stared at Rose.

"I did for a fact. God must be a maniac to allow all this killing. And I've decided that what a Congregationalist can say to the Pope of Rome won't help matters one bit." She looked tired. "You'd think if God loved good people, He'd look after them, wouldn't you? Well, it isn't so. I read in the papers about that Errol Flynn. Someone's filed another paternity suit against him—it makes around the fourth. Well, I don't see anyone striking him down, do you? He's here in all his comfort, climbing in and out of bedrooms, and boys all over the world are being killed. I have half a notion not to go to church tomorrow."

If it had been Errol Flynn alone who had caused Rose to lose her faith—she had lost it before for short periods and for even less weighty reasons—the news would not have been too alarming. But Catherine thought she knew its source. Instead of making any reference to Lucas, however, she chose to tell Rose that Parnell would be hurt if she didn't go to church the next day. "He's been practicing all week."

"It's just a lot of fuss and bother over nothing. What good is God unless He helps people when we need Him? Now, Parnell has everything straightened out in his mind, and he knows his part in the pageant perfectly well. But do you think God will have the time to watch? No, sir. Not when He can be amused by Errol Flynn." She paused, visibly pondering what new threat she could direct at God, whom she treated as one of the family, subject to the scoldings she gave everyone else. "I have half a mind to tell Parnell he can't be a Wise Man this year. It's all tomfoolery anyway."

"The whole idea of religion," Catherine said slowly and seriously, "is life after death. We should pray for the souls of the dead, not for ourselves. That's selfishness. God keeps the dead company, not the living."

From his chair on the other side of the room, Simon watched Rose's face, hoping that she might at last reveal herself or speak Luke's name. She seemed for a moment to be struggling, perhaps beseeching God to answer her prayers now before her faith was entirely lost. As Simon watched her, he saw that she was *listening* to something.

In a moment Rose's face became transfigured, as if visions were parading before her eyes. "Where," she began, "Catherine, do you remember where we packed Luke's star? The one he made when he was a boy?"

Catherine closed her eyes and shook her head. "Don't put it up," she said with finality. "Not this year."

"Why, what a thing to say! Of course I'll put it up. The most amazing thing! The most wondrous thing, Catherine! Just as I was standing here, thinking about what you said, I had the strangest feeling. We never did put it up last year! That's what I remembered. Do you recall? We never did. We forgot all about it."

"I remembered," Catherine said. "I took it out of the box and put it in the hall closet. I didn't think—it should go on the tree."

Resolute now, Rose exclaimed, "Well, it's going up *this* year."

Oh, my God, thought Simon. She was resorting to paganism. If she could no longer gather the attention of one God, if she had worn out the patience of her drawered Pope, she would now try to catch the eyes of all gods in all heavens with a child's star.

"At least wait until Boyd gets home," Catherine said, resigned. "I don't want you falling from any chair."

Rose's strength was fully restored, supported by her final hope. "Well, I can't fall. That's a fact," she said, as if in complaint. "If I fell, who would take care of me? You know, if I ever broke my hip the way Mrs. Johnson did . . . do you know what I'd do? I'd wait until night and crawl out into the back yard and sit down nice as pie in the incinerator and set a match to myself. Yes, I would. I don't intend to be a burden to anyone."

If only she would, Simon thought. If only she would allow herself to be someone else's burden; if only she had the power to need someone in frailty as well as in strength, and the faith that she would be looked after, just as she had looked after Luke. If only she would let herself break down.

"Well!" Rose said, throwing the last of her tinsel at the tree, dissuaded at least for the time being from placing the star on top of it. She stood before it now, taking it all in, moving her eyes from top to bottom. To Simon it seemed that if there remained even one druidic god, Rose was now addressing herself to him.

While Catherine went to the square to do some last-minute shopping, and while Parnell played in the snow, Rose sat on the edge of Simon's bed, washing his face for the second time that day, saying without malice that she didn't want him to look like a pig when Boyd came home. With the washcloth in her hand, she polished his forehead until it shone, and rubbed his cheeks until even his half-deadened muscles tingled.

In the back yard they could see Parnell, looking like an apparition, running up and down banks of snow in the Wise Man costume he had a few minutes ago put on, sneaking out the back door so that Rose wouldn't catch him. It was made from two pairs of old draperies, part of the limited largesse given the family by Cortez, and which otherwise would never have been used because Rose had never *heard* of people putting anything but white curtains at windows. When Rose first spotted Parnell in the snow—a sacrilege if she ever saw one, she said—she was about to tap on the window until Simon indicated with his hand that she was to let him be. Simon liked the look of his grandson in the robe against all the snow, the antiquity of it, even though Parnell now and then made wings of his arms, a kind of winterized Flash Gordon.

The house was warm and smelled of bread, the roast in the oven, of cranberries Rose had been mashing, and of the mince and pumpkin pies she and Catherine had made—both a homecoming smell and a Christmas smell. A dark winter's light, the last of the afternoon, came through the windows to barely color the patterns of the carpet on the floor. From time to time they could hear the furnace grumble and heave as new coal ignited, shaking the chimney at the center of the house, followed by snow sliding from the roof, landing with a thud on the ground.

Rose left the washcloth in the porcelain bowl of warm water, then carefully dried Simon's face, flapping his ears lest water should collect there. He could see that her eyes were worn and tired—tired from her having lain awake at night trying to summon God; tired from having implored the Pope, who didn't even belong to her or to her faith, to intercede and to bring about the miracle. Oh, the absurdity of it. Surely she must know, thought Simon, that some things are irrecoverable.

If any kind of miracle could grow from what had happened to Lucas, it could only be the miracle of bringing the family closer together. Yet Simon knew that Rose had all her life run from emotions, as she had when their son Desmond was killed, as she had when she falsely read the family the telegram, and as she had even when Simon himself was carried into the house on the stretcher. What tormented Simon more than anything was that she would now have to face up to an emotion whether she wanted to or not, and he was afraid that her tears, held so long within her, might be poisoned by hatred. That she might hate God, turning Him out of her drawer just as she had the Pope, that she might hate all people for what they had brought to pass, and hate Simon most of all for what he was going to do.

As she leaned over to snatch the bowl from the top of the marble commode, Simon made a feeble noise in his throat. "Well, what is it you want, Mister Gavin?" she said. "What are you trying to say? Do you want the bedpan?" She watched Simon move his head from side to side.

"Well, I don't know how you can expect me to understand. I'm no lip reader. Do you think you can write it down?"

Over the past few weeks Simon had been practicing with his left hand, writing shaky messages on a note pad that was held for him. He indicated with his head that he wanted to write.

"Goodness me," Rose said. "You won't give me a minute's peace. I have half a mind to pack all my clothes, take the bus to Massillon, and commit myself—yes, commit myself to the state insane asylum. At least I'd get a little rest." She put the note pad before Simon. "Write!"

She placed a yellow pencil in his good hand, then held the pad for him. "You always had a terrible hand for writing," she said. "I don't know how the Pennsylvania Railroad ever understood half the things you wrote." As he finished, she brought the pad before her and held it in the dying light coming through the windows, moving it back and forth to catch the light. Suddenly she dropped it on the bed.

"What's that you're saying! Why, that isn't true, Mister Gavin! You ought to be ashamed of yourself."

On the paper Simon had made large block letters: "LUCAS IS DEAD. TELL THEM."

"The idea! Saying a thing like that. Why, what I'm going to do, I'm going to take this down to the basement and throw it into the furnace. Yes, *sir*."

And she would have, but Simon's left hand had a firm hold of it. With his pencil, he wrote beneath the first words: "I WILL TELL."

As Rose made them out, her face began to display the signs of her confusion and sorrow. The fatigue in her eyes reached into her face, softening it, bringing a tremor to her lip.

"You can't do that, Simon," she said at last, almost inaudibly. "I forbid it. Poor Catherine has nothing else to live for. Do you want to kill her? Do you want to kill Parnell? You can't do that, Simon. I forbid it."

At last, his hand shaking so that the words ran into each other as he formed them, with a desperate effort Simon wrote: "PEOPLE THINK HE RAN AWAY. THEY THINK HE DESERTED."

If it had been painful for Rose to learn that Simon knew the truth, what she now read was the cruelest blow of all. She shook her head back and forth slowly. All life seemed to drain from her. With one hand on the bed, she steadied herself in order to get up, then walked to the window, holding herself there against the frame, saying nothing.

It was a minute before she spoke. "Dear God," she said at last. "Dear God, how could people be so base? How could anyone think that? How could Lucas ever do a thing like that?"

Simon looked at her, imploring, trying to help her, but her eyes would not meet his. "It isn't true," she finally said in a voice so low he could scarcely hear. "His friends came. They came ... they came to tell me what happened. They came to tell me. They came to tell me ..."

She was crying at last. It was as if at this moment she were hearing for the first time what had been told to her more than a year and a half ago; what she had buried in the darkest corner of her mind as she hid the telegram, as she listened to the two officers from Luke's company, as she placed the banner with the blue star in the window. She cried softly, and it was the only sound in the house. Rose cried all the tears she had held back, and Simon, as he listened, was afraid he was losing her. He wanted to call out and tell his wife that he loved and respected her for what she had done for the family, but there were no words in him.

Later—five minutes, ten minutes—she turned from the window and walked toward the bed. She stood apart from him, not coming close to the hand he wanted her to touch. "He never even got to Europe. With all those dreams he had, he never even got to North Africa. He never got anywhere, Simon. The boat ... the boat was sunk. He's dead, Simon. Just as you say. Poor Lucas is dead. I wanted Parnell to be older ... I wanted Catherine to be stronger. That's why I lied. It's a sin, but I lied to you. Will God ever forgive me, Simon?"

She left him, and a minute later he heard her slowly mounting the stairs, pausing at each step. He followed the sound of her feet on the upstairs hall. He heard the door open, shut, and the lock being turned. He knew that God could forgive her, but in the loneliness of her room could she forgive God?

By the time that Boyd came running up to the house on Christmas Eve, racing all the way from the station, Rose was still in her room, the door locked as it had been since late afternoon. Through it she had told Catherine that she felt a little faint, probably because of the homecoming excitement, and that the best place for her was her bed. When Boyd, after he had said hello to everyone, went to her room, tapped, and received no answer, he looked through the keyhole and found that she was sitting on the edge of her bed. From where he stood in the hall, he coaxed her until Catherine asked him to stop. There was no response anyway.

Downstairs they set the table up in the parlor—the dining room couldn't be used, and Catherine said she wouldn't have them eating in the kitchen over the holidays —and they had a late supper, their talk easy and at the same time a little strained, each knowing that Rose had been hurt in some way and that she had sought refuge within herself, as she always did. Afterward Boyd lifted Parnell onto his shoulders for the twentieth time, told

Catherine for the tenth what had happened to Dewey at school, and then said that he would be able to stay home until the last day of the month.

"But that's wonderful," Catherine said happily. "I'm so glad! We were afraid you'd have to go back the day after Christmas."

Boyd said nothing to the family about where he would have to go on the thirty-first, deciding that it would be best to wait until the evening before he left. During the last week in Ann Arbor everyone had been told that the Program was finally being disbanded and that they were being assigned to training units. The long leave over Christmas was to be compensation for the leave they would not be given after they finished training. Boyd was due at Fort Ord, California, on the third of January, and he supposed that he would be sent directly to the Pacific after training. To tell the family now would spoil their Christmas. It was good to be home, and he wanted to savor it as long as he could.

They cleared the table, carrying the dirty dishes into the kitchen, and though Catherine put up a fuss, he and Parnell did the dishes, Boyd washing, Parnell drying, Catherine sitting before the oilclothed table, visibly fatigued, and Simon in his wheel chair. They talked about all the new people in town, how rude even the Rogers sisters now were if you went into their EAT shop on the square while they were serving workmen during the busy lunch hour, how the school board was no longer worried about frogs in the basement of the school but where space could be found for all the new children before September. They talked about who had died, who had given birth, who had a goiter, who had cancer, who had his tonsils out, and even about Dorothy Larson, whom Catherine had seen on the square just that afternoon and who looked, as she put it, like a thousand dollars, dressed fit to kill, leaving it to the imagination how the dollars that enabled her to look that way had been earned in Cleveland. They talked about school buddies of Boyd's who were all over the world, some in the Far East, some in England, some in Italy, and about the Lane boy who had been wounded and was mending in an Army hospital, and about the DeAngelos, whose son had been killed. They talked about the chemical plant and the Ornamental Iron factory, Catherine reporting that the Fosters were investing money from the latter into the former, adding that they would be sitting pretty indeed after the war. At no time did they talk about Francine, the family aware that Boyd and Francine had stopped writing to each other a little before Thanksgiving.

After they had talked themselves out and were able again to relax in the comfortable silences that people who know each other well can enjoy, Boyd said that he thought he might go across the street for a few minutes if they didn't mind. They didn't mind at all. To share Boyd with the Ventrys, saddened because Dewey wasn't home, was what they expected to do.

Boyd went upstairs to throw water on his face and to spruce up his hair, telling Parnell, who was at his footsteps, that he'd teach him how to make his bed the way soldiers did—so tight that a dime could be bounced on it—and also that he wanted to sleep until noon on Christmas. "Like a decaying Vanderbilt," he added, watching the smile form on Parnell's face. He put on his OD jacket, went down the stairs and outside. The Ventrys' garage door, he saw, was open, and inside he could see Dewey's old Ford, perched on four blocks, tires removed, its finish coated with grease to ward off rusting. When he knocked at the front door, Helen Ventry opened it, looking less harried than she had for years, her face older perhaps but tranquil. Tina was in the parlor, dressed in a smart blue jumper instead of one of the white dresses she always used to wear, and her hair had been cut so that it now ended well above her shoulders. Frank and Francine were in the room too, and they both stood up as Boyd walked in, taking everyone's hand by turn, listening to Mrs. Ventry in the background repeating, "Doesn't he make a wonderful-looking soldier?" He saved Francine till last, touching her hand as she offered it. "Hello, Francine."

Before she was able to answer—he was almost afraid to hear her voice—Helen interrupted, full of spirit and animation, saying, "Do you mean nothing looks different?"

Boyd looked from face to face, pausing longest at Francine's, and finally replied, knowing that it would please her, "Tina is prettier than ever. Is that what you mean?"

Boyd searched the girl's face for some memory of what had happened to them in the ravine, but found nothing. Except for her shorter hair, she looked as she always looked, remote and yet incandescent. No, she could not possibly remember; of that he was certain. Whatever dream it was that had brought her onto the lawn that night had been lost or hidden, he knew, just as the evidence itself had been. To Boyd, it seemed that it had happened at some dark time in his childhood, so diffused and unreal had it become.

"She'll talk a leg off you if you give her a chance," Frank volunteered, and as he did, a blush rose to Tina's face. "Pa-pa!" she cried in an embarrassed, put-upon way.

But Francine came to the rescue. "If you don't notice the chair, you'll be an enemy of the people."

"The chair."

The goddamn chair! He hadn't seen it before because his eyes were on Francine. But there it was next to the fireplace, resplendent and unsat on, high and gold, expensive and rare, making everything else in the room look a bit shopworn.

"Papa says he won't sit on it until we put a sheet over it," Francine said. "He says it's a millionaire's chair."

"I'll have to get dressed up every time I want to sit down," Frank added with no little pride. "Have you ever seen a chair like that before?"

"It looks great," Boyd answered truthfully. "Boy, I never thought ... son of a gun, I've been hearing about it for so long, I thought it was something you made up."

"I sent a letter to Dewey as soon as it came," Mrs. Ventry now went on, "and I told him he should have used the money on himself. And then I was going to send it back to the store. But the more I looked at it, the more it seemed ... if we sent it back now we'll never see another one. So there it is!"

"Well, I'm going to mail him the money," Frank said. "He needs every penny the Army gives him. We can take it out of his college money and put it back later."

"But then it wouldn't be a gift," Francine said wisely. "Why don't you just put the money in the bank and then it'll be there for him when the war's over?"

"Why, that's a thought."

"But here I am standing around," Helen interrupted again, "not even offering you coffee and cookies. I'll just be a minute. I sent a whole batch of the cookies to Dewey too."

They sat in the parlor while Mrs. Ventry went into the kitchen, the only vacant seat the new chair, no one daring to sully it—even when Helen Ventry returned to the room. She made space for herself on the crowded sofa, listening to Boyd as he gave her a charitable account of what had befallen Dewey at school, and a rehashing of Dewey's last letter to him in which he had said that things didn't look so bad in Kansas after all. He reassured them that Dewey would almost certainly be given a leave as soon as he finished training, and that he'd be home before they knew it. When Helen, in turn, told him all the kind things Dewey had written in his letters about Boyd and how he had helped him so much, Boyd felt like a cheat and an impostor. He was glad when Frank finally asked him questions—interesting ones—about Army life, and he answered them with zeal, eager to say anything to avoid listening to Dewey's praise of him.

Afterward they induced Tina to play the piano—"Do I *have* to?" she at first whined. Tina agreed, what was once her solace now apparently a nuisance, only if her father sat in his chair.

"Oh, no," Frank said in terrible self-effacement, "I have my old pants on."

"Well, I'm sure Dewey knew you'd have your old pants on," Mrs. Ventry exclaimed. "It's Christmas Eve, and someone has to sit in it."

Embarrassed, Frank Ventry looked once more at the trousers he wore around the house. Tina opened the rosewood piano and sat down at the stool before it, not beginning to play until her father kept his part of the bargain. Once he had, she began to touch the yellowed ivory keys.

It was a prideful chair, and it would take some getting used to, Boyd saw. And in all Frank's hot discomfort at being looked at—perhaps being asked to become the man who would befit the chair, rather than the other way around—Boyd could see the pleasure in his eyes. It was goofy and corny, but it was a precious moment, and Boyd wished Dewey were here to see it. All the rage and injury that had been in the man seemed nothing in comparison to the splendor of the chair, and maybe even in time the splendor would rub off on him.

When it was over—everyone a little self-conscious— Boyd asked Francine if she would like to go for a walk before she went to bed. He waited for her in the hall while she went upstairs to change into a warm sweater and her winter coat. As they left, Boyd told the family that he would see all of them in church the next day.

Making their way down the street past the new houses,

Boyd waited for Francine to speak, and Francine waited for Boyd. When at last she broke the silence it was to say that the new houses were horrid, weren't they? Then, as they turned the corner to Summer, the snow falling lightly now, her voice became more natural as she described the reception the chair had been given when it was delivered, and how both her mother and her father now appeared to value Dewey more. "Before," she said, "it always seemed that each one was trying to give Dewey away to the other, and that Papa really didn't know what to do with him. Now I think they both . . . well, understand him more. They can see him better than they used to. So maybe the war has accomplished something after all." She turned her face toward him and said quickly, "Mother wasn't exaggerating. You *do* look wonderful."

"It's from powdered eggs and Spam."

"It's very becoming."

He asked her how the job in Cleveland was, and she replied that it wasn't. She had left it for good two days before, after having talked things over with her mother. Howard Foster had promised to help her find a secretarial job at one of the two plants in town. When he asked her why she had left Cleveland, she was at first reluctant to answer, telling him that the people there were "different." It wasn't that they were unfriendly, she added, but that they simply didn't like the same things she liked. She had gone, in order to please her mother, to concerts at Severance Hall—she made a point of mentioning that no rich old man had pinched her—but that the music wasn't half so good as it was on records, and that all she could hear from her seat in the cheap section were coughs and groans and dozing people. She had been taken to a few exotic restaurants by friends, had even tried to eat clams— "Filthy clams!" she yelled—but that nothing tasted half as good as what she got at home. She had been invited to several parties in Shaker Heights, and once to Hunting Valley—never-never land, she explained; rich beyond words—but that because she didn't drink she generally found that she was the only sober one around. "Nothing is more depressing than having to listen to people who think they're being charming and who are actually only drunk." In the apartment house where she lived she had befriended a fragile girl on the floor below who was working on her master's at Western Reserve and who was writing a novel on the side; the friendship went to pieces when the girl woke her up by pounding on the door at two in the morning to tell her that thieves had broken into her place and burned her manuscript in the grate, and that one of the men who did it was now standing across the street—sent there by her mother, who hated her. "Well," Francine said, "she was *barmy!* That's all there was to it. What do you call it? Paranoid? It scared the daylights out of me. Do you remember how we always used to say that almost everyone we knew in Ventry was crazy? Well, let me tell *you.* The really crazy people all live out of town."

What she had done mostly, she admitted, was read, and it finally occurred to her that one didn't have to go to Cleveland to do that. As for Boyd's Aunt Cortez, Francine said that she had done a temporary disappearing act. The first time she had called, a man answered the telephone, asked for her name, and a few minutes later told her that Cortez was wintering in Tucson. Because it sounded fishy, Francine called a second time several days later, and Cortez herself answered. "I guess I didn't know what to say, so I just hung up. That's the story. My voyage into the great world. Most of the people I met were really very shabby. I kept telling myself, well, maybe if I got to *know* them they wouldn't be so bad, but they just got shabbier. There you have it."

"It's funny," Boyd said. "Maybe it's just that they have a different . . . ethos. Is that a word? Maybe you have to be born in a city to understand city people. They use each other just the way we do, I expect, but they even do that in double time." He waited for a minute and then decided. "I didn't tell you, but I was in New York over Thanksgiving."

Francine replied that she already knew, Parnell having told her one weekend when she was home. But by that time Boyd's letters had sounded so impersonal, she said, that she thought it was none of her business to know.

"I was seeing a girl."

"That doesn't surprise me either. The last two or three letters I got from you . . . well, they sounded as if you were ashamed to write them. Is she nice?"

"Was. It's all over. And, no, I don't know that she was nice. I think maybe she was . . . mean."

"Mean?" It was a strange, almost childlike word to use.

Boyd appeared to be having trouble saying what he wanted to say. "That's probably the wrong word. Or what it might have been, I think we were both mean. We brought it out in each other. We took what we could get, but I don't know that we ever gave anything. We were . . . sleeping together."

If Francine was surprised, angry, or disgusted, she didn't reveal it. They walked along in the winter silence, listening to their feet crunching against the snow, saying nothing. At last, as they began to turn onto Satin, she spoke. "I sort of figured that too. I knew something like that was going to happen."

"It doesn't mean anything, Francine."

"Yes, it does. *Every*thing means something. If you . . . if you sleep with someone, it has to mean something. But what I was trying to say is that I don't hold it against you. As I said, I knew you would. The night before you left here, I knew that's what you'd have to do." For a moment it seemed that she might cry, but she recovered. "Thank God it didn't work out. All I could think afterwards was that I'd let you go because I wanted you to find something out for yourself, and that maybe I'd made a mistake and that you'd never come back."

"You knew?"

"Maybe not just the way it happened, but something like that." She stopped walking, kicked at the snow. "Can I tell you who you were that last night in town? You weren't anyone I ever knew. You were a stranger and you were treating me as if I were one too. Do you remember? You'd been drinking. I tried . . . to tell you something but it got all muddled up in your head. You almost raped me, Boyd. You almost did that. Okay, so maybe it was because I wouldn't cooperate, but that was still no reason to forget who I am. You weren't even thinking about me. I could have been *any* girl. That's the way I felt." She paused now before continuing. "And what I thought, I thought maybe some other girl could teach you a thing or two. Not by loving you—because I fancy I'm the only one who knows how to do that—but by *not*. I don't even know the name of the girl you knew, but I'm grateful to her."

It was a lot to take in. Francine wasn't talking about something as ephemeral as virginity; she was talking about something as lasting as love—and Boyd tried to understand. "I don't think I'm that way any more, Francine. I've been into the world, and I've seen a lot of things and done a lot that I'm not too proud of. I even . . . I even think I forgot about you for a while. Then all of a sudden

404

you came back. I was all by myself and I saw you as clear as anything, and I could even hear you. It was like you were talking good and loud, and finally I could hear you."

She looked up at Boyd, pleased. "You've changed. You know, when I was watching you in the parlor, I could see that you had. Not just the uniform, but the way you are. All I kept thinking was that maybe you're so disappointed with things that you're tired and empty now. But I don't think so. I think you're stronger."

"I hope like hell I am, Francine. There's something else I better tell you. I won't be coming home again before I go overseas. I have to go out to California on the thirty-first."

"Boyd!"

"I'm going to be all right, Francine. The war's going to be over, I bet, a lot sooner than people think."

They stood before the square, listening to bells echo through the gulf. Two horses pulled a giant sleigh over the top of Tannery Hill, filled with young people coming home from a winter's party. One year before, his own senior class had rented a sleigh and gone on the same ride into the country, but it now seemed a world away to Boyd, an anachronism that had little to do with the life around him. Everything seemed futile. All the travail he and Francine had been through, all they had learned from it, and now there was no way of putting it to use. If he had been to the end of the world and back, as he thought, there were still other ends, far more instructive, that would have to be seen. And as they stood listening to the bells in the distance, envying those whose lives could still accommodate a ride in a sleigh, all he could think was, Damn them and their war. Damn all men who wouldn't let people be.

Still they waited, unwilling to go on and unwilling to turn back toward home, wondering in their separate manners what final, stultifying indignity the world could come up with for their generation, fattened as they were on Depression rice and beans for the sacrifice to come, yanked out of childhood to redeem a world that might be past redemption. As he watched the sleigh pass, Boyd thought of the small lacquered box in Simon's bedroom at home, bought by Simon from a penniless White Russian in Hong Kong years ago. On its lid was painted a troika, racing over the snow, a bundled-up nineteenth-century father, mother, and child in it, their eyes made frantic by the folk artist, and at the horses' feet were three snarling wolves, chasing them. When he was young, Boyd often used to speculate about those three, sometimes saying that they outran the wolves and reached home in safety, and sometimes that he didn't know. But now it seemed to him that perhaps a moment later, seconds after they were rendered by the artist, the wolves had leaped. As wolves always did, and no artist, and no man, could ask otherwise of them.

Afraid of what he might be deprived of, he nonetheless repeated to Francine that he was going to be all right, and that he would be in California for six weeks, by which time the war might be over, although he knew that it couldn't be. She asked him if he would be anywhere near San Francisco before he went overseas. He answered that he didn't know but that he might be.

"Because," she began slowly, "I've always wanted to go there. And don't you think ... don't you think ... if I went out ... I could see you there?"

He led her to a bench in the park, brushed aside the snow with his hand. They sat and he held on to her. It was long after midnight, and Christmas Day, before they were ready to leave each other and make their way home.

On Christmas morning Rose kept to her room, declining breakfast and telling Catherine through the door that she was sorry she wouldn't be able to help with Christmas dinner. "I don't seem to have much spunk today," she said.

As soon as Catherine returned to the parlor, she told the family that she was going to call Dr. Herron, holiday or not, but Simon shook his head, then wrote on his note pad. "IT WILL PASS," written with an optimism he didn't feel. When, during the middle of the day, Rose said that she wasn't quite well enough to come down for dinner but that she had, after all, decided to go to church in the evening, Simon knew that it was still passing.

At ten in the morning, as soon as she learned that Rose was ill and that Catherine would have to do all the kitchen work by herself, Francine had come over, put an apron on, and pitched in. By then the turkey was already in the oven, and had already been well sniffed by Parnell as he returned to the house from delivering his Sunday papers, saying as he walked in, "Are you guys crazy? Who's going to want turkey for breakfast?" Catherine explained to him that breakfast would take a less spectacular turn—just ham and eggs—and that turkeys took a spell to cook. Parnell was dumbfounded that a bird had to languish four or five hours in an oven before it could be eaten.

Which was nothing compared to his surprise, and everyone else's, when Francine showed the ring she was wearing on her hand, placed there the evening before. It wasn't a new one. Such was the thrift of the family that Simon had even once said that they would reuse their coffins if the law allowed. The ring had belonged to Simon's grandmother Nora, and it had probably been bought from an itinerant peddler when Ohio was still part of the Northwest Territory. It was a simple, silver band with a small, unprecious stone set in it, and perhaps it had cost almost nothing when it was purchased. It was a *Gavin* ring, not a Keepsake, not a De Beers, not a Tiffany, and it was finer than the whole lot of them because a Gavin had given it, a Gavin had worn it, and Gavins had kept it out of the pawnshop for untold numbers of years.

For all their talk about putting off any engagement until after the war, Boyd and Francine had decided, while they sat on the park bench, that perilous times required perilous acts. There could be no marriage until after the war—Boyd insisted on this—but at least they could pledge themselves to it. As for the ring, Boyd had taken it from his dresser drawer where Simon had put it long ago, and he hadn't, as he set out from the house the night before, even been sure that there could be a use for it. As it was, a use had been found.

Toward the end of the afternoon, the light already thin and smoky, they sat down to dinner. Francine took her place at the table with them. The wet and gamy dark meat of the turkey was ignored, the dry white flesh alone attracting their holiday appetites. Mostly for Simon, who was unable to do any telling himself, Catherine told the story about Aunt Susan, Uncle Tootie's wife, who would always decline the plainer dishes at Christmas tables, saying, "Goodness, no. I have that at home in my own icebox." And Boyd—again for Simon, who would ordinarily have told it—remembered how when the woman found something especially palatable on her plate, she would say, "Why, I think I'll take a little of this home to Tootie." Tootie, who was the one who had stolen Queen Victoria's hat from the Garfield Museum and burned it, had been too bearish to like parties or family gatherings and seldom went to them. For his contribution, again serving as Simon's mouthpiece, Parnell then recalled the night they drove Aunt Susan home in the old Terraplane, and that upon stepping onto the running board, her arms laden with food for her husband, she had continued to climb up the front seat until she bumped her head against the roof, saying merely, "I can never get used to cars." Which was a fact. Uncle Tootie—bless him, everyone said—had kept a buggy.

They were very merry, talking about old times, not new ones, forgetting the war, and even now and then forgetting Rose, who must have been able to hear their laughter. They decided that just for this once, they would stack all the dishes in the kitchen and not do them until they returned from church. They closed the door between the kitchen and the hall so that no one could see their sloth, should callers come; then made ready for the walk to church. Parnell changed into his robe, looking very inspirational indeed, and hoped that no one would notice that he was wearing his track shoes under his flowing costume. While Francine went across the street to collect her parents and Tina, Catherine and Boyd dressed Simon in his overcoat, drawing the blanket over his lap and his legs. Parnell said that he would push the wheel chair, but before the words were out of his mouth Rose appeared at the top of the stairs and told them that she would see to it that Simon got to church. She was already wearing her Sunday dress, and though her face looked pale, she told them all to go along and that she and Simon would follow by themselves. There was a little something she had to do first.

After they left, Simon waited in the parlor, listening to the voices vanish down the street, and in another minute Rose came down the stairs, carrying the black and worn winter coat the family had been trying to get her to replace for years. She put it on a chair in the hallway, then went to the closet, reaching up until her fingers found what she sought. In the parlor, not looking at Simon at all, she brought a straight chair from the desk and set it down before the tree, heavily lifted herself onto it, then leaned over and placed a small, aged paper star on its topmost part. Once on the floor again, she restored the chair to the desk, rearranged the packages she had upset at the foot of the tree, and stood back, studying what she had done.

As if she were trying to put it off as long as she could, Rose returned to the hall, brushed the lint from her old coat, drew it on, and waited. Soon she picked up from the chair what had been hidden by the coat, carrying it into the parlor. She took one last look at the bay window, stepped up to it, gently removing the banner, hanging the new one—it had been in her drawer for a year and a half—in its place. She pressed the old one into her pocket, returned to the tree and turned on the strings of colored lights, even though the government had asked everyone to conserve electricity. Without a word she began to push Simon's wheel chair into the kitchen, out the door, down the ramp to the back yard, and around to the front of the house. On the walk Rose Gavin paused only for a moment, to look at the window and the gold star hanging there now, then raised her eyes and looked at the other, greater star, on the tree.

Later in the church, antiseptic and plain, built by men who thought that frippery was ungodly, Parnell stood hidden behind one of the two doors that led to what was ordinarily the pulpit. The pulpit, however, had been moved far to one side of the nave and in its stead a crèche had been set up. The Christmas sermon, announced on the sign outside as *Will Jesus Come Again? 7 p.m. Christmas Day* had been delivered, the Reverend Hill intimating that, why, yes, he had half a mind that He would. And he left no doubt but that Jesus would, if the choice were His, come this time to Ventry, avoiding the terrible climate of Jerusalem. To prepare for this, he closed his sermon by urging everyone to buy another war bond or two during the current drive, to keep their houses snug and their morals worthy, and to be sure to attend the bake sale on Thursday of next week, ten until three.

As Parnell bunched his toes back and forth inside his cleated shoes, trying to make his shaking legs stronger for the appearance he would have to make in a few minutes, he watched the black-coated choir in the balcony rise as one and fill the church with song, then let his glance wander over the pews, seeking out his family. Simon, he saw, had been left in the aisle near the entrance, though Rose herself was sitting down near the front. She had in her hands—he wondered what the Reverend Hill made of it—the rosary she had once shown Parnell, the one carried from Ireland and used by men of a different faith. Next to her—a faith more different some could not imagine—were Mr. and Mrs. Levinson, who, though surrendering none of their Jewishness, sent Christmas cards to their Christian friends and attended Christmas service as an act of cordiality, knowing full well that God would not punish them for their lapse. As for other Jews there were none around except Jesus Christ Himself, who couldn't possibly have found fault. Before them, in the next pew, sat Catherine and Boyd, and Francine and the Ventrys.

At the door on the other side of the simple altar, Parnell watched Mary and Joseph, Julie Lindstrom and Richie Glotzbecker on less exalted days. They were both in his class in school, Julie the only one in Ventry who had natural rhythm and could tap dance. She also had pigtails that hung down the back of her costume in a less than Biblical style. As for Richie, his face was white over the purple of his robe. During thunderstorms while they were in school he always put two fingers up in the air for Miss Stickney to excuse him, then went to the washroom and hid under a sink until the lightning passed. He looked now as if he expected lightning to break over his head.

As Parnell waited for the next carol to begin, he turned once more to make certain that the other two Wise Men were still behind him. He fondled the sand-filled matchboxes in his sleeves that constituted his gift to the newborn babe in the crib and that he would have to carry to it as soon as the lights dimmed and a spotlight rested on it. The lights fell, the choir began to sing "It Came Upon a Midnight Clear," and he watched Mary and Joseph make their way to the crèche, Mary playing the scene for all it was worth, little tap-dancing steps beneath her long skirts. Joseph led his St. Bernard—a shaggy, cross animal—to the center of the church and tethered it to a nail that had been driven into the floor, the dog turning toward the congregation and looking as stupid as only a St. Bernard impersonating a donkey could look. Mary then lifted the doll from the crib in a paroxysm of maternal feelings, caressing it, whispering into its ears, and rocking it back and forth in her arms. When the choir began "O, Lit-tle Tow-en of Beth-la-him," Parnell took one last breath and walked with his two friends toward the scene. Over the noise of the voices, his track shoes clopped heavily on the floor, and Parnell's mother in the second pew brought her hand over her mouth to hide her smile.

"I bring you tiding of joy," Parnell said as he reached the crèche. "I bring you frankin-sance, myrrh," he panicked, "and myrrh." As he handed the matchboxes to Mary,

410

he reddened, not even hearing the "Than-kew" which she wasn't expected to say and uttered only to show off her good manners. When the other two Wise Men knelt before the holy pair, something in the church caught Parnell's eye and he looked straight into the pews. The Reverend Hill was walking down the aisle. He stopped next to Frank Ventry, motioned with his head for him to rise from his seat, and the two men walked to the rear of the church. Through the open door Parnell saw them talking in the vestry, and a minute later he watched Frank sit down on one of the chairs there. The Reverend Hill then repeated his walk down the aisle, everyone now turning to look at him, until he stopped at the pew where the Ventrys sat. Helen was up and out of her seat even before he reached her, somehow having divined what was happening, a tremor already begun on her face. Francine followed, then Tina, Catherine, and Boyd. Rose watched the procession for a moment, then she too left her seat, first making the sign of the cross on herself, perhaps the only time it had ever been made in this church. In another minute the Reverend Hill retraced his steps once more, fetching Mr. Foster and Mr. Morrow, talking to them softly as they followed him out.

It was Catherine who finally made her way to Parnell, telling him only that there had been an accident and that she wanted him to push Simon home. The Ventrys and the Gavins were being driven to their houses and she wanted Parnell to follow with his grandfather because the wheel chair could not be got into a car. She made him promise to hurry, and he said that he would. When he asked where Boyd was, she replied only that he had gone.

People huddled around the entrance to the church, talking quietly among themselves, watching Frank and Helen, the latter limp, held by her husband, get in the back of one car with Tina; Francine, Rose, and Catherine entered the second. The cars backed up in the snowy driveway, then moved slowly out into the street.

When the aisle cleared, Parnell walked to Simon, turned his chair around, and began to push it toward the entrance. Two men there helped him get it down the icy steps, lifting it up, then setting it on the sidewalk, asking Parnell if he was sure that he could handle it. Parnell answered that he could.

From where he had been sitting in the rear of the church, Simon had heard everything. First the ringing of

411

the telephone in the tiny office off the lobby, answered by Mrs. Hill, who had run from her seat in order to do it. Then Reverend Hill talking to what Simon guessed was the Western Union operator, who had apparently been told that the Ventrys would be in church. The message from the War Department regretted to inform them that Dewey had died in a training accident in Kansas, followed by a few other words Simon was unable to hear. After that, Simon had listened as the reverend told the family, one by one. Mrs. Ventry had taken it badly, and so had Frank. Boyd hadn't said a word; he simply turned and walked out of the church. As for Rose, she shook her head and clung to the beads in her hands as though they were now her strength.

Well, may the Lord bless and look after Dewey, Simon said to himself as Parnell began to push him over the snow toward Satin Street. It was a strange God who would take both Isaac and the lamb, but Simon supposed there were reasons. It was a strange God who allowed suffering, but men would have to live with it. And it was a strange God who no longer listened to the crying of His children.

Behind him he heard Parnell kick at the robe around his feet, icy from the snow it had collected, humming one of the songs that had been sung in church. He steered him down Summer, then turned onto Priest, making his way toward Saint's Rest at the end. He pushed Simon home slowly, watching the lights in the sky, the blazing windows in the Ventry house, and the colored lights at the tree in the Gavins' window. As he began to bring the chair up the steep driveway, he stopped. His hands fell from the chair, and Simon could feel himself slide back into the street, the chair shaking but still upright. As Parnell looked at the new star in the window, a noise began in his throat—to Simon, it seemed to be the oldest sound in the world—and he began to run. He ran down the street, over the route they had just taken, ran as if he were at last being chased in life by the big gray man of his dreams, ran over the snow, his robe flying at his feet, and all the time the same sound, the same cry, coming from his throat. Ran past Summer, past Spring, past Satin, his voice fading as it got closer to the square.

Simon sat silently in the middle of the empty street, snow falling softly on his head, waiting for someone to find him, and hoping too that someone would find Parnell.

Before Boyd began to make his way up Tannery Hill, he turned one last time and skipped a stone over the frozen water of the river, listening to it hop and cut into the ice. When he walked, he kept to the hard, crushed snow that children had made earlier in the day with new Christmas sleds.

He had wanted to be by himself for a few minutes, and he had been. Upon first hearing the news in church that Dewey had drowned in a training accident, he was unable to believe it. By himself in the gulf, he was still unable to believe it. Dewey had been one of the best swimmers in town. Something had made him choose not to swim. And Boyd thought that he almost knew what it was.

What hurt him most was the needless waste, waste that wouldn't have occurred had Dewey never left home. Good people weren't so plentiful that they could be allowed the luxury of leaving the world at their will. Whatever it was that made Dewey conclude that he was too fragile to remain alive was no more than what almost everyone thought at one time or another. But the unpardonable sin, as Boyd saw it, was that he had been left alone.

If Boyd had thought that the hasty decision he made at school would set in motion this final abandonment, he would honestly have given his life for the mistake. He had let him sleep . . . but he hadn't meant for it to be this kind of sleep. As for whatever aberration might have been involved—Boyd was beginning to think that goodness itself was an aberration—it was no worse than aberrations which occurred, in different forms, in all people. You couldn't permit men to be killed because they were weak or innocent or different. It was what Luke had long ago tried to explain to Boyd, what Boyd had tried to explain to Pipsi, and what he now explained to himself. If there had seemed to Dewey no way out, it was the fault of the world for not showing him one, just as it was even now showing none to the Jews.

It seemed to Boyd a fatal mistake, his own and the world's. There would now be no war at all had men, six short years ago, looked at the sufferings of others and gone to their aid. And Dewey would now be alive if only Boyd had listened to himself and not to the hatred and malice and stupidity of a few men he didn't even know.

Have a good sleep, *paisan*, he said into the night air. Sleep and dream of peace and Ventry.

As Boyd walked over the crest of the hill onto the square, he heard a noise that sounded as if it had traveled across centuries to reach him. He saw an ancient vision running across the snow, a robe flying through the night, a face so frightened that Boyd would remember it until the day he died. He ran toward it, caught the small boy in his arms, and tried to quell the sobs coming from Parnell's throat.

"What's wrong, buddy? Someone scare you? Hell, you don't have to be scared. What's there to be scared about? Come on. It's all over now. Did you think that everyone forgot about you? Well, we didn't. Come on. Here, I'll wipe your face. Son of a gun, you know how fast you were going? You were going like eighty miles an hour in those track shoes. And you want to know something else? I bet you anything you'll break my old record for the mile when you're in high school. Come on. There's nothing to be scared of any more."

Thirteen

It was the last day of the year in Ventry, Ohio, and Parnell Gavin stood with his family on the wooden platform of the Nickel Plate depot, waiting for the early morning train. As a low whistle sounded from the crossing outside of town, he looked down the tracks, then through a window of the station at a wall clock there. Snow was drifting over the line near Erie, he had been told, and the train was running twenty minutes late. Relaxing again, he rested his eyes on a 1943 calendar near the clock, its final month curled from the heat of the radiator beneath it.

The winter sky was gray and burdened, the color of weathered boards on abandoned barns. A thermometer under the deep eaves of the station showed sixteen degrees, and Parnell could feel the pinpricks of cold against his aching cheeks. He brushed his mittened hand across his nose to catch a drop of moisture there.

Except for Boyd Gavin, who wore a heavy GI overcoat, the small party at the depot was dressed in mourning. They surrounded Boyd, almost in a circle, as if to shield him from the wind: Simon in his wheel chair, Rose, Catherine, and Parnell, and Helen and Frank Ventry, Tina, and Francine. There was no talking among them. The only sound came from their galoshes as they moved their feet upon the frozen platform.

Three days before, Boyd and Francine had met a train from the west. They had watched as a casket was removed from the baggage car, lifted to a wagon, rolled to a waiting hearse, and brought to Priest Road. There, it was placed beneath the bay window in the Ventrys' parlor, where the two families sat up with Dewey the night before he was buried. On the following morning they formed a small procession to Chestnut Grove cemetery in the gulf and said their good-bys. And good-by to Luke too, for he could at last be dealt with, and it was his interment as well.

415

They looked now at Boyd, locking what they saw in their minds for succor later on. Francine would, in another six weeks, journey to the West Coast and spend a few hours with him before he boarded his ship at Oakland, using, because Helen Ventry wanted it that way, part of Dewey's college money for the trip. But the others knew that this look might have to last for a long and troublous time.

As they watched, feeding on the young man before them, a giant yellow crane unloaded steel beams from a flatcar at one end of the station onto waiting trucks. When a truck was loaded, it moved urgently across the snow-covered gravel, onto the rutted street, and up the hill. As the crane swooped down again, a worker in a metal helmet looked vacantly down the platform for a second, saw the strangers in black, and turned his attention back to his task.

When at last Boyd heard the train begin to cross the trestle, he lifted his duffel bag to his shoulders, then kissed each one, beginning with Catherine, moving to Rose, to Simon, to Parnell, and the Ventrys, saving Francine till last. The train pulled to a stop, spewing dark smoke and terrible noise, and they walked with Boyd to the steps of a coach where a conductor was standing with a lantern.

"God bless you. We'll miss you. Come home soon."

Boyd touched the hands that reached toward him once more, climbed the steps, and disappeared into the darkness of a coach, reappearing a second later as the train began to move.

And as they looked at the face in the window, caught there in the gray winter sun, the light of a thousand mornings, the shadows of night, smoke, their own faces, the town itself, they could see, each of them, that he was there for all time. And they knew, each of them, that he might never come back, and that it was this way he would have to be remembered. When the train began to inch out of the station, his own eyes cried out to them, and then he was gone.